SIEGE

A NOVEL BY **EDWIN CORLEY**

STEIN AND DAY/*Publishers*/New York

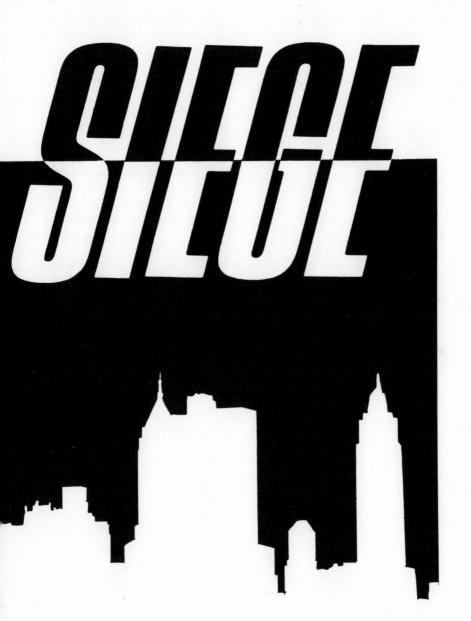

Published simultaneously in Canada by Saunders of Toronto, Ltd.
Designed by Bernard Schleifer
Manufactured in the United States of America
Stein and Day/*Publishers*/7 East 48 Street, New York, N. Y. 10017

SBN 8128-1224-7

SECOND PRINTING, 1969

For my son

RICHARD PATRICK CORLEY

"I had a vision—and I saw white spirits and black spirits engaged in battle, and the sun was darkened—the thunder rolled in the heavens, and blood flowed in streams—and I heard a voice saying, 'Such is your luck, such you are called to see; and let it come rough or smooth, you must surely bear it. . . .' "

—*Nat Turner*

The bridges linking Manhattan Island with the outside world began blowing at precisely twelve minutes after three in the predawn darkness of Saturday, August 30.

The first to go was the Manhattan Bridge between lower Manhattan and Brooklyn. Carefully placed charges dropped wreckage into the East River. Within seconds another explosion wrecked the center span of the Brooklyn Bridge, then the Williamsburg Bridge shuddered under a third impact and splashed down into the outgoing tide. Part of the span crashed onto a small shack near one edge of the handball court in East River Park. Sleeping in it was a forty-eight-year-old vagrant who had wandered eastward from his usual haunts on the Bowery. His name was Harry Dunn, and as the twisted girders of the Williamsburg Bridge crushed the life from his body, he became the first Manhattan casualty of the Three Day Revolution.

By three-thirty, every bridge linking the island with the mainland and the other boroughs had been blasted. But the George Washington still spanned the Hudson. Charges had failed to sever its suspension cables. An air strike had also failed. The mighty bridge swayed and leaned in the brisk breeze that funneled down the edge of the Palisades —but still it stood.

The demolitions experts of the rebel army were busy men that August night. In addition to bridges, there were tunnels to take care of, seven in lower Manhattan alone: the Brooklyn-Battery Tunnel, which carried automobile traffic from the island to Brooklyn; five others that linked Manhattan's subway system with Brooklyn; plus the Tubes under the Hudson River to Jersey City. The Holland Tunnel was left open, mined and defended by heavy machine gun emplacements.

Farther uptown, the Lincoln Tunnel was open, but the Queens-Midtown Tunnel was blasted through its roof. The East River flooded in. No one will ever know how many died in the first thirty minutes of the revolution. Most of the guards and maintenance men in the tunnels were either shot or crushed in the explosions. Those who survived drowned when the water rushed in. Not all the casualties were noncombatants. Rebel demolitions men lost their lives too: some by accident when they misjudged the blasts' effects, some shot down by alert police.

But despite confusion and miscalculation and missed signals, at twenty minutes of four in the darkness of the morning of August 30th, the island of Manhattan was cut off from the outside world and dominated by rebel forces. They held nearly a million hostages, many of them still soundly asleep in their beds and consequently unaware of the events exploding outside their apartment doors.

They would wake in the morning to discover, when they turned on their radios or TV sets, that they were unwilling pawns in what was then being announced as the Afro-American War of Liberation.

SIEGE

ONE

Major General Stanley Shawcross lay soaking in the tile bath of his suite at the Princess Hotel in Danang, in the northeast corner of South Vietnam. The water was scalding hot. Shawcross sighed heavily as he felt the tensions seeping from him, his muscles relaxing, drawing him to the edge of sleep.

He looked at his lower belly; he could barely see the scar from the mortar fragment he had taken near the DMZ six months back. That was when he had been reminded, for the first time in years, of the fascination whites had with a Negro's sex. Shawcross had been lying half-conscious outside the Cong bunkers they'd assaulted that morning. A corpsman cut his fatigue pants away and was applying antibiotic powder to the wound when two passing troopers looked over at him casually.

"Jesus Christ," said one, "take a look at the wang on the old man!"

Shawcross had faded into unconsciousness then and forgotten about the incident until this moment. Well, he thought, grinning, he *was* pretty well built—at least in his relaxed state. What none of those jokers seemed to understand was that he didn't get much bigger when aroused. But you would never be able to tell that to an itchy white world, cowering in imagined sexual inferiority before a distorted image of the black stud.

He remembered riding a freight train through Tennessee one cold winter night in 1938. He was just eighteen then. The night wind whipped particles of ice against him as he huddled in an open coal car. He decided to search for shelter back along the clanging freight train. He found an empty boxcar, and lowered himself carefully down along the door, hanging onto the catwalk and trying to force the door open with one groping foot. He heard voices inside, and kicked—one, two, three! The door slid open and hands caught his legs.

"Okay, buddy," yelled a voice, "we got you. Just swing on down."

Shawcross let go of the catwalk and trusted his life to the strong hands below. They did not fail him. He lurched inside the boxcar and the heavy door swung shut again. A match flared in the darkness to light a stubby candle.

"Sheeit!" said the voice. "He's a nigger."

Shawcross backed into one corner of the car, staring half in fright, half in anger at the three white men who advanced on him. They were a scruffy lot. One wore a faded pair of overalls, bleached pale blue. The suspender rings had long since broken off, and now the straps were pulled through a gaping hole in the bib and tied in a half-knot. This man was in his late twenties, a week's growth of blond beard sprouting like white wires from his narrow cheeks. The other two men were obviously brothers. Both were dark-haired, and each wore a plaid shirt with a north woods flavor. Bright colors vibrated in the flickering light.

"Hold on there," said young Shawcross, putting both hands up in front of him. "I'm not looking for trouble. I just came in out of the cold."

"Well, you just get on out in it again," said white-whiskers. "I don't aim to ride with no nigger."

"I don't know how I'd get back up on top of the car," said Shawcross, "and even if I did, I'd freeze to death by the time we got to Memphis."

"Are you arguing with me?" said white-whiskers.

"No sir. I'm just telling you it'd be simple murder for you to put me outside again."

"He's right," said one of the brothers. "Let him stay, the car's plenty big."

The three men went back to the middle of the car, where they had rigged up a makeshift table. A pot was propped on two bricks over another candle which had gone out when the door opened. The second brother lit it again. The three men sat down, their legs crossed under them, and resumed a game of penny-ante poker. Shawcross leaned against the wall of the jouncing car, weak with relief.

An aroma of something incredibly delicious wafted its way toward him. Slumgullion! The hobo stew that had kept him alive across two-thirds of the continent. It was almost midnight now; he had not eaten since yesterday.

The tall brother studied his cards, pressing their greasy edges together as if he were trying to make two cards into one.

"Come on," white-whiskers growled impatiently. "Them's my cards. Don't rub the spots offen them."

"Hold your water," said the tall brother. He studied the cards even closer. "Let's see. You opened on guts and took three cards on the draw. So maybe you had a pair and maybe you improved. I'll bet a penny." He tossed a penny out into the little pile of coins.

"What you got?" asked white-whiskers.

"Nothing doing, buddy. I paid to see you."

White-whiskers tossed his cards out in the center. "Pair of eights."

The tall brother laughed. "Not good enough," he said. "Three fives." He showed them and raked in the pot.

By now the odor of the stew had Shawcross' stomach cramping.

"How about another hand?" asked the tall brother.

"Naw," said white-whiskers. "You tapped me out. I ought to know better than to play into two brothers anyhow."

"Listen, Mister, you saying we cheated you?" The smaller brother produced a knife and whetted it slowly on his shoe. He rasped the knife blade back and forth, then spit once on the shining point. White-whiskers inched back on his haunches.

"Come on," he whined. "I'd play you a couple more hands to show you I was funning. But you guys tapped me out. I lost fourteen cents."

The two brothers turned away in disgust. White-whiskers hesitated, then shrugged. He bent forward and stirred the slumgullion, establishing ownership.

"Hey, Mister," Shawcross said softly.

White-whiskers ignored him. The two brothers looked around.

"Mister man?" said Shawcross, feeling the words choke in his throat. "Mister, there at the pot?"

White-whiskers looked over, as surprised as if the door had spoken to him. "You talking to me, nigger?"

"Yes sir. Can I see you for a minute?"

"You already see me, nigger. Keep it up and you'll have your frozen ass back out there in the snow."

"Can I talk to you over here?"

"No, you *can't* talk to me over there. Now what do you want?"

"Mister man, I got some money," Shawcross said.

"How do you like that?" said white-whiskers. "Here I am all tapped out and the nigger, he got money."

"How much money?" said the tall brother.

"Just a nickel."

"Where'd you get that nickel, boy?" asked white-whiskers. "Bet you stole it."

"No sir. I worked me a full day in Little Rock for my room, and the man gave me a nickel to travel on."

"You mean you want to get in the *game?*" said the tall brother.

"No sir," said Shawcross. "What I thought was that if you could see your way clear to sell me a little of your slumgullion—"

"This ain't no restaurant," said white-whiskers. "We hardly got enough for ourselves."

"I'm terrible hungry," Shawcross' throat tightened around the words. "I'd give my nickel for just a little smidge of that slumgullion."

"Even if I was to let you," said white-whiskers, "what'd you eat with? You ain't using *my* spoon."

"I've *got* a spoon!" said Shawcross, whipping it out. No one on the road traveled without his own spoon.

"Come on," said the tall brother. "Don't be a shitheel all your life. Sell the nigger some stew."

"What'll I put his stew in? He ain't going to eat from the pot with the rest of us."

Shawcross scrambled around the floor of the boxcar, frantically searching for something to use as a plate. He came up with an asphalt roofing shingle. It was dusty, but he polished off the grime with his shirt sleeve.

"Bring it over here, nigger," said white-whiskers. Hesitantly, Shawcross went over to the table, holding the shingle in front of him. "Where's your nickel?"

Shawcross' hand dove into his pocket. For a terrible instant he thought the nickel was gone, that he had lost it somewhere since Little Rock. Then he found it tucked in a corner of his dungaree pocket.

"Give it here." Shawcross obeyed. White-whiskers examined the nickel carefully in the flickering light of the candle. "Okay, hold out that shingle. Nigger'll eat offen anything," he said to the brothers. "Even a dirty old roofing shingle."

"Give him some meat, too," said the tall brother. White-whiskers cursed, but put a chunk of gristly meat on the shingle along with the carrots and white potatoes.

"Okay," said white-whiskers. "That's more than you deserve."

"Thank you," said Shawcross.

"What'd you say?"

"Thank you, boss," Shawcross mumbled. He backed off into the corner, greasy gravy from the stew running over his cold fingers. He pulled the spoon out of his pocket and began to scrape around the edges of the shingle before any more of the precious liquid could run over. He scooped up a piece of potato and popped it into his mouth. It was fiercely hot, and he sucked in air to cool it.

"Nigger burned his mouth," said white-whiskers.

He gathered up the dog-eared, greasy cards and shuffled them overhand.

Shawcross watched from the corner of the car, as he ate the last tantalizing morsel of slumgullion. The food had not been enough to fill him, only to sharpen his appetite even more.

White-whiskers studied his cards carefully, sweat forming on his forehead even in the coolness of the boxcar. He decided, threw the nickel into the pot.

"Three cents," he said. "Give me two cents' change." He got it and studied his hand. "Cards?"

"Two," said the short brother. The tall brother dropped out. White-whiskers tossed out two cards and gathered up the discards. He examined his own hand again, reluctantly rejected two cards. "Dealer takes two." He squeezed the cards together without looking at them, moving the top card to the bottom of his stack of five, then the next top card to the bottom.

Shawcross was hungrier than ever. He squatted in the corner of the bouncing car and listened to the click-*clack*-click of the wheels.

"Well," said the short brother, "I bet two cents."

White-whiskers tossed his last coins into the pot. "I see you. What you got?"

The short brother flipped over his cards. "Three aces," he said. "Had 'em going in." White-whiskers hurled his cards aside. "Goddammit, I had three queens! Best fucking hand I had all night."

"Don't get your piss hot," said the short brother, raking in the little pile of coins. "Breaks of the game."

White-whiskers got up and cracked the door a bit to watch the snowbound hills slipping by outside.

"Come on, buddy," said the tall brother. "It's colder'n a witch's tit in here. Shut that door and let's chow down."

White-whiskers came back to the table and took out his spoon. He polished it on the bib of his overalls, black with road dirt, and the three men dug in hungrily. Shawcross heard spoons tinkling against the metal rim of the pot, sharp inhalations of pleasure as the men savored the food and smacked their lips over bits of hot potato.

"Sheeit!" white-whiskers said, sitting back on his haunches. "I'm so mad I ain't even hungry."

"Son," said the tall brother, "you are the sorest loser I have ever met. A man who hates to lose as much as you do shouldn't play."

"Mighty good stew," said the short brother, scooting back from the pot and licking his spoon. "There's a little mite left. Do you want it, bro?"

"I'm full up," said his brother. "It's your stew, buddy," he said to white-whiskers. "You want it?"

"I couldn't swallow me another bite. Throw it out the door. We won't eat it before we get into Memphis, and I know you guys want your pot back."

"Maybe we could let the nigger have it," said the tall brother softly. Shawcross heard him and his heart beat faster. Against his will, he began to salivate.

"How come?" growled white-whiskers. "He ain't got no more money, and you wouldn't want any of his nigger clothes. He ain't got nothing to trade."

"Maybe he has," said the tall brother. "Hey, boy, you still hungry?"

"Yes sir," said Shawcross. "It seemed like that little bit just woke my stomach up."

"You got anything to trade for it?"

Shawcross racked his brain. "I guess not," he said finally. "I been on the road two weeks, and everything's already swapped off."

The tall brother laughed gently. "I know just how it is, boy. Well, that's too bad. You see, I'd like to give you what's left of this here stew, but it just wouldn't be right without you giving nothing back, would it?"

"No sir." Shawcross clenched his jaw muscles and sat silently, waiting.

"Friend," said the tall brother to white-whiskers, "you ever see a nigger's pecker?"

"Me? Hell, no. What the hell would I be doing looking at a nigger's cock?"

The tall brother turned to Shawcross. "You know, you don't talk like a southren nigra," he said. "Where you from?"

24

"California."

"California," said the tall brother, as if it were another country. "I guess you went to school out there, didn't you?" Shawcross was silent, not knowing an answer was required. "I *said*, you went to school out there?"

"Yes sir."

"Any white boys at that school you went to in California?"

"Mostly white boys, sir."

The tall brother turned to the other two men. "See," he said, as if he were explaining a secret, "I heard about them California schools." He turned back to Shawcross. "You play football in that California school?"

"Some," said Shawcross.

"You make the team?"

"Just second string."

"What position?"

"Guard."

"You use the same showers as the white boys?"

"Yes sir."

"Now, that just naturally gives you the advantage over us, boy. I mean, seeing as how we was all brought up in separate schools, and even on the job, if there was a shower room, the niggers didn't use it."

Shawcross felt his arms begin to tremble. "I don't know what you mean, sir."

"Well, hell," said the tall brother. "In those football locker rooms, you saw what the white boys had, didn't you? They didn't take showers in their jock straps, did they?"

"No sir, they was naked."

"Then you saw everything they had?"

"I guess so."

"What do you mean, you guess so? Did you or didn't you? Answer me, boy, this slumgullion's getting colder by the minute. You do want some more to eat, don't you?"

"If it don't trouble you none, sir."

"Oh, it don't trouble *me* none, boy," said the tall brother. "What I'm trying to get through to you is that you seen white boys' peckers, and they seen yours, out there in California. But down here, us fellers never had the chance to see what a nigra's got. What the hell, you just can't go around the streets of Meridian asking colored gents to drop their overalls, so all of us southern boys just naturally wonder what all the fuss is about. Now, I got a proposition to make to you. You want this stew?"

"Yes sir," choked Shawcross.

"Fair enough. Now, since you ain't got nothing to trade for it, my offer is you just drop your pants and let us get a good look at what you've got, and the rest of this pot's yours. What do you say?"

"I couldn't do that," Shawcross whispered.

"Look, boy, we ain't going to hurt you," the tall brother said patiently. "I mean, we ain't queer or anything like that. We're just curious. Now, I know it's cold in here, so you come over here by the candle and just give us a good look, and then you can stay over here where it's warm and eat your stew."

"Please," said Shawcross, "I can't do that."

"I don't know what's bothering you," said the tall brother. "You told me yourself you undressed in the same locker room with twenty or thirty other guys, and if you saw what they had, they surely had a chance to see what you got."

"But that was different, sir." Shawcross was almost crying with frustration and a mixture of fear and rage. "I mean, we were only showering. We weren't looking."

"Sure you were looking. You told me you saw what they had."

"Screw him," said white-whiskers. "Gimme that pot. I'm going to chuck the rest of that stew out the door." Shawcross watched him pick up the pot. His stomach clenched.

"Please, sir, don't do that. I'm near starving to death."

"Go ahead and chuck it," said the tall brother without looking at white-whiskers. "He ain't really hungry, or he wouldn't be so standoffish when all we want to do is take a look at something that ain't going to hurt nobody. Go on, chuck it out the door."

White-whiskers unlatched the heavy door and pulled it back. The sound of the wheels clacking over the uneven roadbed increased, and a blast of cold wind swept through the car. White-whiskers scraped his spoon along the bottom of the stew pot and started to turn it upside down.

"No!" shouted Shawcross. "Don't throw it out. I'll do whatever you say. Please, boss!"

The tall brother nodded his head, and white-whiskers slid the door back. The car seemed deathly quiet. Shawcross could feel his temples throbbing, and there was a chilly sickness in the pit of his stomach.

"Okay," said the tall brother, "come on over here by the light, son."

Shawcross stood near the flame of the candle. His knees felt watery and spots swam in front of his eyes.

"Drop 'em, boy," said white-whiskers harshly. The tall brother shushed him. "Don't frighten him," he said softly. "He's a good boy, and there ain't no call to holler at him. Just undo your belt, boy, and let 'em drop."

Frozen in an agony of indecision and panic, Shawcross stood trembling. He knew his eyes were rolled into the white-rimmed parody of fear that Negro comedians used, and he was disgusted and yet unable to do anything to save himself.

"Go on, boy," said the tall brother's gentle voice.

"Drop 'em. Nothing to worry about. I won't let fuckface here hurt you."

Strangers to his mind and will, Shawcross' fingers took it on themselves to unhook his belt, unbutton the fly of his heavy dungarees.

"That's right," breathed the tall brother. "Now, let go."

Shawcross felt the cold air rushing in to nip at his behind as the trousers slid down his legs. He was wearing no shorts, and he could feel the chill from waist to knees.

"Woowie!" said the shorter brother, staring. "Bro, they wasn't lying when they told us about these mothers. Look how this boy is hung."

"He is that," agreed his brother. "It must be some flag-pole when it's hard."

"Make him get it hard," said white-whiskers, moving in close. "Make him get it hard and jack off. That's what I want to see." He reached out toward the boy's crotch. The tall brother slapped his hand down sharply.

"What are you, some kind of queer?" the tall brother asked. "I told him we wasn't going to mess around with him." He moved in fast and put the flat of his hand in white-whiskers face and shoved him back until he thudded against the far end of the car. "If you can't behave like a natural man, you just stay out of sight until you learn how." Over his shoulder, to Shawcross: "Okay, son, pull 'em up. I seen what I wanted to see. Bro, give him the stew. Eat out of the pot, boy—you'll get more of the juice that way."

Shawcross jerked the pants up his trembling legs and fastened the fly.

"You can stay out here where it's warm," said the short brother. But Shawcross backed into the dark corner. He fished out his spoon and dug it into the remaining stew, which had cooled down until it was lukewarm. He pushed it into his mouth mechanically. For a few moments, as he chewed and swallowed the stringy meat—not enjoying it or even tasting it—his hunger fought with his humiliation. Hunger lost.

Vomit rose in his throat, burning as it came. Shawcross ran to the door and flung it open. He leaned out and puked into the freezing wind.

Someone caught him by the belt and said, "I got you, boy. Don't worry. Just get it up."

It was the tall brother.

"Too bad, son. Reckon you ate too fast on an empty stomach. It's a pity, because now it's all gone and we ain't got nothing else to give you."

As another spasm clenched his gut, Shawcross bent his head, trying to bring up something—anything—but a man cannot puke out his injured soul, and that was what had sickened him.

Shawcross stood in the open door, swaying with the movement of the train. They passed a grade crossing, its red lights flashing and the bell clanging.

"You okay, boy?" asked the tall brother.

Shawcross straightened, wiped his mouth and face on his sleeve. "Yeah," he said, stepping back inside the car. The tall brother helped him close the door, and the whistle of the wind stopped. Shawcross leaned against the slats of the car, taking deep breaths. The tall brother held out a half-pint bottle.

"Take a slug of this," he said.

"What is it?" Shawcross asked, deliberately omitting the "sir."

"White lightning. Put a little of that down, it'll settle your stomach."

Shawcross lifted the bottle and took a swig. The whiskey burned all the way down his throat and into his stomach. He suppressed another fit of gagging and then, to his amazement, felt his stomach relax. "Good," he said, wiping the neck of the bottle and handing it back.

"Feel better?" asked the tall brother.

"A little," Shawcross admitted. He went back to his dark corner and crouched down. All sensation of hunger was gone; he felt weak and drained. He must have dozed, because the next thing he knew was a hand shaking his shoulder.

"Hey, boy." It was the tall brother's voice. "Wake up."

"Huh?" mumbled Shawcross.

"We're coming to the outskirts of Memphis. You got to get off before we get into the yards or they'll bend a stick around your head."

Shawcross stood up. The train had slowed, and its mournful whistle sounded far up ahead.

"I know a crossing they almost stop at," said the tall brother. "You jump off there, you're only about half a mile from niggertown. There's an all-night filling station you can put up at until it gets daylight. Now, when you jump off, don't try to run. Just roll up in a ball and let the snow cushion your fall. Otherwise you'll bust a leg and freeze to death before anyone finds you in the morning. Remember what I say—don't cross the tracks. Walk back up the line to the crossing and turn left down the road. It's about half a mile to that filling station. A jig runs it, and he'll let you stay inside and keep warm. He even has sandwiches, so here—" The man pressed something into his hand. "Buy yourself something to eat. I'm sorry you couldn't keep that slum down."

Shawcross wondered how the tall brother could humiliate him one minute and be so concerned for his welfare in the next. Then the white man shouted "Jump!" and Shawcross went flying into the snowbanks along the right of way. As the ground thumped him heavily, he felt snow sliding down the back of his neck. Somewhere in the bank he hit something hard, and his head blazed with pain. Then he lay still on the ground, panting for breath and listening to his heart thump against his ribs. The train was still grinding past him—it was a long one—and as he got to his feet, he remembered the coin the white man had pressed upon him. He opened his hand and, in the pale light of the full moon, saw a quarter. For a rage-filled moment he felt like hurling it after the train, but he did not. A quarter was more money than he had had in the past two weeks.

Instead, he followed the tall brother's directions, and sure enough, there was an all-night service station, presided over by a quiet, very fat Negro who invited Shawcross inside to wait for the dawn. He squandered the quarter on a poor-boy sandwich and two Pepsis and left in the morning, flat broke, heading for Paris Island. Three weeks later he was a buck private in the United States Marines.

More than thirty years later, long after Benjamin Davis and his son had been tokened into generalships in the Army and even the Navy had let two blacks into flag rank, the Marines had relented and Stanley Shawcross had become first a Brigadier and soon after a Major General.

Shawcross stretched out full length in the scalding tub, yawning. He consulted his calendar watch: twenty-four after three on the afternoon of Saturday, November 18. Next week would be Thanksgiving. He wished he could be home in Burbank with Carolyn and the boys. This would be only the third Thanksgiving he had been separated from her since those hectic days in Korea, when he was bucking for bird colonel and making it by being the roughest, gung-ho-est regimental commander in the Marine Corps.

He knew he would never have made it if the pressures

of a changing world had not been working in his favor. His achievements came at the same time as unofficial directives to loosen up and let a few coloreds get into medium-command positions.

Power brought him the occasional forgetfulness that comes over a man who has been successful: he sometimes forgot who he was and what he was. He could still remember how dramatically the Watts riot in 1965 had reminded him that even a major general is still a black man.

He had been home on furlough when the fighting broke out. He was forming up his unit at Camp Pendleton, and this was his final stateside leave before shipping out. Most of his men were on leave, too, and he knew that several of them lived in Los Angeles—one in Watts itself. He tried to phone the man, a young captain named Orin Nelson, and found the telephone out of order.

"I think I'd better go over there and drag Orin out," he told Carolyn. "He loves a good fight so much he might get in this thing just to work out a few of the kinks."

"I wish you wouldn't," said his wife. "The TV says it's getting pretty bad over there."

"Can't be helped," said Shawcross. "I'll have to go. He's got Bob Colgate the ninety-day-wonder with him, and I'd feel awful if anything happened to keep them from making the shipment."

Carolyn Shawcross shook her head. "I don't know what it is with you, Stanley. You're a forty-seven-year-old man with two stars on your shoulders, and you still act like den mother to a bunch of cub scouts."

He smiled, and she pecked him on the lips. He went out and got in the Corvair. For once, it started easily.

The sky was an angry red ahead as he turned off the freeway at Grant Avenue. A smoky, glowing cloud hung over the city. The avenue was curiously empty of traffic, and only a few lights showed in the windows along the sidewalk. Shawcross looked at his watch: it was just after midnight. Grant Avenue should have been in full blast at this early hour. He checked to be sure he had his identification wallet, and cursed out loud. He had left it in his other civilian jacket. Turn back? He rejected that choice without hesitation. The worst that could happen was a citation for driving without a license, and under the circumstances, that was a small enough risk.

At Third Street he turned left. The red glow was closer now, and he smelled the charcoal odor of burning wood. This street was empty of life, too, although there were more cars than usual—many of them parked at haphazard angles near the curb. He drove slowly, ready to stop if necessary. His senses were alert to danger. But when it came, it was so sudden that he had no chance to react.

Something smashed into his windshield. The entire right side collapsed into a network of spider-webbed safety glass, and a red brick fell back onto the Corvair's hood with a thump. Shawcross jammed his foot down on the accelerator, then cursed as the car stalled. He turned the key, heard the starter mutter uselessly. At the edge of his headlights he sensed an approaching line of shadows. As he reached over to snap down the lock on the right-hand door, a voice yelled, "There he is! Let's get the mother!" Before he could lock the other door, it was wrenched open and grasping hands plucked him out into the night. He drove his elbow into the stomach of one of his attackers, drawing forth a painful grunt.

"Hold on," said a voice. "He's blood."

"What are you doing around here, man?" asked another voice. "Don't you know any better than to drive down here without keeping your inside lights on so we can see you're blood?"

Shawcross felt relief tingle through his body. "I didn't know how rough it was," he said.

"Rougher than a cob," said one of the men. "And it's going to get rougher, baby. You from outside?"

"Burbank," said Shawcross, brushing at his trousers. "I got some friends over on Harper Street. Thought I might be able to give them a hand."

"Well, you be careful, you hear?" said one of the men. "We're sorry about your car, but we thought you was Whitey. If you can get her moving again, take it easy and keep your inside lights on. Next time somebody might throw a beer bottle full of gasoline instead of a brick."

"I'll do that," said Shawcross.

To his great relief the engine started on the first try. As the car moved, he glimpsed scurrying figures, caught momentarily in the glare of his headlights. Curiously, he felt no surprise that he was driving down an American street with the same caution he had used so often entering an enemy city under fire. All he lacked was the familiar weight of an automatic rifle strapped to one shoulder and two fragmentation grenades clipped to his belt. "Shawcross' balls," one war correspondent had dubbed them, adding: "The old man would no more go out without those babies than he'd take a walk without his *cojones*."

His headlights picked up something much larger than a man. He mashed his brakes in time to keep from hitting the barricade of garbage cans and furniture piled up in the middle of the street. A crude sign attached to the roadblock read, STOP OR BE SHOT.

"Over here, nigger!" called a voice from the darkness. "Don't make any sudden moves. You're covered."

Shawcross inched the Corvair over to the left side of the street and stopped as three men stepped out of the shadows. Two were California highway patrolmen, carrying short riot guns. The third was a uniformed member of the Los Angeles Police Department. He was the one who had spoken.

"Okay," he said, "get out slow and keep your hands in sight." When Shawcross merely looked at him, the policeman yanked the car door open. "Move!" he yelled.

Shawcross climbed out of the Corvair.

"What happened to your windshield?" asked one of the highway patrolmen.

"Someone put a brick through it."

The patrolman laughed. "Probably couldn't see you in the dark."

"Probably."

"What are you doing around here?" asked the policeman. "Those are Burbank plates."

"I'm an officer in the Marine Corps," said Shawcross. "Two of my men are down here somewhere. I came to get them."

"What kind of officer?"

"Major general."

The policeman snorted. "And I'm Douglas MacArthur." he said. "Let's see some identification, *General*."

Shawcross hesitated. "That's the problem," he said. "I came off in such a hurry, I forgot it."

"No ID?" said the second patrolman. "Mister, you better have a driver's license."

"I do," said Shawcross. "But not with me. I told you—"

"I know what you told us," said the policeman.

"Look at the registration on the steering post," said Shawcross. "It's got my name and address. You can check it with a phone call."

"No time for phone calls tonight, buddy. You bastards have busted the phones as far as I'm concerned. Listen," he told the two patrolmen, "I'm taking this one."

"Wait a minute," said the first patrolman. "I was in

the Corps and I remember hearing about a colored general." Then, to Shawcross: "You must have *something*. What's your name?"

"Shawcross." He looked at him hard. "What unit were you in, son?"

"First Battalion, Third Regiment."

"Commanded by Birdturd McQueen," said Shawcross.

The patrolman nodded, almost smiled. "If you're Shawcross," he said, "you'll know about your brass balls."

"Fragmentation grenades," said Shawcross. "Rumor was I kept them filled with bourbon."

The patrolman looked at his companions. "This guy really is a major general."

"Well, we can still drag him in for driving without a license," said the policeman. "Being a general doesn't make him any better than the rest of these spades."

"The General just forgot his wallet," said the patrolman. "It happens all the time."

"Okay," said the policeman finally. "Go on," he said to Shawcross. "Get about your business."

"My business is over on Harper Street."

"Pretty bad in there," said the ex-Marine patrolman. "Those snipers are firing at anything that moves."

"Two of my men are in there," said Shawcross.

The patrolman nodded. "Okay," he said, "but keep it low, General. This is no place to get your ass shot off after coming through Iwo and Frozen Chosen."

"What about my car?"

"Better leave it here. At least it won't get burned. They've gone wild in there."

"Thanks," said Shawcross. He stepped around the barricade and headed down the street, avoiding dark areas where someone might jump him from concealment.

The street was lit from above by the sky's hazy red glow and a few street lights. The rest had been knocked out by rocks or bullets. Two blocks away from the barricade he heard running feet and stepped into a doorway. Two teen-aged Negro boys ran past, shoes pounding on the pavement, breath rasping with their effort. They vanished, and then Shawcross heard the slap of heavier feet on the sidewalk. He drew himself back into the shadows. Two Los Angeles policemen appeared, puffing for breath.

"Little bastards got away," said one. "Christ, they run fast."

The other policeman answered, but they were now out of earshot, and all Shawcross could hear was the murmur of their voices.

He padded along the sidewalk, eyes and ears alert. Far ahead, he heard shouting and the crash of breaking glass. He approached carefully, found himself on a street that was brightly lighted by flames flickering up along the front of a three-story frame building. The street looked like the wreckage he had seen so often when entering a bombed-out enemy town. Suddenly he was surrounded by running, shouting figures. One of them, a tall, very black boy of perhaps fifteen, shook his fist at the blazing building and screamed, "Burn, baby! *Burn!*"

TWO

Sitting on a stool in the center of a spotlight at The Sands, Las Vegas, comedian Pete Humble took a long drag on his cigarette and went on, his words punctuated by chuckles from his intent audience.

"So after I sat in this Georgia lunch counter for eighteen months waiting for it to get integrated," he said, "when they finally brought me a menu there wasn't anything on there I liked." He absorbed the laugh, waited for it to peak, his eyes flicking from table to table, then shot out the kicker: "Those crackers didn't have any watermelon!"

Pete Humble was a small man, made taller by the white turtleneck sweater and tapered slacks he wore to accentuate his slender body. He scarcely moved, except to pull another cigarette from the leather pouch strapped to his belt.

"So," he said, his black face twisting in mock consternation, "I just plain give up. What's the point of being integrated if you can't even get a slice of watermelon? Between you and me, that's what's wrong with them southern cats. They ain't really mean. They just got a watermelon deficiency!

"Then," he said, "I decided to go up north and get into

show biz. I mean, I had this great sense of rhythm you know. Doobie-doobie-do! So I met this cat, he had the idea he was going to bring back radio. He wanted to kick off with a revival of *The Shadow*, and man, when *I* stand in the shadows, I go *invisible*. Of course, it was too good to be true. We got right up to opening night, and then I blew it. Can you hear me? 'Haw-haw-haw-HEH! The weed of crime bears bitter fruit. Who knows what evil lurks in the hearts of men? *De Shadow do!*' "

Pete Humble held up his hands. "What you gonna do?" he cried. "All them years of listening to Amos 'n Andy *got* to me!"

Pete let the laugh swell, then cut it off with one raised hand. "Well, folks, I guess I got to go now. The only reason I been out here this long is that NBC has been lining up their color cameras and I'm their favorite test pattern. So goodnight one and all, and my parting word is what the French croupier said to the duchess as she bent over to make her roulette bet—'Madame, black is best!' Bye, you-all!"

The light over his head went out, and the band struck up some get-off music.

Backstage, Pete Humble headed for his dressing room, his face running with perspiration. A man stepped up and caught him by the arm. It was Steve Bruno, Pete's press agent.

"Hey, Pete," said Bruno, "that finish is new. You know they love you, baby, but don't you think you ought to use the old one? That 'black is best' is playing it pretty strong."

Pete Humble leaned forward until his breath was hot against the press agent's chin and smiled.

"Fuck you, white man," he said.

THREE

When Shawcross reached the Nelson home, he discovered a barricaded fortress commanded by Captain Orin Nelson, Jr., supported by 2nd Lieutenant Robert Colgate, Orin Nelson, Sr., and two very frightened teen-aged Negro girls.

The house was dark, and at first Shawcross thought it was empty. He went up on the porch anyway.

"All right, Mister," said a cold voice, "don't take another step or I'll blow your head off."

Shawcross froze in half step. He recognized the voice of his junior officer.

"This is Shawcross," he said loudly. "You know my voice, Orin."

"It's him," said the voice of Robert Colgate. "It's the General."

"Come on inside, General," said Captain Orin Nelson.

Shawcross heard the door creak open and saw a dim glimmer of light through its widening gap. He stepped inside quickly and Nelson slammed it shut again.

"Who is it, Junior?" called a voice from the rear of the house.

"No sweat, Pop," said Captain Nelson. "It's General

Shawcross." To his commanding officer, he explained, "Pop's guarding the rear of the house with a shotgun. Up here, we've got these." He showed Shawcross the target pistol in his hand.

"Who are you holed up against?" asked Shawcross.

Nelson grimaced. "Against everybody," he said. "Couple of hours ago, a car came down the road full of white teen-agers. They had what sounded like skeet guns. They shot up the block pretty good. And those black maniacs out there, they're breaking in everywhere they can and burning what they can't take."

"Well, you can't hold them off with a shotgun and two pistols," said Shawcross.

"We can try," said Nelson. He nodded to Robert Colgate. "Keep an eye out," he said. "Me and the General'll go out back." As they walked through the house he indicated the two Negro girls huddled in the alcove. "They turned up about nine o'clock," he said. "A gang of kids were chasing them and they ran in here."

"What kind of kids?" asked Shawcross.

"Black, of course," said Nelson. "The past day or so, anything goes. A girl goes out on the street, she's asking for it. These two didn't know the rules."

They reached the back of the house where the elder Nelson sat watching the open yard, a double-barreled shotgun in his hands.

"Pleased to see you again, Gen'ral," he said. "Pardon the mess. We didn't get a chance to straighten up."

"What are you doing down this way, sir?" asked the younger Nelson.

"I didn't want you and Colgate to miss the shipment," Shawcross said. "My idea was to take you back to my place and keep your asses out of trouble."

"Trouble is the last thing we want," said Captain Nelson.

Shawcross nodded toward the street. "My car's just a few blocks away."

"That's the most tempting offer I've heard all night," said Nelson. "The trouble is, if we leave they'll burn Pop's house down sure as shit. They never have liked him anyway, because he gives them his welfare speech about once a month."

"I'd like to give them the point of my boot, right up their black asses," said the older Nelson. "Sure, I ding them for sitting around drinking and letting the old lady collect welfare for her and the kids. In Watts, Mother's Day comes twice a month."

"Where are the police?" asked Shawcross. "Can't you get protection?"

"You have to be joking, sir," Captain Nelson said. "You must have seen some of the fuzz out there. You think we'd have a chance of getting protection from *them?*"

"From some of them," said Shawcross.

"I'd sure be embarrassed to pick the wrong man to ask for protection and have him remove all my teeth with one bash of his nigger-knocker."

"What do you intend to do?"

"Stay here until things quiet down. My father worked all his life for this house, and I don't aim to sit back and let a bunch of goddamned rioters burn it down. May I remind the General that I am on leave until the end of next week, and what I do when on leave is my own damned business?"

"Simmer down, Nelson," said Shawcross. "I just don't want you to get your ass in a sling and miss the shipment. If those idiots out there call your bluff, they're liable to bust an arm or two before they let you go."

"It's no bluff, sir. If I left my father to shift for himself, you'd never look me in the eye again. Much as I appreciate your coming through the shitstorm to rescue us, I think we'll have to stay here and take what comes."

Shawcross nodded. "I guess I'd do the same thing in these circumstances. But for Christ's sake keep your head down."

"You don't have to worry about that, sir," said Nelson. "I aim to lay so low a snake'd have difficulty looking up to me."

"Son," whispered his father, "there's somebody out there near the orange tree."

The younger Nelson picked up a large flashlight. "Ready?"

The older man lifted the shotgun. "Ready," he said.

Nelson snapped on the light. It caught four black men sneaking up on the house. They blinked at the light, retreated behind the slender trunk of the tree.

"Okay, you guys," yelled Captain Nelson, "we're blood in here. What do you want?"

"White nigger!" one of the men yelled.

Nelson sighed, nodded to his father, who rested the shotgun on the window sill and fired one barrel. The buckshot snipped off leaves and fruit and dropped them down on the huddled men, who began scurrying backward.

"We're white niggers with shotguns!" yelled Nelson. "Next time we shoot to kill."

The men vanished into the darkness. Nelson flicked off the flashlight, and night reclaimed the back yard.

"Wonder what they figure we got in here?" mused the older man. "They must know, no more than a few dollars and an old beat-up television set."

Shawcross wiped the sweat from his forehead. "What's happening to us?"

"That's easy," said Nelson. "You and me, we busted out, but those guys out there didn't. They're just as mad at you and me as they are at the white man. They're screaming, 'Get Whitey!' But what they really mean is get what Whitey owns. Get that whiskey and that money and that new convertible car! And what happens when another black man owns that convertible? Why, take it away from him, he's a white nigger! He's an Uncle Tom! If he wasn't, he wouldn't have all those things that we want. *Right now!*"

He rested the hand that held the target pistol against the window sill. "Well," he went on quietly, "I know we got a rough row to hoe, but I hoed it and so did you, General, and so did Colgate and a lot of other guys. I don't see why we should be expected to carry a lot of burrheads along with us. If they want the cars and TV sets, they can earn them like the rest of us."

Shawcross looked at the younger man, fighting down a flicker of unexplainable anger. He stood up. "I'd better get back to Burbank. My wife is probably worried sick."

Nelson walked him to the front of the house. "I really do appreciate your coming over here like this. We'll see you next week down at Pendleton. That's a promise."

"I'll count on it," said Shawcross.

The older Nelson had come with them to the front door. Lieutenant Colgate looked up from his vigil. "Quiet as sin," he said. "Haven't seen a car or a man on foot since you left off that shotgun blast."

"How about the girls?" asked Shawcross. "Maybe they'd be better off if I took them over to Burbank, or at least out of the area."

"How about it?" called Captain Nelson. "The General here, he's driving over to Burbank. You girls want to go along?"

They looked up and shook their heads violently.

"Guess they're scared to move," said Nelson. "You

just watch out for yourself, sir. We're safe inside walls here, but you're going out on that street again."

"I sure am sorry," said the elder Nelson. "No way to welcome a guest."

"Don't worry about it," said Shawcross. "Just keep this son of yours under control. We need him in the Corps."

"I'll do that, Gen'ral," said the old man. "Orin, you open the door for the Gen'ral and keep him covered till he gets up the street."

"Yes, Pop," he said. "Ready, General?"

"Ready," said Shawcross.

When Nelson swung the door open, Shawcross went out fast and low. He scuttled across the front porch, found solid footing in the front yard and—careful not to get himself silhouetted against the red-clouded sky— began to make his way down Harper Street. He was almost to the corner of Third when he heard a car approaching at high speed. He looked back toward the Nelson house, saw the automobile careening along the empty street without headlights. As it neared the house it lurched up onto the sidewalk, churned across the front lawn, and passed within twenty feet of the porch. Something arched from the right window of the car and Shawcross heard glass shatter. He shouted and began to run toward the house.

The blast flowered within, a brilliant orange flash and a sound that trembled the earth. The entire front of the frame house splintered and collapsed out into the street. The inside was filled with bright blossoms of flame. The car was back on the street by then, and as it approached him, Shawcross found a chunk of rock and when the car went by threw it as hard as he could, straight at the driver's head. His aim was true; he heard a mushy thump as the missile struck.

The car turned, out of control. It struck a fire hydrant, sending a geyser of water fifty feet into the air.

Those bastards! he thought. They're white!

He ran toward the flaming house, but before he could get near it he was cut off by two squad cars that screamed out of the surrounding darkness. Four police officers leaped from the nearest car and blocked his path. He did not stop running, even when one of them lifted his revolver and called "Stop or I'll shoot!" Instead he ran straight at the man, seeing only the paleness of his white face in the flickering light from the burning house. The policeman raised his gun, but another officer struck down his arm as Shawcross closed the distance between them. One policeman thrust his billy club between the General's legs, bringing him down. Thrashing, trying to rise, Shawcross felt the impact of the clubs against his shoulders and neck. Then one blow connected with his temple, and the world exploded around him.

FOUR

Shawcross awoke to the fetid odor of sweat and mold. He was lying on what felt like bare springs. He opened his eyes slowly, could not see through the crusty deposits in his eyes. He licked his fingertips, rubbed away at his eyelids, and gradually brought the room into focus.

He was in a small cell lighted by one wire-caged yellow electric light bulb. The walls were gray and covered with scribbled and scraped messages, most of them obscene. To one side he could see a heavily barred door and, on the other, a tiny screened window high up near the ceiling. Under it, a toilet bowl without a seat.

Shawcross lifted his head and felt the vomit rising in his throat. He barely made it to the toilet, where he was dimly conscious of someone holding his shoulders while he leaned over. Then a hand pressed a wet, cool towel against his face.

The hand belonged to a thin, tall Negro with an intense, hawklike face. His eyes were a piercing light blue, and gave the impression of never blinking.

"How do you feel now, General?" asked the man.

Shawcross looked up in surprise. "You know me?"

"I've been keeping tabs on you for a long time, General. Yes, I know you—and so does the property clerk who took your belongings when you were brought in. He called me and I got my ass over here." The thin man smiled tightly. "It cost me fifty bucks to get locked up in here with you. They don't know who you are yet. You didn't have any ID on you."

"No," groaned Shawcross. "I forgot my wallet. Did they bring anyone else in?"

"Three white guys, busted up from a car wreck. Seems there was a house blown up, and just the four of you were found in the vicinity."

Shawcross told him about the automobile and the bomb. The other man whistled. "Well," he said, "you gave one of them a message to remember you by. His jaw's busted."

"Too bad it wasn't his neck. What about the people in the house?"

"I don't know anything about them. Whitey didn't seem to be worrying too much about the details."

"They've got to let me make one phone call," said Shawcross.

"Pardon me for disagreeing, but they don't have to let you shit unless they want to. You have to remember you aren't a big-shot general to these honkeys, you're a black buck nigger."

Shawcross looked at him steadily. "Who are you anyway?" he asked.

"I'm William Gray," said the man.

"Of course," said Shawcross. "I've read your speeches, you make Rap Brown and Stokely Carmichael look like moderates. Your doctrine is revolution."

"*Black* revolution," said Gray. "But only *my* doctrine, General? Do you mean to say it isn't yours too?"

"Of course I mean to say that," said Shawcross.

"General," said Gray, shaking his head, "this country is filled with thousands of white niggers, but you are not

48

one of them. I know that as well as I know my own name. You're black, General."

"I'm an American citizen who incidentally happens to be black," Shawcross said coldly.

"That's what you say. That may even be what you think. But I *know*, you're one of us, General, and when the day comes you'll be with us."

Shawcross went over and gripped the bars. "Guard!" he called. "Hey, is there anybody out there?"

An uproar went up from the neighboring cells.

"Sure, we here, man! Where else we going to be?"

"Make them feed us!"

"Give the baby a sugar titty!"

"SHUT UP!"

A police officer appeared at the end of the hall, silhouetted against the light from the room beyond.

"It's four in the morning," he said. "Knock off the noise and let people get some sleep."

"Don't you shut us up!" shouted a voice. "You think you so big and hot with your badge and pistol? Man, we going to shut you up with a spadeful of dirt in your dead mouth!"

The policeman came closer. "Who said that?" he asked, his voice tight with anger. His answer was a cry from dozens of men: "Me!" "I said it!" "No, I did!"

"Smart asses," said the officer. He turned to go, then stopped when Shawcross called out to him.

"Guard! Listen to me."

"Sure," said the officer. "And what do you want to do? Spit on me? Or call me a cop pig?"

"Simmer down, son," said Shawcross, unconsciously falling into the tone of voice he used with his troops.

"Don't call me son, you black sonofabitch!" shouted the policeman.

"Go on, boss," said William Gray. "Drag him out of

the cell and bust up his kidneys with that nigger-knocker of yours. That's what you really want to do, ain't it?"

"Shut up, Gray," Shawcross ordered. To the officer: "Simmer down, I said. All I want to do is see whoever's in charge here. Your sergeant or your lieutenant. There's a mistake about my being in here and I—"

"You bet your sweet ass there's a mistake! If I'd been on the arresting squad you wouldn't be in any cell, you'd be in the hospital with those three men you attacked."

"Hey!" yelled someone in a nearby cell. "Who they got in there anyhow? Superjig?"

"I'm entitled to one telephone call," said Shawcross.

"Sure," said the officer. "When you're booked. Until then, shut your big mouth."

Shawcross tried to keep the anger out of his voice. "When will you book me?"

The policeman leaned forward. "When we get damned good and ready," he said softly. He turned and left.

"Well," said Gray. "How does it feel to be an American citizen getting treated like he's only a black man?"

"Why do you keep pushing, Gray?"

"General, it's no accident, us being in the same jail cell," said Gray. "I planned for us to have a talk before you shipped out for Vietnam."

"So far it's talk I don't like to hear."

"If wanting to change things and make them what they ought to be for our people is talk you don't like to hear, I plead guilty."

"There are other ways," said Shawcross. His head ached.

"Like passing a Civil Rights Bill? How can the white man do us a favor by giving us what's already our right? He's had a knife in our backs for three hundred years. Are we supposed to thank him for taking it out? And what good is it to sit in a restaurant if you don't have the

50

bread to buy what's on the menu? Man, Whitey ain't giving us nothing, he's just making headlines to keep down world opinion. We aren't Americans, we're African prisoners. Only now the white man is looking around and he's shit-scared. He sees what's taking place all over the world and it makes his white skin crawl. He sees time swinging in our direction. He sees the dark people of the world losing their fear of the white man. That mealy-mouthed crap about equal rights is just a smokescreen to hoodwink the rest of the world."

"Bullshit," said Shawcross, wearily sinking down to the bare springs of the bunk.

"His days in the saddle are over," said Gray. "The black man knows it, the brown man knows it, the red man knows it, and the yellow man knows it. And most of all Whitey knows it, because all those colored men are engaging him in the one kind of warfare he doesn't stand a chance of winning. They're throwing guerrilla warriors against him, and his heart is down in his stomach because he knows he can't win! That's why there are so many of our brothers in Vietnam, General. Whitey's making cannon fodder out of our young men, because he wants them dead and that's one sure way to get it done."

"Gray," said Shawcross, "why don't you save your breath?"

"You may be a little confused about where your loyalty should lie, but you're no white nigger. You're absorbing what I'm saying, even if the white man has brainwashed your black mind into thinking it's white."

"You must have an asshole for a mouth," mumbled Shawcross, half asleep. "The amount of shit you spray out is fantastic."

Gray laughed. "Mighty colorful talk for a general," he said. "But before you go to sleep, let this slip inside your head and rattle around in there. The guerrilla won in

Algeria and Indochina. The guerrilla won in Cuba. And the black guerrilla is going to win here. When we all live in one place—when we control our own land and keep the white man out—that's not segregation any more, that's separation. Segregation means the white man puts you away from him, far enough so he don't have to smell your black skin but not so far that he can't control you. Separation means you're gone, man. And that's more frightening to the white man than integration. He'll let you integrate before he'll let you separate, because when you have separation you have control! And the only way we're going to get our separation is through guerrilla warfare. Now a man like you knows—General, are you listening to me?"

But Major General Stanley Shawcross was sound asleep.

FIVE

The Reverend Abner Greenbriar raised his hands to quiet the auditorium full of shouting college students.

"We had the March on Washington," he said, "and it did no real good. We had the sit-ins and they did no real good. We tried every form of nonviolence and none of it did any good."

He surveyed his audience.

"Is that what you believe? That is what William Gray and his followers would have you believe, but my friends, I say it is not so. Those things *did* do good!

"Look back to just a few short years ago. The Negro could not vote in many states; he was unable to send his children to decent schools; he was unable to find a job.

"Is it better today?

"Of course it is! A blind man could see how much better it is!

"But the firebrands, the hurry-uppers, run around shouting 'freedom now!' They ignore the fact that they *do* have freedom now, freedom that allows them to castigate white friends because their skins are not black like ours. I look out into this sea of faces, and many of the faces I see are white. Here they are, trying to help. The black man needs that help, the black man appreciates that help—despite the Stokely Carmichaels and Rap Browns and William Grays of this world. Those angry men talk as if they know only how to destroy, not how to build.

"My friends, when I say things are better I do *not* say that things are right. Oh, no, there is still much to be done. But we're on our way!

"Keep cool! Keep working, keep demonstrating, keep marching, keep talking and writing—it's doing the job!

"God bless you and love Jesus."

Greenbriar maneuvered his stocky figure down from the stage and shook hands as he moved through the crowd of young people. As he worked his way toward the exit, a young woman caught up with him.

"Reverend," she said, "I'm Karen Davis. I've been writing to you."

"Oh, yes, Miss Davis, I remember your letters. And the helpful contributions that accompanied them."

"I want to make another contribution," she said.

"That's most generous," he said. "If you'll see my assistant—"

"The contribution is me."

He stopped short and looked at her.

"What did you say?"

"I said the contribution is me." She flushed. "I mean, the contribution is my head and my hands."

"I see. Well, Miss Davis, we can always use more marchers. If you'll—"

"Anyone can march!" she said, tossing her blonde hair. She was, Greenbriar noted, a very attractive young lady. In her early twenties, perhaps late teens. "I didn't come here to march," she went on. "I've been training myself to be useful. I can type eighty words a minute and take shorthand and run a tape recorder and even a movie projector. And I can drive."

"You sound like you're set up to make some man a fine private secretary, Miss Davis," said Greenbriar.

"I am, and that's what I want to be for you. Your private secretary."

Patiently, he said, "But I have a secretary."

"No, you haven't. You don't have a secretary at all. You've got lots of assistants who think they're too important to type a letter or take notes during a meeting so you know later on what you said. You need me, sir."

"Perhaps I do," he said, at the door now. "But I'm afraid—"

"Don't worry about money," she said. "I'll work for nothing. I mean, you'll have to cover my expenses, because I don't have any money of my own, but other than that I won't cost you a penny."

"Miss Davis," Greenbriar said gently, "I can't tell you how much this offer means to me. And we're not so poor that we can't pay a few dollars to our staff. But I'm afraid it just isn't possible for you to be my private secretary. Now, we can find some place for you on the main staff, but—"

"No, you don't!" She followed him to his car. "It's you I mean to work for, not your staff. I made a complete survey of what you need in a secretary, and I fill it in every way. That is—every way but one, and I can't help that." She looked at him sharply, but he did not respond. "All right," she said, "I'll say it. I'm white. That's the reason you don't want me."

"That's the reason I can't want you. Don't you see, Miss Davis, we travel day and night, and much of that travel is in the South. It wouldn't be practical."

"Isn't that what this is all about? So that neither one of

us will ever have to worry about nonsense like that again?"

"Miss Davis," he smiled, "you are a very persistent young woman."

"You don't know how persistent. You might as well give in now, because you'll have to eventually, and it'll save a lot of wear and tear on both of us."

"Very well. Miss Davis," he said, deciding. "Suppose you come to my office tomorrow."

"I've already been to your office. I'm all set up. Your staff was surprised to learn you'd put on a new girl without discussing it with them, but they set me up in the little office outside yours. I brought my own typewriter and stuff, because I wasn't sure what you'd have around."

The Reverend Abner Greenbriar shook his head as if to clear it. "In that case, I suppose all I can do is offer you a lift to wherever you're staying."

"Thank you, I'm at the South Side Y."

As the car pulled away, he turned to her. "How on earth did you ever persuade Mrs. Cochran to vacate that little office? She latched onto it for her files the first day we moved into the building, and she's been immovable ever since."

"It wasn't hard," said his new private secretary. "I told her we were expanding the file department and that she'd better move to the basement now before someone else grabbed all that space she'd need to grow into."

"Amazing," said the Reverend.

SIX

The late afternoon traffic noises of Danang seeped into the hotel bathroom. Shawcross wiggled his toes in the water and flirted with the edges of sleep.

It had been a long time since he had thought of that violent night in Watts—or of Captain Orin Nelson. The young officer had been killed in the bomb blast. So were 2nd Lieutenant Robert Colgate and the two teen-aged Negro girls. Orin Nelson, Sr., escaped with minor burns. Unable to remain stateside for the trial of the three white men, Shawcross had testified by deposition. Months later he learned that they were released because of insufficient evidence.

Then, several years after Watts, he had found himself talking with William Gray again. It was in Saigon, a week after he had shot his mouth off to the press about black casualties.

"Good to see you again, General," Gray said over a drink at the Hotel Paris.

"You're a long way from home," said Shawcross.

"What you told that reporter last week got a big play stateside. That's why I'm here."

"What the hell do you know about casualties?" Shawcross said bitterly. "You're a civilian."

Gray touched his arm. "I'm the civilian who said that whatever else he was, Stanley Shawcross was no white nigger."

Shawcross gulped down most of his second drink. He could not taste it, nor was he aware of the effect it had upon him.

"Okay," he said. "I'll give you that, Gray, you said it first. I didn't believe you back in Watts, but you had me pegged."

"The mission must have been rough," said Gray.

"You don't know what rough is," Shawcross said.

Counting up the casualties after another senseless battle for an unnamed hilltop, Shawcross had seen the name of a Negro captain who had been lost in the action. He added up the total number of Negro dead. Of forty-six men killed in action, eighteen were black.

Drunk and angry, he spoke bitterly that night to a friend of his, a correspondent from an American news magazine.

"Only one out of ten in the States is a Negro, but I lost forty-six good men out there and a third of them were black."

The reporter said nothing, but poured Shawcross another drink.

"What am I—a Judas goat, leading my people to slaughter? I keep seeing their black faces, and they condemn me. Is a black man just something to shove into the line to protect rich white boys who can afford college deferments? The worst part is, the *best* of us are getting killed. Herbert Dean was one of our best! He had no business leading a rifle company in this stinking jungle, fighting a white man's war. He should have been building things somewhere, not blowing up bridges and leading twenty-year-old kids out to die."

"That's the way it's always been," sympathized the reporter.

"Yeah," Shawcross said bitterly, "you bet your ass that's the way it's always been. And what have *I* been?"

"A damned good man," said the reporter, meaning it.

"A white nigger," Shawcross said. "They're using me! They hand me my orders and I send those kids out to die."

"You're a little under the weather, sir," said the reporter, getting up. He made a move to leave. Shawcross pulled him back into the chair.

"Stay," he said harshly. "You won't waste your time. You can quote me if you want to. I'm not that drunk."

The reporter looked at him hard. The General's eyes did not waver.

"All right," the reporter said finally. "But I hope you know what you're doing."

Shawcross answered slowly. "I finally really *do* know what I'm doing." He reached for the whiskey bottle. "Come on, have a drink."

"In a minute," said the reporter.

He reached for his notebook.

"You really told them," said William Gray. "When I saw those headlines I knew that was no white nigger talking. And I started pulling strings to get over here and talk to you."

"About what?"

"You tell me that, General." Gray waited. "I told you there's only one way out for us. That the white man is never going to let us alone in peace unless we make him. The only thing we don't have is the leadership to take control—*control*, General, the one thing the white man doesn't want us to have."

"What does that have to do with me?"

Gray settled back and lit a small cigar. He took his time, and Shawcross could sense that he had pleased Gray by being willing to listen.

"We want recognition as human beings," Gray said finally. "It won't be easy to get it, not even if one hundred percent integration were possible, which it obviously isn't. That leaves only one other direction to go in, separation. That's the only way an imprisoned group can get equality and respect as human beings."

He puffed out blue-gray smoke. "And, along with separation, we must have reparations."

Shawcross put down his drink.

Gray nodded. "Payment for the centuries of labor stolen from our people. What good is it to achieve separation if we remain so poor we're still dependent on the white man's handouts? Part of our revolution's goal is to take back some of those things the whites have stolen from us over the centuries. Land and resources and industry. We must have those, General, because without them we're nothing.

"The black man is where he is today because he had no control over land. Well, all that will be over. The movement is under way, and it will be a violent one. George Washington didn't lead a nonviolent revolution. Patrick Henry didn't say, 'Give me liberty or I'll demonstrate.' Why should *we* turn the other cheek? General, those days are gone for good."

"Why are you putting this to me?" said Shawcross.

"Don't you know?"

Shawcross turned his glass slowly between his fingers. "I was drunk," he said finally. "I remember saying those things, but I don't know what got into me. I guess I just wanted to say Fuck You to the world."

Gray laughed harshly. "You knew what you were doing all right, General. Listen to me. The burning time is coming. You know it. And you know every day you hold off making up your mind is a day of danger for the cause, for yourself, and especially for your people back home."

Shawcross looked up sharply. "What's that supposed to mean?"

"You were in Watts. Who got hurt? Whitey? Or innocent black people who didn't get out of the way fast enough?"

"I think you're trying to stampede me, Gray. You ought to be happy that I'm even listening to your ideas."

"All right," said Gray. "That's enough for now. Just keep listening. I'll get through to you."

"Do you want to bet?" Shawcross asked, smiling. He leaned forward. "All right," he said, "you want land and you want reparations. How do you get them?"

"We're going to take them."

Shawcross blinked. "From the most powerful nation in the world? How in hell do you plan to carry that one off?"

Gray looked at Shawcross over the smoldering cigar. "That might be *your* department," he said.

SEVEN

The water in Shawcross' tub was nearly cool now. Not that it was unpleasant in the heat of Danang, but it was time to get up, put on a fresh uniform, and go down for dinner.

Shawcross had been expecting a rocket from Washington about his lapse of discretion in front of the correspondent but, weeks later, it had not yet arrived. Perhaps it would lie in his records jacket until it was time for his next promotion, then emerge to cause him to be passed over or retired. Somewhere punishment was waiting. Major generals were not supposed to go shooting their mouths off. Shawcross had noticed some tension on the part of his staff after the incident, but many of the white officers had felt impelled to approach him and publicly agree with his statement.

"It's a goddamned shame," said one burly captain from Atlanta. "Those are good fucking men, and they're shoving them into the line like sandbags."

This from a man who would go thirsty rather than drink in a bar that served blacks. Shawcross tightened his lips in a humorless grin.

Dripping, he rose from the tub and wrapped himself in a towel. Water slopped down his ankles and left bear tracks as he padded into the bedroom.

Since his meeting with William Gray in Saigon, he had been following the man's progress. In the past weeks Gray had gone from Saigon to Ghana, where he addressed the African heads of state at the annual conference of the Organization of African Unity. His words made headlines; parts of his speech were reported verbatim: "It would take a blind man not to realize that the efforts of the black man to defend himself by meeting violence with violence might create a racial conflict which could easily escalate into a war more bloody than a thousand Hiroshimas. But what would you have us do? We ask for your help in condemning the white oppressor, we ask for your aid in getting the United Nations to move in our behalf. Are twenty-two million African-Americans any less in the eyes of the world than the oppressed millions in the Congo? Our black brothers across the sea, we beseech your help! May Allah's blessings of good health and wisdom be upon you all. *Salaam Alaikum.*"

Shawcross shook his head as he pulled on his khaki trousers. How could Gray have any hope at all of achieving his goals when he kept shooting his mouth off about them? One of the keys to success in any surprise guerrilla effort would have to be maximum security in the preparatory stage.

In all, Gray had visited eleven countries before returning to the United States. Back in New York, he held a joint press conference with the poet laureate of the Black Nationalist movement, Raymond Carpenter. Carpenter, who had fasted for forty days and written an antiwhite poem each day, had made as many headlines as LeRoi Jones and Eldridge Cleaver in their heyday.

The poet got a laugh from the black audience when he poked fun at the absent Reverend Abner Greenbriar for carrying on with a "white tramp pretending to be his private secretary. There are plenty of good-looking black women around if the Reverend wants to sin a little. Don't he know—*black is best?*"

The purpose of the conference was not to attack the secretary, Karen Davis, but to announce the publication of a weekly newsletter, *The Afro-American Bulletin*, which would be edited by Raymond Carpenter and would carry news of the movement and instructions to "our black brothers and sisters." It was also suggested that any black brother or sister who failed to subscribe to the *Bulletin* would be considered a white nigger.

Shawcross buttoned his shirt and went over to the telephone. When the desk clerk answered, he instructed him to rout out his interpreter from whatever bar he might be inhabiting and have him ready to go in half an hour.

Shawcross was lacing up his combat boots when the telephone rang.

"General," drawled a voice, "is it true you suck eggs and eat the shells?"

"Huh?" said Shawcross. Then, "Dewey? Corncob Dewey?"

"'The one and only. I just blew in from Pleiku, and when I asked the desk clerk who was in residence, he came up with Major General Stanley Shawcross. The one with the big mouth."

"Ouch," said Shawcross. "I'm still waiting for the rocket. It should get in from Washington any day."

"Well, while you're waiting, how about a little bourbon to deaden the pain?"

"Why not? I was just getting ready to go out and look around. I've got a jeep and interpreter coming around in about twenty minutes."

"Send him on his way. No lousy Arvin knows Danang

as well as I do. I know places even Premier Ky never heard of, and as you know, he is the Oriental swinger of all time."

"Okay, put on the desk clerk." Dewey did, and Shawcross canceled his request for the jeep. Then Dewey came back on. "I'll meet you in the bar down here as soon as you get your black ass decently dressed. Let's not have have any more incidents like that time in the Imperial Hotel."

"It's all a lie," said Shawcross. "I did not go swimming in the fountain bare-assed."

"Half of the police in Tokyo will swear to it," said Dewey, "and unless you treat me right, you might be unpleasantly surprised to learn that a certain fast-thinking colonel in the Third Cavalry Airmobile has a photo of the actual event."

"I'll be right down," said Shawcross. He hung up, grinning. He and Clarence Dewey had met in Tokyo the year before and had virtually torn the amusement suburb of Ueno apart before they were banished from the city by Japanese police. Since then their paths had crossed several times in Vietnam, often to the despair of civilian authorities.

He checked his appearance in the mirror. His sidearm was neatly strapped around his waist; he wore his insignia, and his brass belt gleamed. He opened the dresser drawer and took out the two polished fragmentation grenades. Clipping them on, he felt complete again. It was almost time to send them back to Ordnance for their annual repacking and repriming. It wouldn't do to carry them all these years and then have them fail to explode if he needed them.

Shawcross went down the two flights of stairs on foot and into the dimly lit bar. Three overhead fans turned lazily. The room looked like something out of *Casablanca;* he almost expected to see Sidney Greenstreet looking up from a wicker chair.

Instead, he saw Lieutenant Colonel Clarence Dewey, thin and totally unmenacing, sitting atop a bar stool. He noticed how light Dewey was—almost white—and then wondered why the thought had occurred to him.

"General," said Dewey, looking up.

"Corncob," said Shawcross. "Your face looks different. Where is that foul incinerator of yours?"

"Up in the room. The old one finally burned out, and I'm aging the new one in a mixture of tobacco and bourbon." Dewey waved the waiter over. "Gin and tonic for me and a double Wild Turkey for the General." He turned to Shawcross. "I better kill my thirst before I start on the hard stuff. I'm in a mood to get crocked."

"Bad week?"

"Bad day. One of the C-130 shuttles went in on landing and smeared troops and cargo all over the runway. What the hell are we doing over here anyway? Every month I make the indoctrination lecture about how we're in Vietnam to keep from fighting on the Pacific coast, and it sticks in my throat." Their drinks came, and he tossed off half his gin and tonic with one swallow.

"Better watch yourself," said Shawcross. "You might end up being quoted."

"Yeah, wasn't that something? I lift my glass to you, General. I didn't know you had it in you. There are those who had you pegged as a white nigger."

Shawcross laughed. "Look who's talking!"

"Well," said Dewey, "my skin may be white, but I've got a pitch-black heart—like the dogtags when you first come in the service. You remember, they had this little 'N' on them, as if whoever took them off a black neck would have to guess the wearer was Negro."

"How are things going up there?"

Dewey shrugged. "Good enough, I guess. We all know we're never going to win this thing in the field."

He dragged out his wallet and fumbled through it for a color photo. "Here, General. The latest picture of the Dewey clan."

Shawcross looked. Mrs. Dewey was a handsome woman whose face showed only slight traces of her Negro blood. Two of the children were cream-colored. The third was jet black. Shawcross laughed.

"I do hope, General, that you are not laughing at little Clarence Junior."

"If he's the sunburned one, I am."

"I may just have to sunburn your ass, General," said Dewey.

"If you think I'm black," said Shawcross, "you ought to see Carolyn. So naturally both our offspring came out white as sheets."

"So maybe there's an iceman in both our woodpiles. Might even be the same guy."

"Impossible. More likely you're the ice man in my pile and I'm the one in yours."

"The latest thing, I understand," said Dewey. "Those suburbanites are so rich and bored with everything they're wife-swapping all over. Except, I don't know, General, if yours is as black as you say, maybe you ought to throw in a little booty."

"Corncob," Shawcross said, "haven't you heard, black is best?"

Dewey sobered. "That I have, General," he said quietly. "I've been following that bastard's tracks everywhere he goes."

"William Gray?"

Dewey nodded. "Nobody's taking him seriously yet, but I think he may spark the ammo dump. That man isn't kidding, he really wants to start a race war. He wants blood running in the streets. Everybody says oh no, he's just another Malcolm X or a Rap Brown, and believe me, he is not. Unless we're lucky he can set it off for all of us."

Shawcross leaned across the table toward him. "What if Gray did set it off. Where would you be?" Dewey looked at him blankly, then signaled for the waiter for another round. He turned back to Shawcross. "General, you know where I am. I've taken as much shit as you or any other black man in America."

Shawcross knew he should not say what he was about to, but the words came anyway. "That isn't what I asked, Dewey. What I asked was where you would be if Gray did set off his revolution."

"Race war?" said Dewey.

"I said revolution. It may be against the white establishment, but it won't be against the white *people*. What Gray wants is what we all want, a place of our own."

"Well, now," said Dewey, "what he's talking about is a place in the cemetery, not just for whites but for one hell of a lot of blacks, too. That bastard is out of his mind, and if you go along with his way of thinking, you're out of your mind too. Sure, a lot of his proposals make sense. But a lot of them are suicide. We are an underdeveloped, under-respected, underwanted minority. But we're breaking out. I wish it were faster, and maybe there's ways to hustle it up, but open revolution is the fastest way I know to cause a black purge that would make Indonesia look like a Sunday school party."

"Maybe not. You couldn't do it Gray's way, I'll agree. Once it got beyond the riot stage and became a rebellion, the slaughter'd be terrible. But there might be another way."

Dewey sipped at his drink for a moment and then said,

"Are you just theorizing or are you actually proposing something?"

"Just theorizing. A riot is one thing but a planned rebellion is something else again."

"In that case, let's for God's sake drop the subject. It's too fucking dangerous to be theorizing around with."

"Okay," said Shawcross, feeling lightheaded—but from what? The two whiskies? Or the precipice he had walked to, and then drawn back from?

EIGHT

Halfway around the world, in the Watts district of Los Angeles, William Gray stood on a makeshift stage in front of a microphone. His voice blasted from the loudspeakers, and the auditorium rocked with the shouted responses of his audience.

"It is *time* to open your eyes and wake up to the fact that you and me and all our soul brothers, we all of us have a common enemy," he shouted. "He is our enemy no matter where he is, no matter what he says, no matter how friendly he claims to be. He is our enemy because he has blue eyes and blonde hair and pale skin."

"Sing it, baby!" someone cried out.

"Who is our enemy?"

"Whitey!" roared the crowd.

"That's his name all right. I don't care if he is a big-assed liberal from Berkeley or some honkey cop from Chicago. He can sweet-talk you until your black ear drops off, and he is still the same man.

"What is Whitey?

"He is our enemy!"

Gray jabbed his finger into the air with each sentence. "He sent you to the jungles of the South Pacific to fight the Japanese and you bled. He sent you to Germany to

70

fight Hitler and you bled. He sent you to Korea and you bled. Now he is sending you to Vietnam and, oh my brothers, you are still bleeding to death for the white man! You are sacrificing your holy blood for the white man! Will you never learn? You bleed for the white man, but when it comes to seeing your own churches bombed and watching little black girls being blown to pieces, suddenly you have no blood. You kiss his white face as he sics the police dogs on you and blasts your sister's skin with high-pressure hoses! Where was your angry blood when your people cried out in anguish on the streets of Detroit and Newark and Birmingham—or right here in Watts?"

"We busted Whitey good!" yelled a man in the crowd.

"You burned out a few stores and looted a few television sets, and threw out a few poor white trash, but you didn't hurt Whitey! You didn't take nothing that hurt him! You hurt your own! You busted your own supermarkets and your own hardware stores. Why didn't some of you turn a little heat on the rich folks in Beverly Hills or Bel Air?"

"They had the fuzz and the Army," called the man.

"So screw the fuzz and screw the Army," cried Gray. "Can't you be as violent in California as you were in Korea? Can't you be as violent in Beverly Hills as you were on Pork Chop Hill? How can you sit down to your beans and bacon and say 'Brothers and sisters, we are going to have ourselves a non-violent revolution!' Whitey says the black man is simple, and sometimes I think the man is right! How can you be so simple?

"Never in the history of the world, down to this day, has there ever been a non-violent revolution. There's no such thing as a non-violent revolution!

"Revolution is bloody, revolution is hostile, revolution knows no compromise, revolution overturns and destroys everything that gets in its way. Malcolm X said that, and it is no shit, brothers and sisters, it is a simple fact of life that you are unwilling to accept. How can you sit out there like knots on the wall and say 'Lawdy me, I got to love Mr. Whitey, I got to love him no matter how much he hates me!' Where do you think you are going to get singing 'We Shall Overcome'? Just as far as from here to the nearest police cell.

"You know what a revolution is? Ask Whitey. *He* knows. That's why you got him scared and stuttering. Whitey has seen what our brothers in Africa did, what they did in Asia and Latin America. He is very well aware of what a revolution is, and he is hoping and praying that you never find out."

A stout woman stood up and called out, "The Lord, He says, 'Thou shalt not kill'!"

"Yes, sister," answered Gray, "I have read the white man's Bible. What it really says is, 'Thou shalt not kill Whitey!' That's what the White Man's God says, it is perfectly all right for us to kill Koreans and Japanese and Vietnamese children with napalm, but thou shalt not kill Whitey!"

"What are you calling for us to do?" asked a bent, white-haired Negro in the first row.

"Grandfather, I am asking you to be a man," said Gray. "I am asking you to stop kissing the white man's ass! That's the same Uncle Tom route you been going for three hundred years. That's what happens when you work together with the so-called liberals. You water down your strength.

"It's like when you pour out a hot cup of coffee. What kind of coffee is that good coffee? Why, brothers and sisters, it's *black!* What happens when you integrate that coffee with cream? It used to be hot, you make it cool. It used to be strong, you make it weak. It used to wake you up, now it puts you to sleep. It used to be black, and now you've made it white. That's what happens when you let the white man in. You start out strong, and he makes you weak. You start out hot, and he makes you cool. You start out black, and he makes you white.

"Who in this room wants to be white? Come on, I know some of you use skin bleach and hair straightener! Stand up, confess your white hearts! Put on your white clown faces and make us laugh. I know you're out there!"

Gray paused and fixed his eyes on the audience. They shifted uneasily in their seats. Gray waited. No one stood. Then, he shouted suddenly.

"Black is best!"

The audience took up the cry. "Black is best!"

"BLACK IS BEST!"

"*BLACK IS BEST!*"

William Gray went off the stage and headed through the crowd, black hands plucking at his sleeve, out into the night where a Lincoln Continental was waiting at the curb. He got in, and the driver, a short, fat Negro with a bristly black moustache, gave him a grin as he spun the big car away from the curb.

"Sounds like you really got to them," said the driver.

William Gray lit up a thin cigar and settled back into the leather cushions.

"That stuff always gets to those burr-heads," he said.

NINE

"General?"

Shawcross heard the voice from a great distance. Hands were on his shoulders, pulling at him. He resisted, trying to remain in the dream state that was so euphoric. But the hands were insistent, and the voice was suddenly shouting in his ear.

"General! Wake up, sir! It's important, sir. Wake up."

Shawcross sat up. The room was glaring with light.

"Okay," he said. "Okay, I'm awake. What's the problem?"

He did not recognize the Military Police captain who had awakened him.

"Sir," said the MP officer, "I have to be sure. Are you Major General Stanley Shawcross, U.S. Marines?"

"I sure am, son." Shawcross looked at his watch. It was four-thirty A.M. "What's going on? Has there been an attack?"

"Not that I know of, sir. I was instructed to find you and escort you to the Commanding General's office at once."

Shawcross staggered into the bathroom and threw cold water on his face. He glared at his haggard, drink-puffed face in the mirror, and it glared back at him. Well, he thought, this must be it. The rocket from Washington. His eyes were red-lined. He suppressed a grin, touching his kinky hair. At least he didn't have to comb it. There were some benefits.

The jeep sputtered into life on the darkened street. Nice night for a VC bomb to come out of the darkness, thought Shawcross.

But no bomb came to break his reverie. As the jeep rolled through the empty streets, Shawcross could see whole families in doorways—huddled against the stones of the buildings. In the morning they would move on, searching for food or garbage to put in their mouths. Every day a dozen or so would be found dead in their rags. Christ! thought Shawcross, and we think we have it rough. Wait until these people get together and come boiling out of the pot. They make a Georgia sharecropper look like a king.

The jeep arrived at Marine Headquarters. Shawcross got out and looked at the MP. "You coming in with me?"

"No sir." The MP saluted and drove off.

Well, at least he wasn't under any kind of arrest. Shawcross went up the sidewalk, was challenged by the sentry, produced his identification, and went inside. Most of the building was dark, but down one hall he could see a light in the Commanding General's office.

He knocked at the door, heard a deep voice say "Come in," and entered. General Williams came toward him, hand outstretched.

"You sent for me, sir?"

"Yes I did, Shawcross. Sit down, will you?"

Williams drew up a chair near him and held out a yellow envelope.

"When the duty officer received this he took it upon himself to let me see it first. There's nothing I can say. Just read it."

My hands are trembling, thought Shawcross as he opened the envelope. He unfolded the yellow telegram:

MAJOR GENERAL STANLEY SHAWCROSS,
F.P.O.
SAN FRANCISCO, CALIF.

REGRET TO INFORM YOU UNFORTUNATE ACCIDENT CLAIMED LIVES OF MRS. SHAWCROSS AND CHILDREN. ASSUME YOU WILL BE RETURNING BURBANK AND HAVE SO ADVISED AUTHORITIES. AM CONTACTING RELATIVES AND WILL MEET YOU. SINCEREST SYMPATHY.

ROD MCNEAL
AMERICAN RED CROSS
BURBANK

Shawcross replaced the telegram neatly in the envelope. General Williams looked at his watch.

"There's a Pan Am jet out of Saigon in a couple of hours. I reserved space for you on it, and there's a Navy Starfire waiting for you now out at the field. You'll have to ride piggyback, but he'll get you to Saigon in time. If you don't make it right on the button, the tower has authority to hold the Pan Am plane. I'm cutting emergency leave orders, but you don't have to wait for them. They'll catch up. This envelope—" he handed Shawcross a brown manila one "—has enough travel vouchers and payroll authorizations for you to get by until you get organized."

"My outfit . . ." said Shawcross, dazed.

"Your outfit is in good hands," said Williams. "Right now you take care of things at home. That's an order, General."

"Yes sir," said Shawcross, still wrestling with the trivial

because he could not yet face the world-destroying content of the telegram. "But the MP jeep left."

"My staff car's waiting. Let's go."

He led Shawcross down the hall, apologizing. "I'm sorry I had to bring you here, but I wanted to be sure you were set on those flights and it was quicker for you to come to me than for me to go to you. Besides, we're that much closer to the airstrip."

They got into the waiting staff car.

"I left a jeep and an interpreter at the hotel," said Shawcross. "And my gear."

"We'll take care of it. Don't worry about a thing out here, General. Just for Christ's sake take care of yourself. We need you back."

"Don't you worry, sir," said Shawcross numbly. "I'll watch out."

The Navy plane was already plugged into the starting cart. By the time the staff car pulled alongside, the jet was fired up and ready to go. The ground chief handed Shawcross a hard hat and helped him up the aluminum ladder.

"No point in giving you a parachute," he said. "The seat couldn't be jettisoned with you sitting up there anyway."

"No sweat, son." Shawcross inched himself into the crowded piggyback seat, his legs hanging down around the pilot's shoulders. The canopy came down so close that his hard hat bumped against it.

"Hang on, sir," called the pilot. The turbine whine increased inside the cockpit and the Starfire lurched forward. In minutes, the jet was hurtling into the Vietnamese sky. To the east Shawcross could see a red glow.

As the plane rose higher, the sky became steel-gray instead of black, and then—far to the east—Shawcross saw dawn breaking over the horizon.

"This is the time of day I like best," said the pilot. "Everybody's asleep, including Charlie."

"I see what you mean," said Shawcross. He felt oddly calm and very distant from this Navy jet, screaming above the jungle of Vietnam at six hundred miles an hour. His mind was idly plucking the exact words of the telegram from his memory.

UNFORTUNATE ACCIDENT. . . .

What kind of unfortunate accident could get all three? Had the house burned? Was there an earthquake? Had an airplane fallen on them from the sky? Why wasn't McNeal more explicit?

ADVISED AUTHORITIES. . . .

What did the authorities have to be advised about? Which authorities? The highway patrol? The health department? The United States Government? Why say authorities unless you went on to name them? Who are you, Rod McNeal, American Red Cross, Burbank?

The sky was rosy now with the sunrise. Shawcross looked at his watch. It was ten of five. His body was beginning to ache from the cramped position.

The Navy jet streaked through the morning air at thirty-two thousand feet. The pilot grumbled into his microphone and received instructions from tower control at Tan Son Nhut Airfield in Saigon.

SINCEREST SYMPATHY. . . .

What was there to be sorry about? That the Negro Problem had been diminished by three unwanted souls? What did the Rod McNeals of the world know about sympathy? That was a white word, sympathy.

"Going down, sir," said the pilot.

Tan Son Nhut Airfield is the busiest airport in the world. It is busier than Kennedy in New York, busier than O'Hare in Chicago. From the air Shawcross could see the ten-thousand-foot strip—a white scar slashing through the jungle foliage.

This was rush hour for Tan Son Nhut; at any one moment there might be as many as four different aircraft moving along the runway. Those taking off broke left as soon as their wheels left the ground, to clear the runway for anyone who might be coming in. Dozens of ships waited for clearance, little Piper and Cessna spotter planes, heavy-duty fighters—F-104s and F-5s, cargo C-54s and C-118s, and, using all ten thousand feet of the strip, huge C-141 jet transports.

"I think I'd rather fly low-level support against Charlie than go down into that," said the pilot.

His approach was the standard one for Tan Son Nhut, where danger lurked in the sniper-infested jungle around the strip. The jet screamed down in an altitude-eating spiral that minimized exposure to enemy fire and plunked them in the middle of the busy strip. The brakes squealed as the pilot slowed the plane and turned off the runway. Seconds later, an F-102 roared through the space they had just occupied.

"Made it again." The pilot cracked the hatch, and steamy morning air, already unbearably hot, entered the cockpit.

The Starfire passed the black Skyraiders of Premier Ky's famous Coup Squadron parked in a row along the hardstand. A "Follow Me" jeep hustled out and swooped up alongside the Navy jet. A Marine officer sat beside the driver. He yelled up, "General Shawcross?"

"This is him," called the pilot. "Careful getting out, sir," he warned Shawcross, who scrambled out on the wing and slipped down over the trailing edge. His shirt was already plastered to his back. He turned back to the pilot.

"Thanks for a good ride, son," he said. The words sounded phony to him, but the pilot smiled. The Marine captain in the jeep piled into the back, leaving room up front for Shawcross. The General swung his aching legs into the vehicle; it lurched forward, circled the Starfire, and headed off the field.

"The Pan Am plane's been held up by mechanical problems," said the Marine captain. "They expect a delay of a couple of hours. But there's an Air France flight going out by way of Tokyo at noon. You're booked on that, too. Meanwhile, the officer's club is open. You can get something to eat over there."

"Is the bar open?" Shawcross asked.

"The bar? I guess so, sir."

Though it was not yet seven in the morning, the club was jammed with hard-faced men in dark jungle fatigues wearing turned-up Aussie hats or baseball caps. The bar was not only open, but doing a booming business. On one wall, painted in red, white, and blue letters was a huge legend: "FUCK COMMUNISM." On another was the motto of the "Ranch Hand" pilots—the men who flew the C-123 defoliation planes: "ONLY YOU CAN PREVENT FORESTS."

"Jack Daniels on the rocks," Shawcross told the bartender.

"Coke," said the Marine captain. Shawcross laughed. I must be right on the edge, he thought. This guy is only trying to help me.

"I've got runners at both loading gates," said the captain. "Whichever comes first, Pan Am or Air France, one of the runners will get over here and pick you up."

"Well, they won't have any trouble finding me," said Shawcross, turning his glass bottoms-up and waving for another drink.

"In a way this delay is a help," said the captain. "My orderly is putting a kit together for you, fresh linens and shaving gear. He ought to be here pretty soon. But if the Pan Am jet had gone out on schedule you'd have missed him."

"Captain," said Shawcross, feeling an unwanted wave of sentiment sweep over him, "you've been very helpful."

"Thank you, sir," said the Marine.

"Now take that broomstick out of your ass and have a drink with me."

"If the General pleases," said the captain.

"The General pleases. The General damned well makes that an order, if it will ease the captain's conscience."

"Thank you, sir." The captain grinned. "I'll take Scotch and water. Tall glass, lots of water," he told the bartender.

Shawcross started on his third bourbon. The hangover from the night in Danang was gone now. The liquor sat, acrid and burning, on the tense nerves of his stomach. He knew he was on the verge of mawkish, fraudulent comraderie with this young Marine who was only carrying out his commandant's orders. He said suddenly, "Does it bother you, taking orders from a nigger?"

The astonished captain almost dropped his glass. "But sir," he gulped, "you're a general!"

"Sorry," said Shawcross, ashamed. "That was out of line."

"General," said the captain, "you can say anything you damned well please. No one has more right. It's—well, sir, all I can say is I'm damned sorry."

For a second, Shawcross wondered what the captain had done to feel sorry about, and then he realized the man was talking about his own tragedy. He saw Carolyn's face receding before him, dwindling in the far dawn, and he knew suddenly how much of his world had come to an end.

"Oh, my God!" he breathed.

Major General Stanley Shawcross, USMC, sat in the crowded officer's club on Saigon's Tan Son Nhut Airfield and wept.

TEN

"I'm Rod McNeal," said the tall, very black man at the foot of the ramp as Shawcross stumbled down from the Pan Am jet. He had been in the air eighteen hours, not including the refueling stop at Honolulu, and his face was etched with weariness. Even so, it showed his surprise. He had not expected McNeal to be a Negro.

"Thanks for meeting me," he said, gripping McNeal's hand.

"My car's outside," said McNeal. "Let's go."

They went through the corridor to the main ticket area and out through the automatic doors. The air was brisk.

"Feels like winter," said Shawcross, getting into the car.

"Hit thirty-two degrees a couple of days back. Cold for this time of year."

"Any rain?"

"A little. We needed it, too. It was a hot summer. Lot of trouble with forest fires, probably you heard."

"Yes," said Shawcross, and then before he knew what he was saying, "Carolyn wrote me."

He stopped short and looked out the car window. When he spoke again his voice was muffled. "What happened?"

"Are you sure you want to talk about it now?"

"Don't play games with me, Mr. McNeal. Let's have it."

"All right. There were no witnesses, so we can only assume a lot of it. But Mrs. Shawcross and the two children were on their way home from Disneyland. It was already dark, and where she turned off the freeway there's a light that always catches you."

"Yes, I know."

"Ordinarily there would have been a couple of cars waiting there for it to change. But traffic was light. They must have been following her, waiting for a chance. The light was it."

"What do you mean, they?"

"At least two men. They stepped up to the car, and the one on the left side fired three .32 bullets into your wife's head. The other man killed the children with a shotgun. I'm sorry, General, but that's the way it was."

Shawcross gripped McNeal's shoulder so hard that the automobile swerved sharply. A horn blared, and McNeal turned back into his own lane.

"Careful," he said.

They rode in silence for a few minutes, then Shawcross cried out, "I don't believe it!"

McNeal said nothing.

"Who would want to do anything like that to a woman and two children?" He shook his head violently. "Things like that don't happen."

"They do happen, General, they happen all the time. The only difference is, this time they happened to you. I'm sorry."

"Where are they?"

"Forest Lawn."

"How about the rest of it?"

"It can wait," said McNeal.

"In a pig's ass, it can wait! Give it to me now, that's

what I'm here for. There has to be a hell of a lot more to it than you're telling me."

"Well," said McNeal, "the police found a note. It was stuck on the windshield with Scotch tape."

"Let me see it."

"I don't have it, the police are keeping it as evidence. But I made a copy."

"Give it to me," said Shawcross. His voice would have cut glass.

McNeal fumbled in his pocket and got out a piece of paper. Shawcross unfolded it:

THIS IS WHAT HAPPENS TO NIGGER WHORES THAT GET TOO BIG FOR THEIR OWN GOOD. WHITE MEN WAS NEVER MEANT TO TAKE ORDERS FROM NO NIGGER GENERAL. THIS IS A WARNING TO ALL OF YOU BLACK BASTARDS. GO BACK WHERE YOU CAME FROM.

"It was a planned, premeditated act," said McNeal. "They must have followed her for days until they got their chance."

"Of course it was premeditated!" shouted Shawcross. "It's all premeditated! Whitey wants us all dead, and he's planning it this very minute. Jesus Christ, I let it happen to her! I knew what was coming, I was warned, and I let it happen."

"Easy, General. This was the work of mentally disturbed men."

"This *nation* is mentally disturbed," said Shawcross. "Little nigger kids being shot to death in their mother's car. Black men burned to death in Detroit and shot down by the National Guard because they stand up and say 'Give us freedom!' While I was out there in Vietnam, Whitey was laughing up his goddamned sleeve at me. 'We got us a white nigger,' he was saying, 'a white nigger who'll go out and kill for us.' "

McNeal said nothing. They drove in silence for a while, Shawcross staring numbly out the window. They passed downtown Los Angeles, the pyramid-shaped courthouse on their left. "Where are we going?" he asked after a time.

"Burbank. I thought you could use some rest."

"Forest Lawn," said Shawcross. "Take me up there."

"General, you're on the edge. Get some rest first."

"Look, McNeal, I know you're trying to do me good, and I appreciate it. But either take me up there or let me out of this car and I'll get a taxi."

"All right," said the Red Cross man.

They turned off the freeway and started in the direction of the mountains. High on a hill Shawcross could see the huge cross of Forest Lawn glinting in the late afternoon sun. There were only a few minutes of daylight left now.

They drove through the storybook gates of the huge cemetery and turned right to park near one of the mortuaries just inside the gates. As they entered, a slight woman stepped up to Shawcross. Her face was powered white; her eyes were smudged with mascara.

"God has visited you with his punishment," she said in a conversational tone. "Vengeance is mine, saith the Lord. I shall repay."

"Get her OUT OF HERE!" bellowed Shawcross. His mighty arm reached toward the woman, drew back. He knew how close he had come to striking her.

An attendant hustled the woman outside. "I'm sorry, General," he said. "She claimed she was a friend of the family."

"Not your fault," said Shawcross.

"Where are they?"

"In the Golden Slumber Room. I will be happy to—"

"Just me," said Shawcross. "Alone."

"Certainly," said the attendant. He stepped aside. Organ music almost too soft to hear marked Shawcross' steps as he went into the dimly lighted room. The odor of flowers filled his nostrils; then his eyes adjusted to the dimness and he saw the three caskets, draped with velvet and mounded with wreaths. Carolyn's was in the center of the room, and at its foot were two smaller ones for the boys. Shawcross walked over to the bier. His heart seemed to stop beating as he looked down at the peaceful face of his wife. Her skin was purplish-black in the golden light, lips parted slightly in a half-smile. He knew that there must be stitches within to hold those lips so, and he tried to erase that knowledge from his thoughts. Carolyn was lying on one side, her face cupped deep in the velvet pillow. Shawcross knew why: to conceal bullet wounds the cosmetics had been unable to cover. He fought the urge to turn her over. His hand went out and touched her face. It was cool and waxlike to his touch.

"Jesus," said Shawcross.

He stepped down and looked at the silent figures of his two sons. Arthur was holding his favorite toy, a plastic figure of Donald Duck. Harry's fingers were closed over a large silver cross. It had belonged to Shawcross' mother, and for the past eight years had rested atop the family Bible. He reached over to take up the cross. The fingers were rigid and tight around the metal, and he had to strain to free the cross from their clutching grasp. He had it then, and threw it across the room at the stained glass window. It missed and clanged into a corner. McNeal and an attendant entered the room as Shawcross was trying to close the coffin lid. The catch baffled him; he was sweating and cursing when strong hands caught his arms and dragged him back.

"General Shawcross," said the attendant, "Please—you must have respect!"

"You have respect!" shouted Shawcross. "Close those fucking lids! These are my people, not a side show. You got no right to put them on exhibit like pinheads in the circus. Close those goddamned lids!"

"Take it easy, General," said McNeal.

"You take it easy!" Shawcross shouted. "I said, close those lids! Did you hear me?"

The attendant brought the heavy wooden lids down over the still faces.

"Yes sir," he said.

"When I give an order, I expect it to be obeyed."

"He'll obey it, General," said McNeal. "Come on outside, now. You've got to get some rest."

"When's the funeral?"

"Tomorrow. Eleven A.M."

"No one there but blood," said Shawcross. "You see to that, McNeal." The Red Cross man was trying to lead him from the room, but Shawcross kept stopping and issuing fresh instructions. "And no white carnations. Get rid of them. Nothing white. You hear me?"

"I hear you," said McNeal. "Come on, General. Get some rest and you'll feel better."

"About the honor guard," said the attendant.

"What honor guard?" asked Shawcross.

"The Marine honor guard. The officer in charge asked me to inform the General that they will come on duty this evening and remain to escort the procession to the grave site."

"No honor guard," said Shawcross.

"General," McNeal warned quietly.

"Don't General me," cried Shawcross. "I said no honor guard. These are my people, they're not draftees in the white man's fucking white army." He turned to the attendant. "Now you get this, and get it straight. Contact the Marines and tell them, from me, that they are neither expected nor wanted out here. Repeat that."

"The honor guard is neither expected nor wanted," said the frightened attendant.

"That's the message," said Shawcross. "Pass it along and you won't have any trouble."

"The General's naturally upset," said McNeal to the attendant. "But perhaps it would be wise to cancel the guard."

"I'll see to it," the attendant promised.

"Come on." McNeal drew Shawcross after him gently. The General followed, half dazed. The bright lights in the main waiting room made him blink, and at first he did not recognize the man who stepped up to him. He felt a warm, dry hand press his and heard a voice say, "I just got in, General. I was in France and this was the fastest I could make it. Is there anything I can do to help?"

Shawcross blinked at William Gray and shook his head.

"No," he said finally. "Not now. Maybe if I'd listened to you before, you might have helped. But it's too late now."

"It's never too late, Stanley," said Gray, taking the free arm and intruding himself between Shawcross and the Red Cross man. "There are twenty-two million Carolyns for whom it's not too late."

"The General is exhausted," said McNeal.

"He'll go home with me," said Gray. "Won't you, Stanley?"

"I don't have a home," said Shawcross.

"You have mine," said Gray.

"I don't know—" said McNeal.

"The General and I are old friends," said Gray, drawing Shawcross after him. "I'll take care of him. You just go on about your business."

"My instructions—"

Gray stepped up to him and spoke very softly but very intensely. "Shove your instructions, Uncle Tom. This man is ours now, and unless you want a peck of trouble, you get on out of here and let him alone. You hear me, boy?"

McNeal looked at him in disbelief. "You're threatening me."

"You just *know* I'm threatening you," said William Gray.

"The police want to talk with him," said McNeal.

"Fuck the police," said Gray. "Where were they when those white devils were slaughtering his family? Get out of here, man, I'm warning you for the last time. Or you'll wish you had."

McNeal turned to Shawcross. "Do you want me to go and leave you with him, General?"

Shawcross shook his head in an attempt to clear it. "Yes," he said finally, "he's my friend. You go along, McNeal. You're a good man, and thanks for your help. But I'm all right now. Mr. Gray and I have a lot of things to talk about."

"All right," said McNeal, reluctantly. "If you want me to go, I will. But not because some loudmouth radical tells me to."

"Don't push it, Charlie," said Gray.

"My name is Rod."

"You'd better go," said Shawcross.

Gray took his limp arm. "Come on, now." Shawcross followed him from the building and got into the car.

"Any trouble?" asked the driver.

"Just a little lip from a white nigger," said Gray. "His name's McNeal, and he works for the Burbank Red Cross. Somebody ought to teach him a lesson."

"Somebody will," the driver said. Wheels crunched on the gravel of the main drive.

"They won't get away with this," Shawcross mumbled. "I'll find them. I'll find the bastards and kill them."

"Stanley," said Gray quietly, "I doubt if you can find them by yourself. But even if you could, you wouldn't kill the forces that provoked what they did."

"I'll still kill *them*."

"Perhaps I can help."

"How?"

"My organization can deliver them up to you," Gray said. "But more than that, we can deliver up the system that spawned them. We can put Whitey in his place for good and all."

"You're dreaming," said Shawcross.

"Dream with us! What do you have to lose?"

Shawcross watched the brightly stuccoed homes of Los Angeles spinning past the windows.

"Nothing," he said finally. "They've taken it all."

Gray reached over and gripped his forearm hard. "It'll take time," he said, "but we'll find those men for you. More than that, we'll stop things like this from happening again. There's only one real answer. You know that now. Don't you?"

After a long pause, Shawcross said, "Yes."

ELEVEN

The big car turned off the freeway, passed City Hall in Santa Monica. At Montana Avenue it purred into a driveway.

The house was huge, surrounded by acres of lawn. Across Ocean Avenue the rich, deep blue of the Pacific had already swallowed the evening sun. A red afterglow remained, painting rosy traces across the edges of clouds far out to sea.

"The brother has some pad," said Shawcross.

"He should," said Gray. "He makes around two hundred thousand a year."

"What is he—a movie star?"

"Comedian," said Gray. "You've heard of him. Pete Humble."

"Hell, yes, he's a funny man. Except he thinks being black is a big joke."

"Don't kid yourself, General. Pete doesn't think there's anything funny about being black. He just makes the white folks think there is, and he laughs all the way to the bank. Without the money we get from Pete and a couple of others like him, we wouldn't stand a chance of getting off the ground."

"Even if he gave you a whole year's salary, it wouldn't

buy cigarettes for the kind of operation you were talking about in Vietnam."

"Pete's money comes in handy for incidentals. But more than that, he's one of the best couriers I have. He gets to the right places and the right people without attracting any attention."

They got out of the car. "That's more than I can say for you," said Shawcross. "There are times when I think you might just have the biggest mouth in the world."

Gray laughed. "Just think about this—big brother is watching me, all right, but because I *am* such a blabbermouth, no one takes me seriously. Result is I move right under their noses with complete freedom. General, there's a lot you have to learn about me. Once you do, you'll be a lot more positive about this operation."

"You'll have to show me. I don't want to waste any more lives on lost causes, so don't think waving your flag and hollering 'Black is best!' is going to set off skyrockets around here. I'm not interested in sending out suicide squads."

"No problem," said Gray as they entered the house. It was almost dark now, and Shawcross could hear the night birds calling as they swept through the dusk, feeding on flying insects.

They entered a handsome foyer. "Well," said Shawcross, "when you get around to revealing your plan, it had better live up to the advance build-up."

Once again Gray laughed. "You're a forthright man, General, and that's what we need around this place. Don't worry, we'll live up to the billing. . . . Pete'll be back later. Meanwhile he won't mind if we nip a little bit of his booze."

"I think I've had enough. What I really need is some sleep."

"That's easy," said Gray. "Follow me."

He led Shawcross up a winding staircase and into a large bedroom. An artificial fire flickered in a fireplace, adding its soft glow to the room's indirect lighting. The bed was already turned down.

Shawcross had started to strip when a woman came out of the bathroom.

"Hello, General," she said. "I was just checking the towels. Don't pay me no mind. You just go to bed."

Shawcross recognized the striking ebony face of Eloise Gibson. Her recording of *It Takes Two to Tango* had been one of his favorites. He remembered making love with Carolyn to its thrusting rhythm one April night in San Diego.

"I'm a friend of Pete's," she said. Then, in answer to his unasked question, "What you might call a very good friend."

"Pleased to meet you, Miss Gibson."

"Make it Eloise, honey. Nobody around this joint's formal. Come on, now," she said, helping him unbutton his shirt, "you're a tired man and you need some shut-eye. Mr. Gray, if you will cut on out of here, I think the General might be less embarrassed."

"See you in the morning, General."

"All right, Gray," said Shawcross, fatigue slurring his voice. He watched him leave, felt Eloise Gibson's gentle fingers pulling off his shirt, then unhooking his GI belt buckle. He sat down on the edge of the bed.

"Shoot," she said, "these pants won't come off over those big shoes of yours." She bent down and unlaced his GI boots, then pulled them off. "You're a big man with big feet," she observed, peeling off his socks.

"Feet that need a wash," he said, sniffing. Eloise crinkled her nose and laughed.

"If that's the worst you ever smelled, you're a morning glory. Okay, General, off with those pants and hop into bed."

He removed his pants, too tired to be embarrassed by his nakedness. "You're very kind," he said, and then he thought of Carolyn lying in that dimly lit room out at Forest Lawn.

She seemed to read his thoughts. "Let it out, General," she said softly. "No man ought to be put through what you were." She put her arms around him and held his hot face close to her. "It's all right, baby, you got a right to be sad. Don't hold it all inside, let it out."

Against his will, he felt the sobs coming. He tried to keep them silent, but they were loud despite his effort. She hugged his face closer to her and stroked his hair, whispering to him and brushing soft kisses against his forehead.

"You're a good man, General, and when the Lord tests a good man he lays it on hot and heavy. You're doing just fine, don't let anyone tell you it's wrong to cry."

The agony spent itself and Shawcross sat there quietly, feeling the woman's warm body against his cheek. She smelled musky, a little like vanilla.

"Now you just lie down, General." She helped him under the covers. As he felt the coolness of the sheets his eyes opened again. Eloise reached out and took one of his hands. "Don't you worry none. Eloise isn't going anywhere. She'll stay right here. So sleep, baby, sleep."

She hummed a tuneless lullaby and in his mind Shawcross was in his own little bed in Anaheim, forty years ago, in a different world that had somehow always seemed dappled by the sun and filled with fragrant, quiet breezes.

TWELVE

Congressman John Alexander Roberts, Representative of the district of Harlem, sprawled in a canvas camp chair at the end of the long wooden pier and tossed pebbles into the Caribbean. He was being interviewed by Ben Gates, a TV newscaster who had made the long trip down to Eleuthera in the Bahama Out Islands at the specific request of the congressman.

"I have a mandate from the people," said Roberts, with an accent that was a cross between the drawl of the southern Negro and the delightful patois of the Caribbean. "They elected me though I did not seek the office or campaign for the office or even admit that I would accept the office."

All of this was true enough.

John Alexander Roberts had won his seat easily, but near the end of his first term of militant campaigning for Negro rights, he had been caught *in flagrante delicto* with the young wife of a Supreme Court justice.

When Roberts' term expired and he declined to run again, everyone was relieved—everyone except the black men and women who saw in him a defender and a champion of their cause. He was re-elected by a sizable write-in vote.

"Well, Congressman," said Ben Gates, in the well-modulated tones that ordinarily romanced the Late News, "there's no doubt that the people of your district want you. The question is, do you still feel you can serve them?"

"Who can serve them better, Mr. Gates?"

"I was referring to your—ah—difficulties—"

Roberts threw his head back and laughed. "You mean my little escapade down there in Washington? Why, it wouldn't have been more than a fleabite on the hide of the Republican elephant except for one fact—the lady in question is white. I offered my services to the good Justice in case he wanted to challenge me to a duel, but he went and had my name excised from the Social Register instead."

"Still, Congressman, feeling has run high. Do you think you could do your job when there would be reluctance toward inviting you to social functions?"

Roberts looked straight into the camera. "Mr. Gates, I don't know how much of this you are going to be allowed to use, but let me put one thing straight. There was *always* a certain reluctance when my distinguished colleagues from the Southlands were also on the guest list. Meanwhile, I can assure you, sir, once the word got out that I was not as standoffish as folks once thought, I was a very popular midnight caller in old Georgetown."

Gates shook his head slightly and the camera stopped rolling.

"Congressman," he said quietly, "you don't want to talk like that. Bernie, skip the tape back to the beginning of this sequence."

As the sound man rewound the tape Roberts grinned widely.

"What's the matter, Ben? Am I embarrassing you? I thought you television guys had seen and done everything."

"Let's hear where you are, Bernie," said Gates. The

sound man switched on the machine and Roberts' voice squawked from the tiny built-in speaker. "I have a mandate from the people . . ."

"Okay, Bernie," said Ben Gates. "Erase it all from there on. Steve, open up your camera and flash that film."

"Wait a minute," protested the cameraman, "that's a full four-hundred-foot magazine and it's color."

"Whose lousy thirty bucks is it, anyway?"

Grumbling, the cameraman opened the flanges of the magazine perched atop the 16mm Auricon and exposed yellowish coils of film to the sunlight.

"I sure am sorry, Ben," said Roberts, mockingly. "Here you come all this distance, and then you aren't even interested in what I have to say."

"Roberts," said Gates, deliberately eliminating the "Congressman," "let's me and you get one thing straight. I don't care *who* you screw, black or white. But when we turn these gizmoes on, you don't go on record saying things like that. You can't spit in people's eyes on national television."

"*White* people? Why should I give a damn what they think?"

"Because what they think affects black people," said Ben Gates. "Jesus, you know the effect comments like that will have. And not just in the bedrooms of Georgetown. Now if you want to give me a usable interview we'll get on with it."

There was a long pause as the Congressman from Harlem held up his rum fizz, squinting at Gates through its glistening amber.

"You know, Gates," he said finally, "you're a pretty good man. Too bad you're white. We could use men like you on our side."

"I am on your side."

"Maybe," said Roberts. "I guess I had my system put

out of joint yesterday by a visit from an old buddy of ours."

Gates raised his eyebrows.

"Mr. William Gray," said Roberts. "One of these days I think he's going to have a real news story for you. Meanwhile, let's go have a liquid lunch, and then I'll give you the playboy-congressman-on-Eleuthera interview."

THIRTEEN

The honor guard did not appear at the funeral, and the press was barred. Rod McNeal and several friends of Carolyn's were there. Some of the mourners were white; to the infinite relief of the attendants Shawcross did not say anything about it.

William Gray and Eloise Gibson stood beside Shawcross, who wore civilian clothing and a black armband. In the back row was Pete Humble, his head uncovered—one of the few times he had ever been seen without his snappy plaid hat.

The services were soon over. The mourners left before the workmen began replacing the earth in the three cavities scooped from the green hillside.

"Feel up to lunch?" asked William Gray. He and Shawcross sat beside each other in the back of the white Continental. Following them in a red Porsche were Pete Humble and Eloise.

"Maybe a drink," said Shawcross.

"Okay," said Gray, "but take it easy. You still got to talk with them ofay cops this afternoon."

"Screw them," said Shawcross.

Gray smiled tightly. "You know that," he said, "and I

know that—but we don't want them to know that. Just play it cool with the fuzz."

"Don't worry, there won't be any more outbursts like yesterday."

"Hell, baby, what you did yesterday was nothing to be ashamed about, but from here on in you better play it cool."

He lit a thin cigar. "Okay," he said to the driver. "Pull in up there. That's a good place."

The "good place" was a Spanish-style restaurant with a large parking lot in front and tall cactus planted around the door. The Porsche crunched into the lot beside them, and everyone except the driver started inside.

"No room at the inn for drivers?" Shawcross asked.

"Plenty of room," said Gray. "But since you ask, Jerome would as soon go off without his balls as leave that car unprotected. The papers and tapes stashed in it could blow this country right down the middle."

"My mistake," said Shawcross. They went inside.

"Four," Gray told the headwaiter, who led them through an imitation Spanish courtyard to an isolated table near a splashing fountain.

"The lady will have a Marguerita," he said to the table waiter. "Jack Daniels on the rocks for the rest of us."

"Do you always order for everybody?" asked Shawcross.

"Usually," said Gray.

"Not for me," said Shawcross. "I'll have a Marguerita too," he told the waiter.

The drinks came and Eloise lifted hers. "Here's to you, General," she said. The others joined the toast, and Shawcross nodded slightly as he sipped. The coarse salt around the rim of the glass stung his lips.

"Eloise has to fly east tonight," said Gray.

"A job," she said.

Pete Humble snorted. "A job, she says! Three weeks at the Empire Room, that's all."

"Somehow, I lived in California most of my life without ever meeting anyone famous," said Shawcross. "Now all of a sudden I'm surrounded by celebrities."

"General," said Pete, "you're the celebrity. I bet lots of black kids in this country have your picture up on the wall right alongside Cassius Clay's."

"Can't say I care for the company," said Shawcross.

"Maybe you'll get a chance to see me at the Waldorf," said Eloise.

"Might be," Shawcross said. "Something tells me I'm going to have to make a trip to Washington. They won't accept my resignation over the phone."

"Are you sure that's what you really want to do?" she asked.

He looked at her, surprised. Was it possible that she knew nothing of the plans Gray had in store for him?

"The General's put his time in, Eloise," Gray said quickly. "It's time he lived a little for himself."

"Amen!" said Pete. "If you don't live for yourself, nobody else is going to do it for you."

"We're all in the rotten process of saying goodbye," Eloise said softly. "I'm off to New York, Pete's going to Vegas, and you're on your way to Washington. I think we were better off before they invented jet planes. Then, at least, you thought twice before you went scooting off across the country."

Soon Gray asked for the check, and they continued their journey into the heart of Los Angeles. The Porsche left them at the Santa Monica freeway. The Lincoln went on alone.

"I'm going to let you off a couple of blocks from the courthouse," said Gray. "From now on, we'd better not be seen together too much. Come out to Pete's place when you're through."

Shawcross gave Gray a mocking salute as he got out of the car. Gray watched him go.

"He's going to be trouble," said Jerome.

"No, I don't think so," Gray said slowly. "Right now his mind is still a little split between what he was and what we want him to become."

"Oh?" asked the driver. "And what was he?"

"An American," said Gray.

"I want to see Captain Marcus, homicide," said Shawcross, and was quickly ushered through the crowded room to a tiny office at the back. Marcus, a puffy-faced man in his fifties, rose and shook Shawcross' hand.

"Won't keep you long." He opened the file. "You were arrested in 1965, over in Watts."

"I was released without being booked," said Shawcross. "The whole thing happened because three men bombed a private home."

"Yes, that's all here," said Marcus.

"Then what's your point?"

"Have you seen those three men since?"

Shawcross shook his head.

"Heard from them? Received threatening letters or phone calls?"

"Not a peep," said Shawcross. "Do you think they were involved?"

Marcus sighed. "Doubt it. One of them is dead. Another's been inside for over a year on a holdup. The third works as an orderly in the Veterans' Hospital in Frisco."

"Which one died?" asked Shawcross.

"The one you hit with the brick. He blacked out one day at the wheel of his car."

"Good," said Shawcross.

"Not so good," said Marcus. "He jumped lanes and took a couple of college kids with him."

"That's too bad."

"Yeah, I can see it breaks your heart."

"Captain," said Shawcross, "I came down to give you anything I could about my family's murder. I'm sorry that bastard caused a wreck, but I'm not sorry he's dead, and it really doesn't have much to do with this conversation anyway, does it?"

Marcus leaned back in his squeaky wooden chair. "General, this isn't helping either one of us. Why don't we start over, pretend you just walked in that door? I'm not trying to provoke you. All I want to do is find out if you have any information that might help."

"As far as I know, I don't," said Shawcross. "Neither my wife or I ever received threats of any kind. I may have received a few crank letters from old biddies who were against the war and thought I was personally responsible for it—"

"Do you have them?"

"Of course not. I was in the field. You don't keep stuff like that."

"Too bad. You see, that note was just a little too good to be true. Whoever wrote it had more education than he wanted us to know about. And the hit—the attack—was too professional for some crackpot. Have you ever had any trouble with the Syndicate?"

"The Mafia? Hell, no."

"Never leaned a little hard on some Marine who had underworld connections?"

"I've leaned pretty hard on a lot of Marines," said Shawcross. "How the hell do I know what they were in civilian life?"

"It's a possibility, then?"

"Sure, it's a possibility. So is it that Uncle Ho wanted me out of the war and took this way of working it. But it sure as hell isn't a probability."

"No," said Marcus, "I guess it isn't. Well, one more and we're finished."

"Go ahead."

"General, why did you have your wife murdered?"

Suddenly Shawcross had the policeman's throat in his right hand.

"*What did you say?*"

"Let go, General," Marcus said in a quiet voice. "Just testing."

"I could have killed you," Shawcross said numbly.

"Sorry, General," said Marcus. "That was a dirty trick, but it works more often than you'd believe. It's just part of the job."

"Sure," said Shawcross. "We all have dirty jobs to do."

"I'm with you," Shawcross told William Gray. "It took me a long time, but I've made up my mind."

Gray said nothing. He took both of Shawcross' shoulders in his hands and squeezed until his fingers bit into the light suit coat.

Three hours later, the two men drove to Los Angeles International Airport and boarded a TWA jet for New York.

"There's a man I want you to meet," Gray said. "Do you know Ambassador Harumba of Njala?"

"No," said Shawcross.

"You will."

They were seated in the first class section. Outside, at the loading gate, a commotion began. It traveled along the ramp and into the plane itself.

Eloise Gibson was waving both hands and ignoring polite protestations from two airline clerks.

"But you're on the wrong airline," one kept saying.

"That's between you and American Airlines," said Eloise. "You both charge the same price, so my ticket ought to be good here."

"Only if you get it revalidated," he said.

She tapped her foot angrily.

The clerk hesitated, then took the ticket and left. The other clerk followed him.

Eloise Gibson smiled down at the two men.

"Thought you could sneak out on Eloise, did you?" she said. "Well, my motto is, why travel alone when you can go in style with friends?"

Shawcross laughed. William Gray settled back into his seat and said nothing.

FOURTEEN

Raymond Carpenter sat hunched over an IBM Executive typewriter, composing the copy for the next issue of *The Afro-American Bulletin.* A can of Rheingold was at his elbow, and the rough notes for his editorial were pinned to a folding screen that surrounded the work area on three sides. Behind him a portable hi-fi rumbled through the Third Symphony of Beethoven.

"We are dying by the millions," he wrote. "In the slums of Harlem and prison camps of South Africa, in the jungles of Nicaragua and the narrow streets of Calcutta, in the floating villages of Hong Kong harbor and the sugarcane fields of Trinidad, the white man is systematically destroying the non-white.

"Meanwhile, the great white middle class lives in a splendor and comfort unknown to kings two hundred years ago. Their security and isolation from the hundreds of millions of poor throughout the world is so complete that they have convinced themselves such poverty does not even exist. With their television and automobiles and jet planes and air conditioning, they enjoy comforts a Nero would have lusted after—but not the meanest slave in the poorest Roman galley ship would have traded his oar for the conditions under which most of the non-white population of the twentieth century endure their brief, miserable span between painful birth and lonely grave.

"At one time, the poor were needed to till the fields and harvest the crops. Today's poor are unwanted holdovers from the distant past, pawns to be swapped around by politicians.

"Those days are coming to an end. When poverty was silent and alone, each of the countless millions separated from and unaware of the others, when poverty was illiterate and uneducated, when poverty was a closed circle which began and ended at the grave, the oppressors had little to fear.

"But poverty is no longer alone. The motion picture speaks to every village in Africa. The radio is heard in every Indian town in Brazil. Poverty has found a tongue, and as poverty learns to speak, poverty ceases to be alone.

"The white man is all too aware of this. His unity was his strength. Now he sees the non-white reaching for a common unity, and fear dogs the white man's step.

"The racial war has begun, and no one knows where it will lead because the white man may yet choose to destroy the entire world rather than let it be ruled by a black majority. But there is no turning back. Compromise is no longer possible. We will not be bought off with a 'guaranteed annual wage,' or with token integration, or even with the white man's daughters—as if we wanted them! We are on the march, and with the poverty-stricken of the entire world linked together in one nation of oppressed, we shall indeed overcome. Not with words or demonstrations, but with the sword!"

Raymond Carpenter sat back in his chair and read over the last paragraphs. He nodded, satisfied, and reached for his can of beer.

"Man, this revolution jazz makes a man thirsty," he said.

FIFTEEN

It was a quarter of one in the morning, and the TWA jet was high over the state of Nevada. The first-class cabin, dimly lighted, was almost empty. Eloise Gibson dozed in a rear seat. After take-off Shawcross and Gray had moved into the lounge, where they sat facing each other across a formica table. Gray asked for a pack of cards, and now they sat idly playing showdown poker as they talked.

"Well, now," said Shawcross, "maybe you ought to tell me precisely what it is you want, and I'll figure out if it's possible."

"Fair enough," said Gray.

He took a sip of his drink. "When I say equality, I do not mean integration. That's a white man's word and it means nothing to me. Equality, to me, means control."

"Control of what?"

"Land. Unless you control land, you control nothing. The black man with his sweat has earned land that he can control—not just a little dab here and there, but his own separate state."

Shawcross laughed. "Where the hell do you think you can get a whole state?"

"I want a place large enough to move our twenty-two million black brothers into," said Gray. "A state that can be completely self-sufficient, in case Whitey doesn't want to dirty his hands trading with us at first. It should have deep-water ports so we can trade with black nations anywhere in the world. It should have enough factories so we can operate immediately as an industrial society."

"Are you talking about a state that already exists?" asked Shawcross.

"I certainly am. It's called New Jersey."

Shawcross stared at Gray for a long moment. Finally he said, "You're out of your mind."

Gray puffed cigar smoke casually. "It's an audacious dream, but a possible one. I see two prongs to this attack. One is military—and that's your responsibility. The other is political. The two prongs, working together, can pry this reparation—that's what I call it—from the white man's fingers."

"I couldn't take New Jersey with the whole U.S. Army," said Shawcross.

"I know. That's why we have to make Whitey want to give it to us."

"Gray," said Shawcross, "no one can accuse you of thinking small. This is the damnedest thing I ever heard of."

"Spare me your compliments. What I want from you is a workable military plan to get us New Jersey. From there on I promise you we'll have no trouble from outside political intervention."

"How much time would I have?"

"Two years, maybe a little longer. We're dependent on outside sources for help. I've got assurances for two years or so, but no longer."

"What kind of outside sources?"

"African nations, willing to divert funds and arms to our cause. But their commitments can't be guaranteed long-term."

"How about manpower?"

"We've got a top cadre of a thousand or so men right now," said Gray. "Men you can depend on."

"How did you find them?"

"I've been working on it for almost ten years. I've had to start over three different times because of security leaks. The thousand men I'm talking about are the best from over ten thousand."

"Do they know what you're up to?"

"All they know is that I want to lead them to a victory against the white man."

"And they'll follow you on no more than that?"

"Yes," said Gray. "And they'll follow you, too."

"Do any of them have military training?"

"They all do."

"*All?*"

"It wasn't easy."

"What'd you do, raid the Defense Department files?"

Gray laughed. "As a matter of fact, that's exactly what I did."

The head stewardess came over and stood by them. "Who's winning?" she asked.

"He is," said Shawcross. "He has all the aces up his sleeve."

She smiled. "Can I get you gentlemen anything?"

"Nothing, thanks," said Gray. He sipped his drink. "You need a front for the next year. You've got to be as far away from the civil rights movement as a man can get. Your resigning from the service is going to generate some heat. So a friend of yours—maybe you remember meeting him, Sig Warren—is going to hire you as a public relations counsel for Warren Chemicals."

"Sig Warren? I never heard of him."

"You met him in Tulsa during the Chemical Warfare Convention. Eighty-five percent of Warren Chemical's output is devoted to heavy-duty cloth. Synthetics, you know. A lot of military clothing is made from Warren Chemical materials."

"What's the other fifteen percent?"

"Napalm," said Gray. "You can see where he has quite a public relations problem."

"Not one a former Marine general could solve," said Shawcross.

"Doesn't matter. We need the job as cover for the travel you'll be doing, and Sig owes me a favor. If you should happen to solve his problems in the meantime, that's so much gravy for him. A man who's been there and seen it can make a pretty good case for napalm, can't he?"

"Oh?" said Shawcross coldly. "Have you ever seen people die with that stuff burning through their flesh?"

"I've seen black men die with their skulls shattered by honkey cops' nigger knockers," said Gray. "That doesn't make me too pure to advocate a racial war if that's what it's going to take to make them free. If I can send my people out to be cut down by white shotguns, you ought to be able to say a kind word for Sig Warren's napalm."

"You bastard, I ought to throw your ass in the Atlantic Ocean."

"Just so you do it from the Jersey shore," said William Gray.

SIXTEEN

The plane was more than halfway to New York when Shawcross suddenly came alive.

"William," he said, "I think I know a way to get New Jersey for you. It'd take a division. At least twelve thousand crack troops."

"You told me you couldn't take New Jersey."

"We can't. But we can take something to trade for New Jersey."

Gray leaned closer to Shawcross. "What?"

"Manhattan," said Shawcross.

Gray sat back in his seat, thinking. When he spoke, his voice was soft. "If we could hold Manhattan long enough, we could make those bastards come through."

"It's full of if's," said Shawcross. "If we could take Manhattan at all. If we could hold it long enough for you to work out something with the Administration. If they wouldn't promise us the moon and then go back on their word. If we could count on enough world support to keep New Jersey once we got it . . . *if* we got it."

"General," said Gray, "do you know what you have when you take Manhattan? Not just an island with a couple of million people on it. You've got the U.N. You've got the records of almost every major American corporation. You've got the American and New York Stock Exchanges. You've got a hell of a big chunk of the gold boullion reserve. You've got the heart of the communications business—all three TV networks, the radio networks, and for Christ's sake, Bell Tel!"

"But remember, we couldn't hold," said Shawcross. "Not for more than a week, at any rate."

"A week's enough. In a week, we could pull it off."

"A lot of people would get hurt," said Shawcross. "And we'd probably wreck the city. The damage could run to billions."

"White man's money," said **Gray**.

"There's one way to do it. That's to go in hard, blow the bridges and tunnels, take hostages, and zap anyone who gets in the way. That's the only way we could keep the Administration from reacting with a counterblow that would wipe us out. We'd come out of this reeking with blood. What you've got to decide is, can it achieve what you want? And even if it does, is it worth it?"

"It can and it is," said Gray. "Holding a whole damned city for ransom—it's so unbelievable, it could work."

"I'll need the whole two years," said Shawcross. "Getting this kind of force together wouldn't be easy if we were doing it in the open. Trying to do it underground is a ball-buster."

"You got the time," said Gray. "And I can help you locate your men. This has been planned for a long time." He leaned back. "Did I ever tell you about the Redemption?" he asked.

"No," said Shawcross, still preoccupied with the details of his plan.

"Elijah Muhammed taught that Allah visited the world back in 1930 in the person of W. D. Fard. Fard was a light-skinned black who formed the first Muslim sect in

Detroit. In 1934 he disappeared from the face of the earth."

"Probably with a block of concrete around his ankles," said Shawcross.

"Could be. I never trusted the Old Man that much. Neither did Malcolm. For what good it did him. Anyway, according to Elijah Muhammed, mankind began with the black race. The blacks brought civilization to the earth. But they got uppity, so Allah took the white race—which was nothing more than a bastardization of the black strain—and gave it six thousand years to be tried as rulers. At the same time, the black race was tested for faith and courage. According to the Old Man, that six thousand years is just about up, and there's a Day of Judgment on the way. When it gets here, the white devils will go down to Satan and the blacks will come into power again to bring the world to the glories for which it was intended. And that's what Redemption means."

Shawcross said nothing.

"Anyway," said Gray, "that's where a lot of us got our first ideas about separation. Elijah Muhammed says that until the redemption occurs, the black man should stay away from the white. He preached that we either set up an independent black republic within the borders of the United States or else return to Africa. That's where I left him—this is my country, right here. I own part of it. And I want my share."

"Simmer down," said Shawcross. "You're making a speech, and the stewardi are getting interested."

"I believe in Redemption," said Gray, lowering his voice to a harsh whisper. "For that matter, some say I may be the Redeemer."

"Hooray for you," said Shawcross. "But what I really

need to know is how you intend to deliver the stuff we need."

"Sorry," said Gray. "I get wound up sometimes, and it's as if twenty-two million blacks were speaking through me."

"While we're speaking about those twenty-two million blacks, let's not forget that they're going to remain outside Manhattan, in the power of the white man. We'll have to assess the possibility of reprisals."

"Let Whitey reprise! Once we're in the driver's seat it'll be too late. And with a million honkey hostages in our power, he can't even begin to be as ruthless as we are, because he's got something to lose and we haven't."

"Maybe," said Shawcross, stretching.

Gray sighed and shifted his shoulders around in his comfortably padded seat. Funny, he thought, how easily you become used to comfort.

He remembered riding to Chicago in 1947 in a chilly Greyhound bus—half empty because it was Christmas Eve. He had just turned seventeen and was suddenly fed to death with the pastoral backwaters of Thomson, Ohio. He had not yet filled out his application papers for Kent State University, and his mother was uneasy. Perhaps she sensed at that moment that her son's formal education was over, that he was searching for his way into manhood. He had become politically and racially conscious during the summer; she knew he had gone to Detroit several weekends for meetings of a Muslim sect. She prayed he had not yet committed himself to it. When he announced that he was going to Chicago for an indefinite time, she was disturbed—but glad his destination was Chicago instead of Detroit. Her relief would have been shattered had she known he was going to Chicago to join W. D. Callahan.

The bus was cold. One of the passengers passed a pint flask of Canadian Club around, and someone insisted that

Gray have a slug too. Most of the passengers were men, many of them traveling salesmen whose heavy sample cases lined the luggage racks. Even the driver accepted a tiny snort, vowing that he would not let it affect his driving. One of the salesmen had a battery-operated portable radio—a novelty in those pre-transistor days. Soon the bus was filled with the mellow sound of Christmas music, and the passengers began to sing along.

At this point in his life, Gray was still convinced there was good in the white man. It did not disturb him in the least to be riding in a bus filled with whites—and singing *White Christmas* with them in the bargain.

Doris Day and Buddy Clark came on with *Let It Snow* and Gray raised his voice:

> *Oh, the weather outside is frightful,*
> *but the fire is so delightful.*
> *Since there's no place to go—*
> *let it snow, let it snow, let it snow!*

There had been talk of a heavy snowfall, perhaps even a blizzard, and this possibility lent urgency to the flight of the Greyhound bus through the wind-whipped night. No one wanted to spend Christmas Day snowed in at some roadside café.

But fortune was with them: the heavy bus had already turned east on Madison Street in the heart of Chicago before the first huge flakes began to drift down, swirling against the steaming windows. It was well after midnight. The bus bounced on its springs, and the aisle filled with men getting their sample cases down from the overhead racks. The good cheer vanished in grumbles about the lateness of the hour and the coldness of the night. For many Chicago was only a transfer point, and the snow a nuisance. As for William Gray, he had always loved snow and he was happy to see it floating down between the dark hulks of the buildings.

The bus reached the Loop and pulled into its berth. "Chicago, Illinois," said the driver. "End of the line. And Merry Christmas."

A few passengers mumbled holiday greetings back at him as they stumbled off the bus into the biting wind, freshly chilled from its passage over Lake Michigan. Gray, one of the last to leave the bus, was bundled up in a bright red windbreaker, a stocking cap pulled down over his ears. As he stepped to the ground, the driver touched him on the arm in a friendly way. "Take it easy, kid, this ain't a good town for you boys. Watch your step."

In a few years Gray would be able to put such men in their place with a caustic remark. At seventeen he simply mumbled his thanks, uneasy at being black in a city unfriendly to those of his color. He felt, somehow, that it was his fault.

"Where are you going?" persisted the driver.

Gray consulted Callahan's letter. "South Wabash—1820½."

"Wabash is a block that way," said the driver. "Catch the trolley car heading south and tell the motorman to let you off at Eighteenth Street."

"Thanks," said Gray.

"Don't mention it," said the driver. "You just watch yourself, boy. I can tell you're a nice kid, so don't get in any trouble around here. They'll put you *under* the jailhouse."

"I don't want any trouble," said Gray. He descended the steps and shivered in the below-zero night air. He squinted his eyes and made for Wabash Avenue. On the way, he saw a clock in the window of a barbershop. It was twenty after one: Christmas Day.

He waited under the El for the trolley. The streets were almost deserted. He was even colder now as the wind came in off the lake, whistling around the few buildings that stood between him and the frigid water, plucking at his clothing with icy fingers. His feet were so cold they had stopped hurting, and he felt as if he was standing on two stumps of wood. The snow matted the top of his stocking cap and, where it struck his warm flesh, melted and ran down his collar.

He heard a bell, far away, and a grumbling noise of metal on metal, then saw a trolley approaching. He climbed up on its platform and asked the motorman, "Do you go to Eighteenth Street?"

"Unless the tracks are out."

"How much?"

"A nickel," said the motorman. Gray fumbled out a coin, dropped it into the glass-topped collector. The motorman turned a crank and the trolley picked up speed.

The snow, which had lightly frosted the streets and sidewalks, glistened under the lights. Even the rumble of the wheels seemed muffled. Gray, suddenly lonely, wished he was back in Thomson. The Christmas tree would be twinkling from the corner of the living room, strung with popcorn, homemade paper ornaments, candy canes. He had already received his gift from his mother—a handsome alligator wallet with three ten-dollar bills tucked into it—and he had given her the silver-plated candlesticks she had admired in the window of the jewelry shop. But there would still be the stocking to find in the morning, chunky with apples and oranges and hard nuts. He felt a powerful urge to swing down from the trolley car and start back to the bus station, to take the first Greyhound toward home.

"Eighteenth Street," called the motorman. The trolley ground to a stop and Gray swung himself loosely to the pavement. The trolley glided away into the snow-specked night.

He trudged farther south on the silent street. Halfway

through the block he found 1820½, a drab, windowless building with a narrow staircase that climbed steeply to the second floor. Hanging over the entrance was a battered sign, "Royal Hotel." The door was closed but unlocked, and Gray opened it. The wind whistled inside as he entered. He had to lean against the door to get it closed.

"Who's that?" called a voice from the top of the stairs.

"Just me!" Gray yelled, struggling with the door. He kicked the snow off his shoes and started climbing the stairs. At the top a skinny white man appeared, wrapped in a heavy maroon bathrobe.

"Who the hell's me?"

"William Gray. I'm looking for Mr. Callahan."

"Oh," said the white man. "He told me he was expecting someone. Come on, come on, I haven't got all night."

Gray reached the top of the stairs and found himself facing a small desk and a cubbyholed mail rack. The man, impatient, took Gray's arm and steered him toward a hall that led off to the right. "He's down that way, in Room Nine. I had to tell him about his radio a little while ago. You boys be quiet, you hear? There's people trying to sleep."

"I'll tell him," said Gray. "Merry Christmas."

"Sure," said the man, "but be quiet about it."

The hall was dimly lighted by two fifteen-watt bulbs protected by metal cages. He found Room Nine: he could hear music coming through the door. He knocked, and heard footsteps, then the door was flung open and he looked into the round face of W. D. Callahan.

"Billy Gray!" said the man, delighted. "You showed up! Come in, Billy, come in. You look like you're froze clear through."

"It's snowing."

"So I see." Callahan brushed flakes from Gray's dripping shoulders. He shut the door and bustled around the stove while the boy stripped off his soggy windbreaker. "I was just brewing up some coffee. How do you like it, with cream or black?"

"Black," said William Gray.

"That's the spirit," said Callahan. And, perhaps in that moment creating the slogan for a rebellion twenty years later, he added, "Black is best."

Gray accepted the cracked, steaming mug gratefully. The coffee was strong and very hot. He hissed through his teeth as he drank, to cool it. Callahan took out a huge turnip of a pocket watch. "Holy Mackerel!" he said. "It's past two. You can have that bed over there, Billy. You must be wore to a frazzle."

With the words, Gray realized he was. Weariness wrapped him like a heavy cloak. He sat down on the bed and untied his shoes.

"We'll have breakfast when we wake up," said Callahan, "and then there's a big Christmas get-together out on the West Side."

"I thought Muslims didn't believe in Christmas."

"Who ever told you that, son? We believe the white man used Christianity to make us docile and submissive, the same as he did to the black savages in the African jungle, and we reject that. But when you take the malarky and the white propaganda out of Christmas, you're left with a wonderful time of the year."

"Oh," said Gray, slipping under a thin blanket. Then he said: "I have to say, I know an awful lot of good white people."

Callahan sat down in a chair near the bed. "I wouldn't say you was supposed to hate them, son," he said. "Some of us hate them, because we've had so much taken away from us that there's nothing left but hate. But that doesn't mean that you've got to hate. I'd like it if there was some

121

way to do what we have to do without hate, but I'm not man enough to do it. Maybe you will be. But whether you hate or not, you have to remember that we must be apart from the white man. I don't know if you realize this, but if the Japanese had invaded this country in 1942, the black man would have been out there in the street waving rising-sun flags and welcoming them with open arms."

"Still," mumbled Gray, half asleep, "I know some nice white people. I sure wouldn't want to hurt them."

"I hope you don't have to. But if it comes to a show-down between hurting them or hurting your own, what are you going to do?"

Gray's eyes were closed, flicking open every now and then as if he was awake, but weariness caught up with him at last.

The room was dismally cold when he awakened. Pale light seeped in the window overlooking the air shaft. He curled up under the blanket, tucking his hands between his thighs. He could see his breath when he poked his nose above the blanket.

The door opened and Callahan entered, returning from the bathroom down the hall. "You stay under the covers, Billy, until I get up some heat."

He lit the gas oven and left the door open, then used the same match to start the flame under the coffee pot. From the oven, he removed a heavy iron skillet and placed it on a second burner.

"Breakfast coming up," he announced, going over to the air shaft window. He opened it, reached out and brought a brown paper bag into the room. From it he removed a slab of white meat—salted fatback—and cut off four slices with a pocketknife. He put the meat in the skillet, made a little twist of paper and transferred the flame from beneath the coffeepot to the other burner. In seconds the white meat began to sizzle, and Gray could smell the delicious odor wafting through the closeness of the room. Meanwhile Callahan was cutting a half-loaf of bread into four huge slices which he put into the oven. "Coffee's ready," he said, pouring two cups. "Black as my elbow and twice as strong."

Gray leaped out of bed and made a dash for the oven. He stood in front of it, feeling the warmth against his stomach while his behind froze. He sipped the coffee gratefully. Callahan turned the meat and it sizzled again.

"Sorry we don't have no eggs," he said, "but you'll find these white meat drippings on that store bread makes a mighty tasty breakfast."

Gray could not remember ever having been so hungry.

"Wash your hands and face," said Callahan. Gray slipped into his shoes and went over to the sink. He dipped his hands into the numbing water and flicked some on his face. He examined his chin in the mirror and Callahan laughed.

"You don't need a shave yet. Don't hurry it along. Shaving's a big pain in the ass once the novelty wears off."

Gray dried his hands on the seat of his pants and sat down, watching as Callahan moved rapidly around the room, picking up two plates in one huge hand, forking out the meat, two pieces to a plate, then deftly tossing the hot bread out of the oven to join the meat. Finally he poured the drippings over the bread, dividing it with a practiced eye. He handed one plate to Gray.

"You don't need a fork," he said. "Saves washing up. But watch out for that meat, it's hot."

Gingerly, Gray picked up a piece of the white meat. It had browned all over and was crisp and dripped little sparkles of grease. He bit into it, savoring the rich taste of the bacon and the deeper pork flavor. The fat-soaked bread was even better, and his first piece was gone in five great bites. He washed it down with swallows of the coffee.

"You sleep good, Billy?" asked Callahan.

"Pretty good."

"I remember when I was young, I could sleep on a wet log in the water. But when you get older you don't seem to need as much sleep. You spend a lot of time in bed just thinking. Last night I did me a lot of thinking."

"What about?" asked Gray.

"You, mainly," said the older man. "I think maybe I did a wrong thing, letting you come down here. I believe I'm going to have to ask you to leave."

Gray's stomach knotted. "What for?"

"You ought to be home with your Ma, finish up your education."

"I graduated from high school," Gray said in a sullen voice.

"That ain't enough, not for a bright boy like you. I think the world of you, Billy, and that's why it just ain't right to drag you off."

"I want to stay with you," said Gray.

"I know you do, son, and I wish you could. In a couple of years, maybe we'll be working together. But you got to go on and get that sheepskin. Education is one of our weapons, Billy, and not many of us get the chance. You got better things to do with your time than chase around after an old speechifier like me. So listen to me and do what I say. Go on home. I promise to write and let you know how the fight is going. And you keep in touch, too. Will you do that for me, Billy?"

Gray sat numbly on the edge of his bed. "I guess so," he mumbled.

"Good," said Callahan. "I phoned from the desk—the next bus don't come until five-thirty. But that'll get you in before midnight and you can still see your Ma for Christmas."

"Sure," said Gray.

"Do you still want to come over to the West Side for the shindig the brothers have laid on?"

"I guess so," said Gray.

They dressed in their heavy winter garments and went out to catch the trolley back to the Loop. Gray stashed his blue laundry bag in a nickel coin locker in the back of the bus station. They caught another trolley and walked for another block and then entered a storefront church. Its plate glass windows had been painted over, and bright purple letters read, "The West Side Baptist Church."

The small building was jammed with people, all black. They wore their Sunday best, and were grouped around a pot-bellied stove that glowed cherry red. Folding chairs ranged the edge of the room. There was no pulpit or altar. One small, extremely black man rushed over and pumped Callahan's hand.

"Welcome, welcome, welcome," he said. "This surely is a pleasure."

"Reverend Samuel Harris," said Callahan, "this young man is William Gray, a brother from Ohio. He was very active in our work in Detroit."

Harris pumped away at Gray's hand. "Welcome, brother."

Most of the people in the room were men, but there were a few women—buxom middle-aged ladies with floppy hats and flowered dresses. They simpered over Gray. One pressed his hand between hers with such strength that he was sure he would end up with broken fingers, and looking directly into his eyes, she said, "God bless you, brother Gray! We've heard a powerful lot about your good work. You just keep it up." Gray avoided looking at Callahan. He was sure the big man was laughing to himself.

In one corner of the converted store there was a little foot-pumped organ, and a lady sat down and began a series of Christmas carols. Their melodies were scarcely recognizable, but Gray raised his voice along with the others and rattled the walls with "The First Noel" and "Hark, the Herald Angels Sing."

Then Gray watched, awed, as the foolish humor left Callahan's round face and he stood in the center of the room—dominating and controlling it. He looked from black face to black face before he spoke. When he did, his voice was quiet and throbbed with intensity.

"Marcus Garvey said, and I use his words: 'Two hundred and fifty years we have been a race of slaves. For fifty years we have been a race of parasites. Now we propose to end all that. No more fear, no more cringing, no more sycophantic begging and pleading. The Negro must strike straight from the shoulder for manhood rights and for full liberty. Destiny leads us to that freedom, that liberty, that will see us men among men, that will make us a great and powerful people.' I heard Marcus Garvey say those very words. They lodged themselves in my brain like a nail driven into a post. It was twenty years ago that he died in London, England. At one time he had fifty thousand men around him. When he died, there were but five or six lonely followers. I am proud to say that I was one of them."

The listeners leaned forward, as if to get closer to Callahan's words. "Marcus Garvey did more than make speeches. He brought the black man closer to the glory of freedom than he had been for three hundred years. To many of you, the name Marcus Garvey may be just another line from the pages of a history book. But, brothers, I was there—I knew Garvey and what he believed in. When Garvey formed the Universal Negro Improvement Association, he was not an American Negro. Yet he came here—he came to Harlem, U.S.A., to set up the U.N.I.A., because he felt that as bad as the black man had it all over the world, the most terrible inhumanities were practiced right here in the United States."

Callahan took a tattered bit of cloth from his inside pocket and held it high over his head.

"Do you know what this is?" he called. The rectangle of cloth was black, green, and red.

"It's the U.N.I.A. flag," said William Gray. Callahan's flashing smile flicked across the room and then was gone.

"That's right!" he cried. "This is Garvey's flag. I've carried it for more than twenty years, and I aim to carry it to my grave. Take a good look at it, brothers and sisters. The black is for the blackness of our skin. The green is for our hopes. And the red is for our blood! Garvey knew that blood would have to be shed, and he did not shrink away from it. Garvey was twenty years too early; we weren't ready for him then. But we are now—our muscles are strong and our souls are even stronger. It is time to unite—to stop fighting among ourselves and line up against the white man!"

He stopped and observed the effects of his words on the audience. He was making them uneasy. When he spoke of blood, they shrank back a little from him. When he spoke of uniting against the white man, several shook their heads almost imperceptibly. Callahan's lips tightened, and Gray knew that he sensed the audience was going against him. Surely he would now change his tactics, say something to get them nodding with him again. Instead, Callahan launched into a speech so startling in that winter of 1947 that he had no hope of winning their support.

"What's the matter?" he demanded. "Do I scare you?

Are you afraid of freedom? Are you so afraid of the white man that you won't stand up to him and say 'I am a *man?*' Are you so frightened for your miserable lives that you dread risking them in the battle that is surely coming to set you free?"

The Reverend Samuel Harris cleared his throat. "The Good Book tells us to love our enemy," he said.

"That Good Book was written by white men, Reverend!" yelled Callahan. "What do you expect it to tell you? The white man wants you to love him. But how much does he love you? Enough to put clothes on your children's ragged backs? Enough to put food in their hungry mouths? Does he love you enough to let you sit down in the same section of the bus with him? Does he love you enough to let you elect your own government?"

"Progress is slow," said Harris, "but we are making way."

"You're making way because men like Marcus Garvey laid down their lives for you."

Callahan pointed accusingly at the man nearest him. "You! I heard you congratulating me on the work we did in Detroit. Many thanks. But how about *you* doing some work here in Chicago?"

"I do what I can, brother," said the man. "But I can't get involved in riots and that kind of stuff. I got a family to take care of."

"And *I* got a family to take care of, too!" cried Callahan. "Millions and millions of black babies being born every year. What are they going to grow up to? The same polite slavery we're still living in because every time we produce a Marcus Garvey, the white man destroys him? Brothers and sisters, the time to make a stand is now. I do not ask you to bear arms; all I ask is your promise to come forward when the call is given. I ask you to remember what this flag stood for—the black and the green and the red!"

He stood silently, holding Garvey's flag. No one stepped forward.

"So be it," said Callahan. He folded the flag carefully and replaced it in his pocket. Harris filled the silence with his thin voice. "Brothers and sisters, we thank Mr. Callahan for coming here to talk with us today." The crowd applauded politely.

"Come on, Billy, let's get out of here," said Callahan.

Harris bustled after them. "Now remember, brother, you're welcome here any time—and so is your young friend. God will provide."

"God will provide, shit!" said Callahan. The oath startled one buxom lady into dropping her grape punch. The wind whipped in as Callahan threw open the door, and then they were outside and snow was falling again, gently and silently, over a graying city.

SEVENTEEN

William Gray did not take Callahan's advice after all. Although he went home for a few months, he never went to college. Five years after that Christmas in Chicago, he was sitting on a Greenwich Village park bench in Washington Square.

His companion, Raymond Carpenter, was showing Gray the first layouts of a proposed poetry magazine.

Over Carpenter's shoulder, Gray saw a young woman striding toward them. Her short, violently red hair stuck out in all directions. Her car coat was unbuttoned and flapping in the autumn breeze.

"Check that," Gray said.

Carpenter looked around. "Laurie Franklin," he said. "You know her?"

"Sure," said Carpenter. "A poet. Writes some pretty horny stuff. But no talent."

"With a build like that?"

The white girl arrived. "Hello," she said.

"Laurie Franklin, William Gray," Carpenter said in a monotone.

"Listen, Ray," she said, "that last batch of poems you sent back—"

"Stink," he said. "Just because Dianne Di Prima gets

away with it, don't think you can. Little girls shouldn't write dirty."

"You miss the point! What I'm trying to say is—"

Carpenter shrugged. "Sorry, baby, I just don't dig. Try me again." He looked at his watch. "Hell, I got to get back. Six pages to get to the printer by tomorrow morning. See you around, William." He waved absently at Laurie and took off past the old men playing chess.

Laurie exploded. "Sometimes I *hate* him!"

"He's a hard man," said Gray.

She looked at him for the first time. "Are you a writer?"

He shook his head. "Sorry. Just a revolutionary in basic training."

"Don't be sorry, I hate other writers. I'm too competitive—they drive me up the walls. Do you mean that? About being a revolutionary?"

He shrugged. "I mean it," he told her. "But nobody seems disposed to take me seriously."

"You're young," she said. "That's why no one pays too much attention to you yet. But they will, when you find your voice. Just wait and see."

"What do you mean, find my voice?"

"It's a saying they have about poets. At first we're all unformed and confused. We imitate others, search around trying to find out who we are. Until one day it starts coming out right. That's what finding your voice is."

He made a decision. "I think I could find my voice a little better over a beer. How about Louie's?"

"I don't drink beer, but I'll have a brandy if you let me pay for it."

"If you have a brandy, you'll *have* to pay for it. I'm Broke City."

"That's all right, my family sends me plenty of money. Don't be embarrassed."

"I'm not."

In those days, the Circle in the Square Theater was still located on the south side of Sheridan Square. Beneath it, in a cobwebbed basement, was Louie's Bar.

They walked along West Fourth Street toward the Square. The autumn sun slanted into the twisting streets, burnishing the small buildings with golden streaks. The streets were filled with tourists and students from nearby N.Y.U. Laurie's face was flushed and glowing, and her red curls twisted in all directions.

"I bailed out of Vassar in June," she told him, chattering on, filling the short walk with the kind of autobiographical information that has to be gotten out of the way. "I told Moms, I'm free, white, and twenty-one, and I intend to see what it's all about before you get me married off to Harvey Fiddler! So we agreed to a year in New York and here I am."

"Free, white, and twenty-one," said Gray.

"It's just a figure of speech. I didn't mean—"

"Sure," he said, and they turned down the short flight of stairs to Louie's.

She flushed as he held the door for her. Inside, the juke box was blaring Stan Freburg's *Dragnet* parody. He found seats behind a rough wooden pillar and beckoned the waiter. "A stein for me. She's having brandy."

While they waited, Laurie asked, "Where do you live?"

"Over on Cornelia Street. Why? Did you figure I was one of the square niggers down from Harlem?"

"William," she said, "you're so defensive. Please don't be. Not with me. Who knows, I might be your first recruit. You can't lead a revolution without recruits, can you?"

"I guess not," he said. The drinks came and he swallowed a gulp of the cold beer. Laurie cupped her brandy glass in both hands.

"I love brandy," she told him. "It warms me up and makes my heart beat faster, and I feel good all over."

"Sex does the same thing," he said boldly.

"I suppose it does. But you can only have sex in private and with someone you know very well. You can have brandy anywhere."

"I'd make love to you right here with everyone watching," he said.

"That might be nice," she said calmly, "except I'm afraid the police would haul us off before we got the same effect you get from brandy.

"I wouldn't know. I've never had brandy."

"Try some of this. It's really very good."

He sipped the dark brown liquor. It burned his lips and scorched his throat.

"Do you like it?"

"I don't know," he choked.

"Good heavens, drink some of your beer," she said. "You were telling the truth, weren't you? You really never have had brandy before."

She waved for the waiter. "Two double brandies and some ice water." She turned to Gray. "It's handy to have some water around in case your windpipe closes up."

When the drinks came she held up hers in a toasting gesture and they sipped. "Would you like to read some of my poetry?"

"Sure," he said unconvincingly.

"Maybe I'll let you. Except I warn you, I don't have anything that deals with revolutions."

"That's all right," he said, "my revolution doesn't have anything to do with sex."

"You really mean that, don't you, William? You're not just making bar talk to impress a girl."

"I mean it," he said. "You don't know what it's like to wear a permanent sun tan."

"I can imagine," she said.

"You can't imagine one-tenth of it. You think of us as white people with a skin problem. That's crap. We're as different from white people as our skin is different from their skin. We're black inside, too, and that makes it impossible for any white to ever understand us. I wish they wouldn't even try. I don't want to be understood."

"It's made you bitter, hasn't it?"

"Hell yes it's made me bitter." He swallowed the last of the brandy and stood up. "Thanks for the drink, lady, maybe I'll see you around some time."

He heard her protesting, but by then he was out of the door and cutting around the corner onto Seventh Avenue South. He was furious with himself and wanted to go back, but he walked on as if it were a test of his determination.

He spent the rest of the evening in a little bar on Hudson Street, sipping beer and getting mildly high and remembering the first girl he had ever had.

It was the summer of 1947, and the Ohio sun was hot overhead. He was sixteen years old.

That was the year it really got home to him that he was a nigger.

"Hey, Billy," called Les Clayton. Les was the tallest white boy in the senior class of Thomson High School.

"Yeah?" said Billy Gray.

"You ever think of Irma Leakey? That girl who lives out near Twin Forks?"

"What do you mean, think?"

"You know what I mean. How about that set of knockers she's got?"

"They look all right," Gray said, disturbed. He and Les had never discussed sex before. He bent over his hoe.

A day's work hoeing the Clayton corn was worth $2.50 to each boy.

"All right? They make Jane Russell look like a boy!"

"They're pretty big," Gray admitted.

"You know what else? She sells it."

"Sells what?"

"Her ass, moron. Two bucks a hump. I heard it from Howard Morgan. She took him on last Saturday. Without a rubber, too."

"That's the best way," said William Gray—the connoisseur of sex who had never had congress with or without a rubber. "You wouldn't wear a raincoat in the shower, would you?"

"Well," said Clayton, "how about it?"

"How about what?"

"She slipped me her phone number after math. She must want me to call her, huh?"

"Guess so."

"Okay," said Clayton. "After work, let's you and me borrow Pop's car and drive on out there and pick her up. We can go over to Rocky Hollow and have ourselves a piece."

"I don't know, Les. She's your friend. I don't even know her."

"Shoot, she's anyone's friend who has two bucks. I'll call her up and say I want to bring a buddy."

"You'd better tell her who I am," said Gray.

There were few Negroes in Thomson. Gray knew that in the southern part of the state there were unpleasant incidents—but they did not reach him in Thomson, near the Michigan border. He was aware of being black, just as Les Clayton was aware of being a redhead; so far it had not meant much more than that.

He and Les finished the field at five-thirty. Back at the

Clayton house he had fried ham and hot biscuits with white gravy.

After the blueberry pie, Les said—with a wide wink to Gray—"Excuse me, Mom. Got to make a call." He went out in the hall and rang up the operator on the old-fashioned hand-cranked telephone.

"Some more pie, William?" asked Mrs. Clayton.

"No, ma'am," said Gray.

"What are you going to do when you finish school?" she asked.

"Go down to Kent State University. My Mom arranged a scholarship for me there."

"Smart boy like you ought to be able to do better than that," said Mr. Clayton.

"Now, Papa," said Mrs. Clayton, "there's nothing wrong with Kent."

"Didn't say there was. Just said the boy could do better, Mama." And that was that. Mr. Clayton disappeared behind the *Cleveland Plain Dealer*.

Les came back, a wide grin on his face. "Pop, me and Billy are going to the drive-in to see Loretta Young in *The Farmer's Daughter*. Can we take the Pontiac?"

"Pickup truck," said his father.

"We got a *date*, Pop!" The answer was a neutral mumble. Les looked at his mother. She nodded. "Come on, Billy," said Les.

Les coaxed the dusty 1941 Pontiac's engine into grumbling life and threw gravel with the rear wheels.

"We're in like Flynn," he told Gray as the car bounced along the country lane.

"Did you tell her who I was?"

"Sure, I told her."

The sun caught motes of dust on the dingy windshield and turned them into opaque golden frost.

The Pontiac turned north on the main highway. The

worn tires spun it toward Michigan. Suddenly Gray wished they could keep on going, all the way to the state line and beyond. He shifted his behind around on the tattered gray cushions, feeling sweat running down his legs.

"What are you so itchy about?" said Les. "You never screwed a girl before?"

"That ain't it," Gray said. "I just remembered, I left my wallet at home."

"No sweat. I'll let you have two bucks. We owe you for today anyway."

Gray sank despairingly against the rattling door. One hand cupped the warm air that flowed back over the Pontiac's hood.

"Look at that sun," he said, struck with inspiration. "Hell, it ain't going to be dark for hours yet."

"So what? Don't you want to see what you're getting?"

"Well," Gray mumbled, "I just thought, with both of us—"

"The guy in the car can blow the horn when he's through. The other one waits in the woods."

"Oh," said Gray. He closed his eyes and listened to the drone of the engine, to the swish of the tires against the roadway.

Irma Leakey was waiting for them beneath the Pet Milk shelter at the school bus stop. Her eyebrows raised slightly when she saw Gray.

"Hi, Irma," called Les. "Get in."

She opened the back door and got in the car.

"I just want to be able to scrunch down out of sight if we pass another car," she said. "Is this your friend Billy?"

"That's him," said Les, making a U-turn.

"Hello, Irma," said Gray.

"You didn't tell me has was a nigger," she said, then turned to Gray. "No offense, Billy."

"No offense," he said.

"Les Clayton, let's go!" she said. "I told Mama I was going downtown to the movie. What's on?"

"*The Farmer's Daughter*," said Les.

"That's at the drive-in," said Gray. "Downtown, it's *Gentlemen's Agreement*."

"Oh, with Gregory Peck," said the girl. "I wish I was really seeing it. I like him. He's so big."

"They just make him look big for the movies," said Les. "How about a drive up to Rocky Hollow?"

"Rocky Hollow! Oh, Les, whatever do you have on your mind?"

"Well, if you don't want to—"

"I didn't say I didn't want to," she said. "I know you're both nice boys and I can trust you. Can't I?"

"Sure you can," said Les.

"Billy?" She tickled his ear. He jerked his head away. "Can I trust you?"

"I guess so," he mumbled.

Les turned the Pontiac onto a dirt road. It twisted through heavy underbrush and outcroppings of rock. As it sloped down into the hollow, the road was cathedraled with tall trees.

The clearing was littered with trash and beer cans. As Les parked, Gray was horrified to see, less than two feet away from his window, a limp, white condom, draped over a branch.

"Look at that!" Irma cried. "Somebody's been playing with balloons."

"Don't look at me," said Les. "I never use the things."

"Is it yours, Billy? Do you like to play with white balloons?"

"No'm," he said.

"No'm? Is that English?"

"That means no ma'am," said Les. "Billy's very polite."

"Well, I like it," she said. "There's nothing wrong with a boy being polite."

"Billy was just going to take a walk," said Les.

"Yeah," said Gray. He got out of the car.

"I'll honk the horn," Les said in a stage whisper.

"Okay," said Gray. He wandered into the trees, toward the sound of running water. The air was cool and heavy. He smelled the fragrance of leaves and flowers. A bee hummed in the tall grass. Distantly, a crow cawed.

He stood at the edge of the stream and watched the water cascade down a series of terraces, frothing from rock to rock.

He heard the car horn beep three times. He turned and started up the slope. Les met him halfway back to the clearing.

"How was it?" Gray asked.

"Nothing special," Les said, his voice tight.

"Well, then," Gray said, relieved, "I'm not even interested. Let's take her home and the hell with it."

"No," said Les, "she asked me to send you up."

"But I'm not interested."

"Honk the horn when you're finished," Les said, brushing past him.

Gray shrugged and went up to the car. The girl was nowhere to be seen. Then he looked into the car and saw her sprawled out in the back seat. Her blouse was unbuttoned to the waist.

"What took you so long?" she said.

She put one foot against the door. It opened slowly.

"Come on in out of the hot sun."

"Listen, Irma," he said.

"You're not going to disappoint me like your friend, are you?"

"What do you mean?"

"This," she said scornfully, pointing to a viscous smear along one tanned thigh. He recognized the seminal fluid. "Big man," she said, "telling me what all he's going to do and then he pops before he even gets it in." She pulled him toward her. "Would you like to see me?" Her breath was hot against his face. "Would you?"

He licked his dry lips. "Yes."

"Finish taking off my blouse."

The white cotton fell away from her breasts. Unsupported, they had a firm upward tilt. The nipples were blazing red flowers.

"Go ahead," she said, stretching toward him.

Her hands cupped behind his head. He was pulled down into the heady, musky warmth of her bosom. Her flesh felt astoundingly cool to his lips, which moved along the swelling curves until, unexpectedly, a nipple popped into his mouth. It tasted slightly salty. He could feel it harden and enlarge between his lips as the tip of his tongue touched it.

Her hands tightened at the back of his head. "Suck it," she whispered.

He did, first one and then the other. She strained in his grasp and made deep sighing sounds. Her hand fumbled, caressing him through the heavy cloth of the overalls.

"Oh," she said.

He felt himself throbbing in her grasp. He contracted his muscles as her fingers unzipped his fly and clutched him directly. The heat of her palm seared him. He arched his back.

"Careful, Billy," she said. "Save it for Irma." She helped him slip out of his overalls, pulled the rumpled skirt up over her plump hips. She took one of his hands and guided it between her legs. "Use the end of your finger," she whispered.

He slipped it through the tangled hair and into the

warm, moist slit. She thrust her hips up against him. He felt a little rubbery button pressing against his finger, slipping back and forth under her skin as he manipulated her.

"Oh, yes," she cried, "right there. That's it!"

She seemed to widen, then suck his finger deeper. She moved against his hand, slowly at first and then faster. With a shuddering cry, she thumped frantically against the heel of his hand.

"What's wrong?" he said, frightened. He tried to pull away, but she caught his hand with furious strength and held it inside her.

"Aaaaah," she said, shuddering. "Oh, Billy, that was so good."

"What happened?" he asked, still frightened.

"Silly," she giggled. "I came. Didn't you feel me?"

"I didn't know girls came too," he said.

"Sure we do, when a boy knows how to make us. Did you like making me come?"

He nodded.

"I want to come again," she said. "Make me come again."

He put his hand down to her slippery vagina. She pushed it away.

"No," she murmured. "I want you."

"What?"

"I want your cock! Put it in me, right there. Now—push . . . oooooh! Slowly, slowly!"

His penetration was the most exhilarating sensation William Gray had ever felt. He gasped as her muscles tightened around him.

"Ummm," she whispered into his ear. "Are you close, Billy?"

"I think so," he gasped.

She adjusted her body so her legs went around his back, her feet resting on the steering wheel. "I'm almost there again too," she panted, thrusting herself up against his belly. "Shove it to me, daddy! Now!"

Gray arched his hips and drove into her hard. She cried out sharply, "I'm coming again!" Her feet beat a tattoo on the steering wheel. In the distance, he thought he could hear a horn blowing, but he could not have stopped if his life depended on it. He heard her voice, "Don't stop, please don't stop," and the wet smacking of their bodies against each other, and the savage blaring of the horn. Then the shudder began at the base of his spine and exploded outward until it became the world. He heard himself cry out as he spurted in her. All strength left him and he collapsed between her legs. She was still whimpering and gasping. Then her dazed eyes focused and widened as she looked over his shoulder.

Gray turned and saw Les Clayton staring in the open door.

"You blew the horn," Les said numbly.

Irma scrambled to cover her nakedness. Gray slid out the door and onto the ground. He felt warm and full of laziness.

"Man," he grinned up at Les, "if that's what you call nothing special, I'd hate to grab hold of the good stuff."

To Gray's amazement, Les shouted, "You shut up!" He reached inside the car and hauled Irma out. Her naked rump thudded onto the ground and she yelped with pain.

"Is that what it takes to satisfy you?" Les yelled. "A black prick?" He threw out their clothes.

"Hey, Les," Gray said, starting to get up. He was on his hands and knees when Les kicked him.

"Nigger," said Les.

Dimly, Gray heard the Pontiac drive away.

Half drunk on beer and memories, Gray returned to his Village apartment shortly after ten. He opened the

142

battered refrigerator and took out a can of Ballantine Ale. He sipped the rich, malty brew and went back into the living room, stripping off his shirt. His skin felt sticky; a bath would be nice.

Taking a bath in the apartment's tub was an operation. The claw-footed monster had originally sat alone in one end of the kitchen. Gray had covered its top with a large sheet of plywood, hinged for easy entry. But since the top also collected cups and dishes, clearing it for a bath usually took considerable activity.

Fortunately, this week had been a light one for coffee cups. Gray propped the top up against the wall and fastened it there with a hook he had installed the day after the plywood fell down and banged him on the head. He stripped off his trousers and undershorts, turned on the hot water and climbed in.

A tap came on the door to the hallway. "I'm in the tub," he yelled.

"That's all right," said a female voice. The door opened.

He turned his head. It was Laurie Franklin, carrying a huge leather purse. There was one chair in the apartment. She sat in it and looked at him calmly.

"What in hell are you doing here?" he asked.

"You told me you lived on Cornelia Street," she said. "I checked the mailboxes and here I am."

"Well, I'm taking a bath."

"Don't get mad at me," she said, "A revolutionary shouldn't be mad at his first recruit."

"I'm not mad at you." He soaped his feet.

"Good," she said. "What can I get for you, General?"

"I'm no general," he said. "I don't know beans about the military."

"Suppose we make you the premier? That gives you authority to govern *and* to act."

"Sounds pretty good to me." Despite himself, he grinned.

"Even premiers have to dry themselves. Where do you keep your towels?"

"I keep most everything back there," he said, indicating a metal locker in one corner of the other room. Laurie opened it, grimaced at the tumbled mass of clothing and books inside. She rummaged through the piles, found a moderately clean towel and brought it to him.

"Your laundry is disgraceful," she said.

He shrugged, crawled out of the tub. "I get up to the laundromat about once a week."

"Once a month would be more like it. If you're going to be a leader, you should dress like a leader. Leaders don't wear wrinkled clothes, or shirts that smell."

"Does my shirt smell?"

"Like a billy goat. Do you have another one?"

He looked in the closet. There was a bright red plaid that he usually wore in winter.

"An improvement," she said, looking him up and down. "The shirt is a little loud, but at least it's clean."

She gathered up his dirty clothing and piled it in a corner. "Do you have any glasses in this rat's nest?"

He pointed to the top of the gas stove. "Why?"

She opened her huge purse and took out a squat bottle. "Courvoisier," she said. "I thought we might continue our brandy lesson."

"What about the ice water?"

"I don't think we'll need it."

They sat silently, drinking the brandy. He told her about his life in Thomson, Ohio; about the Christmas in Chicago with W. D. Callahan; about bumming around the country and finally coming to Greenwich Village.

"William," she said, "why not *do* something? Even if you don't know exactly how it will fit into your future, action may help shape your mind."

"Like finding my voice?" he asked.

"Something like that." She touched his arm. "I'll help you, William. If you need money, I have some, and I can get more. And I know important people who will listen to you."

"I thought you were a poet," he said, dreaming over the brandy in the darkness of the room. Outside, the street light painted long shadows along the sidewalk.

"Not any more," she said.

"You're kidding."

"Never more serious. I've found a better occupation." They were silent for a few moments. Then she said, "Do you have a moustache? I can't remember." Her forefinger traced his upper lip. "No, you don't. Did you ever have one?"

"Hell no," he said irritably. Did she think all niggers had little thin-pencil moustaches?

"Shhh." She placed her finger on his lips. "Don't get mad. In Psychology they told me no one ever grew a moustache—or cut one off—unless he was undergoing a major personality change. Did you ever hear that?"

"Sounds like book crap to me. Guys grow a moustache because they think it looks good."

"No they don't," said Laurie. "They grow one because they want to look older, or more manly, or cruel."

"I don't like moustaches."

"Right now you don't, but I wouldn't be too surprised if when you really are the Premier you end up wearing one."

"Why do you cut your hair like that?" he asked.

She fluffed it with her hand, and he reached out and touched it gently. "I don't know," she said. "It used to be long and very fine. One morning I got up and whacked it all off with Mom's shears."

"And you're telling me about personality changes," he said, reaching for some more brandy.

The distant night sounds whispered around them, and most of the brandy was drunk or spilled. They argued loudly about trivial things, and lowered their voices to talk about important ones. Her cheek was warm against his, and her breath, fragrant with brandy, warmed him. He kissed her, softly at first, then let his tongue explore. She stiffened and shuddered in his arms.

Slowly, gently, he unbuttoned her blouse. Her breasts were larger than he had thought. He bent to kiss them.

Her fingers, trembling, stroked his face.

"Oh, William, be careful," she whispered. "I never have before."

EIGHTEEN

"What time is it?" asked William Gray, turning in his seat as he struggled back from the brink of sleep. Shawcross looked at his watch. Outside, the night air rushed against the windows of the plane.

"Three-twenty, California time." He was filling pages of a black leather notebook with cramped writing and diagrams. He saw Gray's glance and said, "Rough ideas. Manpower requirements. Logistics. How we seal off the island."

"That's simple. Blow the bridges."

Shawcross shook his head. "For one thing, you can't blow a bridge like the George Washington completely. No, what we have to do is determine the maximum load-carrying capacity we can live with and damage the bridge to that point."

"What do you mean?"

"Well," said Shawcross, "take the George Washington. If we damage it so men on foot can get across but cars can't, we've got one job. If we're willing to let cars across too, it's an easier demolition job. If we're willing to let anything across except tanks, it's easier still. But if we wanted to go whole hog and drop a span into the Hudson, I'd have to fall back on the old answer they taught us in training."

"What was that?"

"It was a trick question. They asked, 'How would you destroy the George Washington Bridge if you were standing on the Jersey side with no weapons and only a nickel in your pocket?' "

"How would you?"

"The right answer is, 'Make a phone call to the Air Force.' "

"These days it'd cost you a dime," said Gray. "But maybe that's still the right answer."

"How do you mean?"

"There's no reason we can't have some of our key people at the controls of a bomber or two."

"It would help," said Shawcross. He scribbled some more notes into the leather book. "I keep checking the figures and they keep saying, one week at the maximum. I'm counting on three or four days' reaction time, then a couple of days of skirmishing. But once they decide to move in force, we've had it."

"We could threaten to kill a million hostages," said Gray. "That ought to keep them out."

"It'd only bring them in faster. The purpose of the hostage is to delay their reaction time—but once they decide to come in, threats to hostages will only speed up their timetable. Anyway, the last thing I want is whole-sale killing."

"Harlem blacks may have other ideas," said Gray.

"They won't have time to get out of line," Shawcross said. "We'll draft every one who can walk. Unreliable as they might be, we can still use them to guard supermarkets."

"Screw the supermarkets," said Gray.

148

"Food is time," said Shawcross. "Those supermarkets are our main source of food and we've got to hold them. Along about the fourth day, when people's supplies start running out, we're going to have to feed them or there'll be hell to pay."

"Let the bastards starve."

"You've obviously never seen a city under siege. Believe me, it's cheaper and easier to feed them. If they lose all hope, they'll climb over piles of their own dead to get at us. Beside, we're not out to commit genocide on the whites. We want table stakes to trade for New Jersey. The less damage we do and the fewer people we hurt, the more we have to trade."

"Okay," said Gray.

"Now," Shawcross went on, "let's assume your estimate is correct, that you can provide the manpower. I'm still worried about armament. You don't just walk into an Army and Navy store and buy twelve thousand M-1 carbines."

"Is that the weapon you want?"

"It's lightweight, simple to operate, and fairly effective at short range. They ought to be easy to come by on the surplus market. They were manufactured by the millions for World War Two and Korea."

"General, if this country is selling anything to anybody, we can get a chunk of it."

"What about heavier stuff? Fifty-cal machine guns, mortars, a lot of bazookas? Those are our first line of defense against a landing."

"But you'd still want the carbines?"

"Yes," said Shawcross. "Although twelve thousand carbines are one hell of a lot of carbines."

"When you meet Mr. Harumba in New York this morning, it'll ease your mind."

"I hope you aren't just pipe dreaming, Gray. We're already talking in terms of four or five million dollars, and we've still got two years to go."

Gray leaned back.

"Don't worry, General," he said. "We're going to make it work."

William Gray stared out the plane window. He was not thinking about logistics or money now. He was remembering the yellow telegram Laurie Franklin had sent him two days after they first met in Washington Square.

It was the first time in his life he had ever received a telegram.

MEET ME APARTMENT 9-C, 268 EAST 78TH STREET, FIVE P.M.   LAURIE

When he pressed the button for 9-C, the front door buzzed open. He took the elevator up to nine and found the apartment opposite the elevator door. He looked at the name under the bell and raised his eyebrows in surprise. It read, W. D. Callahan.

Laurie opened the door to his ring, and he followed her into a large living room furnished with the styleless pieces building owners think is modern.

At that time he did not know the difference. "Mighty fancy," he said. "Callahan would have liked it."

"I thought it would be smart to use another name on the lease," she said. "I didn't think your Mr. Callahan would mind."

"He can't mind," said Gray. "He's dead." Before she could react, he added, "Did you rent this place?"

She nodded. "For us. It wouldn't do your image any good to be seen running around with white girls."

"Screw the image," he said. "I sleep with whoever I please."

"So I've heard," she said. "I did a little checking up on you. If there's any tramp in the Village you haven't banged, she must be locked up in an attic. Those days are over, Mr. Premier."

"Who says?"

"I says," she whispered, unbuttoning her silk blouse.

After the violence of their lovemaking, they sat together in the huge bathtub. He soaped her breasts with an oval cake of Chanel Number Five. "Everybody knew what you were doing with all those poor beatnik girls," she said, stretching under his touch. "But there's a more positive way to begin your battle than by fucking the enemy's women."

"What other nice words do you know?"

"Remember, I used to write dirty poetry," she said. "Do you like to hear me say fuck?"

"Say it again and I'll let you know."

She slapped at his rising penis. "Listen to me, I'm almost through."

"Talk fast," he said, cupping her breast in his hand.

"If you really hope to lead a revolution, you'll need the militant blacks behind you, and they aren't going to feel like following a white nigger."

Startled, he drew his hand back. "Where did you hear that term?"

"A writer named Norman Mailer used it at a party the other night. A white nigger is a black man who tries to achieve goals set by the white man. If you don't want to be a white nigger, you can't fight the white man's battle, you can't want the same rewards he wants—and you can't fuck his women."

"That word again," he said, slipping his fingers between her legs. Laurie wriggled against him. She was breathing quickly, but her words were still careful.

"That's why I rented this place," she said. "We're never going to be seen together again. There's no doorman here. You can come once or twice a week and no one will notice. You're going to be an important man, William. You have to be careful."

He pushed her back into the fragrant water. "Suppose I get this overpowering urge to fuck a white woman?"

Her voice was muffled. "What are you waiting for?" she asked.

Their secret kept. As his power and fame increased, his visits became less frequent—but whenever he was in New York, he tried to get over to East 78th Street at least once.

Laurie's mother had died, leaving her a sizable inheritance. She lived in a high apartment overlooking Gramercy Park, and kept the place on 78th Street only for meetings with Gray.

One afternoon, more than ten years after their hidden affair had begun, she called him at his office.

"Can you meet me at six?"

"Yes," he said, surprised. She rarely telephoned him.

She was waiting anxiously. Pouring a shot of brandy into a snifter she said, "Malcolm X has bolted the Black Muslims."

He took off his coat before answering. "Are you sure?"

She handed him a bourbon. "Positive," she said. "William, I believe he's getting ready to make his move."

"I knew he wasn't getting along too well with Elijah Muhammed," Gray said, sipping his bourbon, "but I thought they'd work it out."

"They didn't," she said. "This is a statement he made to the press. First he said, 'In areas where our people are the constant victims of brutality, and the government seems unable or unwilling to protect them, we should form rifle clubs that can be used to defend our lives and our property.' "

Gray whistled. "That doesn't sound like Malcolm."

"There's more. Listen to this: 'When our people are being bitten by dogs, they are within their rights to kill those dogs. We should be peaceful, law-abiding—but the time has come for the American Negro to fight back in self-defense whenever and wherever he is being unjustly and unlawfully attacked.' "

"I'll be damned," said Gray. "He comes on real strong."

"It's no joke, William. He's obviously making a grab for power. What's worse, you can't break away from the Muslims now—everybody'd just say you were following Malcolm."

"I've got to move soon, though," he said. "I've got men set up in Los Angeles, Detroit, and Newark. They won't wait forever."

"Suppose Malcolm doesn't wait at all?"

Gray looked at his empty glass. "I guess he could set the timetable back twenty years." He sighed. "We'd have to get rid of him."

"Don't wait too long, William."

"I won't." He looked at his watch.

Her voice was disappointed. "Do you have to go now?"

"I'm sorry, Laurie. I canceled two meetings to get over here, and I'm running late for one with Stephen Harumba now. I'll call your answering service in a day or so and we'll get together."

"Not next week," she said. "I'm flying down to Acapulco, and I'll be gone for ten days or so."

"When you get back, then," he said, oddly relieved that he would not see her for a while. "Have a good trip and get lots of sun. You've been looking pale lately."

He knew he had hurt her.

Later that evening he dined with Stephen Harumba, the young ambassador from Njala. Harumba confirmed Laurie's suspicions.

"Malcolm has been in contact with my country," he said. "This is in strictest confidence, of course."

"Of course."

"He came to my office last week to ask for my support in a new endeavor, having nothing to do with the Black Muslims. An offshoot of our own Organization of African Unity. He plans to call it the Organization of Afro-American Unity."

"Very ambitious," said Gray.

"Perhaps too ambitious," said Harumba. "Such a move could possibly endanger planning and preparations made by certain other parties."

"He could wipe us out."

"Might he be reasoned with?"

Gray shook his head. "He may be wrong, but he's not dishonest."

"Then he ought to be stopped."

"I think we'll wait a little longer."

Harumba shook his head. "You Americans," he said. "You school yourselves in terror and preventive action, yet you shrink away from it like little girls from a spider. Do you honestly believe that Malcolm would ever accept a post subordinate to yours? Why, he despises you."

"Still, we'll wait awhile before making up our minds about him." Gray looked at his watch.

"Go on to your appointment," said Harumba. "You mustn't keep a congressman waiting." As Gray started to raise a finger for the check, the African pushed his hand down. "Washington is picking up the check. Just as Washington will eventually pay for your guns."

NINETEEN

Gray took a cab directly from his dinner with Harumba to the rambling town house of Congressman John Alexander Roberts. It overlooked the Hudson River, on Harlem's west side.

Gray's taxi stopped in front. The meter read $2.90, and Gray gave the driver four dollars. He started to get out of the car, then stopped. He had not heard the expected "Thank you."

"Did you say something?" he asked the driver.

"I didn't say a thing, Mac."

"Wait a minute," said Gray. "I gave you a dollar too much."

The driver clutched the bills tighter in his hand. "Thanks a lot."

"Hand it over," said Gray.

"Up yours," said the driver.

Gray leaned back and closed the door. "Let's go."

"What do you mean, let's go?"

"The nearest police station."

"What are you, some kind of a nut?"

"Either hand over that dollar, or take me to the police station."

The driver made a move toward something under the seat.

"Freeze!" shouted Gray. "You bring up a jack handle and I'll bust your nuts with it." The driver, frightened, sat in an awkward position, one hand reaching under the seat, the other crossed over his chest, holding the money. Gray leaned forward and plucked one bill from the man's limp fingers. "Thank you," he said, pushing the door open. "Keep the change."

The driver began cursing as Gray walked up the sidewalk. He put the cab in gear, caught up with Gray, and threw a coin out the window. It bounced off the sidewalk and clinked against a garbage can.

"Take that, you cocksucker," yelled the driver. "You forgot your nigger dime!"

Gray climbed the short flight of granite steps and rang the bell. A maid opened the door and ushered him into the library. The Congressman, mixing a pitcher of martinis at the bar, looked up as Gray entered.

"There you are, William," he said. "We had given up on you."

Gray had never met the second man in the room, but he was familiar with the face of the Reverend Abner Greenbriar.

Greenbriar gripped his hand. "Mr. Gray," he said in deep, booming tones, "your fame has preceded you."

Gray laughed. "By way of the Justice Department?"

"Fortunately, no," said Greenbriar. "Although I must say that you have been very lucky indeed."

"I equate luck with planning," said Gray. "Every time those honkey cops think they have me cold, I set it up carefully with witnesses and even an FBI man or two. They just wind up looking silly."

"You must be careful. They aren't stupid, Mr. Gray."

"Don't you worry, Reverend. The last thing I do is underestimate my enemy."

"I'll grant you that. But I'm afraid you do underestimate the effectiveness of democracy in achieving justice for our people."

"After three hundred years, it's time democracy put up or shut up," said Gray. "If democracy were doing its job, you wouldn't be staging sit-ins."

"There are dangers in moving too fast," Greenbriar said.

"Balls," said Gray.

Greenbriar smiled and went on: "I understand that you intend to speak in Detroit this summer."

"That I do. Detroit's sort of my alma mater. I grew up near there, and I first got involved in the movement in Detroit."

"Detroit's hotter than a firecracker now," said Roberts. "I hope you don't mean to stir up a mess there."

Gray looked from one man to the other. "What is this? Did you ask me up here so you could both jump on me?"

"Oh, hell," said the Congressman, "I know what it sounds like, and that isn't what we meant. Look, I've been told by the President—and this is in the strictest confidence now—that he's going to ramrod the new Civil Rights Bill through. He called me in and asked me off the record to do anything I could to take the heat off for the next year or so. Any disorder or rioting will only make it harder for the bill to pass."

Gray took out one of his thin black cigars and looked at it.

"I'm asking you to cool it," said Roberts. "Hold your demonstrations down. Avoid violence at any cost."

Gray lit the cigar. "Gentlemen," he said, "we've got them on the run." His eyes flicked around the room and the cigar worked in his mouth. "Dammit, this is the time to press harder, not back off. Civil Rights Bills and crap like that is only designed to make the outside world think White America is finally giving us what we've always had a right to. I won't be a party to such a lie." He stared at Roberts. "And you know me better than to ask."

"I had to," said Roberts. "I promised I would."

A knock came at the door and Karen Davis walked into the room. Her blonde hair was loose and shining, her blue eyes direct as they met Gray's. The Reverend Abner Greenbriar made a gesture in her direction. "Gentlemen, my secretary, Miss Davis."

She nodded at them. "Congressman. Mr. Gray. How nice to meet you." Then, to Greenbriar: "Reverend, I hate to disturb you, but you're already overdue at Cooper Union, and it'll take us at least half an hour to get there. I called and they're stretching out the entertainment, but we'd better go soon."

"Time," said the Reverend. "I never have enough of it any more. Goodbye," he said, shaking Gray's hand. "I don't believe in your methods, William, but now that I've met you, I believe that they're honestly motivated."

"My pleasure, sir," said Gray. "I count the trip worthwhile for the privilege of meeting Miss Davis."

"What a flatterer he is," said Karen Davis. "Come along, Reverend. The car's waiting."

They left. Gray turned to find a sardonic smile on Roberts' face.

"The 'Black is Best' champion giving a white girl the eye?"

"Was I that obvious?"

"Baby, you were transparent. You did everything but take your joint out and wave it in her face."

"Sorry," Gray said.

The Congressman laughed. "What's there to be sorry

about? Man, I'd dip my wick there any time I thought I could get away with it. But that chick's never had eyes for any man as far as I know. You don't know how honored you are, William. Up to now I never even saw her smile."

"What's her relationship with the Reverend?"

"Just exactly what it appears to be," said Roberts. "She's his right hand, but that's all. Besides which, I doubt if the good Reverend knows his thing has another use than passing water."

A few days later Malcolm X spoke at a Harlem rally for the Muslim Mosque, Inc. "It's got to be the ballot or the bullet. The ballot or the bullet. If you're afraid to use an expression like that, you should go back to the cotton patch, you should get back in the alley."

Laurie called Gray. "He's getting out of hand, William. For one thing, he's lifting thoughts and ideas right out of your speeches and presenting them as his own. You've got to look at the situation realistically. He's picking up followers who ought to be behind you, he's taking over your movement. You've got to stop him!"

"He's a good man," said Gray. "We'll wait."

In July Malcolm flew to Cairo to speak to the heads of thirty-four member states of the Organization of African Unity.

In his eight-page memorandum to the delegates, he wrote: "America is worse than South Africa, because not only is America racist, she also is deceitful and hypocritical. South Africa preaches segregation—she at least practices what she preaches. South Africa is like a vicious wolf, openly hostile toward black humanity. But America is cunning like a fox, friendly and smiling, but even more vicious and deadly than the wolf."

The next day, on July 18th, the Harlem riots broke out—without the foreknowledge of William Gray, and without the participation of his forces. Molotov cocktails flared in the night, and sniper fire swept the streets.

Gray called an emergency meeting of his New York lieutenants and raged at them. "Goddammit, this wasn't scheduled for months yet! How did it get out of control?"

"No one knows," said one. "The first I heard was when they started shooting out street lights."

"It's that bastard Malcolm," said Gray. "That's it. I've had it with him."

"We don't have any proof," said another man. "All indications are that it was spontaneous. That honkey cop shot without thinking, and the brothers just busted out."

"They weren't supposed to bust out," yelled Gray. "Not yet, not this soon! Where the hell is our control? Where's our intelligence? How could something this big happen without our even getting a whiff of it? Malcolm may not have pushed the button, but he built it, by shooting off his big mouth all over Africa. He'll set everything off too soon and put us back twenty years!"

"You can't knock what he's saying," said the first man. "It's what we've been saying ourselves."

When the rioting and looting were over, the toll of dead and wounded established, another fact was also recorded. The rioters, who booed Bayard Rustin and CORE's James Farmer, had been shouting, "We want Malcolm!"

In late November, Malcolm returned to the United States. At a rally sponsored by his Organization of Afro-American Unity at the Audubon Ballroom in Harlem, he read a message from Cuba: "Dear brothers and sisters of Harlem, I would like to have been with you and Brother Babu, but the actual conditions are not good for this meeting. Receive the warm salutations of the Cuban people and especially those of Fidel, who remembers enthusiastically his visit to Harlem a few years ago. United we will win." The message was signed "Ché Guevara."

This, more than anything else, galvanized Gray into action. He and two of his most trusted men prepared for Malcolm's return from Europe on February 13th, 1965. They watched the late news and were assured that he had actually returned, then they went down and got into the Hertz car. The license plates had been smeared with mud.

Gray, in the right front seat, stared out into the chilly night.

"No waiting around," he reminded the driver. "As soon as you hear the doors shut, get us the hell out of there."

The driver tooled the car through the silent streets carefully, stopping at every traffic light and staying well within the posted speed limits.

"How about his wife and kids?" asked the driver.

"Tough titty," said Gray. "This is the last warning he's going to get. If anything happens to them it's his fault."

"That's it up there." The driver indicated a darkened house.

"Take it easy, now," said Gray.

The car slid up to the curb in front of the house. It was almost two-thirty in the morning.

"Ready?" asked Gray.

"Ready." The man held out two heavy bottles filled with gasoline and cloth wicks. Gray struck a match and lit the wicks. They burned bright yellow in the wind.

"Now," said Gray.

The man threw one, then the other through the window. The glass was shatteringly loud as it broke. Inside, a mushroom of bright orange and flickering red burst toward the ceiling. The men did not wait to see it. They dived into the rented car, slammed the door. Two blocks away the car slowed, turned a corner and headed away from East Elmhurst.

"Jesus," said the driver, "did you hear her screaming?"

"I didn't hear anything," said Gray.

It was not until morning that Gray learned what had happened in East Elmhurst. Malcolm's house had been seriously damaged, but he and his family had escaped into the night without injury.

And Malcolm did not accept the warning. If anything, the frequency of his speeches increased.

"Get him," said Gray.

The Audubon Ballroom, on the downtown side of West 166th Street between Broadway and St. Nicholas Avenue, is a gloomy two-story building which earns its way by being rented out for meetings, dances, and rallies. When the ballroom doors were opened at one-thirty on a clear, unseasonably warm Sunday afternoon, several blacks who had been waiting seated themselves quickly in the front row of the four hundred wooden chairs provided by the management. Dozens of others, including Gray, arrived in the next fifteen minutes.

On Malcolm's express orders, none of them were searched at the door. "It makes people uncomfortable," he said.

Looking at the stage, Gray saw the speakers' stand and, near it, eight straight chairs. Behind everything was a painted backdrop depicting a quiet country scene. By a little after two the auditorium was almost filled, and Benjamin X, Malcolm's assistant, began a long introductory speech. Finally he said, "I present to you one who is willing to put himself on the line for you, a man who

would give his life for you. I want you to hear, to understand, one who is a Trojan for the black man."

From his seat, straining to see over the heads of the
applauding audience, Gray watched Malcolm come out
onto the stage, nod to Benjamin X, and face the crowd.
When the applause lessened, he raised his hand and spoke
the familiar greeting: "*Asalaikum*, brothers and sisters."

Someone from the crowd called back "*Asalaikum
salaam*," and then a disturbance broke out in the middle
of the gathering. A man shouted, "Take your fucking
hand out of my pocket!" and as the audience in the
front rows turned to look, Malcolm called out, "Don't
get excited. Cool it, brother—"

He, and most of the people in the Audubon Ballroom,
had their eyes riveted on the disturbance. But Gray,
watching carefully, saw the assassination from start to
finish. Four men rose in the front row of the wooden
chairs. Two had sawed-off shotguns, two had revolvers.
The shotguns blasted first, and Malcolm's hands flew to
his chest as the pellets tore into him. Then the pistols fired.
He raised one hand and it spurted blood as a bullet
struck a finger; he stiffened and fell backward over the
row of wooden chairs, blood streaming from his thin
goatee. He struck the floor stiffly, his head hitting the
wood with a sickening thud.

In the confusion, the assassins melted into the crowd.

The echoes of the gunshots were still reverberating
through the hall when people began to scramble up on
the stage. A woman knelt over Malcolm and tried to give
him mouth-to-mouth resuscitation. After a few minutes,
a man took her place. Then Gray could see no more,
because the shouting, milling crowd blocked his view. It
took him several minutes to force himself through the
mob. As he climbed to the stage he saw Sister Betty,

Malcolm's wife, on her knees over the blood-soaked body. Four men arrived with a stretcher. As people shoved each other, shouting "Give him air," the men rolled Malcolm's body onto it and carried him out of the building, toward Columbia Presbyterian Hospital.

Gray managed to make himself heard. "Whitey got him," he shouted. "Those white devils found out what he was up to and sent out murdering white niggers to strike down Malcolm. They'll be after me next! Can't you see, Whitey ain't *ever* going to let us get strong? As soon as we show signs of turning into men, they cut us down like old cornstalks. They won't let us have leaders; as soon as we do they lock us up, or they cut us down with lead!"

"They won't get you, too!" yelled a heavy, very black man in rough working clothes. He leaped up onto the stage and stood directly in front of William Gray. "Any motherfucker who wants to shoot this man has got to shoot through me first," he shouted. "Come on, brothers! They took away one of our good men. Are we going to let them have the other one, too?"

"Shit, no!" Another man jumped onto the stage. A circle of men three-deep surrounded Gray. "Okay, brother," said the first man, "what's your pleasure?"

"We got to be hardhearted," said Gray. "They expect us to go to the hospital to see how Brother Malcolm is. But that don't signify. I know how he is. The man is dead, that's all there is to that. My car's outside. Get me in it, then scatter. They got Malcolm, but they didn't get the movement. I want you to spread the news—those plantation niggers killed a *man*, a great man, but they didn't kill his dream. The body is dead, they saw to that, but I aim to see that his dream doesn't die!

"Now, brothers, let's see if we can get to my car."

Gray drove away from the Audubon Ballroom without

incident. By the time he reached his office, the phones were ringing.

He learned that doctors at Columbia Presbyterian had opened Malcolm's chest in a vain attempt to massage his heart back to life. The attempt was abandoned at three-thirty, and a spokesman announced, "The gentleman you know as Malcolm X is dead. He died from gunshot wounds. He was apparently dead before he got here. He was shot in the chest several times and once in the cheek."

Another call notified him that the forty policemen who were to have gone off duty at the 28th Precinct station house on West 123rd Street had been told to remain on.

One call needed no explanation. When he picked up the receiver, Gray heard a woman's voice. It said one word, "Good," and then the connection was broken.

Eloise Gibson returned from the jet's washroom and sat in an empty seat across the way.

"We're almost in," she said. "What have you two birds been doing up half the night, whispering and huddling like a couple of spies?"

"Don't go away mad," said Gray.

"I know," she said. "Just go away. I can take a hint."

She went back to her seat. "Why put her down so hard?" asked Shawcross. "She's a good woman."

"We don't need good women," said Gray. "What we need are closed mouths, and I wouldn't trust my own mother to keep a secret, let alone Eloise Gibson. She's only around because Pete Humble thinks the sun rises and sets in her twat."

"Watch yourself," said Shawcross. "I have a certain fondness for the lady myself."

"Sorry," said Gray. "Nothing personal. It's just that if God had wanted women to keep secrets he wouldn't have equipped them with mouths."

"I don't like to see you leaning on your friends so hard, that's all," said Shawcross. "You might need her some day."

"If I need her, I'll change my opinion."

Shawcross shrugged and turned to the window. The clouds were blazing white now under the morning sun.

"On behalf of Captain Bennis and the crew, we enjoyed having you aboard today and hope you enjoyed your flight," said the stewardess over the loudspeakers. "For your comfort and convenience, passengers will deplane through the forward exit. And thank you again for flying with us."

In the Kennedy International terminal, three blacks came over. "Give this man your baggage checks," Gray told Shawcross, nodding toward the tallest. "He'll meet you over at LaGuardia, at the Eastern shuttle."

As Shawcross handed over the checks, warm hands pressed both his cheeks. "Big brave General," said Eloise. "Abandoning his true friend to the mercy of skycaps!"

"Sorry," said Shawcross. "We've got to get on our horse."

"Well," said Eloise, "write if you get work."

"I'll look you up," said Shawcross.

"Sure, honey." She stood looking after them as they hurried away.

A car pulled up, and the two men got into the front seat. Gray and Shawcross climbed in the back, where a third black man sat.

"General Shawcross," Gray said, "may I present His Excellency, Ambassador Stephen Harumba of Njala?"

Harumba put out his hand. "A great honor," he said. "I am well acquainted with the achievements of the General."

"Mostly luck," said Shawcross.

"A successful man makes his own luck," observed Harumba.

Gray leaned back and lit up a cigar. "We don't have much time," he said, "so I'll get right to it. General Shawcross has agreed to head the military segment of our operation."

"Excellent," said Harumba.

"The Ambassador," said Gray to Shawcross, "meets with us on behalf of the Organization of African Unity rather than as a representative of Njala."

Harumba raised a hand. "Actually, neither my country nor the OAU are officially behind me. Please do not press me for the identity of my backers."

"Fair enough," said Shawcross.

Harumba smiled. "You keep your silence, and I will keep mine. Now, without prying too deeply, I understand that you find yourself in need of certain weapons. And further, that you require extensive sums of money."

"Right on both counts," said Shawcross. "I need around twelve thousand M-1 carbines, plus twenty tons of high explosives, to begin with."

"Twenty *tons* of high explosives? You must be planning to blow up a city."

"Or something. Can you deliver it?"

"The items you mention are large quantities for a private individual," said Harumba, "but they are negligible for a government. Or for several governments. Yes, General, I would say we can deliver."

"The cash we need immediately comes to around six million," Gray said. "And we need it in U.S. dollars."

Harumba shrugged. "Six million? The cost of fifty miles of two-lane highway. In all of Africa, I am sure we could lose fifty miles of highway." He smiled. "In fact, I know men who have already done it."

The car curved past the Unisphere left over from the

World's Fair. Shawcross caught Gray's look, and they both grinned. "A study in stresses," Shawcross said. "Each curving arm both exerts and receives a portion of the load. Blow the right arm and the whole thing comes crashing down."

"You are like two schoolboys admiring a passing coed," said Harumba. "Transparent as glass. So you intend to blow a bridge somewhere."

"As an act of terror," said Gray, "a bridge is impressive."

"And takes twelve thousand carbines to attack? No, William, I know you are up to something much bigger than a simple act of terror. And it's good that I do, because otherwise why would I risk aiding you so massively? Very well, we have an agreement. General Shawcross, it was an honor to meet you, and I shall help you in every way possible. Here is my card—this is my private number. When you return to New York we will begin our work."

"I'll be back in a week or so," said Shawcross.

The car pulled up outside the Eastern Airlines shuttle terminal.

"We're just going to drop you and go right on," said Gray to Shawcross. "The man you gave your luggage checks to will meet you in the bar. His name is Arthur."

Shawcross got out, waved casually as the car drove away. He looked after it, at the buildings of Manhattan thrusting into the morning sky.

The size of the job he had agreed to undertake made him shiver. Manhattan had over a million permanent residents, with another million or so coming in every day for business and pleasure. Their cars could cross ten major bridges or enter by way of four tunnels. Those traveling by rail—either subway or regular trains—used ten more tunnels.

To take and hold Manhattan, every one of those bridges and tunnels would have to be destroyed or blocked. He was going to need every ounce of his twenty tons of high explosives.

But more than explosives, he needed hundreds of skilled men to place and detonate them. Shawcross knew that the success of his mission would lie in the hands of the personnel he was able to locate, recruit, and train in the twenty-one months remaining before he was committed to battle.

At his shoulder, a skycap said, "Can I help you, sir?"

Shawcross turned and looked at the man's dark face, at the servant's smile.

"No thanks," he said, stepping toward the terminal's entrance. "Not today."

TWENTY

It took Shawcross several days in Washington to attend to the painful details of resigning from the Marine Corps. The Marine Commandant, aware of his personal tragedy, was reluctant to permit him to turn in his commission.

As alternatives, he suggested an indefinite leave or a post as assistant to one of the Joint Chiefs of Staff. Shawcross turned them down.

"I suppose you've got a fat civilian job offer you haven't mentioned," the Commandant said finally.

"As a matter of fact I have. I'm going to handle public relations—"

"—you're going to *what?*" The Commandant's face twisted. "One of the best combat generals we got, and you're going to become a flack?"

"I don't know what a flack is," said Shawcross. "But I'm going to attend to the public relations problems of Warren Chemicals."

"Warren? The ones who've had those student demonstrations about napalm?"

"Warren Chemicals makes heavy-duty synthetic cloth," said Shawcross. "Some napalm comes out as a by-product."

"I see you know your line already," said the Commandant. His tone softened. "You know, Shawcross, you've always had a way of saying the right thing." It was the wrong comment to make.

"What you mean, sir," said Shawcross, "is that I'm your tame nigger."

The Commandant stared at him for a full minute, then sighed. "Very well, I'll process your papers. It'll take a little while."

"Please see that they don't get lost," said Shawcross. "Warren Chemicals is going to make an announcement about my appointment a week from today."

"You've made your point," snapped the Commandant. "You're making the mistake of your life. When you come to your senses, it'll probably be too late. Reconsider, man!"

"By your leave, sir," said Shawcross. He did an about-face and left the large office. Behind him he could hear the Commandant punching buttons on the intercom. His stomach clenched and there was a sheen of perspiration on his forehead. He felt ashamed about the way the interview had ended, but knew that otherwise his papers might have been held up indefinitely. Now, at least, they realized he meant business.

"I'm Richard Wilcox," said the strange voice on the hotel phone. "My old buddy William told me you'd be in town. How'd you like to take pot luck with me and my wife?"

"Sounds good," said Shawcross.

He found the address in Chevy Chase. Wilcox, a slim, light-skinned Negro, met him at the door, gripped his hand, and ushered him into a book-lined living room. A pleasant-looking woman fluttered over Shawcross and offered him coffee or a drink. He settled for a beer, and she left the men alone.

"Sarah doesn't have any idea what I'm involved in," said Wilcox, "and that's the way I like it. We got enough problems staying ahead of the tax collector and keeping the kids in shoes. Let her worry about that, and I'll worry about the salvation of the black man."

Shawcross laughed. "You make it sound so cut and dried."

"General," said Wilcox, "for me it is. You know, I started this part of the operation on my own, five, six years back. When Brother Gray arrived, I was already here."

"What do you mean, here?"

Wilcox shook his head. "Didn't he tell you anything at all about me? I was trained in computer analysis and ended up in Washington when the government started to go in for computers and data processing. It's hard to believe, but even as a kid of twenty-five or so, I knew something big was going to come up one of these days, and I figured the guy who had access to the records would be in a good spot. I wormed my way toward that job, and it paid off."

"How?"

"I thought you knew. I'm in charge of the computerized service records of every man and woman in the Armed Services."

"Does that mean you're in a position to pull the names of troops with various military occupational specialties?"

"Better than that," said Wilcox. "An MOS only tells you what a man's doing now. I can get the names of men who are skilled in things they aren't doing as their primary MOS."

"How long does it take?"

"For the read-out? It depends on the quantity. If you asked for the names and pertinent data on every GI who could drive a truck, you'd end up with a couple of million of them, and that'd take a while. But if you added another set of qualifications—for instance, let's say you wanted black truck drivers with a known background of racial antagonism—why, then you'd be down to a workable number."

"Troublemakers?"

"Why not, General. Who do you think will be willing to go along on this operation you're planning? The nice guys? The happy ones? The well-adjusted Uncle Toms? No, sir. But the troublemakers, they'll come in on this kind of deal. The ones who figure they don't have anything to lose. I don't trust the ones who've made it too good."

Shawcross looked around. "You seem to have made it pretty good yourself."

Wilcox laughed. "Not too bad, I admit. It all came out of a setup I devised for security."

"Whose security?"

"The movement's. One of the nightmares we have is that the FBI or the CIA will plant an agent on us. Oh, they've put in plenty of them—but we spot them fast."

"How?"

"Well, we got one team in Internal Revenue. Even FBI men pay taxes, and we're on to the cover jobs they list, so they show up like sore thumbs."

"I'd think the feds would have cover tax returns," said Shawcross.

"Some of them do. So we set up a checking system just in case—a national credit firm. That's where I made all my loot—the damned thing coins money. If this cat we got the eye on says he lived two years in Birmingham, we have the machinery to pull a tight credit check on him there. If he's really a spook, he won't have any credit rating at all, and that's how we nab him. He can have letters of reference, landlords who swear he lived in their apartment for his whole life, but if he's got nothing on the credit books, we've got him. The only way they could have beat this system was to plant men under good covers ten, twenty years ago. I just don't think Whitey had the foresight to do something like that. Now it's too late."

"What do we have to do to get moving?"

"Well, the first thing we need is recruitment teams. We've already done good work in this area. We had teams in Watts and Newark and so on, and got a good idea who would fight with their fists and who would only use their jawbones."

"I'll want to pick my men, though," said Shawcross.

"That's easy. Give me the qualifications and I'll see who I can find."

"Do you keep those records here?"

"Not on your life," Wilcox said. "I keep them in the Pentagon."

"The Pentagon!"

"Sure. Who the hell would think of looking there? We got a whole dummy section, does nothing but handle files and records on the movement—I reckon it sets Uncle back a half-million bucks a year, furnishing us with personnel and equipment. I'll take your specs and have them put through the computer. You ever worked directly with computer tapes?"

Shawcross shook his head.

"Well, they're just like the regular tape you use in a tape recorder. You can hold the tape up to the light, you can look at it, but you can't find out what's on it unless you run it through a recorder. What's more, the tapes are classified on a 'need to know' basis—it's a strange thing, but there's no one in the whole of Washington who has that classification except our men."

"Okay, I'm convinced. What next?"

"How many men do you need, and what do you want in the way of qualifications?"

"Ten, I think," said Shawcross. "They'd better be a hundred per cent cleared, because they'll be close to the heart of things. I want men with command ability. Let's say they should have either been a master sergeant or else held the rank of lieutenant or captain. Of course they must be devoted body and soul to the movement. They must be free to travel, starting immediately. It's best if they have no families to start asking questions, because they're going to be on the road for most of the next year."

Wilcox made notes as Shawcross spoke. "Since you need ten, we'll pull the top twenty to give you a selection."

"Do you think you'll have to go outside the movement?" asked Shawcross.

Wilcox shook his head. "I don't think so. I can get these names for you tomorrow, and then it's up to you. We'll pick guys who are already out of the service. They'll be located all over the country. I think it'd be better if we had them come to you. Preferably on a Sunday, so it won't interfere with their regular jobs."

"How do I arrange that?"

"We have a code system. A phone call, offering a job at some mythical company. It's simple, I'll block it all out for you tomorrow. Now, what do you say to some of Mrs. Wilcox's famous fried Maryland crab?"

"Sounds fine," said Shawcross.

The meal was good. Sitting there in the friendship of Richard Wilcox's home, Shawcross became aware again of the enormity of his loss; it made him fall silent and sip at the wine thoughtfully.

Sarah Wilcox had an enthusiasm for life that spilled over into everything she said and did. She pressed food and coffee and, finally, brandy on Shawcross with all the persistence of a Jewish mother. Despite his original gloom he found himself responding to her warmth.

When he returned to his hotel, much later, he wore a pleasant glow from the wine and brandy. "You had a call at ten-fourteen from a Miss Eloise Gibson," said the clerk. "She said you could reach her at the Waldorf." Shawcross went to his room and placed the call. "Eloise," he said. "What's up?"

"Well, hello, tiger. Say, I want to thank you for looking me up and coming to see the show and everything."

"I'm sorry. Everything down here took longer than I thought."

"Well, I'm getting a long run, but nothing's that long. I can see I'm going to have to apply the screws a little. I have a table reserved for General Shawcross and party this Saturday evening at ten P.M., and if you think that didn't take some doing! I'm a smash, honey."

"Who's 'party'?"

"Me, stupid. We'll have dinner after I finish my act."

"I'll be there," he promised.

"Listen, are you all right? You sound kind of funny."

"Sure I'm all right. I just had a fairly liquid dinner with some friends."

"Well, don't overdo it. You know what they say about the juice. It gives you big ideas, but ideas is all."

"I'd be shocked, if I had any idea what you're talking about."

"I'd get more explicit," she said, "except it's against the law over the phone. So why don't you just go beddy-bye, General, and take a couple of Alka-Seltzers? Tomorrow's Friday, in case you didn't notice, and I want you in good shape for Saturday."

"Good advice," he said. "I'll take it. Good night."

"Good night, honey," she said. "Sleep tight." He heard

her receiver click and hung up his own. He had slipped into bed before he remembered her suggestion about the Alka-Seltzer. It still sounded like a good idea, but he was too tired to get up and do anything about it.

He awoke on Friday morning, heavy-headed and muzzy, but a biting cold shower soon had him feeling his old self. It was a brisk walk from his hotel to a nearby Pennsylvania Avenue restaurant for another appointment arranged by Gray.

The restaurant was filled with lacy curtains and fragile Chippendale furniture. Kenneth Hadley towered over the tiny table like a giant over the castle of Lilliput. He stood as Shawcross arrived, and gripped his hand in a huge black paw.

"Pleased to meet you, General. I don't know about you, but I'm starved. What about we order before we get down to business?"

"Black coffee for me," said Shawcross. "Then some scrambled eggs and toast. And keep the coffee coming."

"Sounds good," said Hadley, giving a nod to the waiter. "Except maybe you better put a little club steak medium well on mine."

The coffee arrived, pleasantly strong, and then their eggs, Hadley's accompanied by a hefty club steak that dripped brown juice along the edge of the plate. The big man sliced it in half, offered a piece to Shawcross, who declined, then began to eat, talking between bites.

"I manage the Brooklyn Bombers," Hadley said. "You ever hear of us?"

"Basketball," said Shawcross.

"Right. Comic basketball. We're an out-and-out imitation of the Harlem Globe Trotters. We play exhibition games with local teams, and usually beat their ears off until the last few minutes when we let them get ahead so there won't be any hard feelings. Anyway, the team gives me a hell of a lot of legitimate travel, and I can tack on side trips. I'm your contact with Brother William, and most of the stuff that demands personal contact will pass back and forth through me. Okay with you?"

"As far as I know," said Shawcross. "Except the cat may already be out of the bag when it comes to contact between Gray and me."

"Could be. We always yell at him for going out on assignments himself, but he does it anyway. In your case I don't know what else we could have done. Hell, we couldn't send a flunky to talk with you. The important thing is that there be no further meetings between the two of you until we're ready to go. When do you expect retirement papers?"

"I put as much heat on them as I could, and I expect they're moving it along at full speed."

"You ought to go to New York or Chicago for your interviews," said Hadley. "You're too noticeable here in Washington."

"New York's fine."

"Good," said Hadley. "When you get the names, turn them over to me. I'll see that they're contacted and a full day of interviews set up."

"I'll get them tonight," said Shawcross. "I'm going to New York tomorrow. If you get the names in the morning, is Sunday too early for the interviews?"

"Shouldn't be."

"Let's shoot for that, then."

"Where will you stay in New York?"

"The Waldorf, I guess."

"All right," Hadley said. "We'll get the names from you in the morning, and by then I'll have a safe place for the interviews. We'll use a business office owned by one of the brothers. The candidates will be there at ten Sunday morning."

They finished another cup of coffee, and Hadley waved away Shawcross' offer to pay the check.

"One more thing," said Shawcross, on the sidewalk. "I want Wilcox in on the full operation. He's got to break out leads for a couple of thousand key personnel, and if he has any brains at all, he'll put two and two together. We might as well tell him. He'll be more effective if he's not working in the dark."

"I'll pass that along. Don't say anything to him until you've received clearance."

"Naturally," said Shawcross.

The two men shook hands and Shawcross stepped off briskly, walking up the hill toward the Capitol dome. The sky was violently blue, and above the rumble of the traffic he could hear birds singing. He stood near the Robert Taft memorial for a few minutes, looking at the Capitol. Silhouetted sharply against the deep sky, the American flag waved slowly in the sunlight.

Shawcross turned and walked slowly back to his hotel.

TWENTY-ONE

In New York City, William Gray was working on a table of organization. With him was Raymond Carpenter. The poet sat quietly in Gray's office, taking notes on yellow paper.

"We can't depend on Shawcross for hostages," said Gray. "He won't sit still for our terror tactics. Once we've got the island he won't have any real choice, but even then I can't see him initiating the kind of terror we're going to need to keep the city in line. He's talking in terms of Public Control, with bull horns and guards at street corners. That sure as hell won't cut the mustard with those honkeys when they realize there's nearly a million of them and only twelve thousand of us. We're going to have to take hostages, and kill hostages, to scare their white asses back inside those fancy apartment buildings."

"We're going to have to scare a few black asses, too," said Raymond Carpenter.

"I know it," said Gray, "and pretty damned soon, too. We've got to impress on them that there's no backing down once they're in the movement. One flapping mouth can blow the whole deal. That's why I want you to head up the Special Forces."

"You can count on me for results—if you leave the methods to me."

"Agreed," said Gray. "Now, you won't need too big a force at first. They'll report directly to you, not to Shawcross, and you report to me. I've got a list of men you can pick from. Men who will do what you tell them to, without asking questions. They'd as soon kill as eat."

"Men like that are sometimes hard to control," said Carpenter. "It might take some measures to convince them I'm boss."

"Take whatever steps you have to. That's your department. Now look, I've got an idea for holding part of the city in line. Just before the strike, we grab up all the ward heelers and hold them as hostages."

"Won't work," said Carpenter. "For one thing, damned few people know who their ward heeler is, and even fewer care. No, I got a better idea."

"Let's have it."

"There isn't a section of Manhattan that doesn't have organized crime running horses and numbers and dope."

"So?"

"So we grab off the Mafia uncles, the bosses of each section, use them to force the mobsters to keep their turf under control. They've got the manpower, and they know their own area better than anyone we could send in."

"Might work," said Gray.

"Those boys know we won't be taking over for keeps. They won't go to the wire to fight us when they can get everything they want by just cooperating a little."

"Sold," said Gray.

Friday night, as Shawcross was dining alone in the hotel restaurant, the headwaiter came over with a message.

"Excuse me, General. A military gentleman outside says he's a friend of yours."

"Bring him in," said Shawcross. He took another swallow of his wine, looked up as the headwaiter returned. Behind him was a familiar figure.

"Corncob!" Shawcross held out his hand. Clarence Dewey, his right hand thrust deep into his uniform pocket, put out his left. The smile faded from Shawcross' face. "What is it?" he asked.

"Let's have a drink first," said Dewey, sitting down awkwardly. He was thinner, Shawcross noticed. How long had it been? Less than three weeks? "A double Jack Daniels," Dewey told the waiter.

Shawcross pushed back his wine glass and said, "Make it two, and quick. This man has a fifteen-thousand-mile thirst."

"What's this I hear, Pappy?" Dewey said. "You're turning in your commission?"

"You heard right," said Shawcross.

"That was a lousy deal about your family," said Dewey. "I still get sick when I think about it. But what good does it do for you to throw your career away, too? You're a Marine, Pappy. You don't know how to be anything else."

The drinks came and Dewey raised his glass. "I bet you're getting a hard time from the Corps," he said.

"Goddammit, stop pumping me. Did they bring you back to find out what old Shawcross is up to?"

Dewey shook his head. "I wish they had. No such luck." He patted his right arm. "I figured if I ever stopped one it would be dramatic—you know, a blast of star shells and the whole bit—smiling, the Colonel fell dead. I was out on inspection of a forward position. I went to return some dumb kid's salute—and I couldn't move my right arm. A VC sniper had plugged me with a .22 slug and I didn't even feel it. It was the kind of wound you could fix yourself with a Band-Aid, but the only trouble was the bullet cut through the main nerve complex and paralyzed my arm. I felt silly as hell. There wasn't even any pain. But the medics took a dim view and stuck me on the next flight out of Saigon, and here I am, stationed at Walter Reed Hospital while the superdocs make up their minds whether or not to try a nerve graft. End of sad story."

"Jesus," said Shawcross, "we can't win for losing, can we?"

"It could have been worse," Dewey said. "They could have shot off my pecker." The expected smile did not come. "Cheer up, Pappy," he said. "Things have to get better. They sure as hell can't get any worse."

Shawcross sipped his drink slowly. "No," he said pensively, "I think things are going to get a hell of a lot worse before they get better. Take my advice, pack up your family and get out of this country. Go where you won't have to fight Whitey for your identity. The fire is coming all right, and you're just the kind of unlucky bastard to get caught right in the middle of it."

"Then running out won't help, Pappy. And neither will that revolution stuff you keep talking."

"I suppose you've got a better solution?"

"I might just have one," said Dewey. "I've been doing a lot of thinking about it lately. Damn it, this country is too big and full of smart people to crumble apart the way it seems to be doing."

"It's too late for those smart people," said Shawcross.

"Man, you've got the gloomies bad," said Dewey. "Are you blaming the race situation for everything that's happened?"

"What else?"

"Look at yourself—you're a major general in the elite

corps of the elite. Do you ever think how many white officers were passed over to give you those stars? Hell, no—you decide you're the Corps's house nigger, and so you shit all over your own achievements. You're one of the best officers in the Corps, white or black, and you chuck a career away because you got the dirty end of the stick."

He gulped down the rest of his drink. "Well, General," he said, standing up, "it's your life. Do what you want to with it. But it cuts me up to see a man like you become a professional nigger."

Stung, Shawcross lashed out. "Well now, that's interesting, because it cuts *me* up to see what you've become, Dewey."

"What's that?"

Shawcross pushed away his unfinished drink. "A white nigger, Colonel."

When William Gray visited the offices of Reverend Abner Greenbriar for the third time that week, he finally found Karen Davis there, transcribing shorthand notes.

"You look mighty efficient," he said.

"I am efficient."

"So I've heard. The Reverend in?"

"He's in Memphis."

"Without his right-hand girl?"

She nodded. "He gets uneasy about taking me into certain cities. Memphis is one of them. I'm told there are standing orders from certain white supremacist groups to shave my head and paint it black."

"Maybe the stories are exaggerated."

"No, they're not. My personal opinion is that I should go down there and let them do it. An example of that kind of senseless brutality might advance our cause more than a dozen speeches."

"Those crackers might get carried away and hurt you worse than they intended."

"Crackers are in Georgia," she said. "I don't know what they call them in Tennessee—ridge-runners, I think. Anyway, here I am, being efficient and bored to death."

"Why do they want to paint you black?"

"Surely you know why, Mr. Gray. They think I sleep with him."

"Do you?"

"What do you think?"

He shook his head. "I don't think you do."

"You're right," she said. "Not that I wouldn't, but he doesn't think of me that way. He's got me up on a marble pedestal."

"White marble?"

"Mr. Gray," she said, "I didn't ask to be born white, any more than you asked to be born black."

"Miss Davis," he said gently, "let us not argue on this lovely Saturday morning. I'll make a deal with you. I won't try to convert you to my beliefs if you don't try to convert me to yours."

The anger in her eyes faded. "Fair enough. I suppose I should apologize. You won't believe this, but the Reverend is very impressed with you. I mean, he doesn't agree with your methods, but I've heard him say more than once that you picked up the mantle dropped by Malcolm X. Sometimes I suspect there's more than a spark of militancy under all his Christianity."

"That's the best thing I've heard all day," Gray said. "When do you expect the Reverend back from Memphis?"

"Monday," she said. "Shall I make an appointment for you?"

"What if I make one for you?"

"What do you mean?"

"I have a table at the Empire Room tonight," he said. "A friend of mine is singing there."

"Eloise *Gibson* is a friend of yours?"

"Kissing cousin," he said. "How about it? Dinner, a good show?"

"I shouldn't go," she said. "But I can work tomorrow night and make up for it. All right, Mr. Gray, it's a deal."

"William," he said. "Where shall I meet you?"

"Well," she said, "this is terribly gauche, but I'm staying at the Barbizon Hotel for Women. The Reverend insisted, and there I am, in the Virgin Village."

"Eight-thirty?"

"Wonderful," she said. "I've got this indecent gown I bought in Paris last year when we went over for the European Conference. I never had a chance to wear it. Do you promise not to be shocked? I mean, it's cut down to there."

"Shocked?" He smiled and gave a gentle wave, then left.

Outside, he hailed a cab. He was already late for his meeting with Laurie Franklin. When he let himself into the apartment, she was standing with her back to the sunlight that glared in through the windows.

"I've been worried about you," she said, her body weaving unsteadily as she turned.

"Business," he said.

"I keep thinking maybe somebody's looking at you the way we did at Malcolm."

"Listen, I'm late. What do you want?"

"It's been forever since I've seen you," she said. "Don't you have time for me any more?"

"I don't have time for anything," he said, looking at his watch.

"I didn't want it to be like this. William, I woke up the other morning, and when I started for the bathroom I saw this wild-eyed woman with hair like straw coming toward me. And my God, she was *me!* I was looking in the mirror and didn't even know it."

He looked at her red eyes, at the tiny spiderwebs of veins on her cheeks and nose.

"I had business with Greenbriar," he said.

"Monkey business! You knew he wasn't there! You just wanted to sniff around that little bitch."

"Laurie, I'm up to here with work. What do you want from me?"

"I want YOU from you! I used to be good enough for the great William Gray. My money bought you your first car, and until I took you to Brooks, you never had a suit that fit. Is it asking so much for you to pay a little attention to me now?"

He turned away. "I'll call you," he said. "I'm late."

"What do you want me to be?" she cried. "Do you want me to stop drinking? I'll try if you ask me."

"It's too late for that, Laurie."

"You made it too late. I used to be white, and that was why you wanted me. You can't fool me, William. You only want to make it with white cunt, and that's all I was to you. Admit it."

"You said it, baby."

"But *you* did it to me You covered me with your blackness and turned me into a nigger. That's why you don't want me any more."

Gray headed for the door.

"You bastard," she whispered. "I know where the body's buried, buddy boy. I know all about Malcolm, remember that."

He closed the door and walked a block to Seventy-ninth Street, where he entered a drugstore phone booth. When Raymond Carpenter answered, Gray said, "Ray, I've got the first assignment for your Special Forces."

At ten minutes after two in the morning, the doorbell rang.

Laurie Franklin staggered to her feet.

"I don't want to!" she called. "I'm asleep. I don't want to wake up."

The bell jangled.

"Oh, all right," she said, stumbling to the door. "I'm coming. Just shut up."

She fumbled with the latch and the door swung open. A man stood there, a black man with an oddly familiar face.

"Who is it?" she said numbly. "Don't I know you? Why, it's Raymond! Raymond Carpenter! Come in, come in. Good Lord, it's been ages. Come in, have a drink. How's the poetry business?"

When he spoke, his voice was low. "Nice place you got here, Laurie. Not like the old Village days."

"No, things change, don't they? Now you're famous, and William's famous, and—" She sat down, feeling sick. "And I'm a drunk. Raymond, do you ever see William?"

"Yes. Frequently."

"Can you do me a favor?"

Moving toward her, he said, "I don't think so, Laurie."

She seemed not to hear him and babbled on. "I made a fool of myself. I said terrible things to him. He won't talk to me now, but he'd listen to you. Tell him I didn't mean any of those terrible things. I was drunk."

"You've been seeing him all of these years, Laurie?"

"Ever since that day we met in the park. We kept it a deep, dark secret. I knew it would hurt him if anyone found out he had a white girl friend."

"So that's been it," said Carpenter. "All this time, it's been you in the background."

"Yes," said Laurie, her head dizzy. "Excuse me, Ray—"

She clapped her hand to her mouth and ran to the bathroom, slamming the door behind her.

When she came out to the living room again, she thought at first that Carpenter was gone. Then she saw him out on the terrace, looking down at the street far below.

"It's a pretty street," she said.

He reached for her. At first she thought he was going to kiss her, and was glad she had brushed her teeth. Then she realized that his hands were pushing against her shoulders.

"Oh, no," she whispered.

Half a block away a janitor was putting out the garbage. He heard a high, piercing scream. The sound seemed to be falling, and then he saw an object tumbling toward the sidewalk.

The screaming stopped. There was a soggy, splatting sound.

In the night, windows began to go up.

TWENTY-TWO

Shawcross chose nine recruiting officers from the seventeen men who had arrived at the offices of Langston Warehouses, a moving and storage firm owned and managed by Negroes. The eight turned down were good men, but family connections, age, and in one case an imminent marriage led Shawcross to reject them.

Ken Hadley sat in as Shawcross explained the situation to the officers.

"Let us say simply that I am involved in forming a black army. You don't have to know what that army is going to do. All you have to do is recruit for it."

"How do we get guys to sign up if we don't tell them what they're getting into?" asked one man.

"Why did you sign up?"

"You promised me a chance to get back at Whitey. And get paid for doing it."

"That's what you tell the recruits. And not even that until you are one hundred per cent sure of your man. All it takes is one blabbermouth to ruin everything. I know this makes for a tremendous security problem, and that's why we've made arrangements to get our men out of their communities as soon as they're committed."

Shawcross pointed to a map of the United States. "We

have the country split up into areas. By the time you go into action, we'll have bases in each one. As soon as you wrap up your man, you get him to the nearest base on the double. Don't let him out of your sight for a minute."

"Who are we recruiting first?" asked one of the men.

"Demolitions experts."

The man whistled slowly.

"Right," said Shawcross. "We're not fooling around."

"All this traveling isn't going to be cheap," said another man.

"That's why we made sure all of you have driver's licenses," said Kenneth Hadley. "I've got a team of men setting up cars with local plates for you to use. You'll be traveling salesman, and we've set up a corporation that'll pay you regular salaries, all tax deductions taken out."

"Who are we working for?" asked a man.

Hadley grinned. "The Uncle Tom Flour Company."

"Hold it down," Shawcross said over the laughter. "Now, you've got the rest of the week to wrap up your personal affairs. Stick to the cover story—you've got a good traveling job that pays well, but it's going to keep you on the road for a while. I'll see you all back here on Saturday morning."

He rolled up the map. "Each of you will report directly to me—no one else. You all hold temporary ranks of major. Later, when the recruiting's done, you'll take over line outfits. In this army, everyone fights. There are no support troops."

He looked at their intent, serious faces.

"Any questions?"

"Jesus H. Christ," said Richard Wilcox to Shawcross. "I knew you and Gray were up to something big, but *Jesus!*" It was Wednesday evening and he had flown up on the shuttle. They were at a secluded table in Longchamps. No one was within earshot; even so, Wilcox looked around nervously.

"We're going for broke," said Shawcross.

"You're not shitting. This is beyond anything I'd imagined. I wish the hell you hadn't told me."

"You need to know," said Shawcross.

"Okay. What's next on the list?"

"I need around fifty good men with experience in supervision, to run first-stage depots we'll set up around the country. As our recruiters get the troops, they'll go through the depot for checking and briefing before we move them into training areas. These first fifty guys have to keep the camps in shape."

"Do you want to interview them?"

"No. I'll split up their initial interviews among our new recruiting team, it'll be good practice for them. This is Wednesday. My guys will be back in town over the weekend. Can we get the first batch in here on Sunday?"

"Sure. Do you want a hundred to pick from?"

"I don't think so," said Shawcross. "The machine did a good job on the last batch. Bring in sixty, that ought to do it."

"Right," said Wilcox. "And I'd better start the runs on your combat personnel. You want nearly a thousand guys with demolitions background. We may have to go all the way back to Korea to fill the quota."

"That's fine with me," said Shawcross. "Let's avoid men on active duty, though. The most important qualification here is motivation. We can train them."

"Done," said Wilcox. "What next?"

"I need to start putting my headquarters section together. Good administrators, but with line experience, too."

"How about me? Once my act with the computers is over, where do I fit in?"

"You're important down there," said Shawcross.

"Only while we're pulling files on personnel. Once that's finished, any one of my assistants can handle the maintenance work. I want in, General."

"If you disappeared it would focus suspicion on the computer department," said Shawcross. "If they ever got into those tapes, we'd be through before we started."

"Not if I was on a normal vacation. I've got almost two years to store up time, and I get four weeks a year. If I come in two months early I can be a hell of a lot of good to you."

Shawcross stirred his drink idly with one forefinger, thinking. "Do you know anything about communications, Dick?"

"Not much," said Wilcox. "But I'm a quick study. What do you have in mind?"

"We're going to put together the communications section along about the time you'd be available. You're a good administrator—you don't have to know how to wire up a walkie-talkie. You could organize the section and keep it running. Interested?"

"You're on. If it's not beyond my need to know, when do you plan to go in?"

"I want a sleeping city," said Shawcross. "I don't want any businessmen in town to worry about, and I want as many people out of the city as possible. That means a long holiday weekend. We'll never make it in time for the Fourth of July."

"Labor Day," said Wilcox.

Shawcross nodded. "We hit New York City on Labor Day weekend."

"Karen, I couldn't feel worse about this if you were my own daughter," the Reverend Abner Greenbriar said. "But if you continue to see Gray, you can't work here any longer. I know it isn't your fault, but that doesn't help. I can't take the risk."

"My beliefs haven't changed," she said. "William hasn't tried to convert me to his way of thinking."

"But you are being converted," Greenbriar said softly. "No, Karen, my files and correspondence must remain private."

"Do you think I'd tell him about your private correspondence?" she flared. "What you're saying is you no longer trust me. I should never have told you—William said you wouldn't understand. He's such an unhappy man, Reverend. If he's cruel and hard, it's because that's what life has made him. I have to try to make him happy. I never intended to get so involved with him—I'm sorry."

"I'm glad you told me. And in all events it couldn't have remained a secret."

"Oh, but it must. You have to keep your promise—I told you this in the strictest confidence. If it were known he's involved with a white woman, it could damage his work. You gave your word."

"I'll keep it," said Greenbriar. "But I cannot keep *you*."

She leaned forward and kissed his cheek.

"Goodbye, Reverend," she said.

"God bless you, daughter," the Reverend Abner Greenbriar told the white girl.

"We've got twelve camps set up," Ken Hadley told Shawcross. "Most are small, two-or-three-day stopovers. The two big ones are located here—near Coolidge, Kansas, and Marfa, Texas."

"Good," said Shawcross. "I've got three permanent men for each small camp, plus fourteen for each big one." He looked at the map. "Aren't those main camp areas in pretty isolated country?"

"One-bus-a-day outposts."

"Won't we stick out conspicuously?"

Hadley shook his head. "We're already putting up regular stockade fences. Our cover is a simple one—basic training camps for U.S. Army Special Forces."

"Won't the fact that all the troops are black cause some comment?"

"For one thing, no one will see them, we're way out in the boondocks. If two cars a day come by, it'll seem like a traffic jam. Then, nobody gets inside the main gate —and the guys inside don't get out."

"What about air traffic?"

"There's an abandoned World War II training strip at Marfa. Nothing lands there. As for Coolidge, the nearest strip is thirty miles away, in Lamarr, Colorado. Just a couple of puddle-jumpers a day in and out. None of the traffic goes over our areas."

"How about guards?"

"We use guys white enough to pass," said Hadley.

Shawcross still felt uneasy. "Word of this is bound to work its way back to the district FBI office."

"We know," said Hadley. "That's why we chose these areas over others we might have used. In both cases the head of the district office is one of our men, and he'll shortstop any reports. Meanwhile, our cover lets us carry out the training programs we want. Personnel will come in at night, by bus."

"What if one of the buses gets stopped?"

"In Kansas we have the Air Force Academy in Colorado on the trip ticket. In Texas, we use Lackland Air Force Base at San Antonio."

Shawcross sat down, satisfied at last. "You've got it pretty well thought out."

"Take supplies—food and stuff," said Hadley. "It comes in by truck, marked with authentic Army numbers. We don't try to keep it secret that there are military bases

out there—what we keep quiet is whose bases they are."
He looked at his watch. "Oh, Gray wanted me to tell
you, he's stationing men from his Special Forces on each
of the bases. They'll be in charge of political indoctrination and discipline. Raymond Carpenter will head them
up."

"What do you mean Special Forces?"

"Our police force," said Hadley. "They make sure
security is maintained, take care of non-military discipline
and so on."

"They'd better not interfere with my discipline," said
Shawcross.

"They won't. They report directly to Gray, but of
course they'll keep you advised of any action they're
taking."

"Such as?"

"Such as, what happens if we find one of the men's an
agent? We'd have to make him talk, find out who his
contact was—maintain his reports until it didn't matter
any more. But that's not likely to happen. It's more likely
one of our own men will decide to desert."

"Desertion's a military problem."

"Not in this case," said Hadley. "It's political, because
the deserter endangers the success of the entire mission.
That point has to be driven home."

"Execution?"

"Probably. We're hardly in a position to maintain
prisoners."

"Any executions under my command will be a matter
of considerable discussion between Gray and myself,"
said Shawcross.

Hadley smiled. "I'm sure they will be."

The Christmas holidays were in full swing by the time

the recruitment teams were fully organized and ready to set out. Thirty-five miles past Marfa, Texas, Shawcross drove up to the main gate of Base Camp #1. A sentry booth was just inside the high wire fence. Over the gate was a sign: "Restricted Area. No Admission Without Pass."

The guard, wearing regulation suntans, raised his rifle to port arms and came to attention.

"Brother," said Shawcross.

"Cain," said the guard, relaxing slightly. "I recognize you, General," he said. "We had to memorize the faces of everyone authorized to enter or leave."

The gate swung open and Shawcross drove in.

The lights were out in most of the buildings, although he could see their shapes in the moonlight. They were standard, prefabricated military barracks—single-story buildings that went up in a matter of hours, and had seen service all over the world.

Even the orderly room looked the same as the hundreds of orderly rooms he had seen during his military career. The picket fence and the stones painted white along the path were clichés that made him think for the first time in months of the huge break he had made with his past.

"Tenshut!" called a voice as he stepped inside. Startled, he returned the salute thrown him by a burly man just behind the swinging gate that separated the waiting area of the room from the office space.

"I'm Captain Marvin Hamilton, sir," said the man. He was dressed in neat khakis and wore twin silver bars on his collar. Shawcross looked around the orderly room. Four other men were present, all uniformed and standing at attention.

"At ease," said Shawcross. He stepped through the gate, feeling conspicuous in his wrinkled civilian clothes.

"The main gate warned us you were on your way in," said Hamilton. "Otherwise you would have interrupted a cutthroat poker game."

Shawcross grinned. "Check and raise?"

"You know it, sir." Hamilton turned his head toward one of the men. "Boyle?" The man stepped forward. "Show the General his quarters."

"Sit down, Boyle," said Shawcross. "I'll be with you in a few minutes. Captain, how many personnel on the base?"

Hamilton picked up a black loose-leaf notebook. "Our version of the morning report," he explained. He looked at the top page. "As of 1700, we have twenty-three permanent party and seventy-eight trainees. There's a contingent of thirty-four trainees due around 0200."

"Do you have room for them?"

"General, we have room for at least fifteen hundred right now, and our capacity is growing at the rate of ten barracks a week. By the end of March we'll be able to handle five thousand men."

"How will you feed that many?" Shawcross asked.

"Sparingly," said Hamilton, smiling. "Most of us could stand to lose a few pounds anyway. I understand we probably won't need all that space for a year, but my thought was it wouldn't hurt to have it ready as soon as possible."

Shawcross nodded. "Well, the training program doesn't get under way until the first week in January, so use the trainees for housekeeping work until then. From what I see, you've made a good start."

"Thank you, sir," said Hamilton. "No criticism implied, General, but the specific instructions weren't all that complete, so we've just been winging it."

"Captain," said Shawcross, "that's the name of this operation."

He followed Boyle to a nearby barracks which had

been split into small rooms. At one end, through a single door, was a three-room suite. On the door were two painted stars. The quarters were sparsely furnished but comfortable, and Shawcross nodded his pleasure.

"How about some coffee, General?" asked Boyle. "The mess hall's going late tonight to feed the new guys when they get in."

"Any chance of getting a roast beef sandwich along with it?"

"Seeing you're the General, I wouldn't be at all surprised," said Boyle. He let himself out. Shawcross sighed and lowered himelf into the canvas camp chair. He had left Denver that morning after inspecting the Kansas installation. It was not as tightly organized as this one; he would appoint a new camp commander here, freeing Hamilton to oversee operations at both base camps. Kansas could use his pushing.

Shawcross was bone-tired. He put his feet up on an issue footlocker that sat at the foot of the GI cot and wished mightily for the fifth of Jack Daniels he had left in his suitcase. His concentration apparently worked, for one of the men who had been in the orderly room knocked and entered, carrying his suitcase.

"Put it on the bunk," said Shawcross. "What's your name, son?"

"Jed Miller, sir."

"Where are you from, Miller?"

"Stockton, California."

"How do you come to be here with us?"

"General, have you ever been in Stockton?"

Shawcross shook his head.

"Then you wouldn't know about the canal," said Miller.

The canal that runs through the poor end of Stockton,

California, laps at piers that are crumbled and decaying from age and disuse. The street fronting on the canal is Stockton's skid row.

The draft had gotten Jed Miller off this blighted street; his service in Vietnam won him his corporal's stripes. He considered remaining in the service, but his ambition, awakened by exposure to the world outside Stockton, drove him into accepting his discharge and returning home.

"That was my mistake," he told Shawcross. "They gave me a taste of freedom and led me to expect that because I did a good job over there, things would be better when I got back. That was a bunch of shit. They didn't tell me that when I got home I'd be just another nigger."

Miller worked in a warehouse and lived with his family in the three-room apartment over a meat market that had been his home for as long as he could remember. Most of his salary went into payments for a flashy blue convertible that had already gotten him two suspended sentences for drunken driving. The rest went for whiskey, and when he lost his job, his unemployment checks paid for the cheap wine that was shipped from the Napa Valley in gallon jugs.

And, always, the canal flowed quietly along the edge of the street, less quietly the morning they found Jed's brother Peter floating in the muddy water, his body ripped with knife wounds. Even today hardly a week went by that some skid row bum didn't stumble, with or without help, into the waiting canal.

In the year and a half he had been out of the Army, Miller was constantly in trouble with the law, and when he heard that a stranger in town was asking about him, he stayed out of sight for a day; he surfaced to find the man waiting at the Red Cap Inn, a noisy hangout for workers from the mill.

"Let me buy you a drink," said the stranger, a large black man in a light brown suit. "You're hard to find, Miller."

"Why were you looking?" Miller accepted the beer suspiciously. "Are you some kind of cop? I haven't done anything." This was not strictly true, of course—he had been involved in minor thefts from parked trucks; for all he knew this stranger was investigating them.

"My name is Dan Brody. Don't worry, I'm not a cop."

"Okay," said Miller, "what do you want?"

"How would you like to give Whitey a kick where it'd do the most good?"

Miller stood up. "Mister," he said, "I don't want trouble. I got plenty of that already."

"Do you know Sam Willis? Oscar Peterson? How about Harry Barber?"

"Sure I know them. I went through basic with Barber and Willis. Peterson was in my outfit in Vietnam. How do you know about them?"

"They're part of the deal I'm talking about."

Miller sat down. "What deal?"

Brody shook his head. "I can't tell you much about it, because I don't know myself. But your buddies are already signed up."

"Signed up for what?"

"We're going to bust Whitey. Bust him good. I don't know where or how or even when, but it's going to be something worth doing. Look, Miller, I know all about you. What have you got to lose around here? You don't have a job, you don't even have a girlfriend."

"Let's take a walk," said Miller. "You never know who's listening in here."

They got up and Brody put down a dollar for the beers. Outside, they walked slowly along the edge of the canal.

"This is crazy," said Miller. "You turn up out of nowhere and say, hey, baby we're going to do something I can't tell you about, but you got my word you'll dig the action." He shook his head. "A guy'd have to be crazy to buy that kind of blind deal."

"Your buddies bought it. This isn't any crap, Miller. Stop for a minute and ask yourself why we'd go to so much trouble to look you up. If all we wanted was muscle, we could get that on any street corner."

"That's what bugs me. I'm nobody special. Hell, I can't even drive a car without getting in jail."

"You can do one thing pretty good. It got you a bronze star."

"Blowing bridges? Sure, in the Army, but . . ."

"We need you, Miller," said Brody. "That's why I put so much time against you."

"Demolitions? Jesus Christ, Peterson's a bridge man, too. What the hell are you guys up to?"

Brody shook his head. "I've told you all I know," he said. "You'll get more information as you need it."

"How long will it take?"

"A year and a half. Maybe two."

Miller whistled. "That's a big chunk, man. What would I tell my folks? A cat can't just take off for two years."

"We've got plans set up for that," said Brody. "You can be working out of the country. Or you can be in jail. Or back in the Army. Take your pick."

Miller grinned. "I kind of like being out of the country," he said.

"Then you're with us?"

"Hell, yes. Like you said, what the hell do I have to lose? My curiosities are up. If I got to join up to find out what the hell is going on, consider me a recruit."

Brody held out his hand and Miller shook it. "I'm glad you decided to come in with us," said Brody. "You were on the top of our list. My car's parked over there. Let's get going."

"Hold on, man, I got to pack some clothes and say goodbye to the folks."

"You won't need any clothes. And you can telephone your folks."

"You sure are all business," said Miller. "Okay, why not? It's no crazier than the rest of it. Sure, baby, let's go." As they walked toward the car, he said, "You know, you told me enough about this operation of yours before I said yes to cause a mess of trouble. What if I'd told you to blow it out your ass, and then went and tipped the fuzz about you?"

"You wouldn't have done that," said Brody, opening the door for Miller.

"How do you know?" asked Miller.

"We had you checked out ninety-nine percent before I ever approached you."

"How about the other one percent?" asked Miller.

Brody started the engine and the car moved along slowly, paralleling the glistening water of the canal.

"That's why I carry this," he said, opening his coat to show Miller a .38 revolver strapped under his arm. "If you'd said no, I would have blown your brains out."

"I think he would have, too," said Jed Miller.

"Son," said Shawcross, "he would have had to."

Miller saluted and left. Shawcross went into the bathroom, looking for a glass. He found one and was unzipping his suitcase when Boyle arrived with a pitcher of coffee and a huge roast beef sandwich. Shawcross thanked him, waited until he left, then poured a slug of bourbon into the glass and drank it neat. He rummaged around under his shirts and came out with his planning notebook, poured some coffee, and put his feet up on the footlocker.

Munching at the sandwich, he opened the notebook to the section tabbed "Timetable":

JANUARY-MARCH:	Form demolition teams. Begin training.
APRIL:	Recruit bus drivers and take through indoctrination period.
JUNE:	Begin shipment of arms and supplies to warehouses in and around City.
JULY:	Get drivers employed by Transit Authority and private lines in City. Others take jobs as taxi drivers to learn City.
AUGUST:	Infiltrate demolitions men into jobs connected with bridges, tunnels, telephone company, subways, and railroads.
JANUARY:	Complete infiltration of intelligence personnel into police, civil defense, city government, Con Edison, and water supply.
MAY:	Set up communications network with intelligence personnel in New Jersey, Bronx, Queens, and Brooklyn. Final date for technical people to be infiltrated into studios and transmitters of television and radio.
JULY:	All arms and explosives, plus emergency rations, to be transshipped from supply dumps to safe warehouses in City.
AUGUST:	Organize diversionary action.
LABOR DAY WEEKEND:	STRIKE.

Folded into the notebook were a series of miniature elevations and floor plans of the Empire State Building. Because of its radio and television outlets, emergency generating plant, and central location, Shawcross had chosen it as Strike Headquarters. In addition, the radio and TV transmitters atop the building would enable him to communicate with his own men—and with the city's hostages—by radio and television.

He sat there until after midnight, the bare bulb in the overhead fixture glaring down on his calculations and plans. At last he sighed, undressed, and fell into bed, the light shining directly onto his trembling eyelids.

"There's something funny going on," said Congressman John Alexander Roberts. His guest, who had come to Roberts in an open bid for Negro support in the coming elections, nodded.

"My antennae are out too," he admitted. "Got any idea what it might be?"

Roberts shook his head. "Something to do with Black Power, you can bet on that," he said. "Every time I try to sniff it out, somebody blocks me. This is a hell of a thing to say to a white man, and a Republican at that, but I'm starting to feel like I've lost contact with my people."

"No idea what's happening?" the visitor asked.

"Baby, your guess is as good as mine. Maybe they're working up a vote boycott. Maybe they're getting ready to draft me as a third party candidate. Who knows? But my mammy always told me that when you hear something rustling around in the bushes, just assume automatically it's a cottonmouth, then you won't go reaching in and get yourself bit."

"You fraud," said the visitor. "Your mammy lived in a co-op apartment overlooking Central Park. There aren't any cottonmouths in the Sheep Meadow."

Roberts grinned. "Maybe she meant muggers," he said.

By the end of January, several African nations had requested and received sizable loans from the United States. Thanks to Stephen Harumba, millions of dollars found their way back to the U.S. and into the accounts of the Uncle Tom Flour Company as capital investments. William Gray was able to accommodate most of the requests that came in from his commanding general.

At first, he balked at uniforms. "Who the hell needs them? Armbands and beards were good enough for Castro."

"Shawcross says uniforms are important psychologically," said Kenneth Hadley. "I agree with him. If we run around with armbands, we're a mob. If we wear decent uniforms, we're an army. What is it, the money? I thought we had plenty."

"No," grumbled Gray, "it's not the money. Okay, tell the bastard he can have his uniforms. The next thing you know, he'll be wanting furloughs."

Gray had designed a special marking for armbands and for shoulder patches, based on the flag of Marcus Garvey. They were being made in Nassau by Chinese seamstresses who thought they were symbols for a professional football team.

Through Hadley, Gray kept urging Shawcross to consider larger, more powerful weapons—and his general kept refusing.

"What the hell do we need 75mm guns for?" he growled one evening in the apartment he had taken permanently in the UN Plaza. "We're not bombarding New Jersey. We aren't going to be able to repel a serious invasion—if it gets beyond the skirmishing phases, we've had it."

When Shawcross submitted his final list of arms, it was essentially as he had presented it months before. M-1 .30 caliber carbines made up the bulk of his weaponry, with light machine guns, bazookas, and mortars. The one major addition was the inclusion of five thousand 12-gauge shotguns.

"A shotgun beats a rifle for crowd control any day," Shawcross pointed out. "And when we start arming our irregulars, they wouldn't be able to hit the inside of a barn with a carbine. But it's hard to miss with a shotgun."

The original plan called for various African nations to order the weapons and then smuggle them back into the country. Shawcross objected to the waste motion involved.

"Why ship all that iron around?" he said. "Let's send empty crates to Africa and keep the hardware here."

In practice, it was not that simple. After being cleared through customs, an outgoing shipment of arms was usually birddogged by a CIA man until it reached its destination. Several shipments actually went to Africa, when it was impossible to get a Movement-loyal CIA man assigned to the weapons. But the supply of order blanks was unlimited, and by the end of the first year Shawcross had his beloved carbines stored safely away in warehouses surrounding New York City.

To his surprise, Shawcross made an effective spokesman for Warren Chemicals. He returned from one cross-country tour, which had won him a half-column write-up in the Wall Street Journal, to find Hadley waiting with an urgent message from Gray.

"You're doing too good a job," he said. "Take it easy. The Administration is thinking of offering you a post. They figure if you can sell napalm, maybe you can sell the whole shitty war."

Shawcross was amused, but he took the advice, and after some months the Administration lost interest in his services.

In April Shawcross took a week off from his public relations duties and went to Marfa, Texas.

The camp now held several hundred men, half of whom were being taught to use explosives effectively. Jed Miller, sporting new sergeant's stripes, took Shawcross around the demolition range, pointing out teams of men who were practicing setting charges to blow the roofs of tunnels.

"These tunnels are supposed to be under water," Miller said. "We punch a hole through to the river bed, the water comes in, and no more tunnel."

"Hard to do?" Shawcross asked.

"It's a matter of focusing the blast. Each charge reinforces the shock wave. Let's hang around. In a minute, these guys are going to blow one."

A noncom ran a red flag up a pole over the "tunnel." The demolitions men retreated behind bunkers. For a silent moment the red flag was the only moving object in view.

"Fire in the hole!" yelled the distant noncom. There was a pause, and then a geyser of earth erupted. Shawcross felt the concussion press against his eardrums. For several seconds dirt fell back to the ground, pattering like rain in the desert.

"Not too bad," commented Miller. "Maybe one charge blew a little late. But that shot would have brought the river in."

Shawcross looked at the young man. His face had thinned out and hardened since their first meeting a few months ago. "How do you know it'll be a river?" he asked.

Miller shrugged. "What else could it be? They don't dig tunnels under oceans."

Marvin Hamilton, now a Lieutenant Colonel, had dinner with Shawcross.

"How are things over in Kansas?" Shawcross asked.

"Coming along," said Hamilton. "We've gotten in our first batch of drivers. Give them a two weeks' refresher and we'll move them out."

"Good. We've set up a central employment bureau in New York for the men to report to on arrival. Delta Employment, 125th Street and Amsterdam."

"General," said Hamilton, "I'm starting to put two and two together, and it adds up to trouble for New York City. But are you really going to turn a couple of thousand men loose in the city carrying what they know about us in their heads?"

"Nobody's going to get out of line. They'll be watched."

"By the goon squad?"

"The what?"

"Those Special Forces of yours." Shawcross started to explain that they weren't his forces, then held his tongue and listened. "They're a mean-looking bunch all right. Half of the trainees come out of their first goon indoctrination wetting their pants."

"Better a few hard words now than a knife later," said Shawcross. "I hope we don't have to go that far, but no one man is going to jeopardize this operation."

"I hope you can keep them under control in New York," said Hamilton.

"There's no choice," said Shawcross. "We've got to infiltrate our demolitions men into certain jobs. Our bus drivers have to drive those streets. By the end of the year, we'll have guys in every part of city government—the police department, even Con Edison."

"In other words," said Hamilton, "you're going to take over the city."

"How many others know besides yourself?"

"Ken Hadley and I see the broad picture—we know what's going on all over the country and we can add it up. I hope no one else."

"My G-4 only knows about the supply operation. G-2 is building up his Intelligence plan, but his picture isn't complete either. I don't have any G-1 yet—you've been sort of handling that administrative end for me. How would you like to take it on full time?"

"I will if you order me to," said Hamilton. "But I know at least three guys who would do a good job for you in administration. I'd prefer the other slot you have open."

"Which is that?" said Shawcross.

"G-3, operations. I think I'm your best bet for number-two man. And I've got my fingers on some damned good number-three guys, all with combat behind them."

"You've got it figured out, haven't you?"

"That's why you hired me."

"Okay, Hamilton, I'll think about it, but I had a few candidates of my own for the job. Whatever happens, there's a top spot for you when we start moving."

"I couldn't ask for anything fairer. Except maybe a little information. You're going to take the city—what I'd like to know is why."

Shawcross smiled at Hamilton. "Back in 1777, a batch of New England slaves petitioned for justice, and the governor of Massachusetts spit in their eye. Our siege of Manhattan is the same petition, but this time they're going to listen. We're using guns instead of paper."

Hamilton shook his head admiringly. "It has class," he said. "I don't think we got a chance in hell of pulling it off, but it sure does have class. But why do you call it a siege? We're taking and holding, not blockading."

"It's a siege from within. Once we take up our positions we're holding New York prisoner until the United States agrees to our terms." He reached for the whiskey bottle. "Now what do you say we pay a little visit to our friend Mr. Daniels?"

He was pouring out the bourbon when the door opened and a man in a sports jacket barged in.

"Who the hell are you?" growled Shawcross. "Don't you ever knock?"

"Sorry," said the man. "I was in a hurry."

"This is Raymond Carpenter," said Hamilton. "I thought you knew him, he's in charge of Special Forces."

"The forces are political," said Shawcross, embarrassed. "They're not under my command." He held out his hand. "I've heard a lot about you, Mr. Carpenter. Now, what's the trouble?"

"We've got our first deserter, General," said Carpenter. "We caught him down in Marfa about an hour ago, lushing it up in a bar with a Mexican waitress. He's in the orderly room."

"How did he get off the base?"

"Over the fence. General, will you muster the men while there's still daylight?"

"What for?"

"To witness punishment."

Shawcross got up slowly. "It sounds to me like the man was AWOL," he said. "If he were deserting, he'd have gotten a hell of a lot further than Marfa."

Carpenter shrugged. "It makes no difference to me. No one leaves this base under any circumstances for any reason. The penalties were clearly spelled out during indoctrination, and the noncoms have repeated them often enough. Colonel Hamilton, you're in charge of these training camps. Haven't you briefed General Shawcross on our operation?"

Hamilton shook his head. "Sorry, General, but I thought you knew all about it. As far as I knew, the Special Forces were under your direct command."

"It's not your fault, Hamilton," said Shawcross. "Get the troops formed. Mr. Carpenter and I will be out in a few minutes."

Hamilton left, and Shawcross turned to Carpenter. "What do you intend to do?"

"Execute him."

"Without a trial?"

"He was found off the base. He admitted going over the fence."

"It's serious, I agree," said Shawcross. "But look at it this way—in a couple of months, we'll be turning these men loose on their own in New York. We'll have to rely on their secrecy then."

"If the men see they can get away with violations of security in training, they'll continue those violations when they're free agents."

"I see," said Shawcross. "You needed this incident, didn't you? If it hadn't happened, you would have had to create it." He sat down heavily.

"General," said Carpenter, "you are so right. Now, I work for the same man you do, and this is the way he wants it. Let's cut the shit, okay? My orders are to step on any deviation fast—and that's what I'm going to do." He turned to go. "Now, are you coming out there with me?"

Shawcross felt numb. A year ago he would have picked this little man up by the seat of the pants and thrown him out the window. "All right," he said. "Let's go."

The sun was a red ball on the horizon when he got to the flat field in the center of the barracks complex. The shadows were long and the men's uniforms were touched with gold.

Two civilians stood in the center of the field. Between them, hands tied behind his back, was a tall Negro. He wore uniform pants and a flowered sports shirt.

Hamilton and two other officers stood near the men. Carpenter took a bull horn from one of them and lifted it. "I am Raymond Carpenter," he said. The flat echoes of his voice bounced off the barracks. "I am in command of the Special Forces which enforce political discipline. Our army is a small, outnumbered force. To succeed, we must be ten times as good as Whitey. We must maintain the element of surprise or everything we are working for will be destroyed. We need one hundred percent security. Not ninety-nine percent, not nine hundred ninety-nine out of a thousand, but *perfect* security. One lapse can destroy us.

"Because this man wanted a drink of whiskey, he risked everything. His crime is against all of us. He is a traitor, and he will be dealt with like a traitor."

He put down the bull horn and nodded to the two Special Forces men. They shoved the bound man down on his knees, and as his eyes met those of Shawcross he called out.

"General," he cried, "don't let them hurt me. I'm sorry, I won't never do nothing like that again, I just got so hungry for a little piece of pussy. . . ." He tried to scramble up to his feet; the two men roughly pushed him down again.

"You wouldn't let them shoot me over a little thing like that!" he pleaded.

Carpenter stepped up behind the man and took out a .38 revolver. As he heard the hammer click back, the condemned man shut his eyes tight and rocked back and forth, moaning. A dark stain spread down the leg of his khaki pants as his bladder emptied.

Carpenter fired the pistol into the back of the man's head. The shot made a flat *crack!* The man spun forward and smashed into the hard-packed desert sand. One leg was still twitching when Carpenter fired a second bullet, into his ear.

The assembled troops let out a soft groan. One man in the front ranks slumped. Shawcross tensed his cheek muscles and swallowed hard.

Carpenter was talking through the bull horn again. "There is no room in this movement for weaklings or traitors," he shouted. "This man was lucky. He had no family. He alone was shot. But if he'd had a family, they would have been executed, too. Remember that. You may get away, but your family can't hide. We've got men in every part of the country. An hour after you turn up missing, your family's dead."

Shawcross heard the men grumbling in the ranks and thought, Carpenter's gone too far now. But he was wrong.

Carpenter held up one hand. "I know that pisses you off," he called. "All right, I don't blame you. But remember, we aren't out to hurt you or your family. We're trying to protect the security of this operation. Keep us out of danger and you'll keep yourself out of trouble." He put the bull horn down and turned to Hamilton. "Dismiss the troops," said Carpenter.

Carpenter and his men moved off.

Shawcross looked at the crumpled body, face down in a widening smear of blood.

"You'd better organize a burial detail," he told Hamilton.

"I'm glad you could get down here, honey," said Eloise Gibson. "I missed you."

She and Shawcross were sitting in the suite provided by the Hotel Pennsylvania management during her engagement in Philadelphia.

"I missed you, too," said Shawcross. They had been drinking champagne, but the fun had gone out of it and now they sat quietly, talking, and looking out over the Philadelphia skyline.

"You act depressed, baby," she said.

"I guess I am," he told her. "I'm just so goddamned sick of pain and killing."

She touched his face. "I thought you left that behind in the Marines."

"So did I," he said, disturbed that he had been on the verge of telling her about the execution at Marfa. He indicated his forehead and said lamely, "It's just that it's all still up here. You can't leave it behind."

"I know just what you mean," she said. "It's a living wonder what you can stuff inside a head and still function. I tell myself over and over that I've left South Carolina back there in antiquity—and then something conjures up a memory and suddenly I'm there again, the same barefoot pickaninny limping stone-bruised to school in that one-room building."

"It was better in California," he said.

"Better? Or different?"

He shrugged.

"Let me tell you about *my* California," she said.

"I'll pour us some champagne first," he said.

He did, and she began.

"I finally got my big break in the late forties. Man, was I dumb. I thought I was going to be a star. I didn't get straight until I had this big biff with my director.

" 'I'm not objecting to the song,' I told him. It was a little funky, but I could have gotten through it. The trouble was, it wasn't hooked up in front or behind, and when I told the director this he finally leveled with me.

" 'Okay, Eloise,' he said, 'I don't know why I have to tell you the facts of life. You grew up in the South, you know what things are like down there.' "

"What does the South have to do with a song in a Hollywood movie?" asked Shawcross.

Eloise laughed bitterly. "That's what *I* asked," she said. "And baby, he laid the truth on me. The reason the song wasn't connected up was so the local distributors could edit it out without hurting the rest of the movie. How about that? There I was busting my ass to get that funky song right, and all the time the whole plan was to cut it out below the Mason-Dixon line."

"I never heard of such a thing," said Shawcross.

"Oh, it wasn't just me. Lena Horne and Ethel Smith went the same route. And you couldn't blame it on the poor director. He didn't *have* to put me in his movie. It just brought him a lot of grief. The poor man was trying. And in the long run, I don't have any complaints. It all worked out in the end. And the times have changed."

"That they have," said Shawcross.

"These days," Eloise went on, "casting agents get a fifty buck bonus for every new black face they can turn up for TV commercials. Do you know, with residuals you can end up making ten or fifteen thousand dollars for one day's shooting? It's too bad I'm over the hill for playing housewife."

"Are you?" he asked.

The tone of his voice made her breath catch in her throat. She looked at him to see if he was joking. He did not smile.

"Stanley," she said softly, "don't mess around with me. When you talk like that you better be serious."

He touched her hand. "Sorry," he said. "I wish I could be serious. Maybe one day soon I can be."

"I'd like that," she said.

In late August, Mayor Clifford Pearson, agonizing over a third set of budget revisions, was visited by his Deputy Mayor, Ben Jacoby.

"You won't believe this, Cliff," said Jacoby. "There seems to be a groundswell of Negroes moving into the city."

"Oh, won't I?" said the Mayor. "Let me show you the welfare rolls, and you'll see how easily I believe it."

"That's not the kind I meant. I've been getting reports from all over. The Transit Authority. The Bridge and Tunnel Works. Even Con Ed. All of a sudden, they're getting job applications—and from pretty damned well-qualified Negroes. Even the Police Department got lucky —they've never had so many good men to choose from."

"Well, I'll be damned," said Pearson.

At summer's end, the first phase of the training program was completed. The demolitions men, the drivers who had to learn New York City, the intelligence personnel who would infiltrate key spots in and around the city, had all been processed through Marfa and Coolidge. Except for a few permanent party men, the bases were empty.

During the summer there were four executions at Marfa and three at Coolidge, all for desertion. One man from Marfa got away completely. His only living relative, a sister in Milwaukee, was run down seven hours later by a milk truck.

Recruitment was suspended for several months. The next contingents would be line troops who had already received their basic training, courtesy of the U.S. Armed Forces. A two-week refresher course would put them in shape.

Operating under cover of a sales convention for the Uncle Tom Flour Company, Ken Hadley leased an entire wing of a Holiday Inn Motel on the outskirts of Denver.

Shawcross flew into the mile-high city Friday afternoon, the 3rd of September. He picked up a Mustang at Avis and made the short drive to the motel. "I'm with the Uncle Tom Flour people," he said to the desk clerk.

"Any relation to Uncle Ben?" It was a gag Shawcross had become used to. "Sure," he said. "He's married to my Aunt Jemima." The clerk laughed. "Welcome to Denver, Mr. Shawcross."

Shawcross smiled, then headed for the bar, where he joined Pete Humble. "Hey, it's good to see your ugly face, man," said Pete, holding out his hand. "How's Eloise? You treating my little girl all right?"

"She's fine. I saw her down in Philadelphia a couple of weeks ago, packing them in as usual."

Humble ordered a beer and leaned forward. "I hear from the big boss that you're doing real fine," he said. "Not that it surprises me. You got the cut of a man who does good at anything he takes a mind to. And Eloise backs that up."

"Look, Pete," said Shawcross uneasily, "I never went after her."

"I know you didn't, man." The comic laughed. "Those are the breaks, and believe me, I'm not mad. I've got all the nooky I want. Not that she wasn't something special, but shit, I wasn't going to marry her or anything."

"I might," said Shawcross. "After this whole thing is over and if we come out of it."

Humble sobered. "Don't talk like that, Pops. Everything is going to fit together like a jigsaw puzzle. Don't go gloomy on a nice day like this."

Shawcross grinned. "Okay," he said. "Tell me, how's the professional nigger business?"

By eight that evening the entire sales force of the Uncle Tom Flour Company had arrived. In addition to Shawcross and Humble, William Gray was there; so were Raymond Carpenter, Kenneth Hadley, Richard Wilcox, and Marvin Hamilton.

With waiters in attendance, dinner conversation was limited to such veiled comments as "How are things going in your area, Mr. Hamilton?" and "I'd say they're slow right now, but we expect them to pick up early in the year."

But when the coffee was drunk and the room cleared

of outsiders, two electronics men went to work. The meeting place had been chosen at random and kept secret until hours before the rendezvous; Gray thought a security leak unlikely. The electronics men made a thorough sweep anyway, and in ten minutes reported the room free of bugs or recorders. When they went off to explore the bar, the door was closed and blocked with a chair.

Gray stood up. "Everyone knows part of what we're doing," he said. "Some of us know it all. Up to now, we've been playing it pretty tight. But it's time the rest of you in this room were filled in.

"You all know I've been preaching separation, there's nothing new about that. What's new is that now we're doing something about it. This country has fed off our flesh and bones for three centuries. While our black hands were building this nation, our black mouths were eating crusts. Well, payday is coming. Every black man, woman, and child in this country is going to get what's owed him."

Flushed, he drank a glass of water.

"I've had this dream for years," he said. "We are going to have ourselves a new nation. And it isn't going to be in some lousy climate, or some wilderness without industry, or anyplace else that Whitey might give us or want us to be. They can keep Alabama and Georgia and Mississippi, what we want is right in the heart of things. Right here—" and his finger stabbed at a map of the United States—"in the industrial northeast.

"Our new nation is going to have factories and farms and raw materials and highways and deep-sea ports. And it's going to be big enough to accommodate us all, those who start with us and those who come later. It's going to be big enough to take in every black man, woman, and child in the United States, and maybe even some of those who've been passing as white."

His finger jabbed the map again. "This is the state that

is going to be our nation. Whitey calls it New Jersey."

"I'll be goddamned," said Pete Humble.

"Now," Gray went on, more quietly, "what makes me think Whitey's going to let us have this new nation? We've seen what his lousy justice is like. And Whitey certainly isn't going to give this to us out of the kindness of his heart. We've seen the kindness of his heart. No sir, we are going to *make* Whitey give us what we want." He pointed dramatically at Shawcross. "And the General here has shown us how."

He pulled down another map. It was a topographical drawing of the island of Manhattan.

He pointed at the Empire State Building. Planted atop it was a tiny flag, red, green, and black. "This is where Whitey lives—in his pocketbook. What the General has planned out for us is an armed seizure of the island of Manhattan." His hand slapped the paper. "Whitey's real Fort Knox. Once we hold it, he has *got* to bargain, because we'll be sitting smack dab on top of his pocketbook, and that's the pressure that squeezes where it hurts. We'll have his banks, we'll have the records and nerve centers of his big businesses, and most of all, we'll have half a million honkey hostages in case anyone starts waving their bombs around."

He stood silently, breathing hard. His eyes went from one man to another. No one spoke.

"That's it," he said softly. "We're in the final months of our preparations. This is the black man's redemption at last." Almost as an afterthought, he said, "We'll call our new nation Redemption."

TWENTY-THREE

As winter approached, Shawcross spent more time in New York. He had chosen Hamilton as head of G-3, Operations, and the two men spent hours walking along the edges of the island, taking notes and photographs. From the cliffs of the Harlem River, down through Washington Heights, all along the Hudson to the very tip of the island at the Verrazano Statue in the Battery, they covered every foot of the West Side—not once, but a dozen times. Then they worked up along the East River, past Hell's Gate and Randall's Island and back to the narrow channel of the Harlem River.

"You know," said Hamilton, "we're going to have to put troops shoulder to shoulder up here. Hell, they could swim guys across."

"I planned a static force," said Shawcross. "Figure three thousand regular troops and around two thousand irregulars. One in four'll be armed by us. The rest will have to use anything they can get their hands on—axes, kitchen knives, anything. We'll assign some heavy machine guns and a couple of dozen bazookas. But my bet is they won't want to hit us in strength."

The two men spent a morning in Central Park. "They could get choppers in here pretty easily," Shawcross said. "We've got to figure some way to slow them down."

They walked around the park, locating landing sites: the Great Lawn behind the Metropolitan Museum of Art, the Sheep Meadow, the Heckscher Playground on the southern third of the park. To the north, above the reservoir, was another danger area.

Hamilton indicated the edges of the park—on the west, high apartment buildings lined Central Park West; on the east, even higher ones ran along Fifth Avenue. "We can get some pretty good fields of fire from those windows," he said. "If we put the landing spots in a crossfire, it'd at least be expensive for them."

"Automobiles," Shawcross said suddenly.

"What?"

"We own every car in New York once we come in. Give a bunch of the draftees a ten-minute course in jumping ignition wires—hell, they could probably teach us—and then we run every car we can find into the park and jam up those landing areas. The cars'll keep out any short-field stuff, and they'll make the choppers hover instead of sitting down. That'll delay unloading and give us a better crack at them. It might even keep them from trying at all."

"We ought to be able to get four or five thousand cars in there in a couple of hours," said Hamilton.

"That'll do it," said Shawcross.

"It's going so smoothly it makes me uneasy," said Gray, sipping coffee with Stephen Harumba in the UN cafeteria. "The laws of chance, if nothing else, ought to be giving us a few problems. But we're right on our time-table, and things look good for the OAU to start putting pressure on the United Nations."

"That, too, is progressing nicely," said Harumba. "I had a meeting with Secretary-General Kogan, and almost gave the poor fellow apoplexy. I would say that we could call for a vote in the middle of May. And we can put many strong voices behind a motion of censure. You can be sure the Soviet Union and her bloc would be delighted to join in."

"Good," said Gray. "We want to get the machinery established so that if a provisional black government should be formed and call for help, the UN will be in a position to act."

"Ah," said Harumba. "This is the way you choose to tell me your secret? Casually over a cup of coffee? But what are you up to? You could never mount a major campaign with the equipment we have helped you get. And your activities will, of necessity, be confined to the Eastern seaboard, probably to the New York area."

"Oh?" said Gray.

"It is simple," said Harumba. "I have traced most of your shipments to warehouses in and around the city. Circumstantial, but clear. Now, to form a provisional black government, you will need a power base. Otherwise the federal troops would simply scoop you up and take you off to prison. Therefore, Mr. Gray, I have come to the conclusion that you intend to take over this very island of Manhattan, by either infiltration or force, and hold it as the center of your new government."

"Close enough," said Gray. "We are going to hold Manhattan until the Administration will listen to reason."

"What do you call reason?"

"We want the state of New Jersey. Lock, stock, and barrel."

"Lock, stock? What does that mean?"

Gray grinned. "It means we want the whole state and everything in it, everything but the white population, that is. They'll have to move somewhere else."

"But how can the government give you such a thing? There must be billions of dollars in private property involved."

"That," said Gray, "is the government's problem. They

can reimburse the whites, for all I care. All I want to do is walk in and take over a going concern."

"You are an amazing man, William Gray," said the African. "Do you seriously believe you can bring this miracle to pass?"

"I do," said Gray. "And *when* we do, it will be because of our friends outside this country—such as yourself. Without you, we wouldn't have a prayer."

"You have our prayers," said Harumba with a smile, "and also our guns."

"I got away," Ed Burgess told the chubby prostitute as he sat on the edge of her bed in San Diego. "Those murdering fuckers killed my sister Jenny, but they never caught up with me. Do you know what they was teaching us to do in that camp?"

"No, baby." The woman yawned.

"Blow up bridges. And tunnels. They said we was going to give Whitey a shot he'd never forget."

"What's wrong with that?"

"Nothing's wrong with it. Hell, you think I got any white friends? It was just the way they treated us—like machines."

Burgess got up and poured out a large shot of Four Roses. He took a healthy swig himself, directly from the bottle.

"Don't kill it, honey," the woman said.

"I paid for it, didn't I?" He handed her the glass. "Hell, a man's got to have a drink once in a while. That's what started it all. Do you know, one cat just went downtown for a drink and a screw, and they drug him back and blew out his brains right in front of us. Well, after that, anyone who took off, he was going all the way. But they got them all. Except me. I got clean away, but they run down Jenny with a milk truck."

"Maybe it was an accident," said the woman.

"No, they told us they'd do it. I didn't believe them."

"Well, next time you will."

"There ain't going to be no next time," said Ed Burgess.

The woman propped herself up on an elbow, trying to decide whether or not to believe this wild story. "Maybe you ought to tell the police or the FBI or somebody."

Burgess sighed and picked up the bottle of Four Roses. "Shit," he said, "who'd listen to *me?*"

The woman made up her mind and pulled the sheet up. "Nobody, honey," she said.

In Spanish Harlem, rookie policeman Jim Matthews walked his beat, swinging his night stick the way he had been taught in Police Academy. He nodded at the store-keepers, who already knew his face. Some of them smiled him inside on cold mornings for a cup of coffee laced with rum.

High in the Empire State Building, William Ferns made final adjustments on the color balance of a program being transmitted over the NBC network, live from New York. Although he had been with the company less than six months, Ferns had made remarkable progress, and tonight he was in virtual command of network facilities.

In City Hall night watchman Jim Clemens made his rounds, testing doors and using his master key to open offices for inspection. Not even the mayor's private bathroom refused to yield to this super key—a fact well known to Clemens, who made it a point to use only that particular toilet.

Joe Kid, a wizard on the complicated switchboard that linked emergency telephones to police headquarters at Broome and Centre Streets, sipped coffee and listened to the endless mumble of police dispatches.

Walking across the Williamsburg Bridge to Brooklyn,

Mike Lewis looked at the heavy steel cables with an appraising eye. He was a member of the bridge maintenance crew, charged with keeping its approaches clear and generally aiding the flow of traffic.

"Throw in Number Six Generator," yelled Jack Walker, acting foreman at the Kips Bay Station of Consolidated Edison, just four blocks south of the United Nations headquarters on Manhattan's East Side. The heavy turbines whirled, and electricity surged into the hungry cables to feed the city.

Fifty feet under the bed of the Hudson river, halfway through the Holland Tunnel, Pete Dundee saw a sleek sedan change lanes illegally. He jotted down the license number, reached into the back of his little booth, and picked up the telephone there. The air was heavy and full of exhaust fumes; he was glad his two-hour tour of duty was almost over.

"I can't help it, lady," said taxi driver Joe Fields. "I'm lost. This is my first haul into Greenwich Village, and any place where Tenth Street crosses Fourth Street is just too much for me. Look—I'm turning the meter off. Now maybe we can ask that cop for directions."

"Go down two blocks and turn right," the cop told him. "Watch out for Leroy Street—it's one way the wrong direction. And next time find out where you're going. You're blocking traffic."

"Yes, sir," said Corporal Joe Fields of the Afro-American Army of Liberation. He did not know he was speaking to Private Jack Thompson, of the same underground force. By now the city was filled with black volunteers, holding down jobs that ranged from policeman to television technician. They reported regularly to an answering service that passed along instructions and kept tabs on their whereabouts; they were spot-checked by the movement's Special Forces, but so far there had been no instances of broken security.

But, as William Gray had speculated, the law of averages always catches up sooner or later.

It happened on New Year's Eve, less than twenty minutes before the lighted ball came down the pole on top of the Allied Chemical Building. Fred Allison, from Toledo, had been given the evening off from his job as assistant traffic manager at the Thirtieth Street Railway Terminal. Since his training at Coolidge and his transfer to New York, Allison had been a model of deportment. With time to kill, he decided to go to Times Square for the year-end festivities. He had seen the frantic crowds before, the searchlights sweeping over them, the signs waved in hopes that their friends would see them on television—but only on his seventeen-inch Philco back in Toledo.

Allison inched his way down the Broadway sidewalk, blinking up at the spotlights. The wind whistled around the corners of the buildings as the minute hand on the huge clock crept around toward the magic midnight mark. Allison waited patiently, hands jammed into his pockets. The crowd was huge. The raucous sound of paper horns filled the air. Someone loosed a balloon, and as it drifted over the crowd, people leaped up, trying to catch the string. It floated over near Allison; feeling for a moment the happiness and gaity of the occasion, he leaped up and caught the string in his right hand. For an instant both his feet were off the sidewalk: a surge in the crowd, like a great human tidal wave, rippled toward him, and several bodies crashed into him. He let go of the balloon and fell backward. The back of his knees hit the window ledge of a store, and with a startled yell he crashed through the large pane. He was lying in the wreckage, dazed but unhurt, when a forty-pound sheet of glass parted from the top of the window molding and fell—a mindless guillotine—cutting through the cloth of his work shirt and severing his jugular.

The screams of people in the immediate area were indistinguishable from the joyous shouts of celebrators, and by the time a policeman was located and dragged over to the gory window, Fred Allison had bled to death. It was midnight and the lighted ball had made its yearly descent before his body, stiff from the cold, was removed.

"Accident," said the police sergeant assigned to the detail. "Poor guy got pushed through a glass window. Never had a chance. DOA."

"There's something funny, though," said his partner, leafing through Allison's wallet. "This one hasn't a scrap of identification."

"A lot of them don't," said the sergeant.

"Wait a minute, here's a phone number."

Fred Allison, unsure of his memory for numbers, had—against orders—written down the number of the answering service.

"Might as well give it a try," the sergeant said.

The policeman dialed the number. "This is Patrolman Schneider of the Police Force, ma'am. We're investigating an accident—no, a man who was killed in Times Square this evening. No, I don't know who he is. He was carrying your number in his wallet." A pause, and then he said, "Well, I wouldn't want to give out those details until we knew if there was a connection between this man and your company . . . I see. All right, and thank you very much."

He hung up the receiver and frowned. "That was an answering service. No help at all."

The sergeant chewed on the end of his pencil. "This

guy didn't look like an actor or anything fancy," he said. "He was just a working slob."

"So?" said his partner.

"So what the hell would he be doing with an answering service?"

William Gray got the news less than half an hour after the police called the service. He was sharing a bottle of champagne with Karen at her apartment when the phone rang.

"It's for you," she said, her voice strained.

"For me? How the hell—" He took the phone. "Hello?"

"William? This is Raymond."

"How did you get this number?"

"Never mind about that now," said Carpenter. "We've got some trouble."

"What kind of trouble?"

"The phone service had a call from the fuzz. They said someone had an accident in Times Square, and he was carrying our number."

"Who was it?"

"Apparently they don't have an ID yet, but my hunch is it's one of our troops, and he's dead."

"When will we know who it is?"

"Tomorrow, when he doesn't report in. We're going to have to set up another service, of course. Hell of a lot of trouble, but this one is blown."

"You're right," said Gray. "Get Davis and Parker moving on a new setup. Have it wrapped up by six in the morning, so when the troops start calling in they can get the new number. And for Christ's sake pass the word— nobody's supposed to be carrying that damned number around with him."

He hung up the receiver, a heavy frown on his face.

"Who was that?" said Karen.

"Raymond Carpenter. He's working on a project with me."

"All about troops and a secret telephone number?"

Gray felt his heart sink. He had completely forgotten her presence. He tried to remember what he had said.

"Just talk, baby," he said. "We've got a little demonstration planned, and the fuzz got onto our private telephone number."

"And how did your friend get onto this one? Did you give it to him?"

He shook his head. "Not me, sweets."

"I thought our relationship was a secret," said Karen.

"Don't bug me, honey," said Gray. "I don't know how Ray found out I was here. Maybe he took a guess."

"And just happened to dial my unlisted number?" said Karen.

"What are you getting so upset for? Are you ashamed of me?"

"I mind because it can hurt you," she said quietly. "How would it look to the world if the ultramilitant William Gray who hates everything white were revealed to have a white mistress?"

"I don't keep you," he flared.

"Do you think anyone would really make the distinction? How do you explain it to them, William? Or to yourself?"

"You're worried about *me?*" said Gray angrily.

Karen put her arms around his neck. "William," she said, "I'm not attacking you. But how can you sleep with me and still say the things you do about the white race?"

"I don't see you as white. You're a piece of ass." He stopped at the door, and added, "Not a very good one!"

He threw open the door and left.

In the empty bedroom, Karen lifted a half-filled glass

of champagne and looked out the window. In the darkness of the night it was starting to snow.

"Happy New Year," she said.

Fred Allison was identified through his fingerprints. Notified of his death, his family flew to New York and created a good deal of commotion.

"Fred was a good boy," said his mother, "and I just know he got mixed up in something funny. Why would he come to New York and work for the railroad? His daddy has a dry cleaning plant in Toledo, and we needed him there. He told us he had this job that would take him out of the country, and for a long time we got those postcards from Panama City. How could he be mailing us postcards from Panama City if he was in New York?"

That was a puzzle, agreed the New York City Police Department. But Panama City was out of their jurisdiction, and they were primarily concerned with the corpus of Fred Allison. Had his death really been accidental? They decided to pay a personal visit to the Washington Answering Service on 125th Street.

The manager, a slim Negro with an earnest smile, seemed anxious to help. No, they had no record of a Fred Allison as a subscriber.

Satisfied, the police departed, and when the Allisons of Toledo, Ohio, took a train back to that city with their son's casket riding in the baggage car, the case was put down as accidental death.

"One less spade for the mayor to worry about," said the duty sergeant.

On the morning of January 1st, Gray shut the door of his private office and whirled on his visitor.

"Carpenter, where do you get off putting a tail on *me?*"

"They're a protection detail. Your love life was of no

interest to me until I had to get hold of you in a hurry. It still isn't, except for the obvious parallel with poor Laurie. I hope you don't decide to get rid of Karen the same way, there's not enough good gash in the world to go around pushing it out of windows."

Gray stared at him. "How the hell did you know about me and Laurie?"

Carpenter shrugged. "She told me, before she took the dive."

"What else did she tell you?"

"Nothing. Look, if you want to fry a little white meat, it doesn't make any difference to me."

"Okay," said Gray, his anger subsiding. "You had your reasons. But now I'm in one hell of a position. What *do* I do about Karen?"

Carpenter laughed. "Shit, man—keep her. Except if you get tired of her, let your buddy move in instead of heaving her off a bridge."

They nodded to each other and got back to their work.

"Put our honorable mayor right up there on top of the list," Gray said. "If we have to make an example of a hostage, that bastard's going to be the first to go. He's been giving the black man in this town a hard time ever since he got in office."

"How about foreign legations, UN delegates?"

"We give them safe passage to the UN area," said Gray. "We don't want trouble with any foreign power."

"The Mafia uncles are staked out," said Carpenter. "We grab them Thursday night and Friday morning, before they head for the Catskills."

"There's a chance the Vice President will be in town over the weekend," said Gray. "He'd be a fine lever to use."

"Done," said Carpenter. "I'm going to have to take over

a hotel to put this bunch up in. Let's go first class and grab the Americana. It'll be easy to guard."

"Okay, but you'll need troops from the regular forces for that. You don't have enough men."

"I've already got a request in with the General for two dozen troops with a couple of machine guns." said Carpenter. "We'll use his forces for general security. I'll take care of the hostages."

"I'm sure you will," said Gray.

"That's the batch," said Richard Wilcox, handing a bulky folder to Shawcross. "Fourteen thousand names and addresses, every man a prospect. Their attitudes are right, and so far as our checks go, they're clean. Still, you'll probably wind up with an agent or two, it just isn't feasible for us to run a Number One depth study on fourteen thousand men."

"Fine," said Shawcross. "We'll start moving them in around the end of July. Even if there is an agent among them, we'll make sure he doesn't get off the base. Once we're in the city it'll be too late for him to do much about it."

"Which brings me to a certain promise you made me over a year ago."

"I haven't forgotten it. When can you start?"

"June fifteenth," said Wilcox.

"Where are you going to stash your family?"

"Toronto. Some friends own a cabin on a lake near there, and I've rented it from June through November. By then everything should be settled.

"Here's what I've planned so far. We'll use commercial radio for any blanket message that everyone ought to get. The police emergency phones all hook in through a central switchboard at Centre Street, and we'll use them to talk back and forth. You'll have mobile radios with every major unit, to talk and receive from central communications.

"As for Bell Tel, I recommend we knock them out of business. Too much risk of calls getting out of the city if we don't. I don't like the idea of federal troops in New Jersey being able to ring up a spotter in the city and ask how are things going. Finally, we want to hear from our intelligence forces outside the city about enemy troop movements. We can do it with Mark Four transceivers. One of my engineers tells me he can beef them up so they'll have an effective range of thirty, forty miles. Strictly against FCC regulations, of course."

"Good work," said Shawcross. "How soon can you try them out?"

"Tomorrow morning," said Wilcox.

TWENTY-FOUR

In May, Stephen Harumba addressed a session of the General Assembly of the United Nations.

Speaking for a coalition of twelve African States, Harumba said, "Our African brothers in America are a kidnapped people, held in slavery and poverty. This is no domestic issue. It is a world issue. The government of the United States has openly refused, time and time again, to free our brothers from oppression. It is time to stop talking and start doing. I call upon this assembly to create a commission to investigate the condition of the Afro-American minority in the United States."

The proposal was voted down, but it created pressure on Washington to move more aggressively in the civil rights arena. Measures which the President had sponsored months before, only to see them languish in committee, came to life and were rushed through both Houses. But these measures came too late. The black forces were moving.

Equipment and supplies stored for months in receiving points around the city were now trucked into Manhattan late at night—rifles, bazookas, mortars, and millions of rounds of ammunition.

The airwaves crackled with radio hams testing their new equipment. Dick Wilcox was pleased to learn that his Mark Four transceivers could reach Manhattan from as far away as Princeton, New Jersey.

In the police stations, in the bus and subway terminals, in the studios and transmission facilities of radio and television studios, the shuffling of duty rosters began. Negro volunteers came forward to work the long weekend shifts over Labor Day, delighting their white co-workers.

"I feel itchy," Shawcross said to Marvin Hamilton. "It's out of my hands now. They pull it off or they don't."

"That's the old football coach syndrome," said Hamilton. "Half an hour before the game, the coach gets that sinking feeling and realizes that if the team's not ready now, it never will be." He smiled. "I've got a touch of it myself. It must be catching."

Two weeks before the Labor Day weekend, Shawcross was walking along Third Avenue when a voice called his name. He turned and almost collided with Clarence Dewey.

"Corncob!" said Shawcross. Dewey was in uniform, wearing colonel's eagles. "And a bird colonel yet! Has the army lost its mind?"

"Let me buy you a drink, Pappy," said Dewey. He hit Shawcross a stout blow on the shoulder with his right hand. Shawcross looked at it, and a grin split Dewey's face. "Yeah," he said, "we took a chance on the nerve graft. I got back my dice-throwing hand again."

He led Shawcross into the nearest bar and ordered for the two of them. "They jumped me over a couple of hundred seniority points," said Dewey. "You'll never guess what I'm doing. I run the whole damned tactical effectiveness section in the Pentagon. New weapons, training procedures—even combat methods—they all come through me. How do you like them apples?"

"I'd say they couldn't have found a better man," said Shawcross.

Their drinks came, and Dewey raised his glass. "Pappy," he said, "it's good to see you. I've thought a hundred times about that crummy argument we had. I think it was just the liquor talking."

"Forget it," said Shawcross. "Are you living in Washington?"

"Right in the middle, Niggertown, U.S.A. If you think Harlem is bad, you ought to take a look twenty blocks from the White House. For Christ's sake, if they can't straighten out the Capital, how do they expect Mississippi to make any progress?"

"What's the general attitude in Washington?" asked Shawcross.

"About the quote Negro Problem unquote? Mostly, I think they wish we'd just shut up and go away. You know, I kept thinking about what you said—I mean, about black casualties and so on. If the troops are thinking like that too, it sure as hell isn't doing much for morale—and that affects combat effectiveness. So I started a pilot program. I sent letters out to a couple of thousand Negro combat veterans—a questionnaire, to find out what they really think now that they're out from under military discipline and can speak honestly."

Shawcross tensed. "What was the result?"

"It's the kookiest thing," said Dewey. "Those letters are bouncing back like rubber balls. I'm having a hell of a time finding most of those ex-GIs. It's like every black man who served in Vietnam has dropped right off the face of the earth."

"Your man Dewey isn't the only one coming up with questions," Gray told Shawcross. "My contacts tell me there are FBI men rooting around all over the country. Can we move up the timetable any?"

"Not possible. We just can't go in next weekend. Half the troops would never get in from the training camps in time. Our men in the city would be working the wrong shifts—we wouldn't be able to get the air strike I need . . . no, it can't be done."

"But what if they blow the whistle on us?"

"We go on with our plans and hope they don't. There's nothing else we can do. Some of the troops are already scheduled to leave the camps three or four days early."

"I don't like it," said Gray. "Too damned many things can go wrong."

"There's nothing we can do except wait," said Shawcross.

"We'd better stay away from each other for the rest of the time. I'll see you at the Empire State Building."

"Right," said Shawcross.

In San Diego, Ed Burgess came to the attention of the FBI. Special Agent Ron Condon was called into the district supervisor's office. "There's a man down on Alvarado Street who's shooting off his mouth about an armed Negro camp somewhere in Texas," he was told. "It's probably nothing, but you'd better check it out."

Condon set off in search of Ed Burgess, and finally caught up with him in a third-rate bar near the beach. Since Condon was a Negro too, and dressed in rough work clothes, it did not take him long to strike up an acquaintanceship with his quarry. Three free whiskies later Burgess reeled off his story, which had gotten more elaborate with each retelling.

"They came to me in the night," he said, "and made

me swear, on my dead mother's grave, I was loyal to the movement."

"What movement is that?" prodded Condon.

"The black movement. They said this was my chance to get back at Whitey. They said, 'We can't tell you what it is—but we'll tell you this, what you know about demolition won't be wasted.'"

"Demolition?" said Condon. "What do you have to do with demolition?"

"Shit," boasted the other man, "I won a silver star in Korea. And they had the names of other guys I knew in the Army. Frank Paulson, Nate Richards—they'd signed up. Paulson was a tech sergeant in my outfit."

"What outfit was that?" said Condon.

"The Twenty-fourth Division," said Burgess. "What'd you say your name was?"

"Ron," said Condon.

"Well, Ron, they took me to this big army camp, out in the desert."

"An army camp? Are you sure?"

"Hell, yes, I'm sure. It had guards and barracks and an orderly room. When I got there, one of those mother-fucking Special Forces guys in civvies told me this camp and everything in it is a military secret. If you go AWOL we'll catch you and kill you. And we'll kill your sister Jenny, too. Well, I didn't believe him. But one guy got caught. They tied his hands behind his back and he was hollering to the General to stop them, but the General just looked at him—and then the little shit in charge of Special Forces stepped up and blew his brains out right there in front of us.

"Man, that shook me," Burgess said. "I knew I was in the wrong pew for sure. So I made my plans, and when I went over the fence, I hitched me a ride and got to El Paso. I tried to call Jenny a couple of times, but when her phone finally answered it was the landlady, and she told me Jenny was dead, a milk truck run over her."

"That big camp in Texas—where was it?"

"I guess near El Paso."

"In which direction?"

"East, I reckon," said Burgess.

"This general," said Condon. "Was he a white man?"

"Black as the ace of spades," said Burgess. "Everybody at the camp was blood."

"What was his name?"

"Never heard it," said Burgess. "Everybody just called him the General. He was a great big bastard, looked like he'd been through it all."

"Did he wear a uniform?"

"Sure. All of us did."

"What else do you remember about him?"

Burgess scratched his jaw. "Nothing," he said finally. "I mean he really was a general, and I didn't have nothing to do with him."

"Some of the men there must have had names," Condon said. He was having a hard time keeping his tone of voice casual.

"Oh, sure. I remember Jed Miller—he was a buck sergeant—training us in shaped charges. You know, to blow out tunnels."

"Who else do you remember?"

"Oh, just guys."

Condon took out his identification, showed it to Burgess.

"I'm an FBI agent. I'd like you to come down to the office with me and tell your story to my boss."

"I'll be damned," said Burgess. "You mean you believe me?"

"Sure," said Condon, wishing he did not, "I believe you."

At the door Burgess stopped and said, "Hey, I just thought of something else about the General."

"What?"

"He always wore two hand grenades clipped to his belt."

Condon looked at his watch. It was twenty after four on the Thursday afternoon of August 28th. He sighed; he had been planning to go down to Mexico over the long weekend, but now it looked like overtime work for sure.

TWENTY-FIVE

In the middle of the night, the telephone on William Gray's night table jangled. He picked it up. "Hello?"

"This is Phillips," said the voice on the other end. "We've got trouble." Phillips was his Washington contact for government bureaus.

"What's up?"

"The FBI picked up a stew bum in San Diego. Claims to have been spirited away to a mysterious black power camp somewhere in Texas. He's shooting off his mouth like a machine gun."

"Did he mention any names?"

"He didn't know the General's name, but it'll take about two minutes for anyone to figure out who's the black General who wears two hand grenades."

"Anything else?" Gray looked at his watch; it was almost one in the morning."

"They know the base is near El Paso. As soon as it's daylight, it'll only take a spotter plane a couple of hours to locate it. I don't know if the CIA's got anything. Harper hasn't reported in yet."

"What the hell is the CIA doing in the act?"

"They started sniffing around after Harumba made his

UN speech. It's a big secret—the FBI doesn't even know they're around."

Gray immediately dialed Shawcross' UN Plaza number. The General answered on the second ring.

"General, do you recognize my voice?"

"Yes," said Shawcross. "What's up?"

"Marfa's been located. Spotter planes will probably go up at first daylight. You'd better get out of your apartment fast, and let me know as soon as you're in the clear. Meanwhile, how do I get in touch with your Number Two? No names."

"He's at the main base," said Shawcross.

"Okay," said Gray. "Now for Christ's sake, get moving."

He hung up, dialed the direct number for the Marfa base. A slow voice answered. "Four hundred eighteenth Provisional Headquarters, Sergeant Clifford."

"Clifford, get Colonel Hamilton on the phone."

"Yes, sir." The receiver was dead for several minutes and then Hamilton identified himself.

"Do you recognize my voice?" asked Gray.

"Yes, sir."

"There's been a leak. Get out tonight. The same goes for Camp Number Two. Get your men here in the smallest groups possible, preferably by private car. Don't travel with them. They may be stopping black faces by morning."

Chester Shoemaker, a CIA man who had let himself be recruited for the Afro-American Army of Liberation, had been waiting for a chance to break away.

By August 24th he was almost desperate enough to go over the fence. Then his barracks was mustered.

"We've been keeping this quiet," said the barracks chief, "but we're moving out early."

Half an hour later they were aboard a bus. A few miles from camp they passed through a small town. Shoemaker strained his eyes and managed to read the sign that said Marfa, Texas.

He and forty-seven other men lived in the bus for the next four days until they unloaded at last in a delivery zone behind a factory in White Plains, New York. There they were split into groups.

"Get into New York by train," said their sergeant. He gave the leader of each group a slip of paper with an address on it. "Memorize it and then tear it up."

Shoemaker tried unsuccessfully to glimpse the address on the paper his section leader tucked into his breast pocket. He followed the other three men cautiously through the early morning streets to the White Plains station, where they boarded a train. The men watched each other warily.

"Where's the john?" asked Shoemaker. One of his companions got up. It was the group leader. "Me too," he said.

Shoemaker looked out the window. The train was slowing for a curve. He stopped suddenly in the aisle, and the group leader collided with him. Shoemaker chopped him across the neck with the side of his hand, then grabbed his breast pocket and tore the cloth away. As the other two men rose and moved toward him, he sprang to the door at the end of the car, slid it open, and entered the vestibule. Hands ripped at his clothing as he leaped over the metal partition. He landed in the cinders of the roadbed, tumbled several times, and smashed against a lineman's shack. The other men did not follow. Shaking, he got to his feet. The torn shirt pocket with its folded wad of paper was still clutched in his hand. He opened it,

244

smoothed out the paper and read, "Harrison Warehouses, 684 West 139th Street."

He limped down from the railroad right-of-way, his clothing torn and blood glistening on one cut knee. A few hundred yards along the highway he came to a weather-beaten roadside diner. As he entered, the counterman looked up.

"Hey, what happened?"

"Car wreck," said Shoemaker. "Can I use your phone?"

"Sure, sure," said the counterman. "Right back here."

Shoemaker sat down and carefully dialed the code series that would connect him directly with CIA headquarters in Washington.

He noted the time: 8:36 A.M. of Friday, August 29.

"No, we don't know what's up yet," said FBI Special Agent Gene Bolt. "We've made a fast check, and those GI buddies of Burgess are nowhere to be found. Meanwhile our El Paso field men are checking to see if this base actually exists."

"Who's in charge of El Paso?" asked the FBI Director.

"Doug Evans," said Bolt.

"Evans is a Negro."

"So what?"

"Replace him."

"But he's one of our best men!"

"Get it out on the teletype. Evans is to report to Washington immediately."

"Yes, sir, but I think you're wrong about him."

"I hope I am," said the Director. "But until this thing is resolved, I want no black agents in positions where they might distort or eliminate reports. Am I understood?"

"I understand. After ten years you've just decided that Doug Evans is nothing but a nigger."

"I'll forget you said that," said the Director, Florida-born Arnold Paulson.

"I won't," said Gene Bolt.

It was 9:25 A.M.

"He's a dependable man, sir," said Eric Maxwell, regional commander of the CIA. "I'd act now without verification."

His superior officer, Henry Sanders, said, "Chester Shoemaker's file shows he was involved in quite a bit of trouble during his service days."

"We knew that when we hired him," said Maxwell. "Anyway, he says they were training him at this military camp in street-fighting techniques." Maxwell paused. "Shoemaker thinks his training indicates a takeover of some sort, perhaps an armed insurrection."

"Ummm," said his superior. "Eric, who do we have near Marfa?"

"Our setup in El Paso is closer," said Maxwell. "But if we use a man out of San Antonio, he can borrow a jet from the Air Force at Randolph Field."

"Get him moving," said Sanders. "If there is a base that size near Marfa, it'll certainly be visible from the air. Meanwhile, get Shoemaker down here right away."

"What about this address in New York? Shoemaker says it's only one of dozens. Shouldn't we move in?"

"Put a couple of men on that address if you want— but no incidents," said Sanders. "Let's confirm Shoemaker's basic story first. Congress is sure death on this racial thing now."

By now, of course, the FBI was already aware of the existence of base camp #1. Their spotter plane, taking off at dawn from El Paso, had radioed its location, size, and the fact that it appeared to be deserted.

FBI District Supervisor Douglas Evans, ordered to return to Washington, vanished mysteriously en route. It was then discovered that field agents had been aware of the base but their reports on it had never been forwarded to Washington.

As for the CIA, they had only the unsupported word of a field agent to go on.

They had already stretched their interpretations of international intelligence considerably to investigate the militant blacks after Harumba's UN speech had pointed up the link between black nationalism and Africa.

Had their information been added to that already in the possession of the FBI, immediate action against the warehouse at 139th Street would have been taken. But since neither group was cooperating with the other, action was postponed—while the leaders of the Afro-American Army of Liberation took frantic measures to preserve the security of their operations.

By the time the CIA received confirmation of the existence of the Marfa Base, it was 11:41 A.M.

"The West 139th Street Warehouse is blown," Ken Hadley told Shawcross. The two men were at their posts in temporary base operations headquarters, a suite of hotel rooms on West 128th Street. "A CIA plant got loose and contacted Washington—he took the warehouse address from his group leader and jumped off a train. The leader was smart—he reported in as soon as he got into the city, and they emptied the place out in less than an hour."

"So the weapons are safe," said Shawcross.

"Safe enough. But there's a couple of hundred guys roaming the streets with instructions to report there tonight. By then, you can bet your ass the CIA'll have the place staked out."

"Can we head them off?"

"How?"

By six that evening Shawcross received word that most of his forces had reached the city safely.

Meanwhile, the annual rush of massed humanity from the city had started. Automobiles jammed the bridges and tunnels. The American Safety Council predicted six hundred fifty traffic fatalities for the long weekend, and pleaded hourly on radio for caution in driving and moderation in drinking.

The oppressive heat of the city broke slightly, and a light breeze came up. Hundreds of thousands of city dwellers, whites and Negroes and Puerto Ricans who had neither intention nor means to leave the city, spilled out into the parks and onto the doorsteps of their slums. Pillows and mattresses were spread on fire escapes. Beer cans popped and young girls laughed softly.

At the southern tip of Long Island, where Brooklyn meets Rockaway Inlet and Lower New York Bay, Coney Island was jammed with more than a million holiday revelers getting a last taste of the sun before they would crowd themselves into coin-operated locker rooms and their sunburned bodies into flowered sports shirts and tight slacks.

Among the million sightseers, no one had any reason to notice the arrival, in small groups, of several hundred Negro men who were quieter, more intent, more purposeful than the throngs around them. The diversionary force got itself into position carefully and waited for the signal to act.

In Washington, Henry Sanders decided to move in on the West 139th Street warehouse. He coordinated the CIA action with the New York City Police Department.

The warehouse was empty. There had obviously been frantic activity just hours before, and apparently the unknown forces had left in a hurry. Behind one closet door was a recent edition of the Hagstrom Map of New York City. Coney Island was circled with red.

"It figures!" said Sanders, who was telephoned directly from the warehouse. "Another riot."

Word was passed to other branches of the government.

"Yes," Sanders said patiently to the Director of the FBI. "We've just confirmed it with a raid on a warehouse in New York. Members of a Black Power militant group have been training for a riot in Coney Island."

"Indeed?" snapped Paulson. "And what does your information say about demolition activity?"

"Demolition? We don't know anything about demolition. What's that got to do with this?"

"Precisely what we'd like to know," said the FBI man. "If you'd bothered to check with us this morning, you would have learned we had already located that secret camp in Texas—"

"Now just a minute," said Sanders. "We've had this group under observation for months."

"If that's so, why don't you know about the demolition training? For your information, the men put through the Marfa camp were demolitions experts. Apparently this Coney Island thing is going to be bigger than you anticipated."

"We were looking into that aspect of it," Sanders said, but his voice lacked conviction.

"I think I had better bring this to the attention of the President," Paulson said.

It was already 6:19 P.M.

"Those ungrateful bastards," said Mayor Clifford Pearson, flipping his cigarette into the fireplace of the office he kept at Gracie Mansion. "That's what happens when you try to be fair."

His Commissioner of Police and Police Chief Phillip Mason listened, embarrassed.

"Christ knows I've leaned over backward," said Pearson. "I've taken their side against the overtaxed white middle class. I've fought for better housing, for jobs, for urban redevelopment. I've tried to tear down the slums, I've started training programs, I've opened Little City Halls in Harlem—and now this! If I had the legal power, I'd move every one of their black asses back to the cotton fields."

Mason coughed. "The question is, sir, what do we do now? The FBI is convinced there's going to be a riot in Coney Island tonight."

"Does the goddamned FBI have to come to me and tell me my city's getting ready to go up in flames? And why Coney Island?"

"It's bursting at the seams tonight. My advice is to shut it down and evacuate, otherwise a hell of a lot of people may get hurt."

"I can see how that would look to the Daily News. They're already giving it to me twice as hard as they ever did to poor John Lindsay. No, we can't evacuate. Can't we go in and bust its back before it happens?"

"The Chief is already pulling men in from as far out as Flushing."

"Well, how about Manhattan? This will be a ghost town in another couple of hours."

"I try not to let the city get too thin," said Mason.

"The city's deserted!" said the Mayor. "Get your men out where they're needed."

"But the merchants insist on protection over a long weekend like this."

"Screw the merchants, that's what they carry insurance for. Get those men out there and head off this thing—now."

"Ordinarily I'd agree with Mason," said the Commissioner. "But these are extraordinary circumstances. Certainly the most important thing is to avert trouble in Coney Island. There are over a million people out there right now. The situation is explosive."

How explosive, none of the men in the room really knew.

It was 7:48 P.M.

"I share your concern," said the President, to the Director of the FBI. "But unless the governor of New York calls us in, this is not a federal matter."

"Those potential rioters crossed state lines. That makes it federal."

The President shook his head. "Not in my book, Paulson. Lately there's been an inclination to federalize everything. Your guys were in here the other day trying to convince me to lock up half a dozen crooked union leaders because they used telephones that could be connected with receivers in another state."

"Mr. President," said Paulson, "we're not just talking about sniping. They have trained demolitions experts with them."

"I know, and that disturbs me. I've already sent the Vice President up to organize the investigation."

"With no disrespect meant," said the FBI man, "the Vice President's experience isn't for this kind of thing. Let me pull in men from our regional offices."

"I hate to keep saying no, but this is out of your jurisdiction. Action must be taken by local authorities."

"If we hadn't uncovered it, there wouldn't be time for any action by local authorities."

"You think I'm making a mistake," the President sighed. "Well, maybe I am. But as long as I sit in this chair, the

FBI is never going to be a super police force with powers that override local government."

"Yes, sir."

Paulson left without saying goodbye.

The President shook his head and pressed a button on his desk. "Barbara, did you get that call through to the governor of New York?"

"I'm sorry, sir. It seems the governor is in Alaska, shooting bear."

The President choked back a gust of laughter. "Put the call through the command circuit," he said. "Have the Air Force track down the great white hunter and set up a direct communications link."

"Yes, Mr. President."

The door opened without a knock. It was Paulson again. The President looked at him, annoyed.

"What is it?"

Paulson nodded his head toward the other office.

"It just occurred to me, sir," he said, "that during this crisis it might be advisable if you had Miss Taylor placed in a less sensitive spot."

"GET OUT OF HERE!" the President bellowed.

The FBI man, startled, stepped back. "But why, sir?"

"You grubby little Napoleon, you heard what I said! Don't open your mouth, don't say one more goddamned word or I'll lay my hands on you, and if I lay my hands on you one of us will wind up in the hospital. Get out of this office and don't come into it again unless I send for you!"

In the nine years Barbara Taylor had worked for him, this was the first time anyone had ever reminded him she was a Negro.

It was 8:12 P.M.

Ben Gates had been off the air for forty-five minutes,

and was enjoying a cold martini at Rattazzi's when an assistant found him.

"Ben," said the boy, "we've been looking all over for you."

Oh-oh, thought Gates, seeing his easy weekend fly out the window onto East 48th Street. "What's up?" he sighed. "Have the Chinese invaded Hawaii?"

"No joke, Ben. Harrison wants you to get out to Coney Island."

"What the hell's in Coney Island except a million sweaty tourists?"

"A riot. We've got the camera and the tape recorder in the car."

"What kind of riot?"

"Black Power."

"Oh, shit," said Gates. "Another one of those."

The driver meshed gears, and the heavily laden Volvo moved off into the nearly empty streets.

"The word is they've got machine guns and high explosives, the whole bit," said the boy.

Gates looked at him, surprised. "If that's true, what are you so damned happy about?"

"It'll make a great story, won't it?"

"Yeah, it'll make a great story. If you live through it."

He sat in the Volvo, his head on his chest. The car turned down Park Avenue and headed for the Queens Midtown Tunnel.

It was now 9:01 P.M.

Raymond Carpenter looked at his watch. In a few hours it would be too late to stop the attack.

"You're making a big mistake," said the fat man who sat with his hands cuffed to a water pipe in a West Side basement. "A mistake we are willing to overlook. Turn me loose now and I give my word we'll forget the whole thing. Johnny Green makes a promise, he sticks by it."

"Maybe Johnny Green does," said Carpenter. "It's John Genelli I'm worried about."

"What do you want with me?" Green/Genelli asked. "Is this a heist? You want the boys should buy me back? How they gonna make a payoff if you won't make contact with them?"

"Maybe we don't want money," said Carpenter, enjoying himself.

"Then what is it?" said the fat man. "A piece of the action? Up in Harlem, I could understand that. But this is midtown. There aren't any of your boys down here."

"You'd be surprised," said Carpenter. "Now why don't you just take it easy? I'll let you know what we want when it's time for you to know."

"You're bucking the wrong outfit," said Genelli. "The brotherhood won't sit still for something like this."

"Like kidnapping all the uncles in New York?"

The prisoner looked at him in disbelief.

Carpenter nodded. "We've got every one of you except Scarpo. He's shacked up in Puerto Rico, and we couldn't lay our hands on him. We took his wife instead."

"All of us?" Genelli was white-faced. "You're out of your skull."

Carpenter shrugged. "It wasn't so hard."

"You got to be kidding," said Genelli. "We don't want no heat with you blacks. But every uncle in town? That means war—you know that, don't you?"

"When the war starts, you may be surprised to find out which side you're on."

It was now 9:38 P.M.

Stephen Harumba moved gracefully through the Embassy ballroom, paying his respects to honored guests from a hundred nations.

254

The plan behind the reception was to keep most UN delegates in the city until their holiday escape was cut off. There had been grumbling among the wives, but their career-minded husbands had recognized where their duty lay.

Russia was represented, and so were France, the United States, and Great Britain.

A number of prominent newsmen were present, along with dozens of celebrities, among them Eloise Gibson and Pete Humble.

Harumba had every intention of keeping the party going until the island was isolated. That meant a very late supper and dancing. He had prevailed on the Soviet Ambassador, without giving reasons, to remain until at least four A.M. As senior ambassador at the party, he would make it difficult for lesser dignitaries to leave earlier.

"Keep them off the streets," Gray had warned. "We want to be sure they're still in the city, but we don't want any of them getting hurt."

From now on, no incoming telephone calls would be accepted. The guests would be kept isolated from the outside world.

It was now 9:42 P.M.

"You can't afford to be out of contact for even an hour," the President told the governor of New York on the radio-telephone. "I've authorized an Air Force jet to pick you up at Ladd Air Force Base. But if the situation should call for federal troops, you've got to authorize your lieutenant governor to call them in."

"That won't be necessary," said the Governor. "Even if New York City can't handle it, we've still got the National Guard."

"I'm only saying *if* federal aid is needed," said the

President patiently. "You ought to prepare for any eventuality."

"I'll keep in touch," promised the Governor.

"Damn it, that's not enough. I want you to give full powers to John Moss."

"He *has* full powers when I'm away, that's what lieutenant governors are for."

"You're wasting time. I have him patched in now."

"Hello, Jack," said a third voice.

"Moss? Is that you?" asked the Governor. "How are things back there?"

"Who knows? The FBI is swarming all over Albany."

"Well, I'm on my way back. I'll see you in the morning."

"Good," said Moss. "Meanwhile—"

"Authorize him to call in federal aid," interrupted the President.

There was a pause. "I don't think I could do that, not with the incomplete information I've got now. Moss, you do what you think you have to. I'll see you as soon as I can."

"Hello?" said the President. "Governor?"

A new voice came in. "This is Captain Shute, sir. The Governor is getting aboard an L-5 that just landed."

"Thank you, Captain," said the President.

"That buck-passing son-of-a-bitch," said John Moss.

"My sentiments exactly," said the President.

It was now 9:48 P.M.

Shawcross had changed into well-worn khakis and was now adjusting the two shiny grenades. "How's it going?" he asked.

"We've got Sectors One through Five on the line," said Wilcox. "Something's interfering with Sector Six.

They're over behind the roller coaster, and maybe all that metal is hashing their transmission."

"Any sign of opposition?" asked Shawcross.

"One hell of a lot of cops reported converging on the area."

Marvin Hamilton, who had arrived from Marfa by a circuitous route through San Francisco, was struggling into a borrowed uniform to replace the one left somewhere in the Texas desert.

Ken Hadley was on a line with William Gray. "Everything's on schedule," he said.

Shawcross consulted his watch, checked it against the Western Union clock on the wall.

"One minute," he said. "Are the lines still open?"

"Sector Six just came in," said Wilcox. "They had transmission failure. They're using the backup transceiver now."

"Stand by," said Shawcross.

"Stand by," said a dozen voices into telephones and radio transmitters. On the wall, the second hand crept toward the end of the last minute of peace left to New York City.

Shawcross had ordered firing for effect only, but he was too realistic to expect that order to be followed. In a few seconds, people would start dying.

"Thirty seconds," he said.

"Thirty seconds," repeated the chorus of voices. "Stand by."

"Fifteen," said Shawcross.

"Fifteen seconds," said the voices.

"Ten."

"Ten."

"Five."

"Five."

"Four. Three. Two. One."
"SHOOT!"

Ben Gates smiled his professional smile as the floodlights were turned on at the edge of the Coney Island boardwalk. The cameraman signaled; Gates cleared his throat and lifted his microphone.

Far above him, there was an almost noiseless *pop!*

Ben Gates fell dead with a .30 caliber steel-jacketed bullet in his brain.

It was three seconds past ten P.M.

TWENTY-SIX

While echoes of the first shot fired at Coney Island were still bouncing off the walls of the Bobsled Ride, thousands of men reported to assembly points in Manhattan.

Kenneth Hadley risked half a dozen men in civilian clothes to head off the two hundred who were scheduled to report to the warehouse on 139th Street. Most were successfully turned back. A few got through and walked into the waiting arms of the authorities.

Their interrogators were anything but gentle. Several rebels broke down in minutes and told what little they knew. The captives were taken to the nearest precinct house, on West 143rd Street, and booked for vagrancy.

In Coney Island itself, the diversionary force concentrated on shooting out street lights and throwing hundreds of cherry bomb firecrackers into air shafts and parking lots. The holiday crowd fled screaming into the water, where three more casualties occurred. Mrs. Louis Goldthorpe, from Far Rockaway, dragged her twin sons into the surf, in an attempt to escape the turmoil on the beach. A wave knocked her down, and when she came up, gasping, one of the twins—young Morton Goldthorpe, aged three—was gone. Mrs. Goldthorpe began to scream, but the throngs paid no attention to her.

Nesbitt Kasinow, a retired salesman, stepped into a deep hole, twisted his ankle and, held down by his water-logged clothing, drowned.

The third victim was young Bruno Ferrieri, a champion swimmer on the YMCA squad. When he heard someone in the darkness calling for help, he kicked off his shoes and trousers and set off in the general direction of the shouts, toward a sixteen-foot sailboat, the *Silky II*, becalmed at the entrance to Rockaway Inlet. He suffered a sudden cramp, cried for help, and disappeared under the waves.

Under orders from the Mayor to avoid an open confrontation with the rioters, the police concentrated on isolating the area. Anyone who wanted out was passed through the police lines; no one could enter.

The police set up a human barricade along Surf Avenue, preventing the shouting crowds from pressing inland. Thousands ran along the beach and crowded into Manhattan Beach Park. Other thousands jammed their way into the New York Aquarium, where some fainted from heat prostration.

By eleven-thirty, although the booming of the cherry bombs could still be heard, Chief Mason was receiving encouraging reports from his field officers. The rioters were making no attempt to break out of their perimeter. Direct exchanges of shots between them and the police were few.

Patched in on the command link between Centre Street and Coney Island, Mayor Clifford Pearson sounded pleased. "I told you, Mason. Keep the pressure on—they'll break by morning."

To Albert Grant, the entire day was unreal. Bussed to Newark from Coolidge, Kansas, he arrived tired, dirty, and hungry. He and five other black soldiers had been given their rendezvous point and sent into Manhattan to kill time until ten P.M. that night.

They pooled their money and had a giant spaghetti dinner on Forty-second Street, then holed up in a triple-feature movie for the rest of the day. By seven P.M. even the staunchest among them was heartily sick of *The Revenge of the Night People*, and they left the theater to wander in the garish neon dusk of Times Square.

The night was hot and humid. Hands reached out to them from doorways, plucking at their sleeves, urging them to come upstairs for a little fun. Two male prostitutes, both black, camped for them, running fluttery hands through their slick hair. Albert Grant had to be restrained from punching one who offered to blow him right there in the darkened doorway.

The crowds were elbow to elbow, and the six men had a hard time staying together. There was a flurry of panic when one man was missed—but he was found inside a cubbyhole of a bookstore, leafing through a nudist magazine which showed the hairy pubics of men and women in full color.

"Shee-it!" he said, when pulled back out on the street. "Never saw nothing like that in the Akron drugstore!"

The neoned windows of the bars beckoned them.

"How about a beer?" said one man.

"No dice," said the leader.

"Why not? It might be our last chance for a while."

"Okay, but no more than two apiece."

They went into one of the brightly lit, neon-and-chrome-decorated bars and crowded into a red plastic booth. A blowsy waitress came over.

"What'll it be, boys?" she asked.

"Six beers," said the leader. The waitress flounced

away, and he passed around their last pack of cigarettes. "Hold the talk down," he said. "We don't want to attract any attention."

The beer came and vanished quickly. They ordered a second round.

"It's just like shipping out for Vietnam," said Grant. "I got the same hollow feeling in my belly. I mean, when it's the real thing, you know it."

As the time for their rendezvous came around, they walked west toward Fortieth Street and Eleventh Avenue, pausing at the bus station to pick up their suitcases. The men fell silent now, each walking in the privacy of his own thoughts.

It sure don't seem real, thought Private Albert Grant, foot soldier in the Afro-American Army of Liberation.

"Of all the guys to kill!" roared William Gray. "Ben Gates! Just about the only TV commentater on *our* side!"

Shawcross, on the other end of the line, said, "Those things happen. It could have been worse."

"What's the situation so far?"

"The police are getting overconfident. When Phase Two pops thirty minutes from now, it'll shake them up even more."

"What are our chances?" Gray asked.

Shawcross laughed. "Getting better every minute."

Hadley came on the line. "There's a shitstorm brewing in Washington," he told Gray. "The President is in the act already. I'd look for federal intervention before morning."

"Just so they all head for Coney Island," said Gray.

"Here's another juicy bit, the President sent the Veep up to look things over."

"Where's he coming in?"

"Newark," said Hadley. "Any minute now. Then he's going to take a chopper to the Pan Am Building and scoot up to Gracie Mansion to chin-chin with His Honor the Mayor."

"Let's hope he decides to spend the night," said Gray.

The radio and television stations went on the air at eleven P.M. with live coverage from the scene, relayed by microwave and cable from the beach area.

Walter Cronkite appeared for a few minutes on pool coverage, carried by all three networks. He spoke of the breakdown in communications between the races as a "national disgrace," apologized for any part the news media might have had in fanning the flames, and pleaded for wisdom and forebearance on the part of whites and blacks alike on this hot August night.

"Ben Gates would not have cried for vengeance," he said. "Ben was an honest man with a unique sense of reality. In a case like this, I know he would have said what I am going to say. Pack it up, take it home, cool the violence, and let judgment prevail in the morning."

Stephen Harumba had sneaked away from his guests to catch the news broadcast. It begins well, he thought. He went back to the party radiating good will and hospitality.

At Stewart Air Base, nearly a hundred miles away, Air Reserve pilots drank coffee and checked their watches against the official clock on the wall.

"Hell of a time for a training mission," grumbled one pilot.

"Sure is," agreed a pilot near him, rubbing one finger against his black cheek.

"I'll be go to hell," said Albert Grant, crouching in the

gloom of the warehouse on West Fortieth Street. "Here we get our asses shanghaied, sweat our balls off in the desert for a month, haul freight all the way across the country to New York, go through this cloak and dagger act of tapping on doors and saying 'Joe sent me,' and this is what they put us to doing." He bent closer to his work so he could see how the stitches were lining up. "Shoulder patches, for Christ's sake!"

In this and a hundred other Manhattan warehouses, men were crouched over needles and thread, affixing the red, black, and green insignia of the Afro-American Army to their khaki shirts.

"Wearing that patch may keep some trigger-happy sentry from shooting a hole in your burr head," one noncom said to Grant. "So fasten it on good."

It was now after ten P.M., but the unventilated warehouse was still stifling hot.

"You know," said Grant as he held up his shirt to admire the patch, sewn on with a delicately interlaced cross-stitching he had learned in the Combat Engineers, "Whitey's right about one thing."

"What's that?" asked the man next to him.

His teeth gleaming in a grin, sweat streaming down his neck and pooling in his armpits, Grant said, "Niggers do stink—especially you!"

"Have you had any word from the Mayor?" the President asked John Moss.

"Not a peep," said the Lieutenant Governor. "He's hacking it on his own so far."

"My reports are that there was some sniping."

"One TV reporter got killed. A couple of flesh wounds and that's about it. There's been a lot of shooting but damned little hitting."

"Still," said the President, "I'd certainly keep the National Guard on the alert."

"I've got the 411th and the 318th both standing by. I can have them moving in thirty minutes."

"You know, Moss, sometimes I wonder why you're not the Governor instead of our friend in Alaska."

"Well, sir," said the Lieutenant Governor, "lately I've been sort of wondering that myself."

"This is terrible," said the Reverend Abner Greenbriar, watching his television set. "What set it off?"

"I heard a cop shot a black child," said a secretary.

"You always hear that. Does anyone have any hard facts?" No one answered. "Then we can assume the cause is unknown," said the Reverend. "Well, there's no help for it. I've got to get out there."

"No, sir," said his assistant. "This isn't just brick-throwing. There are snipers up on the roofs, and they're shooting everything in sight."

"That's not what it sounds like to me," said Greenbriar.

"But Ben Gates—"

"That good man," Greenbriar said softly. "Why did it have to be him? I'd vow it was an accident. The blood would be running in the gutters if they actually wanted to kill people." He took the cup of coffee someone handed him. "What's been the official reaction to this so far?"

"The TV said police were being drawn in from all over," one of the women said.

"I checked with the Deputy Mayor," said the assistant. "No one can get to His Honor."

"Get back to the Deputy Mayor, then," said Greenbriar. "Tell him I'm on my way out there, and if he can have a prowl car pick me up and clear the way it would help. I'll tie a white handkerchief to my radio antenna.

I'll be on the Prospect Expressway, and then Ocean Parkway."

"Yes, sir," said the assistant.

Greenbriar gulped down the rest of his coffee and went out the door, waving back those who wanted to accompany him.

"Stay here, stay here," he told them.

Although the night was hot and humid, Greenbriar felt a chill.

It never ends, he thought.

The Vice President fought down a moment of vertigo as the wind whipped the tiny helicopter over the edge of the landing pad and he stared down at the converging steel pillars of Manhattan. The helicopter righted itself and made a smooth touchdown on the Pan Am building roof.

"Sorry, sir," said the pilot. "The wind gets pretty rough up here for these small babies. But you ought to fly one of our scheduled ships."

"I'll do that," promised the Vice President. The wind knocked his thirty-dollar hat off his head and sent it over the edge into the night. He grimaced. "Try burying that on the expense account," he muttered.

The Deputy Mayor was waiting inside. "Good to see you, sir," he said. "The Mayor asked me to pick you up."

The swift elevator ride to street level, the police-escorted drive up Park Avenue, the sirens clearing traffic, the screeching stop in front of Gracie Mansion—all took less than ten minutes, and left the Vice President nervous and twitchy. He was escorted into Pearson's private office, which was crammed with temporary communications equipment. The Mayor met him with a firm handshake and a mumbled apology.

"Had to stay on top of things here," he said gruffly. "You know how it is."

"How is it?"

"We've got it under control," said Pearson. "I knew they wouldn't have the commitment to go all the way. We've contained them, and it seems to be burning itself out."

"Are there fires?"

"No, no," said Pearson impatiently. "Just sniping. Damned poor sniping at that. They hit four or five people, but only one of them died."

"Only Ben Gates," said the Vice President.

Pearson shrugged. "Manner of speaking," he said.

Shaw sat down and put both feet on the Mayor's desk. "The President said for me to give you any help you wanted, so what's the word?"

"Thanks," said Pearson, "but the truth is we've got this pretty well under control by ourselves, and there's no reason we can't go along that way."

"Have you been in touch with Albany?"

"No need to. As I said, things are settling down here and there's really no need for outside interference—"

"No?" said the Vice President. "What makes you think outside help—or interference as you choose to call it— won't be needed before the night is over?"

Pearson spread his hands. "What can they do? We've got them encircled—they'll come peacefully enough. They haven't got the punch for this kind of thing. Hit and run, yes. Burn defenseless stores, throw bricks. But now they're surrounded and they're outnumbered, and that's the end to it as far as I can see."

"For Christ's sake, what do you have inside that glamor-boy head, steel wool? Didn't our agents tell you those men were specially trained for this operation?"

"You can't change their nature," said Pearson. "Training's one thing. Having the balls to put it into action is another."

"Oh?" the Vice President flicked his cigarette ash on the Mayor's rug. "Do you know where these men came from? Every one of them put in a tour in Vietnam, so don't talk to me about balls. If they're laying back, it's because they have a reason for it and because it's part of their plan. Don't start dreaming of headlines about how the golden boy mayor of New York put down an uprising from his comfortable command post in Gracie Mansion. The President is very unhappy about this scene —he wants it shut down. Right now, not tomorrow, and not when those men on those roofs get hungry. You're acting like that idiot who thinks he's governor. Thank God, Moss at least has brains—he's got the Guard alerted and ready to move."

"We don't need the Guard," Pearson said.

"I'll believe that when we sit down with the leader of those black men on the rooftops and find out what it is they want."

"I know what they want. They want a free ride with someone else paying for the ticket. That's why I won't deal with them."

"And that's probably why they're on your rooftops instead of marching in Mississippi," said the Vice President. "To think this city could elect *you* after John Lindsay."

Pearson mumbled, "I need a chance to think."

"I need an answer. Now."

The Mayor of New York looked out the window at the East River flowing by his back lawn, at the twinkling lights across the water, saw it all receding from him as if it had never been his.

"All right," he said. "I'll ask for the Guard."

On a platform at one end of a West Fortieth Street warehouse, a tall black man wearing the silver bars of a captain was instructing his men.

"Nobody goes in or out any more until we get the word from Headquarters," he said. "We're Company B for Bravo, and our job is Mobile Defense West."

He unrolled a Hagstrom's map, about three feet long, brightly colored, and showing every street and block in the city.

"Maybe you guys from out of town don't realize it, but Manhattan is an island. This is the Hudson River along the left—and across it, New Jersey. Down here at the island's end is Upper New York Bay. The East River goes up along the right-hand side of the island until it splits off. This is the Harlem River, and it goes all the way up and across the top. End of circle."

The Captain looked from one intent face to another. "Our assignment is to take this island away from Whitey and hold it."

No one spoke. "I don't know how long we've got to hold—or what we hold against. But they've given us this sector—" he indicated a strip along the left edge of the island. "From Fifty-ninth Street, here, at the south edge of the railroad yards, down to Thirty-fourth Street. Buses will move us to where we're needed. If the West Side Highway—here—is out of action, we move on this street —Eleventh Avenue. We'll commandeer private cars for smaller groups."

He raised his voice slightly. "I don't know what Whitey will throw against us—if anything. But if he comes across that river, our job is to stop him with everything we've got. In a few minutes, Sergeant Casey will issue weapons. For the rest of the night we're on our own, so we'll be spread pretty thin. But sometime in the morning I've been promised a contingent of draftees.

You'll each get four or five of them to help out. We have arms for some, the rest can be used as lookouts.

"One more thing. Until this is over, every man is on duty twenty-four hours a day. You sleep and eat where and when you can, we don't have enough men to set up shifts. If you have to shoot, shoot to kill. We don't have ammunition to waste. Any questions?"

Albert Grant had a dozen, but he was damned if he was going to be the first man to put his hand up. He sat silently until Master Sergeant Casey started bellowing. "Okay, fall in line for weapons. Squad Leaders first. You get both carbines and pistols, you lucky bastards. Line troops get carbines and fragmentation grenades. Mortar men and bazooka teams, wait until last. Keep moving, we don't have all night!"

It was just like being back in the Regular Army, thought Grant.

Shortly after midnight, the diversionary action in Coney Island increased in intensity.

The cherry bombs, which had been exploding off and on all evening, took on a new sound. At first the police, on the outskirts of the area, did not respond. Then one ex-Marine, standing near a corner of Neptune Avenue, heard the blast and felt the shock wave.

"That's a concussion grenade!" he yelled.

The word was relayed to Chief Mason, who had moved his mobile headquarters to a position outside the Coney Island Hospital.

"I was afraid of this," he said. He had his communications man connect him with the mayor's office. "Sir," he told Pearson, "they've started throwing concussion grenades out here."

"Any casualties?" asked the Mayor.

"Not yet, but there will be. I think we ought to go in after them. The longer we wait, the better they get themselves dug in."

"How about tear gas?"

"Ineffective on those roofs."

"You've got to hold off awhile," said the Mayor. "This is a big commitment, and I have to think about it. How are you on manpower?"

"We've got more than half of our twenty-eight thousand men out here. God help us if anything breaks out anywhere else."

"Well, just hold off," said the Mayor. "I'll get back to you as soon as I can."

"Wait a minute, there's something coming in." Mason read the slip of paper a trooper handed him. "Now we've had it," he said, forgetting the open microphone.

"What is it?"

"Sir," said Mason, "I've just gotten word that bands of Negroes in automobiles are throwing fire bombs into homes at Bensonhurst, Bath Beach, and Sheepshead Bay."

"Jesus Christ," said Pearson.

"A patrol car tried to intercept one band, and both officers were killed with machine-gun fire."

"How many are there?"

"Who knows?"

"I'm declaring an emergency," said Pearson. "The National Guard is on stand-by. I can have them in the area in a couple of hours."

"In a couple of hours Brooklyn could be burned to the ground."

"Broadcast a Code Thirteen," said the Mayor. "Get every man who can carry a gun out there."

"It'll strip the rest of the city, we—"

"Strip it!" yelled the Mayor.

"Right." The Chief sighed. "Signing off." He turned to his communications man. "Code Thirteen," he said. "Get every man who can walk—on duty or off. We'll move our headquarters to Prospect Park. Have them report there. In uniform or out—we can't spare time for them to check in at the station houses."

"Yes, sir," said the policeman, his hands making the rapid connections that would start teams of operators calling the home of every off-duty policeman in the five boroughs. Radio stations and television programs interrupted their scheduled broadcasts and ordered police to report to Prospect Park in Brooklyn.

By one A.M. most of the patrolmen so far unaffected by the activities in Coney Island were on their way to Brooklyn.

The Reverend Abner Greenbriar was having trouble getting permission to talk to the rioters.

"They're not listening to anyone," a patrolman said.

"They'll listen to me." Greenbriar's voice, at least, sounded perfectly convinced.

"What can we lose?" said another patrolman. "Let him use your bull horn."

"Thank you," said the Reverend.

He turned up the volume on the bull horn and took a step out into the open. "This is the Reverend Abner Greenbriar. I am unarmed. I want to talk to you."

From across the square a voice called, "Go back, Reverend! You're wasting your time."

"Just *listen* to me," shouted Greenbriar.

"Go back," repeated the voice. "Some of the guys over here think you're a white nigger, Reverend."

"At least you can listen!" cried Greenbriar. "At least you can think on what you're doing!"

"We know what we're doing!" called another voice. "And we know what you're doing. You're fronting for the white man! Get your ass back behind that building or we'll shoot it off for you."

"I beg of you—" Greenbriar began.

Something kicked up white dust from the pavement near him, went spanging off.

"You misunderstand me—"

Another bullet smashed into the sidewalk. Two policemen dashed out from behind the buildings, grabbed Greenbriar by both arms and dragged him, protesting, to shelter.

"They shot at me," he said numbly.

The arsonists' cars careened through the streets of Brooklyn. Bensonhurst, Bath Beach, Sheepshead Bay—all blazed under fire bombs within the first half-hour. Then the raids spread into Borough Park and Flatlands, near Brooklyn College.

Because many of those attacked were asleep, the first warning they had was the sound of breaking glass. Opening their bedroom doors, they were met by a glaring wall of flame. Some, warned by the broadcasts or by shouts and noise in the streets, were looking out their front doors when the raiders arrived. These were the unlucky ones: by now blind destruction had taken over, and bullets from carbines cut down dozens of sleepy-eyed Brooklynites.

Fire departments responded to the disaster, but there was little they could do. There were too many homes flaming to let them choose which few to save; they established perimeters outside the stricken blocks and concentrated on keeping the fires from spreading.

Four raider cars skidded around a curve in Flatbush and found themselves facing a police barricade. Shooting as they tried to turn, the raiders were hit by a fusillade of police bullets that punched through the thin metal of the cars. In less than twenty seconds, nine of the raiders were dead and four others seriously wounded. They were pulled from the wreckage of their vehicles and dragged behind the barricade, where a doctor dressed their wounds and police officers hurled questions at them.

"Who put you up to this?"

"Who gives your orders?"

"Why are you doing it?"

"What were your plans for the rest of the night?"

"Where is your headquarters?"

"Shit, man," said one of the raiders, choking on his own blood, "they just said go out there and burn Whitey down, so that's what we did." He fought for breath, and died.

"It's working," said Dick Wilcox. "The police have put out a Code Thirteen and set up mobile headquarters in Prospect Park. There isn't a fully staffed station house in Manhattan."

"Any reports on casualties?" asked Shawcross.

"The troops are shooting up everything in sight."

"What did you expect? You can't hold troops back once they start killing."

"The Guard's been called in," Wilcox reported a few minutes later.

"Are they federalized?"

"Not yet."

"They will be by morning," said Shawcross. "It's a bad break, having the Governor away. I was sure he would resist federalization for a couple of days at least."

He glanced at the maps on the bare wall. Each was covered with clear plastic, and marks had been made on them with grease pencils. By now demolitions men would be making their first cautious probes against the bridges and tunnels.

Some of the bridges—minor ones across the Harlem River—would be easy. But the huge Triborough Bridge would be a monster to handle, almost as difficult as the George Washington.

The question now was whether the bridges and tunnels would be ready to blow before the authorities suddenly realized how vulnerable Manhattan was.

Wilcox was in communication with the various teams by radio. If radio failed, they would use the excellent facilities of the New York Telephone Company, at a dime per bridge.

At Stewart Air Base, black pilots Stan Putnam and Harry Cranford made final cockpit checks in their two Republic F-105 Thunderchiefs. The pilots of the other two planes would be surprised when Putnam and Cranford broke out of formation over Westchester County and made screaming bomb runs down the Hudson River.

Tonight, the Thunderchiefs were loaded with eight thousand pounds of bombs in their bomb bays. Bullpup missiles were mounted on wing pylons. Their orders were to climb to fifty thousand feet, proceed toward Cape Cod, make a simulated run on Rockport, Massachusetts, and then return.

It was on the homeward leg that the two black pilots intended to break off from the formation. Ordinarily, their bombs would not be armed. This night, thanks to a team of black ground crewman, the weapons aboard the planes flown by Putnam and Cranford were fully operational.

At the Njalaian Embassy, Eloise Gibson fought back a yawn as Harumba's long introduction to her act droned on. It seemed unusually late to be starting entertainment on any night other than a New Year's celebration. She wondered if Harumba meant for the affair to go on until dawn.

In an adjoining room, a bored British aide plumped down in a chair, lit a cigar, and turned on the television set to watch Johnny Carson.

One of Harumba's assistants stepped into the room.

"I'm sorry," he said, "the television is out of order. Perhaps you would join me in the garden for a drink."

"Why not?" The aide left, noticing that the set's plug had been pulled out of the wall.

The third rail was a constant hazard as the four demolitions men worked their way cautiously into the IRT subway tunnel between Manhattan's East Forty-second Street and tiny Belmont Island, halfway across the East River.

Three of the four men were strangers to this tunnel. The fourth, Clyde Dean of Rock Rapids, Iowa, was a twenty-four-year-old IRT night-duty volunteer who had undergone intensive training at the Coolidge base.

They walked along the tracks, under Second and First Avenues, then, finally, the Franklin D. Roosevelt Drive.

"The river starts here," said Dean, indicating a portion of track. They stepped off another quarter of a mile and began to place the charges carefully.

Two sets were positioned fifty feet apart, wired to go off at the same time. If one did not punch through to the river, the other would.

When it did, the East River would rush into the tunnel and flood it, cascading along the rails all the way to Grand Central Station.

Karen Davis sat in front of her television set, numb with shock. So this was what William Gray had been planning! She tried to call him and got no answer. Then she tried Abner Greenbriar.

"We don't know where he is," said Greenbriar's secretary. "He went out to Coney Island hours ago to see if he could help, and we haven't had a word since. We're all sure something's happened to him."

"The news broadcasts would have mentioned it," said Karen, trying to quiet the panic in the secretary's voice, and her own.

"I suppose you're right, but we're so worried. What could have brought it on? We were sure we'd get through the summer—why did they have to start shooting?"

"I wish I knew," said Karen.

Helen Pearson, pregnant with her first child, was also watching television, her face expressionless.

Her mind raced over the events of the past three years. Had Cliff's attitude toward Negroes contributed to this chaos?

In past riots, blacks had remained in their ghettos, burning their own tenements and looting stores owned by absentee whites. This one was different. They were raging through white areas.

Helen Pearson felt as helpless at that hour as all the other well-meaning liberals in New York who had hoped that the inevitable confrontation between black and white would never come.

In Brooklyn, at two A.M., first contingents of the National Guard arrived, wearing green fatigues and steel helmets, and riding light personnel carriers mounted with machine guns.

The first encounter between the Guard and the raiders

was a massacre. A squad of Guardsmen, their boyish faces half hidden under heavy steel helmets, marched toward raider cars stopped at a road block. One black man gave a signal. Thompson machine guns opened up, and steel-jacketed slugs ripped through green fatigue cloth, tearing bloody gouts of flesh from the bodies that toppled to the cement.

From then on, frequent fire-fights broke out. Mistakes were made. Several houses went up in flames from National Guard tracer bullets. Negroes were pulled out of their automobiles and subjected to rough searches. Several cars that attempted to run the road blocks were blasted with machine guns, and dozens of travelers were wounded.

By now the flames raging over a hundred square blocks could be seen by aircraft making approaches to nearby John F. Kennedy International Airport.

The President, exceeding the requests of Lieutenant Governor John Moss, had mobilized a full division of regular troops stationed at Fort Dix in New Jersey. If the riot followed previous patterns, it would die down as morning approached, lie dormant, and then break out even more violently after dusk of the second night. The President was determined to provide federal aid by that time, whether the state of New York requested it or not.

As the hands of the clock in provisional headquarters passed two A.M., Shawcross began receiving reports from his demolitions teams.

The first—not surprisingly—came from teams assigned to the small footbridge between Ward's Island Park and the East River Housing Project on Manhattan's East Side at 102nd Street. It was set and ready to blow.

Elsewhere, things were not going so smoothly.

One of the demolitions men assigned to the Willis Avenue Bridge, connecting the northern end of First

Avenue and the Bronx, missed his footing. He screamed as he fell and struck the water with a flat, slapping sound. The other men worked grimly, trying not to listen to his shouts for help as he splashed frantically below them.

The Macombs Dam Bridge and the 145th Street Bridge were prepared without incident, as were the Madison Avenue and Third Avenue Bridges. But a man assigned to the Queensboro Bridge made an unknowing slip with his sidecutters and severed the hot line leading to the charges. This mistake would cost lives later.

"The Williamsburg is ready to go," said Wilcox. "So is the Manhattan."

Shawcross himself received the report from the George Washington Bridge. He turned to Wilcox and smiled. "The bastard's set," he said, "but if the air strike doesn't take it out, my bet is it'll stay up."

As the violence in Brooklyn increased, Manhattan fell silent and empty. Forty-second Street, which ordinarily plied its gaudy wares until dawn, was almost deserted. The bars stayed open, neon tubing alight, two or three steadies seated at their regular stools. There were few black men in these bars now; most had cleared out when they heard that another race riot was in progress. The few who remained shook their heads and spoke loudly against the violence. No sir, that ain't the way to get things done.

Few taxis were on the streets; as the crowds thinned, cab drivers pulled in for coffee or went back to their garages.

In Greenwich Village, Bleeker and MacDougal Streets were empty of tourists and hippies. A few Italian ladies, dressed in black as they had been all their lives, sat in their third-story windows and looked down at the silent street, or spoke to each other in whispers.

The Wall Street area was deserted. Whole blocks stood empty of cars and people. To the east, the Fulton Fish Market stirred sleepily.

Most restaurants were closing for the night. The thirty-foot broiling wall of fireplaces at La Fonda del Sol in the Time-Life Building had burned down to the coals, and less than thirty people remained in the seven dining areas which ordinarily seated four hundred. Nearby, on the sixty-fifth floor of Rockefeller Plaza, the Rainbow Room was empty except for a private party which had spilled over from the Grill. The view of the city was spectacular, but even to the uninitiated, Manhattan was obviously going to sleep.

Sardi's, The Four Seasons, Toots Shor's, Lindy's, The Forum of the Twelve Caesars, Trader Vic's, Twenty-One, the Colony, and the Tavern on the Green in Central Park —all were preparing to shut down for what their managers thought would be a few hours to get ready for the weekend crowds. No one knew that it would be weeks before some of them reopened, and that others would never open again at all.

As the last minutes sped by, diplomats danced at the Njalaian Embassy; soldiers, rousted from their bunks at Fort Dix, grumbled; men shouted and died in the streets of Coney Island; four Thunderchiefs made a simulated bomb run and began their return flight to New York; black policemen and firemen and technicians for dozens of plants and city services reported for duty.

The complacent world of white America would end in eleven minutes.

"Redemption Headquarters, this is Angel One. Come in, please. Over."

"Angel One, this is Redemption Headquarters. We read you. Over."

The messages were crackling back and forth between the communications center at Shawcross' headquarters and the two black-piloted Thunderchiefs, high in their dark void of sixty degrees below zero. The transmissions were no doubt being monitored, but in a few minutes it would make no difference.

"I estimate nine minutes to target. Are we still Go? Over."

"Affirmative, Angel One. You are still Go. We will expect you in exactly nine minutes. Confirm. Over."

"Confirm. Nine minutes. Over and out."

It was now four minutes after three in the morning. Although violence was raging within ten miles, Manhattan was quiet. As the minutes ticked away, the black troops chomped nervously at wads of gum, lit cigarettes from the butt ends of previous ones, talked quietly in the hot darkness.

Until it was possible to take action instead of waiting in basements and warehouses, the troops of the Afro-American Army of Liberation were just going to have to sweat it out.

At eight minutes after three A.M., Eastern Daylight Time, the Hustler bomber carrying the Governor of New York passed over two peaks of the Bitter Root Range of the Rockies and struck violent clear-air turbulence. In an attempt to turn away, the pilot put the bomber into an unintentional slip; the turbulence threw up one swept-back wing, and the other stalled out completely. The heavy bomber flipped over before the pilot was able to reverse his controls and plowed, upside down, into a glacier, exploding with a bright orange ball of flame.

John Moss was now Acting Governor of New York

State, although it would be another two hours before he knew it.

"Redemption Headquarters, this is Angel One. We are breaking off in one minute. Target ETA is three minutes, forty-five seconds. Over."

"Angel One, proceed as planned. Good luck. Over."

In the command headquarters of the 582nd Tactical Air Defense at Wild Duck Pond, New Jersey, the duty officer riffled through his code book.

"Sergeant," he said, "is this thing up to date? I don't find any Redemption listed here."

"That's the book for today, sir."

"Have you got anything on the scope?"

"Local stuff coming out of Kennedy," said the sergeant. "And there's an Air Force training flight on their way up to Stewart."

As the duty officer looked at the radar scope, two white dots broke away from the group over Westchester and streaked down the dark shadow of the Hudson River valley. After a moment's hesitation, the two others followed.

"This is Flight Leader Jenkins, 280th Combat Wing. Two Thunderchiefs with me on a training mission have just broken away from our flight plan and are heading down the Hudson Valley toward New York. We are following. They don't answer radio communications."

The duty officer pressed an alarm button and brought the missile base to red alert.

"This is it," said Shawcross. "Cut in full command network."

"It's in," said Dick Wilcox.

Shawcross took the microphone. "All units, stand by."

He was heard by men crouching on the walkways of

towering bridges, men in police stations and fire halls throughout the city. He was heard by nine leaders of the crime syndicate as they sat, frightened and hostile, under the muzzles of three submachine guns held by members of Raymond Carpenter's Special Forces. He was heard by more than a thousand mobile units in New Jersey, Staten Island, Queens, the Bronx, and Westchester County; by FBI agents and police radiomen who cursed and tried to triangulate the transmitter's location.

The two F-105 Thunderchiefs roared down the Hudson Valley, five hundred feet above the water. Shawcross' voice came clearly into the headphones of the pilots.

"This is General Shawcross. The time has come to strike for freedom. All units, Plan One is now in effect."

As the carrier wave faded, the bridges and tunnels connecting Manhattan to the outside world began to shudder and collapse under massive explosions.

The siege had begun.

TWENTY-SEVEN

At precisely twelve minutes after three A.M., the team assigned to the Manhattan Bridge received the Go signal from rebel headquarters, and Henry Logan, chief of the demolitions team, depressed the firing lever of his detonater. The charges had been planted carefully; split seconds after the dull boom of the explosion, an entire span of the bridge dropped into the East River.

The Brooklyn Bridge, a few hundred yards south, shuddered under the impact of almost a thousand pounds of high explosives, its center span completely wrecked. George Peabody of Hackensack, New Jersey, had just driven across it. The explosion caught his Rambler in a savage shock wave and threw it against a pillar. Peabody, strapped in with a shoulder belt, was unharmed—but his car, less than a month old, was smashed beyond repair. He stood overlooking the wreckage of the city's oldest bridge and could see only his shiny red automobile, now just metal twisted against one of the bridge's granite towers.

He barely noticed when the Williamsburg Bridge, which had served New York since 1903, lurched under the impact of an explosion and crashed into the murky waters of the river. As part of the wreckage tumbled onto a small shack in the East River Park, the first Manhattan fatality occurred. The girders crushed the life out of a forty-eight-year-old derelict sleeping in the shack. His drinking companion, urinating against a tree a few yards away, was unharmed.

The two F-105 Thunderchiefs arrived at the George Washington Bridge. Stan Putnam's plane went in first, followed closely by Harry Cranford's. Putnam dropped a pair of thousand-pound bombs. Cranford, following, saw one explosion burst on the upper roadway. The other erupted harmlessly in the river.

Putnam's Thunderchief turned and made a second pass at the bridge. Motorists stopped their cars on the mile-long roadway and looked up in amazement at the approaching aircraft. Meanwhile both of Cranford's bombs hit the roadway, and now, although the physical structure of the bridge was still intact, there was a gaping hole through the concrete.

The motorists, aware of their danger, began trying to get off the bridge but were trapped by the cars piled up behind them. One man jumped from his pickup truck; as the second load of bombs burst a hundred yards away, he climbed up on the rail and leaped into the darkness to certain death in the river two hundred fifty feet below.

People abandoned their cars and began to run toward the nearest shore, using the pedestrian walks along the sides of the bridge. Several cars, overturned by bomb blasts, were burning. The night was filled with screams.

On their third pass the Thunderchiefs aimed at the area where the cables reached their lowest point, hoping the bombs would cut a cable and tumble the whole structure into the river. Two of the four bombs missed, but the other two widened the roadway's gap to almost ninety feet.

By now the other two planes had caught up. As Stan Putnam straightened for another pass at the bridge, he was trapped in converging fire from .50 caliber machine guns. A bullet hit his bomb load, and the plane exploded into a red blossom, cascading wreckage along the edge of Inwood Hill Park on the northern tip of Manhattan.

Cranford, unaware that his companion had been blown out of the air, was on another bomb run. The gap in the roadway widened to a hundred thirty feet, but the supporting structure stood. Cranford's Thunderchief arced over the New Jersey village of Edgewater and turned toward the bridge again. He saw the two pursuing jets and flew through a stream of tracers, his plane shuddering under their impact. A piece of metal tore from his port wing.

Cranford aimed directly at the massive towers of the bridge. The Bullpup missiles whooshed from their mountings and flamed through the darkness. One burst against a tower, and for the first time the bridge trembled and swayed.

"Redemption, this is Angel Two," said Cranford into his open microphone. "I'm out of bombs and missiles. Angel One must have been shot down. The bridge is still standing. What do I do now? Over."

"Angel Two, this is Redemption Headquarters. Stand by while the ground team tries to cut the cables. Keep this frequency open. Over."

"All right," said Cranford, "but I'm under attack and your guys had better hustle. Over and out."

He flew an evasive pattern, trying to keep the other two jets from closing on him. Meanwhile a team of demolitions men on the New York side of the bridge set off a series of charges. One packet misfired, distorting the pattern of the explosion. The cable held, although the bridge swayed alarmingly.

When Shawcross received this information, he sighed and took up the microphone again.

"Angel Two," he said, "this is Redemption."

"I read you, Redemption. What are your instructions? Over."

"The ground team messed it up," said Shawcross. "We've only got one chance now and it's your show. Ram the top of the northwest tower. Confirm. Over."

"Ram the top of the northwest tower," repeated the pilot. His voice was flat and without emotion. "Wilco. Out."

"Thanks, son," said Shawcross.

The radio sputtered, then Cranford's voice said, "Balls. This isn't exactly what I had in mind."

"Angel Two," called Shawcross, "what are you doing? Come in, please. Over."

The carrier wave went dead. "He's switched off his radio," said Wilcox.

"Check with the bridge team," said Shawcross.

"He's turned away from the bridge," the team's radioman reported. "He's flying up the Hudson with the other two planes chasing him."

Richard Wilcox cursed. "He's cutting out on us."

"I don't blame him," said Shawcross. "Ramming the tower probably wouldn't have done much good anyway."

Reports were coming in rapidly. The Triborough was down now, as were the other eleven bridges across the Harlem River.

The Fifty-ninth Street Queensboro Bridge was still standing. The demolitions team there was attempting to find a break in their detonation wires. Meanwhile they were under attack from a contingent of policemen who had started late for Brooklyn.

"Which ground force is nearest them?" asked Shawcross.

"The Mobile East. They're in the warehouse at East Fifty-seventh and First Avenue," Marvin Hamilton said.

"Use them," said Shawcross. "That bridge has to come down."

As Hamilton spoke into a telephone, Shawcross received other reports.

The blowing of the tunnels had proceeded without serious hindrance. There were occasional gun battles between surprised guards and determined demolitions men, but now, at three-thirty in the morning, all of the railroad and subway tunnels into the city had been destroyed.

The Holland and Lincoln tunnels were left open, heavily barricaded and mined with explosives.

The Queens Midtown Tunnel was blasted. A dozen motorists died when the waters of the East River cascaded in through the damaged roof.

The last tunnel to go was the Brooklyn-Battery, after a pitched battle which claimed the lives of four rebels and eleven guards. Because so many people were fleeing from Brooklyn, this tunnel was more crowded than the Midtown, and more than a hundred fifty people drowned.

Three hundred men of the Mobile East force came up behind the thirty-odd policemen who were keeping the demolitions men from blowing the Queensboro Bridge and opened fire with carbines and light machine guns. In less than five minutes the police force was captured. The officer in charge, himself wounded, surrendered his shattered command to the rebel captain. The rebels stripped the police of weapons and, as the demolitions men worked frantically to get their charges reset, allowed the wounded policemen to seek shelter in a nearby apartment building.

At exactly twenty minutes of four, a leaden explosion shattered the center of the Queensboro Bridge.

Only the George Washington Bridge still stood—and it was impassable.

The island of Manhattan was cut off from the outside world.

The first explosion occurred at 3:12 A.M.; the last at 3:40. From start to finish, the isolation of Manhattan had taken exactly twenty-eight minutes.

TWENTY-EIGHT

The Njalaian Embassy was so close to the Queensboro
Bridge that the explosion blew out a bank of windows
facing East Sixty-third Street. That was the end of
Stephen Harumba's grand ball.

By cajoling, pleading, and tricking his guests, Harumba
had managed to keep them from rebelling at the lateness
of the hour.

Now there was no need for trickery. Using the public
address system, Harumba instructed his guests to gather
in the main ballroom. They arrived, nervous and trying
to shake off the effects of the food and liquor they had
consumed during the past six hours. Most wanted to use
the telephones and, on Harumba's instructions, were told
they were out of order. Those who wanted to leave immediately were kept from doing so by barricaded doors.

"Ladies and gentlemen, please!" Harumba called out,
trying to still the babble in the room. "You must listen
to me." His shouting quieted the guests, and they stood
in hostile little groups, anxious to get away.

"Thank you," said Harumba. "I know you are disturbed, and that is precisely why you must listen. First,
let me assure you that there is no danger to anyone in this
room." This was an unfortunate way of putting it, for

many had families elsewhere in the city. A jumble of voices drowned out Harumba's for a few minutes. The room finally quieted when Soviet Ambassador Rudenkov held up his arms for silence. "Your Excellency, we have heard explosions and shots. I have tried to use the telephone and have been told that it is out of order. I have tried to leave and been told that it is not safe for me to do so. An explanation is in order."

Harumba tried to answer and was shouted down. Only when the Soviet Ambassador called for silence was he able to make himself heard.

"You are here because I took precautions to insure your safety," Harumba said. "You have heard explosions and shots. Well, at this moment in the streets outside, a civil war is raging. Out of bloody combat a new nation is being born."

The Assistant Ambassador to the United Nations from the United States, Talcott Burgard, started toward the door.

"Mr. Burgard, please!" called out Stephen Harumba. "I have no wish to offend you, but you would not be safe on the streets."

"The hell you say." When Burgard got to the door, he found it locked and pounded at it angrily.

"I apologize for keeping my knowledge of the revolt secret," said Harumba, "but I could not risk the chance that the authorities would be notified should I warn you in a more orthodox way. I wanted to protect your safety."

"What's going on out there?" asked Talcott Burgard.

"I think," said Harumba, "the black man of the United States has just seceded."

"A riot," said Burgard.

"A civil war," said Harumba. "I do not know at this moment whether the rebellion will be successful, but I do not think it will be safe for anyone—white or black—

to be on the streets. My information is that there are almost no policemen remaining in the city. There are thousands of rebels securing the island. Doubtless they have no desire to injure any law-abiding citizen, but accidents are certain to happen. In the morning you will be allowed to go from here to United Nations soil. It will be respected by the rebels. Your families will join you there."

"Rebellion?" said Soviet Ambassador Rudenkov. "This is a lawless riot, and when this episode is over I assure you that my government and yours will have things to discuss."

"I am sorry you feel that way, Your Excellency," said Harumba.

"I'm going to my office," said Talcott Burgard.

"I have done my duty in warning you of the danger," said Harumba. He nodded and a Njalaian aide near the door tapped on it three times. A key turned and the door swung open.

"You'll be sorry you pulled this, Harumba," said Burgard.

In a corner of the room, Pete Humble handed Eloise a straight bourbon. She sipped at it; it tasted like tap water.

"Is it Gray?" she asked.

Humble nodded.

"Stanley was mixed up in it, too."

"Right up to his neck," said Humble.

"He got out of the Marines because he was sick of war and killing—he told me he never wanted to see another dead man in his life."

"He got out of the Marines because William Gray wanted him to head up a rebel army," Humble said bluntly. "I was there the day Shawcross came back from Vietnam, and Gray was waiting for him."

"So was I," she said. "Or have you forgotten?"

"No, I haven't. Those days were good. When Shaw-cross came, the good days went."

"Poor Pete." She touched his cheek. "Neither of us intended it. But you've got part of it wrong. Gray couldn't have been waiting—he was in Paris."

"Honey, you don't have to trust my memory, it was in all the papers. What difference does it make? The important thing is that Gray and Shawcross got together."

"And you were in it from the very beginning, too—weren't you, Pete?"

"All the way."

Even before the last bridge was down, the ground forces of the Afro-American Army of Liberation moved carefully into position.

To the few inhabitants of the city who were on the streets at that hour, the uniformed troops were a terrify-ing sight. Every man was armed with a rifle or machine gun. They moved quietly but rapidly to their destinations. Those who watched them stepped back into doorways and withdrew from windows as the black men went by.

Ten minutes after the first bridge fell into the East River, the Director of the FBI was in the President's office recommending a massive pickup of black leaders all over the nation. "We've got to get them out of action," Paulson said. "Until this is over, none of them should be trusted."

"In 1941," said the President, "we put two hundred thousand loyal Americans of Japanese ancestry in prison camps because they weren't to be trusted. The Nisei soldiers needed so much to prove they were loyal, the cemeteries of Italy are crammed with their bones."

"It isn't the same, sir," said the FBI man. "This is a racial thing. These people put loyalty to blood first."

"No pickup," said the President.

"I can't be held responsible if—"

"The responsibility," said the President, "is mine."

Shortly after four A.M. every radio station in New York City was overrun and taken off the air. The exceptions were two Civil Defense frequencies, both of which began transmitting a tape loop of William Gray's voice.

"This is an emergency," it said. "Remain in your homes. Do not go out onto the streets. The forces of the Afro-American Army of Liberation have occupied Manhattan. You will not be harmed if you obey instructions. Do not use the telephone. Conserve water. Above all, do not leave your homes."

A pause, then the tape began to repeat: "This is an emergency. Remain in your homes. . . ."

Gray wanted to broadcast a live message no later than five A.M. This meant that the technicians in the Empire State Building had to work feverishly to get the hookup ready. Although the TV cameras were not yet patched in to the makeshift network, the technicians were transmitting a title card that read "Stand by for an important message." This card was being received by sets within range of the transmitters—a radius of roughly eighty miles around the city—but it was also piped along the coaxial cable to the affiliated stations of the three networks. Those stations, more than a hundred fifty for CBS alone, were burning up the wires with queries to network headquarters in New York. The messages were ignored. The hundreds of stations located in the cities and towns of America knew only that something big was happening, and that they'd have to stand by to find out what.

Each of Manhattan's seventeen police precincts had its own plan for combatting any possible riot action, down to such details as how to prevent buses, subways, or automobiles from entering the area. Every Wednesday morning since the 1967 Newark riots, a meeting had been held at Centre Street to update the riot plans and to discuss the possible use of these carefully designed blueprints against civil disorder.

The police department's plans were coordinated with other plans: the civil defense headquarters, the fire department, the New York National Guard.

The plans took into account every variable the human mind could conceive. Staging areas were set up, command centers were established. Telephones to the governor, the mayor, and the police commissioner were hooked up in each precinct.

When Mayor Clifford Pearson ordered Chief Phillip Mason to strip the island of every available man to combat the arsonists in Brooklyn, the plan for Manhattan's defense was short-circuited. Its forces were scattered over twenty square miles of Long Island. Equipped with the latest in riot-control devices—ranging from a thirty-thousand-dollar Command Police Vehicle to deadly Stoner Assault Guns, tiny carbinelike weapons that could fire through a brick wall—the police and their equipment were on the wrong side of the East River.

The National Guard, which had the most complete set of plans of all, called *Skyhawk*, was no better off. John Moss would not leave the scene of the riots, and the state legislature delayed its official recognition of Moss as the head of government. This put the military chieftains of the National Guard into a quandary: some leaped instantly to obey Moss's orders; others procrastinated. Still others planned action on their own.

Although the rebels had been able to silence radio and television stations located in Manhattan, the residents of the island could still receive signals originating from outside. Channel 13, the educational television station, which had recently moved its transmitter to Jersey City, was taken over by order of New Jersey's governor. So were such powerful New Jersey radio stations as WPAT and WVNJ. These stations soon began to urge Manhattan residents to heed the orders given by the rebels and remain inside. Those who possessed firearms were instructed to keep them loaded—and their doors locked.

The radio and TV stations under control of the authorities also urged National Guardsmen to report to their units. It was this instruction that resulted in the first series of military casualties on the island. Men who attempted to report in to the 1st Battalion of the 69th Infantry, at 68 Lexington Avenue, were roughed up by rebels assigned to take over that unit. Several Guardsmen, though weaponless, tried to put up a fight and were shot down by the black troops.

This scene was repeated all over the city: on Fifth Avenue, with the 1st Howitzer Battalion of the 369th Infantry; on East Thirty-third Street, with the 1st Battalion of the 71st Infantry; at the building which housed Troop A of the 1st Squadron, 101st Cavalry; and, most wasteful of all, at 643 Park Avenue, where members of the 199th Army Band tried vainly to report with their instruments.

The New York Police Department did no better. Precinct houses were taken over by fast-moving Afro-American troops minutes after the bridges began to blow. Each station house had at least one and in some cases several black troops who had infiltrated in months before as patrolmen or civilian employees. These men knew the layout of the building, the location of weapons and ammunition; some actually had the few remaining patrolmen under arrest with their hands in the air when rebel forces entered.

When off-duty policemen tried to report in they were greeted with a shout of "Get your hands up, *now!*" and if they hesitated or went for their service revolvers—and many did—they were blasted down.

Perhaps fifteen hundred policemen were on the island, fully armed and capable of action—except that they had no means by which to communicate with each other, no way to assemble into an effective force. Their car radios could transmit only to central communications, not from car to car, and this left them helpless once the black forces took over the radio facilities.

A few civilians who found themselves on the street—as they returned from after-hours clubs, or from late dates, or from night jobs—walked blithely through the entire attack, unaware that death brushed their shoulders a dozen times. Others were not so lucky. Arne Lindstrom, a porter at the Playboy Club, left the club, walked around the corner of East Fifty-ninth Street to Madison Avenue, and was blasted down by an itchy rebel soldier who put two carbine slugs into his left kneecap. He lay on the sidewalk, screaming, until a passing patrol found him and dragged him inside the Standard Brands Building across the street. A night man was on duty; huddled in the lobby with him was the creative director of an advertising agency located in the building, who had just awakened from his weekly Friday night drunk. They made Lindstrom as comfortable as they could. He remained with them for two days, subsisting on food and water taken from the adjoining Schrafft's Restaurant and watching his wounded leg fester and turn gangrenous. Finally taken to a hospital, Lindstrom lost the leg on September 4th.

Hundreds of others were wounded or killed when they tried to run from patrols. Most of the black forces were trying not to injure citizens—but in the night it was difficult to tell civilians from policemen or National Guardsmen.

The hordes of Negroes who poured out of Harlem were also impeding the orderly occupation of the city.

Like liberated people anywhere, the blacks streamed out into the streets to greet their rescuers. They carried gifts with them: beer from neighborhood stores; colorful cushions to sit on; anything and everything they imagined might please the black troops. As they progressed southward toward where they imagined the invaders might be (it never occurred to them that their own ghetto areas were also occupied), they frequently ran on to bands of troops who were startled—even frightened—by them. Several black men and women were killed in these unfortunate confrontations.

As the eastern sky lightened with false dawn, Afro-American troops fanned out from the dispersal areas, equipped with bull horns and rifles. Where bull horns failed, the rifles did not. People on the streets—black as well as white—were ordered inside. Those who did not obey were shot.

From the heights overlooking the Harlem River, the Mother Cabrini Shrine near Fort Washington Avenue, the Polo Grounds and City College, Grant's Tomb and Riverside Park, Gracie Mansion and Columbus Circle, Bellevue Hospital on East Twenty-eighth Street, Washington Square in Greenwich Village, City Hall and nearby Chinatown—from Battery Park on the southern tip of the island to Inwood Hill Park on the north, Manhattan was completely in the hands of the rebels by five A.M.

TWENTY-NINE

General David Magid, Provost Marshal General of the United States Army, officially in charge of heading up the Military Police, was also responsible to the Justice Department for supervising any situations in which civilians might come under the authority of military personnel.

Although the FBI is the official voice by which riot control information is disseminated to local authorities, it was Magid's office which actually prepared the information. Under a previous Provost Marshal General, Carl C. Turner, the Provost Marshal office had written the FBI's famous manual *Prevention and Control of Mobs and Riots*, published in 1967.

That this very manual had come under considerable dispute from police officials did not reduce in the slightest the authority in General Magid's voice as he spoke to the President of the United States.

"They aren't revolutionaries, sir," he said. "They're criminals, rioters—and that's the way we have to treat them."

"Do you mean that they're criminals when they're committing criminal acts or that they're criminals because they're black radicals?" the President asked softly.

"Semantics," said Magid. "Begging your pardon, sir,

but my office has had considerable experience with this kind of action. The police officers have a saying for what we have to do. 'Flood the area with blue.' Blue refers to police uniforms."

"Thank you for the explanation," the President said.

"Our reaction to riots is usually one step behind the rioters. When we ought to be using clubs, we're still talking. When we ought to be using gas, we've just moved up to clubs. When we ought to be peppering them with birdshot, we're just getting around to gas. They stay one step ahead of us all the time, and that's why the thing escalates and we end up with property damage and casualties."

"I'd say we're a little beyond birdshot at this moment," said the President. "These rioters, if that's what you want to call them, have destroyed every bridge leading into Manhattan Island?"

"The George Washington is still standing."

"Of course. I forgot that one. Thank you, General."

"You can't be expected to remember every detail," Magid said. "My recommendation is to flood them with khaki."

"Very neat, General. And that is how we'll stay one step ahead of them?"

"Precisely," said Magid. He sat down, resting his case.

"The situation has gone far beyond that of a riot," said Attorney General Hugh McLeod. "My opinion is that we must treat it as an insurrection."

"Why not go all the way and accept it as a rebellion?"

"Too dangerous. As insurgents, the incident remains an internal matter which, I hope, can be put down quickly. If we become involved in a rebellion, especially one with racial significance, the door is open for foreign powers to recognize the rebel government and take their side."

"A rebellion," said General Magid, "is a rebellion."

"A revolution," the Attorney General said patiently, "is a successful insurrection. Let's hope that the situation in New York, whatever else we decide to call it, never becomes a revolution."

"In any case," said the President, "it calls for an immediate response from this government."

"Prudence suggests that we delay a little longer to see what the insurgents want," said McLeod.

"I'm declaring a national emergency," said the President. "We'll start the machinery moving, but make no announcement yet. Apparently there's going to be a broadcast from Manhattan at five A.M."

"Twenty minutes from now," said the Attorney General. "And the first explosion was less than two hours ago? They don't waste any time, do they?"

"No," agreed the President, "that seems to be *our* talent."

Half a dozen men came out of the darkness into the floodlit area surrounding Gracie Mansion. One, a black officer, carried a white flag. The others had automatic rifles at the ready.

"Who's in charge?" asked the man with the white flag.

A police officer stepped forward.

"This island is now under our occupation," said the man with the flag. "I am Lieutenant Harrison of the Afro-American Army of Liberation. I am instructed to speak with the Mayor."

"Like hell you will," said the police officer. "My men are inside and they've got you covered. Tell your men to throw down their arms."

"On the contrary," said the black officer. "Your men will throw down their arms."

"How do you plan to make us?"

Harrison raised one hand, let it drop. There was a whooshing noise and something streaked past him and exploded against the mayor's limousine. The car began to burn.

"That was a shell from a three-five rocket launcher," Harrison said. "We don't have many to spare, so the next one goes through a window of the Mansion. If the Mayor's in there he's liable to get hurt."

"What do you want?"

"Have your men come out, hands on their heads. No tricks, or that bazooka fires again."

"Everybody outside!" called the police officer. "Hands on your heads. Leave your weapons on the floor. Hurry it up. That's an order."

The rebel lieutenant threw down the white flag, took out his service automatic and, as the policemen left the Mansion, brushed his way past them. He entered, caught one policeman by the shoulder, asked, "Where's the Mayor's office?"

The man, too angry to speak, pointed. Harrison kicked the door open. Several men were grouped around a radio transmitter.

"Which one of you is Mayor Pearson?" asked Harrison.

Pearson stepped forward.

"You are to come with me," said Harrison.

"By what authority?" asked one of the men. "For what purpose?"

"By authority of the Afro-American Army of Liberation," said Lieutenant Harrison. "And my purpose is to place the Mayor under arrest."

"Arrest?" Pearson said numbly. "On what grounds?"

"War crimes against the black citizens of New York," said Harrison. He waved his pistol toward the door, and Clifford Pearson, Mayor of the occupied city of New

York, stumbled outside into the grayness of the first dawn of the siege of Manhattan.

By now the cables carrying telephone and teletype messages out of the city had been cut.

Con Edison's generating plants did not falter. At the moment of the strike at the bridges, black men had taken over the operation of the generators—forcing white workers to continue with their ordinary duties.

"You're here for the duration," they were told. "We'll feed you, and we'll let you sleep when you get tired. Keep the generators turning and you'll be okay. Louse them up and we'll shoot you through your empty white heads."

A good deal of the city's power came past the rivers from upstate generators, and there was nothing the rebels could do to insure its continuation except rely on the fact that the hostages would be worse off than the rebels if the power were cut.

The same held true for water. The reservoir in Central Park would be sucked dry in a matter of hours if the giant mains bringing water from upstate were closed down. But, again, the hostages would suffer far worse than the rebels.

All over the city, those buses which had not already been abandoned by frightened drivers were comandeered by the rebels. The transfer of drivers was almost casual. A car filled with rebels would force the bus over to the curb, a pair of armed men would get out and order the terrified driver from the wheel. The new driver would get in and proceed to the nearest assembly point, while the former driver was ordered inside the nearest building and told that if he put his head out it would be shot off. One driver, hard of hearing, did, and it was.

The car bearing Assistant Ambassador to the United Nations Talcott Burgard came under fire three times as it was driven frantically across town to Burgard's offices. One bullet shattered a window just inches away from his face and a sliver of glass grazed his temple, causing blood to trickle down his cheek. Burgard leaped from his car and rushed inside the office building.

He opened the office door and came face to face with the blazing muzzle of a revolver. Two of the bullets caught him in the chest and, as he fell, he saw the terrified face of an aide over the smoking gun.

"You silly shit," Burgard choked. "Why don't you look before you shoot?" Then he passed out.

In his room at the New York Hilton, the Vice President balanced the importance of staying in touch with the President against the very real possibility that the rebels would take him prisoner. He came to the conclusion that it was more important for him to remain free, left his suite, walked down three flights of stairs to keep the elevator man from seeing him, and came out in a carpeted hallway. He moved along it quietly, trying doorknobs until he found one that opened.

"I'll scream," said a woman's voice.

"Don't do that," he said, and entered the room. A handsome blonde in her early fifties was sitting upright in the king-size bed. An open book lay across her knees. The sheet was pulled up around her neck.

"I'm the Vice President of the United States," he said.

"And I'm Sarah Bernhardt. You don't look like the ordinary bedroom creeper, so just get the hell out of here."

"I've got identification. Here."

He tossed his wallet to her. She leafed through it, looked at his AGO card and other official identification, then tossed the wallet back. The sheet slipped a little bit.

"All right," she said. "You *are* the Vice President of the United States. What are you doing busting into my room?"

"I'm hiding," he said. "There's an armed insurrection going on. They'd probably like me as a hostage."

"Okay, Mr. Vice President, if you're really hiding I'd suggest you lock that door. Then we can figure out what to do."

He pushed the lock button.

"Locked," he said. "Thank you for your hospitality, Miss—"

"Mrs.," she said, getting up. She wore a white night-gown, over which she now pulled a blue dressing robe. "Mrs. Elvira Mooney, of the Kansas City Mooneys. Now what's this about an armed insurrection? Have the Russians landed?"

"I don't think so," he said. "My information is that there's a Negro army out there taking over Manhattan."

"Do they know you're here?"

"If they don't, they will. And whatever they're up to, it wouldn't hurt them any to have the Vice President as hostage."

"Well, if they start searching this hotel, they won't have any trouble finding you." She looked at him carefully. "You'd better cut off that moustache." She rummaged through her suitcase. "Here, thank your stars I'm too old-fashioned to use a depilatory." She handed him a small razor. "And then we'll do something about that shock of hair."

"Like what?"

"At fifty-two you don't suppose I'm an innocent blonde, do you? Get rid of the moustache and I'll give you a beauty treatment."

Half an hour later, as he waited for the bleach to work,

he sipped a cup of coffee she had made with the sink's hot water and a jar of Maxim from her suitcase.

He turned on the television set, switched from channel to channel, and saw only the "Stand By" message. Then he found Channel 13 and recognized the Governor of New Jersey.

". . . not panic," he was saying. "It is important that you remain in your homes. All New Jersey cities along the Hudson River are under martial law until further notice. Do not leave your homes. As for the residents of Manhattan, I am in communication with the White House, and your government urges that you avoid unnecessary risks. The rioters plan to present a message to the nation at five A.M., and this station will transmit that message. We urge you to keep your sets tuned to Channel 13. Do not leave your homes. Above all, do not panic."

"Panic?" said Elvira Mooney. "I'm scared shitless."

"Me, too," said the Vice President of the United States.

In the Empire State Building, William Gray was looking over the speech he intended to give in a few minutes. With the streets in rebel hands, both he and Shawcross were moving their headquarters into the building.

Shawcross, en route from his uptown headquarters, rode through the deserted streets in a black Oldsmobile, the red, black, and green flag of the Liberation forces flying from its radio antenna.

Black troops moved quietly along the side streets and up and down the broad avenues. There were few incidents; most people were inside. Telephone calls had roused many of them as frenzied relatives or friends called to ask if they were safe. These calls ceased shortly after 4:46, when the central switching system of the

New York Telephone Company was shut down by a black technician.

Grim-jawed white men took hunting shotguns from their closets, loaded them, and foraged through drawers for more ammunition. Those without guns armed themselves with kitchen knives. In many buildings leaders emerged, going from apartment to apartment gathering a vigilante force to guard the entrances into the building with whatever weapons were available.

Racially integrated buildings had the most trouble. White residents mistrusted Negro neighbors, and more often than not, Negro families were terrified of revenge from their white neighbors and remained behind double-locked doors.

Those who had television sets—over ninety percent of the population—had them turned on. Most viewers were tuned into Channel 13, preferring its skimpy news to the other channels' "Stand By" signals.

At three minutes to five, the signal from the rebel stations flickered and a picture came in. It showed a simple podium and, behind it, an unfamiliar flag. Channel 13 instantly fed this signal to its own transmitters.

The studio clock in the background indicated exactly five A.M. when a tall, dark man stepped into the center of the picture. He placed a sheaf of notes on the shelf of the podium, looked at the camera, nodded once, and began to speak.

"I want you all to listen—you people of the City of New York and the nation of the United States of America!

"My name is William Gray. I am the Premier of a new state, which we have named Redemption. I use the term 'state' advisedly. This is no empty riot, no demonstration. At this moment, the twenty-two million black people who have been prisoners of white America are free at last, after three centuries of slavery.

"The long-awaited revolt of the black man in America has taken place. Why did we do it? What pushed us over the edge? What are we asking for? Why did we choose Manhattan?

"Our numbers are small. We are only the fuse to the powder keg of twenty-two million oppressed blacks. The powder keg is always bigger than the fuse. Touch a match to the powder keg and nothing will happen. But touch a match to the fuse and you set off the explosion.

"We are the fuse leading to a black explosion that could destroy this country. We do not want to see such an explosion. No one, white or black, would benefit.

"And that is why we have occupied Manhattan. Had we thrown our army in direct opposition to the white establishment, the battle would have been terrible. I can tell you frankly that there are outside forces, outside nations, ready to rally to our cause should we ask for help. But were we to do so, the black explosion in America could be the opening shell burst of World War III.

"So we have tried to act with moderation. We are laying siege to the largest and most important city White America owns. We have tried to limit damage to a minimum and will continue to act with moderation so long as the White Administration does the same.

"This city is vital to the life of White America. We do not want it. We want only what we have earned down through centuries of oppression. And that is the reason for our military action.

"At this moment, a statement of our position is being delivered to the President of the United States. Copies have been sent to newspapers through the nation.

"Our new state will be called Redemption. It is bordered on the East by the Atlantic Ocean, on the West by the Delaware River, and on the north by what is now the New York-New Jersey border. In short, the state of New Jersey, in its entirety, for the lawful uses of the Black Nation of Redemption.

"New Jersey is only seven thousand five hundred twenty-one square miles in size. There are forty-five states which are larger. If we took the ten percent of the nation that our population entitles us to, we would be entitled to three hundred fifty thousand square miles of territory. We are asking for less than three percent of that.

"Redemption is a concept with precedent. In 1948, the state of Israel was formed from lands which belonged to certain Arab states. World opinion was on Israel's side, for the Israelis had been deprived of the land their sweat and blood had drenched over the centuries. We, the black people of America, are in a similar situation now —and the same world opinion is on our side.

"The nation of Redemption has existed, legally, since three A.M. this morning. We are a government in exile, but even so, I am pleased to read the following message: 'We are pleased to recognize your government and to offer whatever aid may be appropriate.' It is signed by the President of the African nation of Njala.

"I have other similar messages here. They are arriving every five minutes. They are signed by the leaders of such nations as Nigeria, Ghana, Albania, Chile, Tunisia, the United Arab Republic, and Kenya.

"I hope that it will not be necessary for us to accept these offers of aid. That is why we have occupied only Manhattan. Every day that the United States is deprived of the records and business facilities here is a day that will cost her billions of dollars in lost revenue. Finally, more than half a million of her white citizens are here, as hostages to our safety. A black life taken in Los

Angeles will result in two white lives taken in Manhattan. That is my promise.

"Likewise, the troops here will be served first. If authorities outside the city shut off the water supply, our troops will drink first. It is the civilian hostages who will suffer. The same goes for electric power and for food.

"We will not be deterred from meeting force with force, bloodshed with bloodshed. As a last resort, we will accept the foreign assistance that has been offered to us.

"How much simpler it will be if the government of the United States will listen to reason. I know it represents a wrenching upheaval for the six million people of New Jersey to be moved to other states. But there is plenty of room elsewhere for them. How the government of the United States will reimburse those firms and individuals who suffer losses is up to them. I might say that the release of funds designated for the welfare rolls of the country would easily make up the repayment, if the black man were truly such a great burden. But that is facetious. I will content myself by saying that the price is small—less than one month's financing of the unwanted Vietnamese war.

"If it surprises the white man to see us in this act of revolt, if it disturbs him to consider the possibility of a black nation is his own back yard, if it worries him to see his white supremacy declining—all I can say is that it has been a long time coming and that he brought it on himself."

Gray stepped back, stumbling slightly as he moved out of the picture.

A parade of officials came to the podium, giving explicit instructions to the residents of the city.

"Any white person seen on the streets, until further notice, will be shot without warning."

"Conserve water."

"Use food in refrigerators first, then freezers. Save canned goods for last."

"Each building will elect a building commander. All firearms must be turned over to the building commander. We have the registration records from City Hall telling us who's got guns." Marvin Hamilton, impressive in his sharply creased uniform, did not add that no one had time to go through all those records.

"Disturbances in the streets or the buildings themselves will be severely dealt with. Black troops will remain out of the residential districts, but white citizens' committees will be formed to keep order." Raymond Carpenter and a frightened John Genelli made this announcement. Genelli, speaking an argot that was only partly understood by the viewers, gave explicit orders to the Syndicate members throughout the city. The meaning was clear: keep your areas under control, or they're going to cut our throats.

"All residents of apartments overlooking the rivers or Central Park will move into other quarters immediately." This order led to general confusion and despair on the part of those affected. Often they did not even know their neighbors by name, and now they had to ask them for shelter during the emergency. Some simply huddled in hallways until black troops arrived and forced neighbors to take them in. Others took to the streets, heading for apartments which belonged to relatives or friends. A few of these were shot or molested by the tense black troops, but most reached their destinations unharmed.

"Doctors and nurses on duty at hospitals must remain there. Troops have been assigned to screen all hospitals and prepare them to handle casualties."

"All food stores are off limits. Anyone caught looting a food store will be executed on the spot."

Finally, William Gray reappeared.

"We do not know how long this campaign will go on," he said. "We advise the citizens of this city to assume the worst, that it will be a matter of weeks, and plan for it.

"The curfew will remain in effect through the rest of today, Saturday, and through the night. If all goes well, it will be lifted for the daylight hours Sunday. At that time, we will permit the Staten Island ferry boats to resume operation, and those who wish to leave the city may do so. But it will be up to them to get to South Ferry on foot. No civilian cars may be driven.

"At nine each morning, beginning tomorrow, Sunday, we will permit twenty-five food trucks to come into the city through the Lincoln Tunnel. We want only flour, sugar, canned meats, fruits, and vegetables. When they are unloaded, we will put thirty hostages on each truck and allow them to leave."

Gray looked straight into the camera. "If the trucks do not come," he said, "the hostages will be shot."

Marvin Hamilton stepped forward and said, "General Stanley Shawcross, Commander of the Afro-American Army of Liberation, has ordered every able-bodied black male in Manhattan, whether or not he knows how to use firearms, to report immediately for duty.

"Those living above West 155th Street report at seven A.M. to the southern end of High Bridge Park. Those living between 155th Street and Ninety-sixth report to the north end of Central Park, near the lake. All black men between Ninety-sixth Street and the Battery, report to Washington Square Park in Greenwich Village. That's seven A.M., an hour and a half from now. If you are any distance at all from your assigned place of induction, you'd better start walking now.

"If you have a friend who doesn't have a radio or TV set, warn him and bring him with you. After twelve noon

312

today, any black man seen on the streets without an identifying armband will be treated as a deserter. The penalty for desertion is execution."

"My plan is to get in there fast," said Police Chief Phillip Mason. "Flood them with blue before they know what hit them."

He was standing on a pier near West Street in Brooklyn, facing New York's lower East Side.

"How do we get across?" said a police lieutenant, looking toward the shattered bridges.

"Small boats," said Mason. "Plenty of them around here. We can get a couple of thousand men over before it gets too light."

"National Guard too?"

"Hell no. We want to end this riot, not extend it. Policemen only."

"Okay," said the lieutenant.

"Forget the owners," said Chief Mason. "Short the ignitions. And start loading."

"I suggest an air strike," said General David Magid.

"On what?" flared the President. "How do you separate the troops from the hostages?"

"By color," Magid said. "We'll send in a squadron of Huey gun ships, soften them up for an assault by Marines in personnel-carrying choppers."

"Absolutely not," said the President. He turned to his Attorney General. "What do you think, Hugh?"

"I think we've lost our comforting little label of insurrection," said Hugh McLeod. "Gray may be lying, but my hunch is that he's leveling about those governments recognizing Redemption. We've got a revolution on our hands, and the only thing we can do is put it down."

The President sighed. "Start all available forces converging on the area," he said to the Joint Chiefs of Staff, "but keep well away from Manhattan. I don't want an airplane to fly over it, I don't want so much as a stray sparrow to cross its borders."

The Joint Chiefs of Staff began to answer, all three men talking at once.

"Dammit!" said the President. "One at a time."

"We've got one hell of a lot of colored boys in every one of our units," said General James Hazzard, Army Chief of Staff. "My advice is to pull them out before we start to move."

"You're telling me a black soldier can't be depended on to put down a black riot?"

"It's a revolution, Mr. President," said Hazzard, "and that's exactly what I'm telling you. My further advice is that we'd be wise to put all black troops under arrest until this thing is settled."

"No sir!" said the President. "You have my permission to exclude Negro troops from this operation—but anyone who starts arresting them will have to answer to me."

"Yes sir." Hazzard sat down.

"How many revolutionaries can there be in the city?" said the President. "Twenty thousand? Thirty?"

"Maybe when they started," said Magid, "but by seven o'clock this morning they'll be up to a hundred thousand. They're not fooling around. You heard what he said, they want every black man who can walk."

"All right," said the President. "No matter how many, they're all on that island. We must have some non-fatal gas we can use to put them out for an hour or so. How about MACE?"

"MACE isn't a gas, it's a liquid," Magid said patiently. "You have to squirt it right in a man's eyes to make it work—or at least, get it on his skin."

314

"How about CS?" said General Hazzard. "It's a military version of tear gas, and goes further—it gets the eyes, but it also gives a strong, gagging sense of suffocation."

"CS might be it," agreed Magid. "You give a guy a whiff of that stuff, he isn't going to be too much trouble for a while. It's like having a steel band around your chest."

"It sounds just like what the old people with emphysema and asthma need to put them out for good," said the President.

"We might lose a few civilians with respiratory trouble," said Hazzard. "It can't be helped."

"How do you disperse the stuff?"

"The Ranch Hand planes we used in Vietnam for defoliation," said the Air Force General, Scott Sedwin. "Standard C-123's, fitted out with huge tanks. They could go up and down the city streets, blanketing an area four or five blocks wide on each pass."

"Would they start shooting hostages if we did that?" asked the President.

Magid shrugged. "Once a jig got a good sniff of the stuff he wouldn't be able to shoot more than one or two, I guarantee that."

"How soon can you have enough planes at Newark Airport?"

"Say one o'clock this afternoon. I'll have to pull them in from Illinois."

"Do it." The President turned to General Hazzard. "You'll have to get enough CS to Newark."

"No problem." said Hazzard. "Three plants on the East Coat make the stuff. We'll send tank trucks and take their entire on-hand supply. But I don't know if we can have it all at Newark by one P.M."

"Do what you can. We've got to knock them out for a couple of hours."

315

"More like one," said Hazzard. "The stuff wears off pretty quick."

"Can we put enough troops in there to have the situation in hand by the time they're able to shoot again?" the President asked.

"It's tight," said Hazzard. "We'll make an air drop into Central Park. No heavy equipment, just paratroops and light weapons. At the same time make amphibious landings along the piers. Use anything that floats."

"What about my idea of sending in gun ships?" asked Magid. "The hostages will just have to take their chances."

"Maybe they will," said the President, "but not right now." He looked around at the tense men in the room. "All right, gentlemen, you know what your assignments are. Keep me informed. We'll be in contact again in two hours."

The room emptied and he sighed, looking at his watch. It was twenty of six in the morning, and he was very tired. He pressed his call button. "I could use a cup of coffee, Barbara," he said.

When she came in, Paula Burke, the Vice President's secretary, was with her.

"Hello, Paula," he said. "What brings you down here so early?"

"I called her and asked her to come in," said his secretary.

"Why?" He was surprised.

"You're going to need a good secretary," she said, "and Paula's the best one in the city."

"I don't understand, Barbara, you've been—"

"I'm sorry, Mr. President, but I've been watching TV too. I can't work for you any more."

"Why not?"

"Because I want William Gray and his men to win,"

she said. "And if I stay around here, I'm afraid I might do something to help them."

At that moment, the area around Central Park in Manhattan was a roaring growl of auto motors. A team of two thousand black troops in the area around the park were crossing ignition wires as fast as they could and driving the vehicles into the park. Soon the green was a giant, haphazard parking lot.

The Americana Hotel was emptied of its paying guests and staff. Four members of Raymond Carpenter's Special Forces surveyed the hotel register carefully and detained the best-known hostages, including film celebrities Sid Caesar, Jean-Paul Belmondo, Jack Parr, Jack Lemmon, and Alec Guinness, who were in town for a motion picture scheduled to start shooting on September 6th.

The syndicate leaders were hosteled on one floor, political prisoners on another, celebrities on a third. Mayor Clifford Pearson and other priority prisoners were placed in a heavily guarded suite.

Into the Empire State Building came one radio report from Brooklyn advising Wilcox that police forces were gathering along the far banks of the East River. Wilcox passed that information to Shawcross immediately.

"Better get some of the fast-fire small arms men into the area opposite," Shawcross told his Mobile East commander. He received a confirmation and clicked off the radio microphone.

"It's too easy," Wilcox said.

"They're still in shock," said Shawcross. "We froze them. That's the secret of any successful surprise attack. I remember a paperback I read, *Modesty Blaise*. She was a lady spy, and when she went out on a kill assignment she'd strip to the waist and burst in on her victim that way.

"That's what we did. We busted into the room with our bare titties hanging out, and they're still in a state of shock. Now's when every minute counts like five for us. Later on, they'll come back to life and start giving us a hard time. I hope we've reached an agreement by then."

By six-thirty A.M., the evacuation into the sanctuary of the United Nations had begun.

The Secretariat Building contained twenty acres of office space, framed between thirty-nine stories of Vermont marble, much of it now being turned into impromptu sleeping quarters for delegates and their families.

As the refugees arrived, an emergency meeting of the United Nations itself was already under way in the huge Assembly Hall. The issue before the Assembly was the recognition of Redemption by the UN, and such recognition had come under attack by the representative of the United States—a junior delegate, the only one available now that Talcott Burgard had been shot. Not expected was the position of the USSR representative, who spoke eloquently about the rights of a nation to settle its own internal problems. Many delegates, relieved as they received word that their families were safe in the Secretariat Building, allowed themselves to fall into a half-slumber as simultaneous translations of the speeches droned on. They had been present at enough assemblies like this one to know that nothing was going to be decided in the next few hours.

When Chief Phillip Mason's forces started across the East River in their lashed-up armada of small fishing boats and pleasure craft, Redemption forces were waiting for them.

There was a light fog on the river, and the coolness of the morning air made the mist clammy and damp. Mason's forces came out of the mists and into view halfway across the river.

On the Manhattan shore, the rebels were hidden behind abutments of the Franklin D. Roosevelt Drive. Teams of bazooka men with heavy cases of rockets piled beside them were strategically placed on the Gulf Oil Pier at the foot of East Twenty-third Street and on the U.S. Trucking Pier, at the foot of East Twentieth. Along the other piers—several belonging to New York City and to the Sanitation Department—were squads of black riflemen and machine gunners. The police boats pushed against the oil flecked water, splashing their way toward Manhattan.

When the lead boat was less than fifty yards away from the tip of the Gulf Oil Pier, the rebel officer gave the signal. The first rockets streaked flatly over the water and exploded against the sides of the larger boats. Debris splattered into the air. Men shrieked in pain and terror as the light machine guns opened up and sprayed lead into the smaller craft. Fourteen boats were sunk in the first forty seconds of the ambush, and with them went one hundred fourteen policemen. Dozens of others fell wounded into their damaged boats. Chief Mason was never seen again after a rocket blasted the lead boat into oil-soaked debris.

Two minutes after the battle began it was over. In addition to the fourteen boats sunk in the first seconds, three more failed to make it back to the Brooklyn shore. Most of their passengers drowned. The boats scattered as they fled, and some wound up as far downriver as the abandoned New York Naval Shipyard.

Under fire from invisible attackers for less than five minutes, New York's Finest suffered more casualties than had been received in the entire century's war against the underworld.

The rebel forces did not take a single casualty. Their leader radioed to Shawcross: "Enemy force retreated under fire, sir. Fourteen boats sunk, and the rest are out of sight in the fog."

"Well done," said Shawcross. It was their first combat victory.

A year and a half earlier, the Defense Department had set aside seven brigade-size army task forces for use during riots.

This force, numbering more than fifteen thousand men, was trained to support the National Guard. The troops were equipped with the most modern communications equipment, with body armor that would stop a .22 bullet, powerful searchlights, and mobile gas dispensers. Strategically located drop points had been selected where equipment, maps, food, and other supplies were stored for these troops.

These supplies were now in the hands of the rebels. And the brigade assigned to the New York area, staging out of Fort Dix near Trenton, New Jersey, gathered impotently on the wrong side of the Hudson River, its movements reported to the rebel headquarters by roving spotters with powerful radio transceivers.

The Army communications men were aware of the rebel transmissions—but since each message lasted only a few seconds, they were unable to fix the transmitter positions with their radio direction finders. Like invisible gnats, the rebel spotters harassed the military forces.

The burning and shootings in Brooklyn had ceased. Once the bridges started exploding, the arsonists sped away from the flaming streets of Brooklyn and Coney Island and vanished into the protection of the black ghettos. Behind them were hundreds of flaming homes, many of which would burn down to their foundations.

Acting Governor John Moss, advised that Mayor Clifford Pearson had been captured by the rebels, mobilized the rest of the New York National Guard and formally requested federal assistance. As might be expected, communications links between the improvised battle headquarters in Long Island City and the White House were erratic. And, despite attempts at cooperation between the federal government and the state, neither was able to tell the other precisely what it was doing. Moss knew that federal troops were moving to encircle Manhattan; he did not know of the proposed gas strike and the simultaneous landing of troops.

Nor did he have full authority over the National Guard. The Guard, with its citizen soldiers led by professional military men, was splintered into several factions, often acting independently without consulting other units.

So it was that a force consisting of two infantry companies readied itself along the Bronx side of the Harlem River, eight hundred feet from Manhattan. Their commander, out of touch with both John Moss and the Department of the Army, was planning an assault on the abutments of the Harlem River Drive.

His mistake was in underestimating the black forces. Shawcross had assigned three thousand of his best troops as a static force to protect the dangerous Harlem River perimeter, from Randall's Island on the south to the Hudson River on the northwest.

As black draftees massed in the parks, hundreds were assigned to the Harlem River static unit. Many arrived bearing whatever arms they or their friends had: small caliber rifles, 12-gauge shotguns. Several had CO_2-powered air pistols.

Meanwhile, a special supply team working out of the G-4 group had been making interesting use of the yellow pages of the New York telephone book. Under Guns & Gunsmiths, they found two and a half pages of listings, ranging from AARON ROBT INC., Antique Firearms, Bought, Sold, Appraised, Corner of Madison, 3rd floor, 257 E. 84 . . . 744-6016, to ZERMAT CO INC., 209 West End, RI 4-3740.

Driving pickup trucks, supply teams plundered every gun store in the city, as well as the gun departments of large department stores.

Even so, only one out of three of the irregular troops had a firearm. The rest were armed with knives, hatchets, or whatever they could take from the shattered windows of hardware stores.

As soon as the city was under rebel control, teams were put on duty guarding the supermarkets and larger food stores. At first two black troops were assigned to each store. When draftees became available, the regular force was reduced to one rebel per store, aided by three irregulars.

In the Harlem area, several stores were broken into and looted by black men and women while the guards stood by watching. In one case, witnessed by more than forty residents of the apartment building across the street, a command car carrying a lieutenant and a squad of soldiers arrived while looting was still in progress. The black troops dismounted and fired into the crowd, felling several. The rest ran, leaving the dead and wounded behind.

Disarmed and standing against the brick wall of the market, the rebel guard shouted, "They was our own people, they wasn't Whitey!" The lieutenant did not answer. He took a pistol and stepped up to the man, who suddenly realized what was going to happen. He tried to grab for the weapon. The officer fired directly into the soldier's face. The man was smashed back into the plate glass window, bounced off it and fell down on the sidewalk, twitching. The officer fired a second bullet into his ear, and the horrified watchers saw the rippling tremor slow and stop.

The officer assigned two more troops to guard the store. The command car drove away. After a while, people crept out of doorways and dragged away their dead and wounded. The executed soldier lay where he had fallen until Sunday morning, when the stench became too great and he was dragged into the middle of the street and burned with a mountain of garbage.

Although Shawcross had not intended that the white curfew be enforced as strictly as promised in the television broadcast, some troops shot before thinking, or disregarded the standing order to avoid unnecessary bloodshed.

There were a few unfortunate civilians who had gone to bed the night before, slept through the tumult of the early morning hours, got up without turning on a radio or television set, and wandered out onto the strangely quiet streets to find themselves face to face with armed Negroes.

Some broke and ran. Others advanced, asking, "What the hell's going on here?" Many froze where they were, terrified. In most cases they were ordered back inside the buildings—aided by shoves and pushes—and experienced nothing worse than a bad fright. Others, not so lucky, were shot as they stood—or as they advanced, or as they ran—and were left to die. Only rarely did those who watched from nearby windows come out to give aid to the wounded after the troops were gone.

Marvin Hamilton's plan to equip all draftees with the red, black, and green armbands was short-circuited by the discovery that several cases of armbands had been lost. This made it impossible to tell which black civilian had been assigned to a specific post and which one had simply tied a white handkerchief around his arm—the emergency substitute for the armbands—and was on his way to loot a jewelry store.

Syndicate criminals did an amazing job of keeping order in their districts. They were well-armed, and had no compunctions about pistol-whipping any loudmouth trying to start trouble. Where the Mafia was clearly in charge, looting and destruction were kept to a minimum.

On the hundredth floor of the Empire State Building, incoming reports advised Shawcross that most areas were secure.

"It's looking good," said Hamilton. "Except for those cops. They should have had better sense."

"Not as good as you think," said Shawcross. "We're getting reports about a build-up of National Guardsmen along the Harlem River."

"What sector?"

"High Bridge. They're using Yankee Stadium as a staging area."

"Don't those idiots realize we've got those areas spotted?"

"You'd think they would," said Shawcross. "We'd better beef up the static unit. Pull your Mobile East forces up from as far south as Forty-second Street."

"I could drop a couple of dozen mortar shells right down into that stadium," Hamilton said.

"Not yet," said Shawcross. "Maybe Washington'll come around and let us have what we want."

"Sure," said Hamilton, in a voice that carried no conviction.

THIRTY

William Gray's suite in the Empire State Building, formerly occupied by the World Wide Rubber Company, was on the eighty-sixth floor. In addition to several hundred feet of office space, it contained a handsome apartment which had been used by the president of the company. At this moment he was in Acapulco, still unaware that this was anything other than an ordinary Saturday morning.

"Has there been any response from Washington?" Raymond Carpenter asked Gray.

"Nothing yet. They're probably having an emergency session of Congress. It will take them awhile to accept the situation."

"What happens if they don't come around?"

Gray shrugged. "We get help from outside."

Carpenter snorted. "If they send in a real counterattack, we can't hold them off."

"They won't," said Gray. "Any assault they make would be more dangerous to the hostages than to us."

"Then why aren't they dickering?"

"It's still too early. They have the documents, and they're probably examining a videotape of my speech. Give them time."

"If they take much more time, we ought to start cutting a few throats," growled Carpenter. "Maybe they'd like to see Johnny Carson's head on a plate."

"Shut up," said Gray. Carpenter got up. "Where are you going?"

"Up to the communications section, if it's all right with you."

"Simmer down, will you?"

"You forgot the 'son,' " said Carpenter.

Shortly after nine A.M., the boroughs surrounding Manhattan began to evacuate Negroes. The order came from the Acting Chief of Police, and no one questioned it. The Bronx, Queens, Brooklyn—all saw house-to-house searches by grim-faced policemen. They were angry, and their treatment of the bewildered Negroes was rough.

The same thing happened in Jersey City, Hoboken, Weehawken, West New York, Fort Lee, and other riverside New Jersey towns along the Hudson. Buses were brought into the areas and loaded with Negro residents. There was no time for packing; the evacuees were permitted to take along only what they could snatch up as they were ordered out of their homes.

On Long Island, Negroes were herded into any enclosure that could be guarded. Aqueduct Race Track became one such informal prison, as did the fence-enclosed area of Floyd Bennett Field. In New Jersey, cleared areas in Overpeck County Park and swamp flats along Sawmill Creek were used. There was no shelter; in the heat of the forenoon, children began to cry from thirst and hunger. Emergency kitchens and water supply trucks were set up, but there was not enough food or water to go around.

Both New York State and New Jersey were placed

under martial law. Federal troops converged on the banks of the Hudson, swarmed along the New Jersey Turnpike and Route 17. Civilians were forbidden to leave their immediate areas. Non-military cars were forced off the road and their distributor caps removed. Thousands of sightseers who had headed for the Palisades to stare through field glasses at the occupied city across the Hudson were stranded there, forbidden to use the highways to return home.

The quietest place in a hundred square miles was the besieged city itself. The black troops were in their positions; the civilian population was indoors. Along the Harlem River, rebel troops crouched behind abutments and stood in high windows overlooking the river. Quietly, they waited for whatever might come from the direction of Yankee Stadium.

On the west side of the island, combat engineers from the New Jersey side of the George Washington Bridge ventured out to the center of the span to examine damage from the night's bombing. They were driven back by machine gun fire.

An Army tank moved slowly out along the roadway. When it stopped, there was a flash at the New York end of the bridge, and a rocket burst against the tank turret. The rebels had bore-sighted three bazookas along the roadway. The tank went into reverse and retreated with only minor damage. After the brief skirmish, the bridge area was quiet, too.

Before the first day's shooting began, Colonel Clarence Dewey had sneaked away from his office at three in the heat of Friday afternoon, climbed into his red Mustang, and headed for Williamsburg, Virginia. Thousands of other government workers had the same idea, and his first ten miles took half an hour, but then he was rolling along toward Richmond on the broad concrete ribbon of Interstate Highway 95.

At Richmond he turned east on Route 60, through Sandston, and by seven in the evening he was showering in his Williamsburg motel room.

His wife and children were spending the summer with Marsha's family in Rochester, and Dewey was a summer bachelor for another two weeks. He dressed, had a beer in the motel cocktail lounge, then got back into the car for a four-mile drive to his favorite Williamsburg restaurant, The Oaks, near The College of William and Mary.

He began the meal with a glass of cold wine, since he could not be served liquor in Virginia. He took his time over his charcoal broiled steak; it was after ten P.M. when he paid the check and strolled out, puffing on his pipe.

Driving back to the motel, he listened absentmindedly to music from the car radio. The news broadcast was well under way before the words penetrated his consciousness.

". . . snipers firing at police and bystanders from the roofs of Coney Island. Newsman Ben Gates was shot and killed by one of the rioters. Mayor Clifford Pearson has said that the situation will not be allowed to get out of hand, and that the National Guard will not be needed. Stay tuned for. . . ."

Dewey swept the dial, searching for more news, but found only gospel music and an interminable commercial for *Changing Times*. When he got back to the motel he turned on the television set. NBC had interrupted its regular program to bring a report from Coney Island. It consisted principally of guesses as to the purpose and identity of the rioters, followed by a pool coverage statement from Walter Cronkite, who urged everyone to cool it. Dewey poured a shot of Jack Daniels into a bathroom glass and sipped at it, switching channels to see if he could find any harder news. But the coverage was all speculation.

What he could pick out of the rumor and opinions disturbed him. This was more than an ordinary riot. He found himself hoping that Marsha had not picked this weekend to pay a visit to New York. He dialed his mother-in-law's number, and was relieved when his wife answered.

"I was just sitting here watching TV and got lonely," he said.

"Then you must know about the riot."

"I saw a news report."

"Did you hear about your friend?"

"What friend?"

"It was on the first report. They said the FBI had linked him with the group that planned the riots. I *think* it was the FBI that found out about him."

Dewey struggled to keep annoyance out of his voice. "Can you think of his name, honey?"

"Oh, that general you knew, in Vietnam. Shawcross."

When Dewey hung up the receiver, he opened the dresser drawer and began to repack his suitcase.

The temperature was almost a hundred degrees, and the air was oppressively humid along the Harlem River.

"I think they're starting to move out," reported a black observer perched on the roof of a six-floor tenement on the Bronx side of the river. His message was received in the Empire State Building and relayed to the static force along the river.

"For Christ's sake," Shawcross said, "doesn't that National Guard idiot know we've got him boxed in with a crossfire?"

The National Guard commander did not even know that he had been forbidden to attack the island of Manhattan.

At ten minutes before twelve, his troops were ordered into the water. Some rode in rubber rafts, some in rowboats. Many started to swim across the Harlem River, holding onto life jackets.

The rebel static force commander looked down at the river from his position in the heights above the Harlem River Drive and felt slightly sick.

The National Guard commander sent nearly twelve hundred men into action against the Harlem Heights. They never had a chance.

When the rebels opened fire, the river, which at one point looked like an incredibly crowded swimming pool, became a bloody, frothy torrent of sinking rafts and thrashing men.

Some, near the Manhattan shore, managed to climb out of the river, right into the muzzles of rebel guns.

The slaughter lasted less than twelve minutes. After the last shot echoed against the rock-clad Heights, an oppressive silence settled over the battleground.

Three hundred eighty Guardsmen were dead or missing in the swift current of the Harlem River. Four hundred nineteen others were wounded. Most got back to the Bronx shore; twenty-one were captured by the rebels.

This was the second time a well-armed force had failed to seize the Harlem Heights. The first force had been British, fighting against General Washington, who had defended the island with another army of rebels during the first Revolutionary War.

Two hours later, Shawcross made a tour of the area.

"Watch it, sir," said one of the black troops. "They're still sniping at us from over there."

Shawcross could hear the occasional flat slap of small arms fire from the other side of the river.

By now the current had carried the bodies and the shattered boats downriver, but the bodies of Guardsmen who had made it to the Harlem River Drive before being killed were sprawled everywhere.

"See if they'll honor a white flag so we can get those bodies out of there," Shawcross said.

"We tried that. They hit two of our men."

"Okay," Shawcross said, "but when it gets dark, I want those men buried. Dig a mass grave in the park. And check dog tags, wallets, anything you can find. Those poor bastards had wives and families. When this thing's over, they'll want to know where their men are buried."

"Yes sir," said the officer.

"What were our losses?"

"Very light. Twenty-eight dead. We've sent the wounded over to the New York Medical Center."

It was unlikely the Guard would try a river crossing again, but Shawcross was disturbed by the size of the counterattack. It meant that the Administration was going to fight instead of talk. Because he had no way of knowing that this abortive attempt was under the direction of one misguided commander who had acted without specific instructions, Shawcross returned to the Empire State Building full of apprehension and reported to Gray that it seemed likely they were to be met with force instead of negotiation

It did not take long for young black men of Harlem and the East Side to discover that a white handkerchief tied around their arms would protect them against all but the most persistent questions. Hundreds descended into the city's midtown area, where Liberation troops were scarce anyway, and systematically began looting the stores on Fifth and Madison Avenues.

While gunfire echoed sharply across the Harlem River, the loudest sound in the heart of the city was the clanging of dozens of burglar alarms.

Looters broke into Tiffany & Company, at the corner of Fifty-seventh Street and Fifth Avenue. A guard who had remained inside since the takeover fired on them, wounded two, and then was overcome and kicked to death under the famed clock supported by a figure of Atlas. Looters fought with each other over their spoils. Just inside the door, the yellow Tiffany diamond, mined in South Africa in 1877, glowed dully—ignored by men who went after rings and watches.

They ran up Fifth Avenue toward the Plaza Hotel, carrying armloads of expensive dresses from Bonwit Teller and Bergdorf Goodman.

Dozens of young people staggered out of F.A.O. Schwarz onto the sidewalk, laughing, carrying huge stuffed animals.

When looters occasionally were challenged by occupation troops, they dropped their booty and ran for cover, pointing at their white armbands. In some instances black soldiers joined in the looting.

Most watchmen assigned to the stores stood by and did not interfere. Those who did were severely beaten. Several were killed.

St. Patrick's Cathedral was spared by the looters only because black soldiers were patrolling its entrances. One half-drunk boy tried to throw a brick through a stained glass window and was shot in the leg by an outraged soldier.

At the Museum of Modern Art, on West Fifty-third Street, vandals slit paintings with knives and wrote obscenities across statues.

The Zenith, Motorola, and Sony showrooms were broken into and stripped of portable television sets. Three determined looters made off with a six-hundred-dollar color set and lugged it as far as Seventy-second Street, where they abandoned it on the sidewalk.

Amazingly, real damage was slight. The looters, shouting and laughing, smashed windows and showcases, scooped watches and rings into their pockets, but rarely penetrated above the first floors.

There was no serious fire yet in Manhattan on this first day of the siege. But with the fire departments shut down and refuse and debris starting to pile up in the streets, the hot August breezes soon began to smell of burning wood.

"It's all set," said Pete Humble, around a mouthful of the sandwich he had mooched from the chef of the Njalaian Embassy. "I spotted this cat with a walkie-talkie, he passed my message along to Uncle William, and the General's sending a car for us."

"Not for me," said Eloise Gibson.

"Sweetie, you're being silly," said the comic. "Your everloving Stan is over there at the helm. Don't you want to fly to his side?"

"Don't snow me, Pete. I'm worried sick. But he knows where to find me. And if he doesn't have time for me now, I'm not going to go pushing in."

"I thought maybe you didn't agree with what he's doing."

"As a matter of fact I don't."

"Shall I tell the brave General that when I see him?"

"That's up to you," she said. "Personally, I think our friend Gray is taking every black person in America for a royal sleigh ride."

"This is John Alexander Roberts," said a voice from the

radio speaker, "Congressman for the Twenty-seventh District. I am speaking from my home in Harlem, and I want you to go next door and tell your neighbor to tune in to me. Go on, right now—I'll keep talking so you can find me on the dial. All of you black people in New York, tune me in and listen to me, because what I got to say is going to open your ears, baby. Like I said, this is your friendly neighborhood Congressman, John Alexander Roberts, and I am speaking now mainly for the purpose of giving your next door neighbor a chance to tune me in, so everybody lean out the window right now and holler, 'You all got Roberts tuned in?' Hear me, you holler that out right now."

Throughout Manhattan, windows already opened to the warm air flew up even wider, and heads poked out into the late afternoon and shouted: "Hey, the Congressman's on the radio. He wants you to listen." There was no need to name him; to black New Yorkers, there was only one congressman.

The communications experts had overlooked one AM transmitter in upper Harlem. Station WXOB, originally operated by the now defunct *Harlem Enterprise*, had been off the air for over a year and thus left alone. Tie-lines had now been run into Roberts' home.

Roberts knew that urging listeners to get their neighbors tuned in would gain him the widest possible audience; he knew, also, that it would be only a matter of time before the signal was picked up, traced, and eliminated.

"Okay, children," he said, "here we go. I don't know how much time I have to speak with you, so listen hard because there will be no reruns of this program.

"You must know by now that this island of Manhattan has been taken over by an armed force which refers to itself as the Afro-American Army of Liberation. Right off the bat, children, that is a bare-faced lie.

334

"Did anyone ask you if you wanted to be part of a rebellion? Did they ask anyone you know? Has anyone breathed a word of a black nation called Redemption until this morning?

"The answer to all these questions has to be no, baby—you never heard about any of these things because these mighty black leaders did not dare ask you what you thought. They did not dare because they knew full well what the answer might be.

"You all know where I stand with regard to the black man in America. I've been fighting a long time to get injustices remedied. But with all my anger at the way the black man is treated here, I am an American and proud of that fact. So don't tell me to abandon my country, turn against my flag, and pretend I am an *African!*

"When you come up to me and talk like that, baby, I call you what you are. What you are is a traitor.

"I don't know how much longer you're going to be able to hear my voice, because you can bet your black asses—sorry about that, Mr. FCC—that the rebels are on their way here right now to shut me off. That shows you how much justice and freedom you can expect from this gang who pretend to be speaking for you. How can they speak for you without giving you a chance to speak for yourself?

"Stay out of their way. Do not try to fight them head-on, they've already proven they are killers—but don't go out of your way to help them. You all know how to put on the slow-down. Slow down, children, show Mr. William Gray that he cannot get away with—"

There were noises in the background. A new voice said, "That's enough, get away from that microphone."

Roberts raised his voice, and thousands of listeners heard, "You're black Americans. Don't—"

The station went off the air.

"Where the fuck does he come off going on the radio and attacking the movement?" said Gray. "I figured him for our side."

"He's an honest man," said Shawcross.

"Crap," said Carpenter. "He wasn't talking to Harlem. He was talking to Washington, to let Mr. Charlie know he's right in there Uncle Tomming."

"You know as well as I do that Roberts is no Uncle Tom," said Gray.

"You lilies," said Carpenter, "are going to sit here and let the whole thing fall apart around our ears. I say we go on the air and tell the President that if he doesn't come through soon we start killing hostages."

"Wait a minute," said Shawcross. Before he could say more, Gray stepped up to Carpenter.

"Ray," he said, "that's the second time you've shot off your mouth about killing hostages. It better be the last."

Carpenter started to splutter, decided against it, and stalked out of the room.

"Ray's all right," said Gray. "He's just a hothead."

The Prime Minister of Canada, disturbed by the influx of refugees, ordered the U.S.-Canadian border closed until further notice.

Students in Mexico rioted, demanding that their President recognize the government of Redemption. The Army was called out, and thirty-one students were shot down in the Zocalo of Mexico City.

Fidel Castro, in a television speech that lasted two hours and thirteen minutes, hotly denied any complicity in the second American Revolution, but formally recognized the new government. He moved two divisions to the perimeter of the U.S. base at Guantanamo.

Red China's Ambassador to Warsaw advised U.S. representatives there that if the government of Redemption requested it, China would send volunteers to help defend the "new republic."

Discussion in the United Nations bogged down as always, and the Assembly recessed at two in the afternoon for private meetings. By that time messages had been received from the Prime Ministers of Great Britain and Japan, both offering to act as mediator between the adversaries. The acting Ambassador from the United States refused both offers. "This," he declared, "is an internal affair."

Non-military flights in and out of Newark Airport were canceled. Dozens of Ranch Hand planes requistioned by the Air Force, parked on a taxi ramp near the control tower, were being pumped full of a liquid from tank trucks.

All the servicemen working near the planes wore gas masks.

THIRTY-ONE

In mid-afternoon, Special Forces men worked their way from floor to floor of the Hilton, looking for the Vice President of the United States. "Tear up every room in that hotel, but get him," Carpenter had said.

Eventually the troops found their way to the door of Elvira Mooney's room and knocked.

"Who's there?"

"Police. Open up." The Special Forces men had found this the most effective way of getting doors opened.

Elvira Mooney opened hers and was pushed aside.

"Hold on there," said a slim, blond-haired man, coming out of the bathroom. "You have no right to push my wife around like that."

"We don't want no trouble, mister," said one of the black men. "Just stand still for a minute and we'll be on our way."

One of the searchers looked under the bed; another checked the bathroom, the closet.

"That's all folks," said the first man. "Thanks for your help. My advice to you is to stay in this room. Don't go roaming around, or you might get in trouble."

A flight of C-123 Ranch Hand planes appeared out of

the south, sweeping up from Staten Island and over Upper New York Bay to converge on Manhattan. They angled around the skyscrapers on the lower tip of the island.

Another flight of the same ungainly aircraft appeared in the Hudson River Valley. They swept over Yonkers and the Bronx, and at five-fourteen P.M. on Saturday, August 30, crossed the Harlem River and were over occupied territory.

As each plane flew its assigned path, a white, misty liquid floated down between the buildings, swirling in clouds between the Hudson and East Rivers. The planes flew slowly, trembling on the very edge of the stall; it took them almost five minutes to go from one end of the island to the other. The planes flying north were at eight hundred feet; the ones flying south, at one thousand feet. At a point near Seventy-second Street, the aircraft at the lower level had to fly through the choking mist released by planes at the higher altitude. The crews wore protective clothing and gas masks, but even so they became uncomfortable as minute quantities of the CS found its way through their protective garments.

People caught out in the open heard the planes approaching, looked up, and saw the mist floating down. Tears and a fierce burning in the throat were the first sensations. Then, as the gas penetrated the skin's pores, an overwhelming sense of suffocation came over each victim. In cases where the gassed person suffered from a serious respiratory or heart condition, suffocation was often permanent.

Ninety-three people died in the first ten minutes. Many were elderly men and women, lying in their beds near open windows, who were unable to escape the penetrating gas.

Redemption troops caught in the streets sprawled in doorways, vomiting, tears streaming down their faces.

Those in air-conditioned buildings suffered just as badly: the giant fans caught the gas and pumped it through the buildings in seconds—in many cases delivering a dose that exceeded what a man might have received outdoors. The central air conditioning in the Empire State Building was efficient, and the pilots had released a particularly heavy dosage over its spire.

Shawcross, choking, dragged himself to the radio room and prodded a weeping Richard Wilcox into switching the transmitter to the Command network.

"All personnel, protect yourselves from the gas," Shawcross called. "Put your heads under running water. Use towels wrapped around your faces. Get off the streets for the next ten minutes and protect yourselves the best you can. I repeat, all mobile forces, protect yourselves against gas for the next ten minutes and then converge on Central Park. Be ready for an air drop in the next half-hour. Mobile West observers along the Hudson, warn us of any amphibious action." He turned to Wilcox. "Transmit an all-points alert—I want to know what they're sending in. I'd guess drop planes and helicopters, but we've got to know if they're sending any hogs."

"They wouldn't send in gun ships; they'd kill more civilians than—"

"Don't tell me what they won't send in!" shouted Shawcross. "Just get on the horn and pass the word."

"Yes sir."

Wilcox moved to his equipment.

"I *told* you!" Raymond Carpenter choked, running cold water over his face. He and Gray had both shut themselves in the bathroom of Gray's apartment. "They're not dealing, they're launching a counterattack. I told you what we had to do and you wouldn't listen. Now it's too late!"

Gray started to answer, was struck with a paroxysm of vomiting, and could not speak. When he looked up from the toilet bowl, Carpenter was gone.

Between the dropping of the gas and the assault, Hazzard had planned an interval of twenty minutes. Two things combined to rob him of his victory. Thanks to a mix-up in take-off procedures, his troop carriers were eight minutes late reaching the drop zone. By the time the formation shaped up over the New Jersey flatlands, eight precious minutes had been lost. Because of a boat shortage, any attempts at an amphibious operation had been abandoned.

Minutes after the CS gas blanketed the city, a stiff breeze sprang up from the west, blowing much of the heavy gas out over the East River into Queens and Brooklyn, where already harassed citizens now had one more thing to worry about. As a result the defenders had less exposure to the gas than had been planned. The lost eight minutes helped them to recover even more—and by the time radio reports alerted Shawcross to the aerial armada approaching from the west, his troops were in position, little the worse for wear.

"They're sending in hogs," he reported to his field commanders. This was their signal to move their troops from the boundaries of the park, and men in windows back into inner rooms.

The helicopter gun ships swept in over Riverside Park, bumped up over the brownstones and apartment buildings, and made a circuit of Central Park.

Their firepower was astonishing. Machine gun bullets shattered the sidewalks, striking sparks and throwing up concrete dust. They riddled clumps of bushes where suspected defenders might be hiding and broke parkside windows.

On Shawcross' instructions the fire of the gun ships was not returned; the squadron commander assumed that the gas had done its job. He reported this conclusion to the airborne jumpmaster.

The breeze dropped for a few moments, and it was then that the gun ships made their attack. But it started up again just as troop carriers appeared over the city.

"It's starting to blow down here," warned the gun ship squadron commander. "Coming in from the west, maybe fifteen knots."

"Roger," replied the jumpmaster. Fifteen knots of breeze approached the limits of safety for an ordinary drop, but this was an extraordinary situation. He reported to Hazzard, received a confirmation that the risk should be taken, and the troop carriers proceeded toward their drop zone.

An entire airborne division hurled itself into the heat of the August sky that afternoon. Men threw themselves into the slip streams of the troop carriers, felt static lines rip the parachutes from their packs, then found themselves in the horror of a turbulent wind that seemed to come from nowhere.

Those troops who were lucky enough to remain within the boundaries of the park had trouble enough. They wound up splashing in the lakes, where dozens, dragged down by their heavy equipment, drowned. Some were impaled on the tops of trees or smashed against the metal sides of the automobiles parked in every flat area. Many were injured and out of action before a shot was fired.

The rest of the division had even worse problems. The wind carried them into the buildings along the eastern boundary of the park. Hundreds smashed into the sides of buildings on Fifth Avenue, falling to the pavements with broken limbs and bleeding faces. Others, higher still, were dragged over roof tops and scattered from Fifth Avenue to the East River—and beyond. Nineteen paratroopers drowned in the river itself.

General Hazzard's counterrevolutionary force, which had had every expectation of an almost bloodless victory, was demolished that afternoon.

Hundreds of men lay tangled in their shroud lines, bleeding from injuries suffered during the drop. The cluster of troops which would have formed in the park and then moved out to retake the city was scattered and disconnected so badly that few forces of squad strength or better managed to form up. In the main, it was individual men and improvised squads who engaged the Redemption troops in the one-sided battle.

The gun ships, which had retreated from the drop zone to avoid fouling the chutes of the paratroopers, returned and found themselves unable to offer covering fire: U.S. troops were scattered so widely that there was no perimeter to defend.

When three Huey helicopters were blasted out of the sky by a concentration of bazooka and recoilless-rifle fire, the others were ordered away from the park. The facades of buildings along the avenue were draped with the white nylon parachutes of unfortunate paratroopers who hung helplessly from cornices, from chimneys, from flagpoles. Many swayed limply, unconscious. Others were too injured to lower themselves to safety with the coil of rope they carried for that purpose.

In Washington, hooked in to the U.S. Command Circuit, the President shut his eyes tightly and shook his head.

"Hazzard?" he said thickly.

"Yes sir?" came the General's voice from the New Jersey banks of the Hudson.

"Can you communicate with your men?"

"We've lost our radio links."

"There must be some way you can talk to them, even if they can't talk back."

"We've got public address systems in some of the choppers."

"Use them. Tell your men to throw down their arms and surrender."

"I can't do that, sir," protested the General.

"Like hell you can't!" shouted the President. "Do you want to kill them all? You've lost, Hazzard. Save the ones you can."

In minutes the troops in Central Park were surprised to see three helicopters approaching the park again with white flags dangling from open hatches. Some of the rebels fired, but most waited as the ships got closer.

"Attention," rasped a loudspeaker from the nearest helicopter. "Hold your fire. Both sides, please hold your fire. I have a message from the President of the United States."

The men—black and white—lay in their positions and listened.

"My instructions are to order the men of the Ninety-fourth Airborne Division to lay down their arms and surrender to the forces of the rebellion. I repeat, men of the Ninety-fourth Airborne Division, you are ordered to lay down your arms and surrender. That is a direct order from the Commander-in-Chief."

On his command frequency, Shawcross spoke. "Watch out for tricks. But if they come out with their hands up, hold your fire."

There were no tricks. The United States had surrendered a full division of men.

Nations around the world, advised of the air drop by United Nations communications headquarters, reacted with concern for their nationals marooned in the captured city.

Strong protests to Washington jammed the cables. Dozens of messages urged restraint in dealing with the rebels, pointing out that thousands of lives were involved and suggesting that negotiation be tried.

"Idiots," muttered Attorney General Hugh McLeod. "You don't negotiate with rebels. Half of those countries had their own revolutions. They didn't negotiate."

"We may have to," said the President.

Paula Burke rushed in. "Excuse me, Mr. President, the rebels are on television again."

"Thank you," he said, switching on the portable TV that had been set up on the corner of his desk. He heard an unfamiliar voice speaking.

". . . a posture of accommodation to the United States," said the voice. "But this posture has not succeeded."

Now the picture came in, and the President was looking at a black face he had never seen before.

"Accordingly, the Redemption Army is forced to take additional steps."

"Who is he?" asked the President.

"Raymond Carpenter," said Paula Burke. "He used to be a militant poet."

A militant *poet?* he thought. It's like a bad dream!

"Our original demands were modest," said Carpenter. "Barely enough living space for our current population, space we have earned a thousand times over. Every step we made was taken with care to avoid a dangerous confrontation. Every effort was made to avoid unnecessary bloodshed and damage. What has been the reaction to this accommodation?"

Carpenter's voice took on a fierceness. "The white police attacked us across the East River. Their forces were destroyed, and we took no further action. But the honkeys did not learn. At noon, a large military force struck at us across the Harlem River. Again, they were driven back by Redemption fighting men. And we took no further action.

"Five hours later, the entire city was gassed from the air. Against all civilized rules of warfare and humanity, an entire city was blanketed with choking gas, injuring civilians and troops alike, making no distinction between race or sex, suffocating babies and old people. This attack was followed by a massive assault from an entire Airborne Division—gunship helicopters of the United States Army roamed up and down the streets, shooting at anything that moved, military or civilian. Every building along Fifth Avenue was riddled with heavy caliber machine gun bullets. Hundreds of civilians were killed or wounded.

"Despite the treachery with which it was carried out, the military attack by the United States failed. Several thousand paratroopers are now our prisoners.

"Our word to the United States is that it must halt here. We asked only for a moderate settlement, in partial reparation for the centuries of abuse and exploitation our people have suffered. The answer was a vicious, bloody series of attacks.

"Well, we will sit still no longer. This is our final warning. Respond to our demands or else. If the Administration does not heed this warning, our response will be swift and terrible.

"It is obvious that the President of the United States still needs convincing that we mean business. Very well, Mr. President, here is your proof."

The camera angle widened and the President started as he recognized Clifford Pearson. The Mayor was in a chair, hands tied behind his back.

"This man is the Mayor of New York," said Raymond Carpenter. "In his short term of office, he has harassed and tormented the black citizens of this city, he has spoken of them in terms of contempt and hatred.

"It was our wish to be merciful, even to our enemies. But that mercy is fast waning. In the case of this creature who has used his high office to destroy black pride, mercy is exhausted."

The three people in the President's office joined millions of others throughout the country and watched with horror as Raymond Carpenter turned to Pearson.

"You have been tried and found guilty of war crimes against the black people of this city," Carpenter said.

"Six rioters in a TV studio do not make a trial," said Pearson.

"The sentence is death by shooting." Carpenter moved closer to the bound man.

"He can't be going to—" McLeod began, then stopped.

Carpenter stood behind Pearson. He pressed a pistol against the back of the Mayor's head. Pearson winced as the metal touched him.

The cords in his neck stood out as he shouted, "Helen, don't watch!"

Carpenter fired.

"I want that man killed," said the President. "I want him found and shot without mercy."

"Yes sir," said Hugh McLeod as he sat numbly on the edge of the sofa and listened to Paula Burke's sobbing. The President held her hand and stroked her hair.

Night came over Manhattan. While Saturday nights in New York are usually festive and noisy, this one was distinguished by empty streets, dark theater marquees, and closed restaurants.

Cats ran furtively up the shadow-filled sidewalks, clattering through overturned garbage cans.

Except for the roving forces of the rebel army, not a

car moved along the streets. Buses stuck out into the middle of streets where they had been abandoned.

The city still had electricity, but many of the apartment windows were dark, their residents huddled inside, fearful of attracting attention with a light.

Thousands of city dwellers had started toward the Battery, hoping to ride the ferry to Staten Island. They huddled in hallways and abandoned stores—miles from their homes—trapped first by the gas attack and later by darkness.

For the most part, the looting had stopped. Some of the looters now sat around on door stoops and sipped at better whiskey than they had been used to, taken from smashed liquor store windows.

Occasionally the crash and whine of a distant shot was heard.

It was not surprising that, as night came on, white men with military backgrounds sought out others. Organized resistance to the rebel force formed in the darkness of hundreds of apartment buildings.

Shawcross and Wilcox looked up as the door of the radio room burst open. Five carbine-carrying Special Forces men fanned out as Raymond Carpenter came in.

Richard Wilcox reached for his sidearm. Shawcross stopped him with a sweep of his arm.

"That's better," said Carpenter.

"What is this?" asked Shawcross. "Where's Gray?"

"In his apartment downstairs. How did you like my speech?"

"Get Gray up here."

"You don't give me orders, General."

"Get Gray."

"No," said Carpenter. "Mister Gray is under guard.

From now on both of you are taking instructions from me."

Shawcross took a step toward the small man.

"Hold it right there," warned Carpenter. Two of the Special Forces men caught Shawcross by the arms. Shawcross glimpsed Wilcox going for his sidearm again. He yelled, "Don't!" but his command came just as one of the Special Forces men caught Wilcox full in the face with the butt of his carbine. Blood sprang from Wilcox's nose and mouth as he fell backward, crashing to the floor. He was still trying to get his pistol up when the first bullets from the other man's carbine slammed into his chest, his belly; and then one slug made a small, black, fatal hole just over his right eye.

Shawcross strained at the strong hands that held him. He was unable to speak.

"See what I mean?" said Carpenter. "It takes blood to shake people up. I didn't have anything against Wilcox. I didn't even have anything against poor old Pearson. I just needed somebody to nail to the wall. Now, are you going to cool down and listen to reason?"

"I'll kill you, Carpenter."

"Just sit down, General. You're not killing anyone. I need you, baby. Those troops out there like their Mister General, so cool it. We're going to win this one yet, but not the way you and Gray were going. Now, what's it going to be? Are you going to work with me? Or do you join Gray downstairs and let me finish up alone?"

Shawcross looked at the quiet body of Wilcox. He shrugged his way free from the restraining hands and sat down. After a long pause, he nodded.

"I'll work with you," he said quietly. "But just until this revolution is back on the track. And I warn you, I won't put up with any more of this killing."

"Fair enough," said Carpenter. "We've made our point, so we probably won't need to do any more anyway." He sat down and took out a thin cigar. It was the first time Shawcross had ever seen him smoke. "Now, let's talk some turkey about what we're going to do next."

THIRTY-TWO

Attorney General Hugh McLeod arrived in the Oval Office of the White House a few minutes after ten P.M. With him was Colonel Clarence Dewey.

"Mr. President," said McLeod, "I know how busy you are. But the Colonel here has persuaded me that what he has to say is important enough to put everything else aside."

"Sit down, Colonel," said the President.

"Mr. President," said Dewey, "I won't mince words. I think your plans for handling the rebellion are a terrible mistake."

"Plans?"

"It's no secret in the Pentagon that you're assembling another counterrevolutionary force for a major assault on Manhattan."

"What choice is there? Give in to their demands?"

"No sir. This is a black problem. Turn it over to blacks to handle."

"What do you mean by handle?"

"Gray didn't ask the rest of us if we wanted this revolution, at least the kind he's running. Plenty of us are sickened by what's happened. But if you mount a massive attack, if you escalate the killing, you'll force every black man in this country to take sides."

"There doesn't seem to be any choice," the President said.

"There is! Let me take a team of black troops into the city, go in fast and penetrate their command structure. When we do, we can cut the rebellion off at the top. Even if it doesn't work, what have you lost? You can still go ahead with your build-up."

"How would you do it?"

"Swim in at night. Teams of four. Every man a trained killer—what we call the zap squad."

"And once you're in the city?"

"Infiltrate rebel headquarters. That's the only way to do it, sir."

The President sat for a moment, thinking.

"All right, Dewey. What would you need?"

"These men." Dewey handed him a sheet of paper covered with names. "While we're gearing up, I'll send in a pathfinder team to scout the situation."

The President pressed his intercom button. "Paula, will you get General Hazzard in here."

"Mr. President," said McLeod, "the Colonel's plan will help us even more if we detach him and his men from our government."

"It sounds like we're ashamed of what we're asking them to do."

"Maybe. But it would cool some of the heat from other nations. There's a hell of a lot of difference between the Administration sending in the zap squad and other blacks doing it."

When General Hazzard entered, the President handed him the sheet of paper. "The Colonel's requested these men to form a commando force," he said. "Give him any other help he needs as well."

Hazzard frowned. "I hope we can locate these men," he said to Dewey.

"Most of them are here in the city, sir."

"Well—unfortunately, they probably aren't."

"What do you mean, General?" asked the President.

"Most Negro troops have been detached from their regular organizations, sir."

"What!"

"It was a request from the FBI, sir."

"Are you trying to tell me you've put them under arrest?"

"Detention, sir, not arrest. Detention for the duration of the emergency."

"Why wasn't I told?"

"I don't know, sir. I assumed you had authorized it."

The President punched the intercom button. "Paula, get that bastard Paulson over here on the double."

"I'm sorry, sir," said Hazzard. "I was acting under orders."

"You should have questioned those orders. I want you to get moving and see if you can undo this mess. Locate those men. Authorize Colonel Dewey—"

"—*Mister* Dewey," said McLeod.

"—to take complete charge of the situation up to and including Mr. Dewey's assuming command of certain military forces in the area. Do you understand those orders, General?"

"Yes sir. Thank you, sir." Hazzard turned and left, dazed.

"What can I say, Dewey?" said the President.

"I won't shuffle my feet and say everything's all right, sir, because it sure as hell isn't. We'll go in and pull your hot potatoes out of the fire, but there's going to have to be a whole new deal around here. After this, if you think we're going to settle for a bunch of promises and civil rights bills and antipoverty programs, you've got another think coming. Sir."

"We earned that," said the President. "What exactly do you want?"

"Hold on," McLeod yelled. "Now *he's* blackmailing us!"

"Call it what you want," said Dewey. "We'll get your city back for you, but don't think we're packing up and going home afterward with a chestful of tin medals and your handshakes."

"Go on," said the President.

"Mr. President, we've had a lot of abstract freedoms thrown at us, along with abstract programs and promises. The trouble is, you can't eat abstractions. We want concrete things. Things like food, clothing, shelter. This goddamned country's full of silos crammed to the top with food surpluses. Well, silos don't have to eat. But people do—poor white people as well as poor black people. It's time you stopped worrying about offending a few local politicians who want to keep the price of wheat up and started using that wheat to make bread for our own hungry people."

"Proposals like that have been made before," said the President. "They're not as simple to carry out as you think."

"Mr. President," said Dewey, "you don't have any choice."

"I agree," said the President. "But while we're being frank, how can you trust me? I might tell you anything now for the sake of expediency, and go back on it all tomorrow."

"I think you can take the President's word," said McLeod.

"Sorry, sir," said Dewey. "Not good enough."

Furious, McLeod stood up. The President touched his

arm. "In other words," he said, "no tickee, no washee."

Dewey nodded. McLeod swore and turned away.

"It's all right, Hugh," said the President. "I don't blame them for not trusting us any more. Colonel, I'm planning an address to the nation later tonight. Suppose we spend some time now working out a first step program for your people. Then I'll announce the results during my address. You'll have the entire world in your corner as witnesses."

"Mr. President," said Dewey, "you've got yourself a deal."

THIRTY-THREE

Saturday night passed quietly in Manhattan. An occasional shot boomed in the empty streets. Buildings burned, untended by firemen. Someone in the Empire State Building suggested running an old movie over the rebel-controlled TV channels. Raymond Carpenter approved. "It'll give those honkeys something to do," he said.

The Wolf Man, featuring a young Lon Chaney, Jr., contrasted oddly with the genuine terror of the night. As Chaney frothed his way through acres of wolfbane, hundreds of white men slipped out into the darkened streets, weapons ready, taking up positions. They were commanded by former noncoms and officers who had seen combat in Vietnam, or Korea, or even World War II— all determined to fight for their lives.

The broadcasts from Newark kept them aware of the situation. Then, at midnight, the President made an address to the nation.

"We regret our original military reaction," he said. "It was an error.

"Serious consultation with Negro leaders has convinced us that the desperate men in Manhattan do not speak for all of black America. We have been asked to stand aside and allow negotiations to begin between the factions of the black community.

"Equally important, this Administration has been forced to take note of the mistakes we have made in the past. We have agreed to a three-point—drastic but necessary—proposal made by responsible members of the black community, and I tell you this: I have taken a personal vow as strong as my original oath of office to see these steps given life so that the plight of twenty-two million black Americans is changed—not slowly, but dramatically and immediately.

"The days of food surpluses being stored to maintain prices are over. That food is going to be distributed. By the end of the week, if there is a single hungry man in this nation, it will be because we haven't been able to find him. I know this is going to cause problems for the farm industry, but somehow we'll work them out. In the meantime, we intend to erase the word *hunger* from the dictionary.

"Housing comes next. Eighty-seven percent of Harlem housing is substandard. This government has always been able to build a Boulder Dam or send a man to the moon by applying massive resources to the problem. Well, those same resources are going to be applied to the housing renewal problem of this nation. We are already in contact with such energetic builders as Mr. Levitt, and within the week we will launch a massive housing project unparalleled in world history. Substandard housing is going to be a thing of the past. And note that this new approach to housing will not be a government project. The people who live in those houses, white and black, are going to own them, if we have to let them buy them a brick at a time. This nation has resources enough to support this program, and we intend to do it.

"Finally, point three. Education. Money for education

comes from three sources today. There are federal dollars, and local dollars, and foundation dollars. It has been suggested, and we are going to look into the proposal very hard, that all of these dollars be pooled and divided per capita among all school children in this nation. Roughly, what we intend to do is arrive at a figure to which each child is entitled. Then, that child will be permitted to choose the school he wants to attend. Any school, anywhere, private, public, parochial, black, white, or zebra— wherever the child goes, that's where his dollars go. Now, this is going to take some working out, but it is not going to be shelved or sidetracked, and within a very few months I assure you, my fellow Americans, that the face of education in this country will be changed drastically."

The President took a long drink from a water glass. He looked out at the camera silently.

"Some are going to say," he continued, "that I had no right to agree to these proposals. Well, that may be so. President Truman decided to drop the atomic bomb, President Eisenhower decided to send troops to the Middle East, President Kennedy decided to enforce the Cuban quarantine, President Johnson committed us to a land war in Southeast Asia. I have determined to commit us to another war, a war against injustice and poverty and hunger. With your help, and God's, we will win.

"Meanwhile, this nation's mantle of protection still covers embattled Manhattan Island, and any foreign power thinking to benefit by the present confusion would be well advised to reconsider. We will brook no interference with the internal affairs of this nation, whether that interference is well-intentioned or not. In plain language, no trespassing."

"The Director is waiting," Paula Burke said over the intercom.

"I'm his boss," Hugh McLeod protested, in the Oval Office. "I ought to stay here."

"I'm *your* boss," said the President. "Leave this one to me, will you, Hugh?" McLeod left, and passed Paulson on his way in without a word.

The FBI man stood stiffly inside the office, waiting to be invited to sit down.

"You have made a mistake you will not be allowed to make again," said the President. "I am ordering you to tender your resignation, effective immediately."

"You forget, Mr. President, that this job is not a political appointment. Mr. Hoover made that clear when he took over in 1924, and I repeated that viewpoint when I assumed the job."

"I don't give a damn what you repeated. Your duty is to this nation and to this government. How dare you order General Hazzard to detain Negro servicemen?"

"My duty," said Paulson, "is to avoid any possible escalation of the unfortunate situation in Manhattan. This is a black rebellion, and therefore we must guard against black citizens who could seek to contribute to its success. I realize that my position might not seem a popular one to an official who wants to be reelected, and that is exactly why I made it so clear that my post must not be dependent on public opinion."

"That's so much crap and you know it," said the President. "I want you out of that office right now. Harris will take over as Acting Director."

"Mr. President, I ask you to reconsider," said Paulson, softening his tone. "The directorship is not a political football to be kicked around by whichever party happens to be in office. Our nation's security—"

"Very nice speech, the Police Academy sleeping pill. I've heard you give it at least a dozen times."

"Is it really necessary for you to be so unpleasant, Mr. President?"

"It is. I've got to get some of this bile out of my system before I have to apologize again for your idiocy. Please, do us both a favor. Leave now and don't come back. Don't go to your office, I've already given instructions that you are not to be admitted. Just get out of here and be thankful that I'm not pressing charges."

Shawcross, busy at the radio, looked up in annoyance. "What are you doing here?" he asked.

"Eloise got to worrying about you," said Pete Humble.

"Where is she?"

"I stashed her down on the next floor," said Humble. "I figured things might be a little hot up here."

"Well if it isn't the funny man," said Raymond Carpenter, entering the room. He wore trim, neat khakis. On his shoulder was a circle of five gold stars.

"Been out raiding the Army-Navy stores, Ray?" asked Humble.

"Watch your mouth," said Carpenter.

The communications man who had taken over after Wilcox was killed looked up.

"Mr. Carpenter, there's a radio message for you." He handed Carpenter a microphone.

"This is Carpenter."

The radio speaker squawked with static. "Captain Ben Harris, sir. I'm at United Nations communications center. Ambassador Harumba wants to speak with you."

"Put him on."

A new voice spoke. "Carpenter? I've been trying to find Mr. Gray."

"I'm in charge now, Mr. Harumba."

"Very well. Carpenter, your exhibition on television

leaves my government no choice. We are forced to with-
draw our support for your movement."

"It's a little late, baby," said Carpenter. "We've already
got what we wanted."

"You are a fool, Mr. Carpenter. You've got nothing. It
was only a matter of days until you would have succeeded. Then you had to destroy it all with a meaningless
gesture. You've set the black movement back fifty years."

"Shove it," said Carpenter, clicking off the radio.

He looked around the room. "Why are you all looking
at me?" No one answered. He cursed and hurried out.

The Secretary-General sat in his office at the United
Nations and pushed his face into his hands. He had not
slept for over thirty-six hours, and he was not a young
man.

The Vice President's wife picked up the telephone,
started to dial the President's private number. Then she
put the receiver back in its cradle. The poor man, she
thought. The last thing he needs is me pestering him
about my husband.

General James Hazzard raised his voice. "Yes, you
heard me right. The orders come straight from the President. This man Dewey's a civilian and you *will* consider
yourself under his command from the moment he arrives.
How the hell do I know when he's going to arrive? And
listen carefully, I don't want any incidents. Incidents,
goddammit, incidents! Why? Because Dewey and his
men are niggers, that's why!"

Karen Davis heard a heavy knocking on her apartment
door.

"Who's there?"

"Police," said a voice. "Open up."

She released the double lock, and the door swung open. When she saw the black faces outside, she tried to push it shut again, but the first man's foot was in the way.

"You Karen Davis?"

She nodded.

"Mr. Gray sent us to fetch you," he said, not unkindly.

"Oh," she said. "Is he all right?"

"Right as rain," said the man.

John Genelli sat in his room at the Americana Hotel, tilting a bottle of beer. "They'll get theirs," he said. "Wait'll we're out of here. We'll show those spades who's boss."

"Sure," said another syndicate leader. "And while you're at it, think up what we're going to tell Mr. D'Amato when he asks us how something like this could build up without us getting a whiff of it. It better be convincing."

Shawcross warned Marvin Hamilton that he expected some action from the whites this night.

Hamilton agreed. "They've been too quiet," he said. "And we never got around to picking up their guns."

Private Albert Grant, exhausted by almost two days without sleep, sat behind the retaining wall of the Christopher Columbus Fountain in Columbus Circle. He had been sipping on a half-pint of Carstairs he had liberated from a nearby liquor store, and was pleasantly warm and sleepy. He jammed the bottle into his hip pocket and stood up to look around the darkened entrance to Central Park. At that moment he thought he saw a bright flash to one side, but before he could turn his head a bullet struck his temple, ripping out blood and brains and all the thoughts and memories that had made him the individual called Albert Grant.

At four-thirty in the morning, a giant power line feeding electricity into the city from upstate power plants first smoked, then shorted. Light bulbs dimmed to a deep yellow, then went out. Television pictures shrank, flickered, and disappeared. Elevators hesitated, then stopped between floors.

Power to upper Manhattan was cut off. To spotter planes orbiting the city, the upper portion of the island seemed to flicker and vanish.

"Now it gets rough," said Shawcross.

"The snipers'll really go to town," said Hamilton.

"Keep them isolated from one another and go in and get them."

"We may have to burn a couple of buildings."

"Burn them," said Shawcross.

THIRTY-FOUR

A Redemption soldier, one of several moving cautiously along Lenox Avenue, was suddenly slammed back by a shot from a high-powered rifle. A companion tried to hold him up, but the wounded man seemed to have lost all strength in his legs. Another shot from the same rooftop hit the second soldier, his right temple exploding in a pink spray of flesh and bone chips.

"Take cover!" yelled a black officer.

An NCO, hustling around the corner of 136th Street, said, "We can't get above them. They got all the high spots."

The officer pointed to a tall brownstone that dominated the corner. "That's where it's coming from! Give me that bull horn." He took it up and from the protection of a parked car shouted, "You up on the roof. Cease firing. You're surrounded. Come down the fire escape with your hands up."

His answer was a volley of shots that shattered the car's windshield.

"Burn the building," said the officer.

The NCO waved three of his men forward. They ran, swerving, dodging the fire from the rooftop. Safe up against the building, they threw two white phosphorous grenades through the ground floor windows and ran for cover as the flames mushroomed inside.

"That'll bring the bastards down."

Either the snipers did not realize their danger until the flames burst through the roof, or they waited too long. As the blaze cut them off from the fire escape and the heat intensified, several jumped. One, his clothing on fire, screamed all the way to the pavement seven flights below.

At nine A.M. on Sunday, one of the scheduled food trucks failed to arrive. Raymond Carpenter waited impatiently at the exit of the Lincoln Tunnel, glancing at his wrist watch.

"Okay," he said at nine-ten. "Those honkeys over there—" he pointed to one huddled group of hostages—"line them up."

The thirty hostages cut out of the crowd stood against the wall of the tunnel, dazed. A moment ago they were on their way to safety and now—

"Okay," said Carpenter.

The machine guns opened up. Some awaited the bullets passively. Others hid behind shaking hands, like a child in kindergarten who believes that because his finger hides the teacher from him, the teacher cannot see him. One man ran at the black troops. The bullets caught him in the head and he fell back, his face a red mask.

Just then, the missing truck drove out of the tunnel. The driver slammed on the brakes, stopping just at the edge of the carnage. Shaking, he got out of the cab and looked down at the sprawled bodies.

"I had a flat tire," he said. "It wasn't my fault!"

A narrow lane of bubbles formed in the Hudson River, pointing across it like an arrow directed at midtown Manhattan. Ten feet under the oily surface, three frogmen swam carefully, plotting their course with an illuminated compass. They cut through a wire mesh screen and penetrated a huge tunnel where the water was warmer and less turbulent.

They surfaced, found a ladder that led up to a walkway, and climbed it. Even though they were out of the water, they continued to breathe bottled air from the cylinders on their backs.

"Smells nice," mumbled one, getting a whiff of the sewer gas through his face mask. The leader motioned for silence. The men slipped out of their flippers and padded along in the darkness like three creatures from a science fiction movie.

The flames and smoke over the northern end of the city now towered high enough to be seen from the opposite side of the river.

"It's worse than Detroit," said Patrolman Larry Brickson to his partner.

"Hook me up to full Command network," Shawcross told a technician when he heard of the executions. The technician's fingers flew over the connections as he muttered instructions into his throat microphone. "Ready, sir."

"This is General Shawcross. Now hear this. No matter what orders you are given by your superiors, any man in this army who kills a hostage is guilty of murder and will be shot. I repeat, no matter *who* orders it, the killing of a hostage is forbidden unless you want to be executed for murder. We can still win if we stay together, but senseless atrocities are no answer. Now hold it down! That's an order. Shawcross over and out."

"Do those orders apply to Carpenter?" asked Hamilton.

"Especially to him," said Shawcross.

The second day of the siege was much worse for the prisoners of Manhattan. Apartment-house residents broke down the doors of those who had gone away for the weekend—and fought over cans of Campbell's soup.

The black troops were uneasy. Having become the targets of snipers, they were less inclined to be gentle toward whites found roaming the streets. More than one light-skinned Negro was beaten and sent bleeding into the nearest building, his white armband no protection against the anger of the troops.

The heat was oppressive. A pall of smoke hung over the city. The odor of burning wood was everywhere, along with the smell of garbage, excrement, and death.

When Shawcross tried to see Gray, the Special Forces men guarding the apartment would not let him enter.

"Besides, General," said one, "he's got his woman in there. You wouldn't want to interrupt now, would you?"

The Air Force weather experts were pessimistic.

"We're likely to get an inversion sometime tonight," one said. "And if we do, with all that combustion, those folks are going to have one hell of a job breathing."

His colleague examined the figures again. Neither mentioned out loud the possibility that frightened them more than the polluted air.

With the heat and burning gasses from the fires trapped under a summer inversion, conditions were almost perfect for the freak of nature that had destroyed Hamburg and Dresden in World War II.

Fire storm.

Karen Davis tried to keep Gray from pouring another slug of brandy. "Please, please don't get drunk."

Gray shrugged.

"But with all that killing," she cried, "no one will win. Can't you or the General control him?"

"Get your hand off that bottle."

"Please, William, do *something*."

"I couldn't get past the guards outside that door even if I had a gun. And what difference does it make? The country's split right down the middle, and Nat Turner didn't do it, I did it, that's what they'll remember, that's what counts. Now stop crying."

"We couldn't get inside the building," said the leader of the frogman team. He had returned alone from the mission across the Hudson. One of his companions was now lying motionless in the dark sludge of the sewer, overcome by wounds received when he and the third frogman were shot by an alert Empire State Building guard.

The leader handed Dewey a red, black, and green strip of cloth. "You need these armbands. And ordinary issue khakis."

Dewey took the armband and turned to a cutaway plan of the Empire State Building. "Thirty men," he said finally. "Ten to hold the entrances while the other twenty go to the top."

"Okay," said the frogman.

"Get cleaned up and catch some sleep. We won't be going over until slack tide, after midnight." The frogman nodded and left. Dewey handed the Redemption armband to an army sergeant. "Get fifty of these made up by 1700 hours."

"Where do I do that, sir?"

"How the hell do I know? Open up a tailor shop, just get it done."

"Yes sir."

Dewey had decided that if they left from Pier H just

above Weehawken Cove at slack tide, it would be an easy underwater swim straight across to the B&O Railroad pier at the foot of West Twenty-sixth Street. There, they would open their watertight plastic bags, don khaki uniforms, and head for the Empire State Building. It had to work.

Raymond Carpenter stopped his jeep at West 135th Street, on the edge of the burning area.

"Man, it's jumping from block to block," one of the black troops told him. "Those buildings are nothing but tinder."

"Let them burn," said Carpenter. "We're better off without them. Whitey can plant corn in the ashes, because us niggers are going to be long gone."

Refugees streamed out, carrying bundles of clothing and cardboard boxes.

"We're putting them in Lenox Terrace right now," said a black officer. "Every family there is doubling up with refugees. When we run out of space, we'll move into Abraham Lincoln and Riverton Houses."

"Don't sweat any over Whitey," said Carpenter. "Just take care of blood."

"Yes sir," said the officer, privately determined to disobey the instructions. The poor white families being driven out of their pitiful apartments in this predominantly black section of the city were in as much need as the colored. One family was accompanied by a black neighbor who called out to the soldiers, "This man's all right. He's a good man. He's been a good neighbor. Please don't hurt this man, he's all right."

A white sniper stepped nimbly from the roof of a building onto one that was blazing and disappeared inside. He reappeared with two squalling Negro babies, carried them back over to the other building, and handed them to a family who were evacuating the top floor. Then he returned to the roof with his rifle. No one ever found out who he was.

A blind man, white underneath layers of accumulated dirt, was pulled through smoke-filled streets in a wagon by three Negro boys. When adults approached their strange procession, the children shouted and threw rocks, making it clear they would protect their helpless charge.

One supermarket, directly in the path of the fire, was still being guarded by a black soldier and three draftees. The crowd begged the guard to let them remove the food before the fire reached the store, but the soldier was afraid to disobey his orders. Finally one of the draftees looked to heaven, said, "Lord, forgive me," and bashed the guard behind the ear with a shovel.

By midafternoon the fire had built a flaming wall across the northern end of Manhattan. On the west, it crept down as far as the campus of Columbia University at West 120th Street. On the east, it was further downtown, to East 106th Street, raging through Spanish Harlem.

At four-thirteen in the afternoon, a squadron of planes appeared over the Hudson River. The black troops, fearing gas again, hurried inside. But this time the aircraft were on a peaceful mission. Their huge belly tanks contained fire-fighting compound, which they scattered along the edges of the flames. It had little effect, however, and when the planes disappeared toward New Jersey, the fires seemed as fierce as ever.

"I don't think I'm in direct contact with more than half our units," Hamilton told Shawcross. "The rest are being pushed out of their areas by the fire."

"I made a mistake," said Shawcross. "When I said burn

a building or two to get the snipers out, I didn't realize the flames would spread so far."

"What are you going to do now?"

"Get Carpenter to parley with the government," said Shawcross. "It's our only chance."

"What are we waiting for?" John Moss yelled over the radio link with the White House. "They're burning the goddamned city to the ground!"

"Take it easy, John," said the President. "We're sending in a hunter-killer team tonight to get the leadership."

"Well, it better be damned soon, or there won't be any reason to take the exercise. The whole north end of the island's covered with smoke."

"I'm aware of that. My weather people are worried as hell about a fire storm."

Moss groaned. "That's all we need. What if tonight's plan doesn't work?"

"We'll be able to mount an assault by Tuesday. But we don't want that. The casualties on both sides would be terrible. You were in Europe, you know what house-to-house fighting can do to a city."

"It's a disgrace," Moss said quietly.

The President sighed. "The hell of it is that we knew this was coming for years, and we didn't move. They rioted, we beefed up the riot squads. The President's Commission warned us that black and white polarization was nearly complete—we argued in Congress."

"Have you considered giving them what they want?"

"What who wants?" said the President. "Shawcross? Gray? Carpenter? Greenbriar? Stop and think, Moss. The rebels in Manhattan speak for the black man's frustration and rage, but getting a separate state won't solve anything. If we give them New Jersey, what do we give the Indians? Do we give Detroit to the Poles? And what about blacks who don't want to live in Redemption? Do we establish a quota for immigrating Negroes moving back into the United States? And who's going to run those factories and industrial complexes they want so badly? How soon will Redemption turn into a nation in need of outside technical assistance? Who will provide it? Africa? Russia? John, it just doesn't make sense."

"No," said Moss, "I guess it doesn't."

Fear descended over Manhattan as darkness swept in from the east. The summer sunset was invisible behind a pall of smoke that drifted down over the island.

Spreading westward with the wind, the fire invaded the city. High-pressure hoses might have contained the flames, but the fire departments of Manhattan were no longer functioning. As the conflagration spread, most people just concentrated on getting the hell out.

For the black dwellers of the ghetto, there was no sense of triumph as their slums crumbled under the flames. They fled for their lives, abandoning the meager treasures of generations to the fire.

Every few minutes, planes appeared overhead and dumped chemicals on the flames. To the eye there was no noticeable result. Then a rumor spread that the Air Force was helping the fires along with flammable chemicals, and black troops began to fire at the planes.

"We'll go in around three in the morning," said Clarence Dewey. "Four-man teams. When we get into the city, we put on khakis and armbands, head for the Empire State. Their Chief of Operations is named Hamilton. If we're challenged we say Hamilton has ordered us to reinforce the security force there.

"When we get inside, here's how we split up." He showed Hazzard his plan.

"Can you capture Shawcross?" Hazzard asked.

"I doubt it," said Dewey. "I don't see him surrendering peacefully. My guess is he'll start heaving those lousy grenades at us. I hope not, but that's the way I read it."

"I know you'll do your best to bring him out," said Hazzard. "It's important that he go before a court-martial for his part in this."

"Really, General?" said Dewey. "Is *that* important? I thought what's important is that we somehow keep this country of ours from going down the chute."

"You've made your point, Dewey," said Hazzard. "Now, after you've completed your mission, you'll want to get off the island. I've arranged for two Navy PT boats—"

"We're going over to cut off the revolution's head," Dewey said. "Without a head, it will die."

"And if it doesn't?"

"Why then, General, we're going to be in one whole mess of trouble, and PT boats aren't going to do anybody much good."

By midnight, the worst fears of the experts came to pass.

The flames, feeding on thousands of tenements in upper Manhattan, erupted into a fire storm.

With a tower of heated air rising directly above the burning area, and fresh supplies of cool air being drawn in from the sides, a breeze began to move toward the wall of flame. The breeze became a wind, and the wind became a gale.

Shawcross drove up to East Ninety-sixth Street, the nearest safe approach to the fire. The streets going south were choked with refugees, their shouts hardly audible above the roar of the fire and the howl of the rising wind.

Breathing had become frighteningly difficult. The very oxygen was being sucked into the blaze.

"Everybody get out of here!" Shawcross yelled with his bull horn. "There's a fire storm building up! Get out of the area. Keep moving south."

A slight figure detached itself from a group of soldiers and came over to his jeep. It was Raymond Carpenter, his natty uniform streaked with soot.

"Where the hell have you been," said Shawcross. "We needed you back at headquarters. They'll never let us off the hook now, between what you did and the god-dammed fire."

"We'll make them," Carpenter said. "We'll kill every white motherfucker on this island if they don't wise up."

"Is that all you can think of?" yelled Shawcross. "Your tactics have turned every ally we had against us."

"All I did was shoot a few hostages. *You* started this fire."

The flames, violent splashes of color just blocks away, threw garish highlights over the strained faces of the two men. The streets near them were emptying.

"That mistake," said Shawcross, "wasn't as bad as the one I made two years ago. The stupidity of allowing men like you to get involved—I knew better and yet I did nothing about it."

"Men like what?" said Carpenter. "Men who don't flinch? We're *all* like that! You've killed, I have, and so has Gray."

"No," said Shawcross. "Not Gray. His hands are clean. And that's why he must pick up the pieces of this revolt. What's left of it."

"Gray's hands clean?" Carpenter laughed. "You'd be surprised at your friend Gray."

374

"After what you did on TV—"

"—At least, nobody can say the man I killed was completely innocent. He wasn't a helpless child. And it's not as if I enjoyed it."

"I don't believe that," said Shawcross.

Carpenter caught his arm as he started to turn away. Shawcross whirled and shoved the smaller man violently.

"You've been tricked!" Carpenter shouted, sprawled on the sidewalk. "You want to hand this revolution back to your precious Gray because you think he's so pure and noble? He's the worst of us all!"

"You're a liar," said Shawcross, starting for the jeep.

"Where are you going?"

Shawcross did not look around.

"You're going to give it all back to Gray again?"

Shawcross climbed into his jeep.

"Goddammit, Shawcross, listen to me!" Shawcross turned the key. "Don't you care about what happened to your family?"

Shawcross turned slowly. "What did you say?"

Carpenter spat. "There's your honest man for you!" He waved a hand toward the burning buildings. "That's the man who sent you out to burn a city. That's the man who sat around with his finger up his ass while I had to kill hostages to convince Whitey we meant business."

Shawcross caught him by the collar. "I asked you, what did you say?"

"Do I have to write it on the sidewalk? Where do you think your friend was when your family was being cut down with honkey bullets?"

"He was in Paris."

"He was shit! He was in Los Angeles, masterminding the execution."

"That's a lie!"

"Why the hell would I lie to you? You've been had!

375

Gray wanted you so bad he was willing to pay five thousand bucks to have your family killed."

Shawcross caught Carpenter by the throat. His hand tightened. The smaller man's face twisted. "Get away," he whispered.

"No one will help you," Shawcross said calmly.

Carpenter gasped, "It's—still—true."

The fingers around his throat relaxed. Shawcross straightened, Carpenter fell down to the street, coughing. As his hand reached for the pistol strapped to his belt, Shawcross' heavy boot crushed his fingers. Carpenter shrieked.

Shawcross threw the pistol across the street. "You little snake," he said.

Carpenter's lip trembled. Tears of pain streaked his soot-grimed cheeks.

Shawcross got back into his jeep, ground the starter, and headed down Madison Avenue.

Behind him, silhouetted against the flames, Raymond Carpenter dragged himself to his feet.

"Come back!" he yelled.

The jeep turned the corner.

"Shawcross! Don't leave me!"

The sound of the flames was a mighty roar—an angry mixture of crashing timbers and crackling tongues of flame.

Carpenter choked. The wind blew harder toward the center of the fire, and he started down Madison Avenue.

Papers swirled around him and were sucked into the pillar of flame.

The wind rose. Cardboard boxes and plastic garbage cans tumbled past him.

Carpenter realized that the flames had encircled him.

He made a small, mewing sound.

Slowly, without hope, he began to run.

THIRTY-FIVE

It was almost dawn when Shawcross managed to reach his headquarters. The streets were so choked with people that it was impossible to drive, and he abandoned his jeep. The journey downtown on foot, through hordes of terrified refugees, was like a descent into hell. All semblance of order had broken down. The rebellion was swallowed up in the individual fears and terrors of a million people.

Horrified by the destruction around them, some black soldiers abandoned their weapons to carry the aged and the infirm. Only one color predominated in the streets of Manhattan on this oppressive Labor Day morning—the black color of soot.

Amazingly, less than two thousand perished, due to the slow build-up of the conflagration. Morningside Park, the campus of Columbia University, Barnard College, and Riverside Park, all linked up to provide a barrier to the advance of the flames.

Power supplies to the city were cut off by the fires. The Empire State Building was running on emergency power, and the elevator to the hundredth floor was slow to reach its destination.

Shawcross was met by Eloise Gibson. She came toward him slowly, her eyes very wide.

377

"We thought you were dead," she said tonelessly.

He took her hands in his own. They felt cold.

"Eloise," he said, "do you remember when my family was murdered?"

"Of course! How could I forget?"

"Where was William Gray that day?"

Pete Humble looked up from a radio he had been monitoring. "In Watts," he said.

"Not in Paris?"

"He was giving a speech in Watts," said Humble.

Shawcross sighed. "Pete, I want you to take Eloise out of here. Right now."

"I won't go."

"Yes you will. I want you safe."

"It's done," said Humble.

"Hurry," said Shawcross. Perspiration beaded his upper lip. "Go down a few floors and get away from the elevators. Break into an office. Don't go out of the building. Things are rough out there. Now get going. I've got work to do."

The swim across the river had been tiring. Now Dewey and his men were dressed and moving cautiously off the B&O Railroad pier. Although it was hours yet to full daylight, the city was brightly lit by the pyre of flame in the north.

"If we don't hurry, there ain't going to be any city left to save," muttered one of the men.

"I think it's burning itself out," said Dewey. "It was higher when we started across."

He was right. With almost everything combustible consumed, the fire storm had begun to subside. From a line drawn across Manhattan—just below the Recreation Pier at 107th Street and the East River—the island had been cut in half by a black swath. Smaller fires that had leaped over the natural fire breaks still burned, but they were not serious.

To the north, the line had been held where the island narrowed. The flames had not crossed the width of West 155th Street, which extended from the wreckage of the Macombs Dam Bridge in the Harlem River to Trinity Cemetery near the Hudson.

Between these two extremes, not a living person breathed, not a building was intact. Empty shells stood, burned out, their roofs fallen in. From the air they looked like thousands of boxes piled in the rubble.

What Civil Rights demonstrations could not do, what could not be wrought by Presidential decrees or by the speeches and writings of black leaders, had been accomplished by the senseless chance of violent accident.

The slums of Harlem were gone.

"Am I hooked into the Command network?" Shawcross asked.

"Yes sir," said the technician.

"And we're patched into the radio transmitters and the TV channels?"

"Everything we can get."

"Okay," said Shawcross. "Take off. And thanks."

He sat in the deserted TV studio. The television camera was on, its red light glowing—but there was no technician behind it. It was locked down on its pedestal. Shawcross could see himself on the monitor. He shifted his position so that he was in the center of the screen.

He looked into the unblinking eye of the camera and spoke quietly. "I am Stanley Shawcross," he said, "Commanding General of the Redemption movement for black nationalism.

"Our purpose was not to destroy but to build. But our purpose has gone awry, as purposes often do.

"We did not wish destruction. But our plans went wrong, and we caused destruction. At this moment, more than twenty percent of the island of Manhattan lies in ashes because I, as leader of this military operation, miscalculated.

"I say now to all of the men who have followed my flag, lay down your arms. The war is over. Help as many as you can to safety, avoid further conflict. You fought well, and your names will be honored. The failure is not yours.

"You were failed by your leaders, myself in particular. You were failed because I concentrated so deeply on what I considered to be my primary responsibility—the military leadership of this movement—that I did not see what was going on around me. I did not see the way our ideals were being subverted by a handful of men.

"To the officials of the government of the United States, I say the soldiers of this revolution were fighting to redress a wrong. They are ordinary men, possessing all the greatness that ordinary men can find within themselves. They deserve your understanding and mercy."

He lowered his hand, which had been raised to emphasize the point. Looking at it, he said, "This hand served the government of the United States well for twenty-five years. For the past two years, it has been turned against that government. Now I hold this hand out to that government on behalf of my people—hold it out to touch, if possible, the consciences of the white majority in this country. Ask yourselves this question. If the Negro has been driven to revolution, who drove him there?

"I hurl no accusations, voice no recriminations. I sit here a defeated man, champion of a cause that deserved better than it got. To the twenty-two million black people I have failed, I say, forgive me. Our cause was just, but this was not the way.

380

"I make no excuses. We blew it! We came charging in, shaking our fists, and tore down the house it took so long to put up. But that doesn't mean something can't be salvaged out of this mess. Something *has* to come out of it, or else all those good men on both sides have died for stupidity and blind anarchy. I wish we had it to do over again. We can't, it's too late for us. But it's not too late for you out there. Remember this weekend! And remember that it can happen again, unless you find some way to change.

"Are you going to learn from it? Or are you going to shove it into the backs of your minds and continue down the same path to chaos?

"It's up to you. I've had it.

"The siege is over.

"*This* time!"

THIRTY-SIX

The door to the television studio opened. William Gray came in, a .38 pistol in his hand.

"You bastard," he said, "you've thrown it all away." He waved the pistol. "Let me have your gun."

With his fingertips, Shawcross drew his .45 from its holster and handed it to Gray.

Gray put it in his hip pocket. "God damn you, why did you do it?" he asked. "I worked my whole life for this."

"Because we didn't deserve to win."

Gray looked around the room. "Where are the technicians?"

Shawcross laughed. "Don't worry, William. There aren't any witnesses. I sent them away."

"You seem pretty sure of something."

"I'm sure you intend to kill me."

"Why would I do that?" Gray tucked the .38 into his belt.

"Why would you have a mother and her two children shot down on the highway?"

Gray sighed.

"I figured as much," he said. "It was the only way, Stanley."

"Don't call me Stanley. Was that all you could think

of to swing me over to your side? What a waste of three lives!"

"The hell you say!" shouted Gray. "You fouled this one up, General! It wasn't me who burned down the goddamned city. Maybe you're not going on, but *I* am! I'm not a man who gives up."

"You're a sack of corruption," said Shawcross, "and I'm sick of the sight of you. I guess I'm sick of myself, too." He plucked the pins from both shiny grenades on his belt.

They made a double popping noise. The sputtering of their fuses was unnaturally loud in the soundproofed room.

"What did you do?" screamed William Gray. "Shut them off!"

"Can't be done," Shawcross said calmly. "I've carried these babies for twenty years. It's funny as hell to finally have to use them."

Gray fumbled for the pistol. "I'll shoot you!"

"Shoot and be damned," said Shawcross. He tossed the grenades out on the heavy rug between them. They lay in the thick nap, tiny wisps of white smoke rising from their metal necks.

Gray screamed with rage, dropped the pistol, and ran toward the door.

Clarence Dewey, followed by three enlisted men, dashed into the hallway of the 101st floor.

"That's the studio," one man pointed.

Dewey leveled his M-16 at the closed door, ready to blast the lock open. Before he could press the trigger, an explosion inside threw the door ajar.

Sagging from it, still clutching the knob, fell the lifeless body of William Gray.

Dewey ran into the smoke-clouded room. It smelled of cordite.

He saw Shawcross, sitting against an overturned TV camera near the pockmarked wall. Both of his hands were clasped over a great wound in his chest. It welled blood with every beat of his heart. He looked up.

"Jesus Christ, Pappy!" groaned Dewey, bending over his friend. He made hesitant, grasping motions toward the gaping wound.

"What the hell," said Shawcross, his eyes shifting in and out of focus. He tried a smile, but only one corner of his mouth lifted. "What the hell," he repeated.

He raised one hand a little and pointed his bloody index finger at his friend.

"Zap," said Stanley Shawcross, and died.